Beauty and the Barbarian

Highland Force Book Three

Amy Jarecki

Rapture Books

Copyright © 2014, Amy Jarecki

Jarecki, Amy

Beauty and the Barbarian

Paperback ISBN: 9781942442455

ISBN: 9780692208175

First Release: May, 2014

Heartfelt thanks to all my readers.

Chapter One

Sprinting onto a thin strip of beach, Ian raced for the shore. Rain pelted his face as he skidded to a stop. Gasping for air, he sucked in deep breaths and peered through the dark night—north, then south. Thank God. A lone skiff sat askew, poorly camouflaged at the tree-line edge.

His side cramping from his frantic escape, he darted to the tiny boat with a pained hitch to his step. The deerhounds' barks grew closer. If he hesitated, they'd be upon him in a blink of an eye.

Ian's heart hammered his chest as he bore down on the skiff and shoved it into the angry swells. He jumped over the bow and snatched an oar. With every muscle, every sinew, he paddled against the surf and ignored his fatigue. A single oar made the boat fishtail, but there was no time to set them in their locks. Ian gritted his teeth and slammed the oar into the white swells in a hurried rhythm, side to side.

Over the roar of the surf and the driving rain, dogs yelped in an excited frenzy. Men shouted. Ian didn't turn around—he needed more distance. As sure as he breathed, they were ramming lead balls down their muskets. With luck, the rain had soaked their slow matches, rendering the guns useless.

Ian sped his determined paddling and squinted through the pelting rain—across to his home, the Isle of Raasay. He hadn't set foot there since he was four and ten, but the sight of the island enlivened him. He could barely make out the black outline of Dùn Caan, the flat-topped peak that forever identified the isle as Clan MacLeod land.

A sharp jab struck him from behind. Ian's body propelled forward. His nose slammed into the wooden hull. An ear-shattering musket clap followed, piercing through the wind. Something stung, burned his back. Ian slid his hand over the screaming pain. Hot blood oozed through his fingers.

More claps blasted from the beach, thudding into the tiny skiff. Ian rolled to his side. Icy water spurted over him. Frantically, he worked to hug both wooden oars against his chest. A thousand knives attacked his skin as salt water swallowed his lifeline to Raasay. The last thing he saw was the looming outline of Dùn Caan.

Blackness engulfed him.

Chapter Two

*E*ilean Fladda, Scotland. The year of our Lord, 1584.

Merrin had never seen a dead man before. As she peeked over the rocky crag, the image of the Highlander face down on the beach did not repulse her. From her vantage point, the man appeared in his prime, well-muscled like a warrior. Why had he washed up on the *caol*—the narrow span of land that connected the tiny islet of Fladda to the Isle of Raasay? From whither had he come? What caused his death?

Dry at low tide, soon the narrow gap would fill with sea water and wash the body into the Sound of Raasay. Merrin dropped the shell she'd found. Reaching beneath her cloak, she lifted her kirtle skirts and climbed over the rock. She glanced at the deerhound behind her. "Gar, come."

After scanning the scene for danger—any sign of life—she crept down to the Highlander.

Gar sniffed, nudging the man with his nose. Merrin stood at the Highlander's side for a moment. Powerfully built, he wasn't anything like her father or Friar Pat. His face was turned to the side, his damp flaxen hair pasted over his cheek and mouth. Clad in a dirty linen shirt, his broad shoulders tapered to narrow hips supporting a red-and-black kilt, a bold plaid. *Perhaps he's one of the clansmen from Brochel Castle.*

Dark red blood soaked one side of his shirt. It clung against him, the wound still oozing. The Highlander's kilt hitched awkwardly up over his thighs. Merrin stared, her pulse quickening. The kilt exposed the lower half of his buttock. It wasn't rounded and soft, but chiseled, as if hewn from stone. At the apex of his powerful legs was something soft, strewn with downy curls.

Pushing the hood from her head, Merrin stepped over the oars that rested askew beside him and knelt for a closer look. He had ballocks just like Bucky, the ram...and Gar. That it surprised her—a man had ballocks—seemed odd when she considered it. *How else would he breed?*

Her gaze swept across his muscular form and a stirring deep inside augmented her curiosity. Her breasts ached like they did just before she started her courses. Merrin licked her lips and cast her stare back to his face. With a soft whimper, Gar sat and leaned against her like he always did—the big sook.

She looked closer. Though bloodied and bruised, the Highlander had a pleasant face with an angular nose and a bold jaw, thinnish lips, but not too thin. She scooted up to brush the hair away from his face. Strands stuck to the stubble of his beard. Merrin gasped when the coarse bristles prickled her fingers as she swept the hair aside. Her fingers stopped at the back of his neck—a long, very warm neck.

Warm.

Merrin's gut clenched and she placed her finger just under his nose and held it still.

He wasn't dead.

Her trembling palms clapped over her mouth. *Merciful Father.* Instinctively, her hand slid down and covered the red mark on her neck. She'd forgotten her scarf. *What if he woke? He'd see me.*

She snapped her gaze to Gar. "Stay." Merrin pulled the hood over her head, quickly scanned her surroundings for intruders and ran for the cottage.

She raced into the rickety lean-to her father used for a workshop, latched on to Niall's arm and tugged. "Da. Quickly. Ye must come."

A portly man, the herbalist hardly moved. He pointed his pestle her way. It smelled of mint, which did nothing to allay the foul odor of horehound. "The friar needs this tincture straight away. There's a nasty cough spreading at the castle."

"Ye do no' understand." Merrin tugged harder. "Th...there's a dead man on the *caol*. But...he's no' dead." Shaking, she rushed to explain, "I thought he was dead when I saw him, b-but he was warm to the touch and then I..."

"Slow down, lass, me head's spinning with your babble." Niall rested the pestle in the mortar. "There's a man washed ashore, ye say?"

"Aye, with blood oozing from his side." Merrin dragged him toward the door. "Gar's guarding him, come. We need the barrow."

Niall shrugged out of Merrin's grasp and followed. "Ye're becoming bossier every day—just like your mother, God rest her soul."

Merrin couldn't help the roll of her eyes. She loved her father dearly, but he forever chastised her for everything—or nothing. "Ye need someone to keep ye to rights."

Niall lifted the barrow handles and pointed it toward the *caol*. "I need someone to stay quiet, cook me meals and keep the cottage."

Merrin rushed ahead, pulling up her hood and clasping it closed at the neck. "I do all that."

"Not the quiet part."

"Och, quit your bellyaching, Da."

Merrin stopped at the top of the bluff, which was covered with verdant green grass. Gar stood and barked up at her, wagging his tail. She pointed. "There."

Huffing, Niall wheeled the barrow beside her. His mouth drew down in a grimace. "Come. We must hurry."

Now he sees the urgency—couldn't listen to the likes of me. Merrin scuttled after him, having never seen her father move so fast.

Niall knelt and tugged the Highlander's kilt to cover his buttocks.

I should have done that.

He pulled up the blood-encrusted shirt and leaned close, his lips pursed. A jagged puncture wound seeped. Carefully placing two fingers either side, Niall examined it. A thick line formed between his brows and he swirled his fingers in a circular pattern. "There's a musket ball inside."

Merrin dropped to her knees beside her father and studied the wound. "Shot?"

"Aye, and left for dead, I'd wager." Niall stood. "He's a big fella. I'll need your help lifting him into the barrow."

Merrin moved to his shoulders. "Do ye recognize him?"

"Nay."

He rolled the man over. The hilt of his dirk glistened in the sun with brilliant reds and blues sparkling. Merrin looked closer. "Are those jewels?"

Niall brushed the sand off the hilt. "I daresay 'tis an heirloom a man would carry with pride—definitely not a piece worn by a common sentry. That's for certain." Da pointed to the matted fur sporran. "And his purse is ermine. The only man I know around these parts with an ermine sporran is our chieftain, Alexander MacLeod."

Merrin puzzled—a bejeweled dirk and an ermine purse? Where on earth had the Highlander come from?

Niall levered his hands under a shoulder. "Latch on to the other one and we'll lift together."

After a fair amount of hefting, they got him in with legs dangling so far over the barrow rim, his toes nearly touched ground. The poor blighter would have been bellowing like a castrated bull had he been awake.

Niall picked up the wooden handles. "Run ahead and stoke the fire. We'll need to remove that musket ball straight away."

Merrin slapped her hip. "Gar, come." Along the way, she snatched an arm full of peat from the workshop. She pushed through the cottage door and tossed it on the fire, then swung a kettle of water into place. After setting fire to a twig, she went about lighting every candle in the main room, including a tallow column with three wicks upon the enormous hearth. She pulled aside one of three wooden chairs to access a candelabra on the rectangular table. Next, she crossed the room and lit the oil lamp that rested on the small table beside her mother's oak rocking chair. Merrin's favorite, it sat in the corner beside her loom.

When the wheels crunched across the path, she held the door. "Barrow him straight inside."

Niall pushed the cart beside the table. "We'll put him on the board where I can work."

Merrin moved the candles and together they rolled the Highlander from the barrow, which was a mite easier than lifting him into it. Resting on his stomach, the man grunted. Merrin examined his face to see if his eyes had opened—no, he still looked dead, his skin a pale bluish-yellow in the candlelight. Bruises spread beneath his closed lashes.

Niall's iron knife scraped against the whetstone. "I dunna ken if I can save him, but I'd be no kind of healer if I didn't try."

Merrin nodded. "How can I help?"

"Put a poker in the flame. We'll need it red hot. Fetch a pile of rags—and grab a pot of honey poultice from the cupboard."

Once Merrin followed her father's orders, she stood beside him, cloth in hand.

Niall ran his dagger through the candle flame. "Hold the cloth beside the wound to sop up the blood."

Merrin swallowed and looked down at the peaceful form unconscious on the table. "Do ye think he'll wake?"

Niall pulled up the shirt, exposing the angry wound, encrusted with dark blood. "Mayhap. It'll hurt like the devil, nonetheless."

"Do we have to do it now?"

"The longer the lead ball stays in him, the sicker he'll become." Niall nodded toward her hands. "Hold the rag firm."

The Highlander's muscles remained flaccid while Niall probed with his knife. "'Tis not too deep."

An exhale whistled past Merrin's lips. "'Tis a good sign."

"I nearly have it." With a twist of Da's wrist, the musket ball popped out. Niall grasped it in his pincher fingers. "Nasty piece of lead."

Blood drained from the cut. Merrin worked quickly to sop it up, but it flowed too fast to stanch it.

"Put pressure on the wound," Niall snapped. He turned to the fire and reached for the poker. "Stand back."

Merrin pulled away the blood saturated cloth and tossed it into the fire. Drawing in a ragged breath, she clutched her fists to her chest.

Niall hesitated. "He may thrash a bit. Ye'd best bear down on his shoulders."

Merrin moved to the end of the table. Her fingers sank into muscle, thick with banded sinew and ever so warm to the touch. Her insides tumbled like a rolling brook. These were the shoulders of a powerful warrior. Merrin leaned her weight into him just as Niall rammed the glowing poker into the wound.

The Highlander bucked so violently, Merrin's small hands were useless holding him down. The pungent stench of burning flesh wafted from his back. The man bellowed louder than a braying bull. Arching up, his eyes flashed open and focused on her—ice-blue eyes filled with agony stared at Merrin as if she'd murdered him and all his kin.

He thudded back to the table, the wind wheezing through his throat. His body shuddered. Wide-eyed, Merrin stepped away. The Highlander's eyes closed and his back rose and fell in a steady rhythm. Merrin glanced to the wound. The bleeding had ebbed considerably. "Ye did it."

Niall jabbed the poker in the flame. It sizzled and stank as he turned it over. "Did ye doubt me, lass?"

"I kent ye could, I just feared he would be too weak to withstand it."

He hung the poker on its black nail against the hearth. "He's not healed yet. Rub the honey poultice into the puncture, then bind it. I've got to finish mixing the tincture before Friar Pat arrives."

Merrin pulled the stopper off the pot. "Do ye think he'll help us move him? The Highlander cannot stay on the table."

"Aye." Niall wiped his hands on a rag. "Ye'd best bring in some straw and fashion a pallet for him."

She glopped the poultice over the Highlander's angry-red flesh and gently rubbed it in. "Should we put him on me bed?"

"And where would ye sleep?"

Her shoulder ticked up. "I could use the pallet."

"Nay. We'll put him out here where we can keep an eye on him. God only knows how he ended up with a musket ball in his back."

"Ye think he might be evil?" Merrin studied the man's face. She didn't have a sense of foreboding like she did when marauding pirates from Rona were about. She sensed no wickedness at all.

Niall grasped the door latch. "I dunna ken, but I'll no' have him sleeping in your bed, or mine for that matter. We can make him comfortable enough with a bit of straw."

"I'll see to it, then."

Merrin glanced back to the door that led to her room. Once a larder, the small space had a bed, a trunk for her things and pegs on the wall where she hung her two kirtles. Niall's chamber was much larger, with a bed big enough for two. It even had a chest of drawers with a mirror atop—the nicest piece of furniture they owned.

The Highlander would be far more comfortable on her bed, though. She'd recently finished making a mattress of downy feathers. She could sink into it and sleep like a bairn. Alas, Niall said no. There was no use arguing—at least not today.

Merrin poured some water in the basin and doused a cloth. Wringing it out, she turned to the patient, hair hanging over his face. He couldn't possibly be comfortable strewn across the table on his stomach, but she'd see him cleaned up before the friar came. She ran the cloth over his brow and dabbed the broken skin on his nose. From the blood encrusted below it, she guessed he'd been hit with considerable force.

"What happened to ye?" she asked aloud. From his spot on the rug in front of the hearth, Gar whined, pricking his ears as if she'd spoken to him. "Not you, ye big hound."

She cleaned the blood and grime from the man's face and neck, sliding the cloth under his collar as far as it would go. Though he smelled of sweat, blood and seaweed, propriety got the better of her and she opted not to cleanse anything else. Had she known he was alive when she examined his ballocks, she never would have looked. She bit her lip against a tight fluttering sensation low in her midsection. She could not deny the experience had been interesting.

The cloth slipped from her fingers and dropped to the floor. Reaching for it, she made the mistake of bracing a hand on the

Highlander's thigh. Solid muscle filled her palm. Merrin stood straight and stared. Every inch of him was so *hard*.

She averted her attention to the leather boots that covered his ankles. Pulling the laces, she removed them with his hose. *He doesn't need footgear if he'll be abed for days.*

Voices came from the workshop. Good. Friar Pat had arrived. *Mayhap he'd ken the Highlander.* Though she recognized the ancient timbre of his voice, Merrin didn't need to. Friar Pat was the only person who visited. The clan, who mostly resided within the walls of Brochel Castle on the eastern side of Raasay, gave Eilean Fladda to the west a wide berth. They all feared her mark—but the friar was different. He said Jesus walked among the lepers and healed them. The friar didn't fear her, but he was the only one.

Merrin headed to the door just as Niall burst through with Friar Pat close behind, hobbling in with his walking stick. Gar did nothing but open an eye—vicious watchdog he was.

The aging friar spread his arms wide. "Merrin, my dear lassie. Give an old man a squeeze." His hug was warm and filled with kindness—he even smelled of sugared dates. Pat held her at arm's length. "I reckon ye grow bonnier every time I pay a visit."

Heat spread over Merrin's cheeks. "It seems like forever since we saw ye last."

"Aye, I'm not as agile as I once was."

"And how is your rheumatism?" Niall asked.

"It hurts." The friar smiled and patted Merrin's shoulder. "But the good Lord has seen fit to grant me with a long life, and for that I am grateful." He regarded the Highlander and frowned. "So this is what washed ashore?"

"Aye." Niall moved beside the patient. "Is he from Brochel?"

Merrin's heart stuttered with hope as the friar bent down to inspect the Highlander's face. "Bruised a bit, is he not?" The friar pushed aside the patient's hair. "Och, I'll be a monk of Judas."

That was the closest Merrin had ever heard the holy man come to swearing. "What is it?" She craned her neck around the friar's stout frame and scanned the Highlander's face—had she missed a red mark like hers?

"If I didn't know better, aside from the blond tresses, I'd say he was the likeness of Laird Calum MacLeod." The friar crossed himself. "God rest his soul."

Merrin and Niall both made the sign of the cross at the mention of the legendary first Laird of Raasay, who died "seeking the Holy Grail" in Tortuga—at least that was how the friar told it, though the island was a fair distance from the Holy Land.

"But do ye recognize him?" Niall asked.

Friar Pat frowned. "Nay. He doesn't hail from Raasay. Of that I am certain."

After Merrin fashioned a pallet of straw at the side of the hearth, they moved the Highlander, which proved no easy feat. Merrin took hold of his ankles while the two men wrestled with his shoulders. If she'd known how heavy his legs were, she'd have opted to switch with Da. Merrin would have sworn the patient was hewn from stone if she hadn't seen him bleed. But they rested him on the hay gently enough. Merrin draped a newly woven plaid across him, pleased to see her handiwork put to good use.

She insisted upon serving up bowls of potage before the friar made his return journey. Niall washed down a bite with a gulp of ale. He pointed his spoon at the unconscious form across the room. "I thought we'd try to spoon some broth into him on the morrow."

Pat nodded. "And ale. Give him a thimble of poppy juice if he starts thrashing about. That'll calm him."

Merrin studied the man. He looked peaceful with his hands folded over the plaid she'd tucked around his body. "Anything else we can do for Caolman?"

"Who?" Niall asked.

Merrin bit her lip. "We have to call him something—and I found him on the *caol*."

"Caolman it is, until he wakes and can tell us his name." The friar chuckled and patted her shoulder. "Keep applying your honey poultice and cleanse it with St. John's wort morning and evening."

"Thank ye, friar, I'll tend him as if he were me own."

"Very good." Pat nodded toward Niall. "Your da's a better healer than I, lass. If he cannot bring the poor soul to rights, no one can."

Chapter Three

I an MacLeod's eyes flew open with a violent bellow. Someone just stabbed him in the back with a scorching, sharp poker. For an instant he beheld the most beautiful woman he'd ever seen in his life—long, luminous hair, eyes the color of blueberries, pure skin with a rosy glow to her cheeks. *How can an angel cause such unimaginable pain? Have I passed into purgatory?* Collapsing, Ian fell toward blackness again—falling, tumbling over and over, but never crashing to the ground.

When later his consciousness registered a door opening, he had no idea how much time had passed. He couldn't make out the conversation, but he recognized a voice—one that took him back to his childhood, one he trusted unconditionally. Could he ever forget Friar Pat's merry rumble?

By the grace of God, he'd made it home to Raasay. Ian's brother, Alexander, would be near—he'd face him soon. The bond of kinship ran deep in the Highlands. Ian could sleep now.

As consciousness slipped again, his mind drifted to the woman's unbound tresses. If only he could open his eyes, he'd reach out and run his fingers through them. The color of polished mahogany, her hair cascaded to her slender waist in luxurious waves.

A dog barked. Ian twitched, his heart thundered. He tried to open his eyes again. Where had the beauty gone? His foggy mind refused to focus.

Ian's heart raced as he slipped deeper and deeper into blackness. More dogs growled and barked, frothing at the mouth, chasing him, snapping their teeth and snarling. Ian ran for his life, the dogs on his heels, nipping at him. He had to run faster...had to save her...had to fight...

Merrin sprinkled oatmeal over Caolman's body to ensure the bogles didn't try to take him during the night. Shifty creatures they were, always trying to play tricks. Niall continually warned the bogles would be after her if she strayed. *The bogles and the evil pirates from Rona.* Merrin was content to stay on Fladda, especially after the pirates had crept onto the islet and tried to steal food. When they'd cornered her, she'd feared for her life until she bared her mark and spat out she'd put a curse on them all. To her surprise, they turned tail and ran to their galleys faster than Gar could chase them down.

Niall had long since gone to bed, but Merrin held vigil beside Caolman, constantly watching his face to see if his eyes opened. During the day, his fever rose. She swathed his forehead with moist cloths. He'd begun mumbling imperceptibly, but Merrin caught words, "no" being the first and most frequently used.

Caolman grew more restless as the night progressed, his shirt damp with sweat. His head thrashed from side to side. "Janet, ye cannot give up. We're nearly there!"

Those were the clearest words he'd spoken. Merrin leaned closer, hoping he'd say more, but he thrashed his head and garbled, making a racket.

Janet? She'd never heard Friar Pat or Niall speak that name. Lead filled the void in her stomach. Was Janet his woman? Where was she now? Had she drowned? Merrin looked toward the *caol.* Waves crashing on the shore always rumbled louder at night. Would another body wash ashore?

"I love you," Caolman said as clear as day. His voice resonated with meaning, flowed like honey from a spigot.

Merrin's heart squeezed. Often she'd dreamt of hearing those words. She slid her gaze to his face. Heaven help her, he was beautiful. If only a man would speak like that to her. Merrin wrung the cloth between her hands. If only *someone* would love her. But there was little chance of that.

People feared her. To outsiders she was a witch—*a bana-bhuidseach*. She wished she might actually be a witch, if only for a moment. She would cast away Caolman's ills. Of course, if she were a witch, she would be a good-hearted one—if such a thing existed.

Six months shy of her twentieth birthday, she remained trapped on Eilean Fladda, where she would live out her life as an old maid. Her poor mother had died of childbed fever. Even as an infant, Merrin had been a demon. She was responsible for her mother's death. Though Niall never alluded to it, his fanatic superstitions confirmed Merrin's fears. Niall nailed crosses over every door and window to ensure no spirits came and stole her away and turned her into a witch.

One thing worried her continually. Merrin would most likely outlive her father. That was the natural way of things. She'd watched Friar Pat's hair turn grey and fall out—and now the poor bald man lumbered painfully, plagued by bouts of rheumatism.

Niall turned nine and forty last winter. Though the friar had lived well beyond that, many a man met his end before his fortieth birthday—and now her father pushed a half-century. Merrin had no inkling what she would do if she lost him. She prayed for his health every night, but the signs of aging were there—the greying hair, the stooped shoulders, the weathered flesh upon his weary face.

"Who are ye?" Caolman's deep voice was but a whisper, pulling Merrin from her thoughts.

Her gaze darted to him. Muted by the candlelight, his soft blue eyes stared directly at her, his lips slightly parted. She ran her hand across the scarf that covered her neck. Thank heavens, it was still in place. "I'm Merrin, the healer's daughter."

He swallowed and closed his eyes.

Merrin reached for a tankard of mead. "Can ye drink?"

Caolman didn't respond.

She spooned a bit of mead between his lips, as she had done several times that day. "Drink."

His Adam's apple moved and then he started to shiver. Merrin placed her hand on his head. His skin was afire. Quickly, she doused the rag and pressed it over his face. He panted, sucking in arrhythmic gasps while Merrin maintained her vigil, constantly applying the cool cloth.

"No!" Caolman shouted. Merrin jerked her hands away. "Ruairi will kill ye!"

Ruairi? Merrin had heard that name. He was the most notorious chieftain in all the Hebrides. Legend had it he'd sold his soul to the devil for everlasting life—making the Isle of Lewis a living hell for his clansmen. The ancient chieftain would never die. Had Caolman deceived him—mayhap swindled or cheated? Merrin's hands trembled and she looked to the window. There could be far more than bogles and fairies after Caolman's soul. Crossing Ruairi MacLeod would mean no one was safe—not even on the tiny islet of Fladda.

She mustn't tell Niall. He might insist they throw poor Caolman into the sound and watch until he drowned.

Merrin stirred at the tip of Niall's boot rocking her shoulder. Daylight streamed in through the window. The rooster crowed. She clasped her hands to her head. Had she been hit with a mallet? Her temples throbbed as if she'd been bludgeoned.

"And what are ye doing asleep out here beside *him*?" Niall said "him" as if Caolman robbed them of their last farthing during the night.

Merrin stretched and shook out her skirts. "I must have drifted off. He had the sweat all night—fevered he was. I haven't been asleep for long."

"Ye should have gone to bed. The Highlander's mind is deep amidst his troubles. He wouldn't have noticed whether ye were dousing his head with a cool cloth or no'."

Merrin headed to the hearth and reached for an iron frying pan. She wouldn't tell Niall Caolman woke—she wasn't even certain he had—though his voice sounded so clear. *"Who are ye?"* Besides, he was sleeping without a care at the moment

Niall poured two tankards of ale. "I'm away to Brochel after I break me fast."

Merrin cracked four eggs into a bowl and added cream. "When we've a patient to mind?"

"Ye've got him well in hand. Besides, we're low on oats."

She poured the eggs into a pan and stirred. "It seems we're always low on something, and every Wednesday, too. Ye're making a habit of it."

"And why not? Ye're old enough to fend for yourself for a time."

She set a basket of bread on the table. "Aye? I tend the herbs and livestock while ye go about with the clan at the castle?"

Niall tore off a chunk of bread. "A man has needs."

Merrin turned her attention to the eggs, flipping them furiously. Of course Niall would need more than her companionship. Holy fairy feathers, she yearned for companionship with someone her own age. *But that could never be.* She used a potholder to lift the pan off the grill and spooned a mound of eggs onto Niall's trencher—a bit too vigorously.

He gave her a sideways glance and shoved the rest of his bread in his mouth. "Sit down and break your fast."

After serving herself, Merrin rested the hot pan on the table where Gar couldn't reach it. She raised her spoon. "I should like to go to the castle with ye one day."

"'Tis too risky." Niall shook his head. "Even with your neck covered, they still ken who ye are."

Merrin pushed her eggs around her trencher. She'd lived in isolation all her life, yet it was still lonely. She couldn't eat. "Will I always be a monster?"

Niall reached over and smoothed his hand across her hair. "Ye're no demon. When I lost your mother, the clan was so angry—the women screaming for your death. But ye were too beautiful to put under the knife." He kissed her forehead. "They're all wrong about you. Ye're an angel. I just dunna ken how to prove it, and it would kill me to see ye burned or worse."

Merrin shuddered. "Merciful Father, what's worse than being burned?"

Niall's face grew dark as if he'd seen horrors beyond Merrin's imagination. "Never mind that." With a belch, he stood and headed for the door. "Give your patient a bath. The cottage reeks of him."

"Caolman."

"What?"

"Ye ken, we're calling him Caolman until he wakes and gives us his name."

"Right." Niall shoved a bonnet over his head. "Do no' wait up for me."

"Will ye be back tonight?"

"Most likely on the morrow." Niall strode outside, slamming the door behind him.

Merrin pushed up from the table and dashed to the window. Father had a spring to his step. Clearly, visiting the castle brought him amusement he couldn't find at home. So many times he'd told stories of pipers and fiddlers. She'd listen to him play his flute and imagine the cottage filled with people dancing and drinking ale—just like Da described it. If only she could go along. She'd hide behind a curtain and watch—if Da would allow her to do so.

Caolman moaned. With a gasp, Merrin faced his pallet. *Bathe a man? Da really asked me to do that? Am I expected to strip him bare? Mayhap I can cleanse him beneath his clothing.*

She'd never even seen Niall bathe. On the odd occasion when he filled the tub, he'd made her close the door to her room and remain within until he called her—not that she wanted to see her father naked. *Merciful Father, that would be disgusting.* She took a step toward the sleeping Highlander. Odd. The idea of seeing *him* naked didn't disgust her in the slightest.

Merrin prepared a basin of water and scented it with rose oil. She knelt beside Caolman. Beads of sweat dotted his forehead. Gently, she fingered the collar of his shirt. Salt crusted on her hands. She raised the blanket and looked beneath. A bit of seaweed stuck out from his belt. Truly, his clothes were so full of salt, his skin must be chafing. Perhaps they needed washing more than he did.

Gar pattered beside her and sniffed under the blanket. He licked the errant seaweed and shook his head, flicking his tongue in and out until the salty morsel dropped to the floor.

"Tis not nice is it, laddie?"

With a whine, the dog returned to his mat in front of the hearth.

"Ye see that." She stared at Caolman's closed eyes. The bruising beneath had cleared some. "Ye even stink too much for me mangy mutt."

With a sigh, she folded the blanket and loosed the laces of his shirt. She tugged it up one side at a time until it finally freed over his head, practically knocking her on her backside with the last fervent tug.

Merrin lathered the cloth and ran it over his brow. She hummed as she caressed his eyes and ran the cloth through his hair and around his neck. She sang the words when she slid the cloth across his chest, trying her best not to ogle the muscular, taut flesh. Caolman shivered. Merrin sucked in a sharp breath at his response and apologized.

His nipples grew erect, as hers did when cold. But his chest was nothing like Merrin's. The sinew beneath his skin stood proud, masculine. Merrin swirled the cloth down to his banded abdominals, which constricted against her touch. She stopped singing and stared at his chiseled muscles. A longing washed over her, so intense it made her entire body ache. How could a mere man, a stranger, fill her with yearning? Merrin's mouth went dry and she steadied her breathing. Heaven help her, he was beautiful far beyond anything she'd ever imagined.

Regaining control, she continued the song and tenderly reached beneath him to wash his back. Merrin could have sworn Caolman rose ever so slightly. Once she'd gone over every inch of his upper body, she rocked back on her heels and stared at his belt buckle. The palms of her hands perspired and she hummed to calm her nerves. At near twenty years of age, it was time she learned all that made a man different from a woman. Her fingers trembled as she slid the belt from its buckle.

Ian shivered violently when the cold cloth swiped across his chest.

"Apologies, but the cool water will help your fever."

The woman's dreamy voice soothed him, as did the rose oil she used to scent the water. When she began to sing, Ian's flesh tingled. *Is this heaven?* She hummed at first, then her voice grew stronger, more self-assured. She lifted his arm, singing a woeful ballad about a lover lost at sea. Her voice was clear as a warbler's call, yet it carried emotion much akin to someone who had endured tragedy and pain.

Her deft fingers caressed him ever so gently, as if bathing a bairn. The throbbing pain in his back ebbed as he relaxed with her heavenly ministrations. She pulled her hands away for a moment, once again humming. If only she would keep touching him and never stop. Not now. Ian tried to open his eyes—heard himself moan.

"Forgive me, but me da says a bath. Ye need to be washed there too and I cannot very well avert me eyes."

Her soft lilt mesmerized him. His belt was pulled taut and then released. Struck by the sensation of floating, Ian had an inkling she'd exposed his manhood, but he hadn't a mind to wake. His nakedness was as natural as breathing.

The cool caresses resumed, this time along his lower abdomen. His skin enlivened, aroused by her touch. In a swirling pattern, she moved lower. The woman no longer hummed. Her breathing became labored.

"Ye're beautiful," she whispered, her small hand sliding between his legs.

Ian had no control over the moan that escaped his throat. With languid strokes, she cleansed every inch of him, but her breath caught when his erection shot to rigid. "Merciful Father, Ye're like a stallion with a mare in heat."

Ian opened his eyes. She pulled her hands away, gaping at his hard manhood. He tried to speak, but his tongue was dry and swollen in his mouth. He moaned again, his eyes closing. Licking his lips, he managed, "Do no' stop."

She gasped again. "Ye're awake, are ye not?"

Ian was neither asleep nor awake, but he was definitely very aware. The cloth ran down his legs with rapid strokes, water squirted through his toes. Her touch became much more brisk and soon she sopped up the droplets with a drying cloth. Ian again opened his eyes as the woman draped a plaid over him.

She tucked the blanket around his sides. "There ye are."

Shaped like a supple hour glass, the woman was exquisite. She smelled of fresh bread and sunshine.

"Are ye an angel?"

She stared at him, mouth agape.

Ian tried to talk again, but all he could manage was, "Are ye?"

"Nay." The woman's hand went to her neck and pressed against her plaid scarf. "Do ye remember I told ye me name is Merrin, the healer's daughter?"

Ian remembered very little, not even how he came to be in the tiny cottage. "Merrin? 'Tis a lovely name. I'll no' forget it now." Ian's tongue rasped like sandpaper attached to the roof of his mouth. "Where am I?"

"Eilean Fladda."

His vision clouded—she must be mistaken. "Not Raasay?"

"The islet is attached to Raasay by the *caol,* where I found ye."

Ian closed his eyes and searched his memory. He recalled seeing Fladda when he was a lad. It was forbidden to explore the islet, though he couldn't remember why. Mayhap it was another of the rules set down by his overly protective mother.

"What is your name?" Merrin asked, lifting a tankard and spoon.

"Ian."

She carefully emptied the contents of the spoon into his mouth. Sweet honey mead slid across his tongue—nearly as sweet as the soft lilt of her voice. "Ian is a nice name. Do ye have a clan?"

Should he tell her? *Why not?* "MacLeod."

She offered him another spoon, which Ian lapped up greedily. He watched her eyes—large, caring, amazingly blue and radiating with innocence. They registered no hint of recognition. Of course, everyone was aligned with the MacLeod around these parts.

She looked directly at him, making his heart race, as if she could see into his soul. "Raasay? Dunvegan? Lewis?"

The lass was persistent. "Raasay." That was the truth. Merrin's lips pursed and her eyes darted away. Ian sensed his answer displeased her.

"Are ye in pain?" she asked with an unmistakable edge.

"Aye, me back feels skewered."

"Mayhap because it was." Her features softened when she smiled. If she had wings, Ian would swear on his life she was an angel. "I have a tincture to ease your discomfort."

Before he could say a word, Merrin shoved a spoon of bitter-tasting potion in his mouth. Ian sputtered while the foul liquid slid down his gullet. "Are ye trying to poison me?"

"'Twill help ye sleep." She put her hand on his forehead. "Ye're still fevered, though no' as bad as last eve."

Ian closed his eyes, the tincture taking effect quickly on his empty stomach. He tried to open them again. If only he could gaze upon her face for a bit longer. He managed to force his lids to a squint and watched her bustle about. When she collected his clothes from the floor, Ian remembered he was naked. She'd cleansed his privates and had not a word uttered. The lass didn't even appear to be embarrassed. Was she married? But she said she was the healer's daughter—such a statement would indicate she was not yet spoken for.

There were so many questions he wanted to ask Merrin. How could such a beauty be hidden from the world on a piece of rock too small to be an island?

Chapter Four

M errin took Ian's clothes outside to the washbasin. She needed the fresh air to clear her head. After tossing in some lard soap, she hiked up her skirts and set to stomping Ian's shirt and kilt clean. A hundred warring thoughts swarmed through her mind. Her hands still trembled. Ian—if that was his real name—took her breath away.

When she removed his clothing, she'd expected him to be different, but not so amazingly so. Merrin's body reacted in ways she'd never before experienced. He took possession of her mind—as if *he* was an actual witch sent by the fairy folk to trick her. Merrin glanced at the cross above the door where her father had nailed it. If Ian were sent to trick her, his charms should not work within the cottage. But she was rattled, tramping on his clothes like she'd gone mad.

Merrin stomped harder. She could not shake the image of his manhood from her mind. Were all men thus endowed? He was like a stallion—far bigger than a ram or a dog, not to mention his exquisite beauty. Deep inside, her body inflamed at the sight of him. Blasted bogle's breath, was she to be tormented by the memory of his sex for the rest of her days?

Merrin clutched her arms across her ribs and scrubbed the clothing with her toes. He'd lied to her. That had her twisted up inside as much as anything. *More.* He said he was aligned with the MacLeods of Raasay, yet Friar Pat gazed upon his face and professed he was indeed not. What was Ian hiding? If he *was* a MacLeod, he most likely hailed from Lewis—was on the run from Ruairi, the tyrant chieftain. But why would a man like Ian lie to the likes of her? She posed no threat. What else was he hiding?

Her mind's eye conjured him naked again. Merrin pressed her hands to her face and shook her head. Merciful Father, why could she not pull her mind away from his magnificence?

Dear Lord, please, please help Ian heal quickly. I cannot bear to have him in the cottage, looking at me with those penetrating eyes. He makes me tremble...I...I must have caught the fever from him.

After hanging the washing to dry, Merrin busied herself feeding the livestock, checking the store of peat, anything so that she wouldn't have to go back into the cottage. While she worked, she continually glanced toward the door, expecting Ian to hobble through it at any moment—hoping he would be on his way, blast him.

But the Highlander would need tending soon, and she grew hungry for the noon meal. Merrin bore up her courage and marched through the door. Half convinced Ian would be holding court with the King of the Fairies, she hesitated and peered through the dim room. Ian hadn't moved from his pallet—the plaid still draped over his sleeping form, just as she'd left him.

Ian tilted his chin. "Ye were the only one who ever showed me kindness."

Merrin tiptoed up to him. A bead of sweat trickled from his temple. She knelt down and put her hand to his forehead. The fever had returned. She doused a cloth and wiped the sweat.

Ian pushed her hand away. "Mother, please do no' make me go to Lewis. I want to stay here with you and Alexander."

Merrin sat on her haunches. *Another piece of the mystery unfolds. Mayhap if I play along...* "Ye must go."

Ian grimaced like a wee lad tasting a bitter brew. "Me uncle hates me."

Uncle? Was Ian reliving a scene from his childhood? Merrin acted on her guess. "Is it Ruairi Ye're afraid of?"

Ian bared his teeth, his face suddenly scary, hateful. "Ruairi will kill her!"

Merrin pressed her hands to her face. His ravings were incomprehensible. With a sigh, she applied the cool cloth to his forehead. "Is Janet in danger?"

He grabbed Merrin's arm and his fingers bored into her flesh. Ian's eyes flashed open, wild with terror, but vacant as if not seeing her. "Ye cannot survive here. He will kill you."

Moaning, Ian released his hold and thrashed about. Merrin pressed down on his shoulders. "Calm yourself. No harm will come to ye today. Lie back, Ian, and let me tend ye."

Merrin prayed no ill would befall them. Merrin knew little of the world outside Fladda, but of one thing she had no doubt, if Ian had crossed the great Lewis Chieftain Ruairi, there would be retribution. Soon.

Gradually, Ian's breathing resumed the slow cadence of sleep. Gar lumbered over from his mat in front of the hearth and curled up beside Ian's leg. Merrin stared at the deerhound. The dog was fiercely protective of her, and yet he lay beside Ian to give comfort. "So 'tis ye who's playing the traitor now? We'll see who ye prefer come meal time."

Merrin turned her attention to the day's work and brought in Ian's damp clothes to hang on the pegs over the mantel. She mixed oatcakes and tended mending, along with other chores. That Ian was in trouble she had no doubt. Whether he was a scoundrel or not was an entirely different matter. But Merrin intended to uncover his secrets—hopefully before her father returned.

Something creaked against the floorboards with a steady rocking sound, reminding Ian of the groaning of a ship's hull when at sea, except softer. The pain in his back throbbed, burned like someone held a flame to his skin. With effort, he rolled to his side and realized a dog rested against his leg. The wiry deerhound whined, complaining his sleep had been interrupted. With a shake of his head, the dog turned in two circles and plopped down again, his back pushing against Ian's legs. "Do no' mind me, just make yourself comfortable."

The rocking stopped. Ian blinked. Across the room, Merrin put her sewing aside and stood, the firelight glowed against her fair skin. From his pallet, she appeared tall, sturdy and incredibly shapely. She had the hips of a goddess, and her cleavage blossomed over her kirtle's neckline as if sending him a wrapped invitation. If only he could rise from his damnable pallet and open the present. He groaned. Merrin's porcelain skin had to be softer than satin. His fingers itched to touch it. Though simply dressed, no woman could ever look more beautiful.

"Are ye hungry?" she asked, her voice soothing.

His stomach growled. "I could cut the heart out of a stag and eat it raw."

She chuckled. "Fortunately, we do no' have to go to such extremes."

"How long have I been here?"

Merrin picked up a bowl and knelt beside him. "I found ye morning last."

Ian closed his eyes—it all started to come back—fleeing from the Isle of Lewis to save Janet from further abuse by his uncle. How much time did he have before they found him—or did they think him already dead?

When Merrin leaned closer, his senses filled with the intoxicating fragrance of primrose. He shuddered when she grasped his shoulder and piled pillows behind him. Their eyes met. Their gaze locked. Fathomless, unspoken meaning passed between them—mutual respect, raw attraction, fervent attachment, none of which Ian understood. *She's a common lass, for Christ's sake.*

She brushed a strand of hair from his brow, easing the intensity of their connection. Merrin's hand trembled when she held the spoon to his lips. "See if ye can take some broth." Her soft voice warbled.

Ian opened his mouth and allowed her to feed him. His gaze fixed on her face, smooth, unblemished skin, eyes as clear as the deep blue of dusk. His stomach complained with pangs of emptiness. "Have ye anything more substantial?" When she frowned, he feared he'd hurt her feelings. He blinked. The last thing he wanted was to be discourteous. "The broth is fine, indeed. 'Tis only me stomach is as hollow as a woodpecker's nest."

Merrin frowned and ran her fingers over the woolen plaid tied around her neck. *Why is she wearing a scarf? 'Tis not cold in the least.*

"If ye can hold this down, we'll see about giving ye a morsel of haggis. I made a fresh batch today—it should go easy enough on your stomach."

Ian cringed—haggis was a garnish. He craved a slice of beef or a hearty lamb pottage. "If I eat your haggis, will ye give me a morsel of meat?"

Merrin frowned and shoved another spoon of miserable broth into his mouth, which Ian swallowed with pleasure upon meeting her gaze again. "Aye, but no' so fast. One thing at a time."

Honestly, Ian didn't mind being fed by an incredibly beautiful woman. He imagined he could take to a life of a royal rather easily, his every need attended by servants. But Merrin could be no servant. If anything, Ian should attend her. A woman blessed with such beauty should be pampered, loved and held in the highest esteem, regardless of a common birth.

When he'd eaten all the broth, Ian grasped Merrin's wrist. She froze. Wariness darkened her eyes and she yanked her hand away as if she feared him.

Ian clenched his fist, his fingers still searing from brushing the silkiness of her skin. "Apologies. I just wanted to ask..." *So many things. What is a beautiful woman doing isolated on a tiny island? Why would her father leave her alone with a stranger, albeit unconscious, with nothing but a dog to protect her?*

Her lovely blue eyes widened. "Ye wanted to ask?"

He ran his fingers across the soft woolen plaid that hid his nakedness. "Why do ye wear that scarf? 'Tis quite warm with the fire blazing in the hearth."

Her eyes drifted down the length of his body. He liked it when a beautiful woman drank him in. She'd bathed him, caressed every inch of his flesh—knew him intimately, yet remained bashful. Merrin pulled the scarf tighter. "I always wear it."

She was hiding something. Had she been badly burned? Ian dropped his gaze to her chest. Milky white breasts swelled over her kirtle's scooped neckline. There was no sign of mottled flesh. Had she a scar? 'Twas a mystery he would like to solve. His gaze slipped back to her cleavage. God, he'd never seen breasts more lovely.

Ian ran a hand over his bare chest. "Where are me clothes?" His gut clenched—had he lost his dirk?

"I washed them." She dipped her chin with an adorable blush and pointed to the hearth. "They're drying."

Ian pushed up on his elbows and peered at the big fireplace. Sure enough, his clothes were hanging from the mantel with his belt, dirk and sporran neatly placed beneath. He became lightheaded from his effort. Oh how he wished he'd been fully conscious when she'd removed them. The maid must have flushed scarlet for certain.

She crossed the room, leaned over a pot and stirred. Ian watched her, fascinated. Her every movement was graceful. She wore her inordinately long chestnut locks unbound. Reaching below her waist, they shimmered in the candlelight with the slightest movement. Stirring intently, she focused on her task as if it were gravely important. Had something irritated her?

"Are ye upset?"

Merrin stopped and looked out the window, rather than at him. "Why would ye ask that?"

"Ye've beat whatever Ye're stirring pretty well. I wouldn't want to be in that pot being thrashed about by a spoon as forceful as yours."

She sighed and stared into the bowl. "Who are ye, and why are ye on the run from Ruairi, Chieftain of Lewis?"

Ian's gut clenched. How in God's name did she know? Clutching the plaid against his waist, he tried to stand. If only he could make it to his clothes, he might find a boat. His very presence put her in danger.

Merrin dashed across the floor and pressed against his shoulders. "What are ye doing? Ye're too weak to rise."

Stabbing pain brought stars across his vision. Ian dropped back like a sack of grain. His strength sapped, bested by a wisp of a lass. "As long as I remain in your cottage, your life is in peril."

She stood straight, tapping her foot against the floorboards impatiently. "Aye? Ye think I dunna ken 'tis a risk having ye here?"

"Well, I…"

"I found ye on the caol with a musket ball in your back. Ye've been fevered and moaning 'bout some lassie named Janet and how ye need to steal away from Ruairi—ye didn't want to go there as a wee lad, but your ma said ye must." Merrin folded her arms. "Tell me I'm wrong."

Ian closed his eyes. His head pounded as he tried to make sense of it all. "Nay, ye are not."

"And why didn't Friar Pat recognize ye?" She pointed a long, slender finger, her accusing eyes pinning him to the pallet. "Who are ye, and do no' dare lie to me."

Hot air whistled through Ian's lips. He owed her the truth—at least as much as he could reveal. "I am Ian MacLeod of Raasay."

"How could—"

Ian held up his hand. "If ye want to hear the truth, ye'll allow me to finish."

Chin raised, she offered a sharp nod.

"I'm the second son of Laird Calum MacLeod. I was only a lad when he died, and ten year' ago at four and ten, me ma considered it best to be fostered by me uncle."

"Ruairi?"

"Aye. The man's near twenty years older than me father, but still he lives—and as the years pass, the worse he grows."

"A tyrant, aye?"

"Of the worst sort. He prays on the weak—children and women." Ian rubbed his hip. "I've felt the sting of his lash more than once."

Merrin tapped her foot. "So what happened with Janet?"

"When his third wife passed, Ruairi cast his sights on Janet MacKenzie—three and sixty years his younger, mind ye. He kept her locked in the tower, very jealous of any man who looked her way."

"She was beautiful?"

"Aye."

Slender fingers touched her mouth. "Did ye love her?" she asked softly.

Of course he did. Ian never could resist strong feelings for a fine-looking woman in need of rescue, but for some reason, he couldn't admit it. "Thought I did."

Merrin stepped back, one eyebrow arched. "And how did ye end up with a musket ball in your back?"

The fire smoldering in the pit of Ian's stomach inflamed. The frantic race to deliver Janet to the MacKenzie stronghold flashed through his mind. He'd done the right thing, no matter what anyone else thought, and now he'd pay for it the rest of his life. "'Tis complicated."

Again she crossed her arms, accenting the cleavage above her neckline. It was enough to unman any poor blighter. Merrin inclined her head, oblivious to the stirring effect she had on him. "I'm no' daft, and I've no other place to go."

A low chuckle growled from Ian's throat—she may not be aware of her allure, but she sure knew how to make a man squirm. "Ye're a clever one, 'tis for certain." If he revealed more, she could betray him and send word to Lewis—but then she already knew enough to damn him to hell.

"If ye want more food, ye'll be honest with me. I'll no' betray you. On that ye have me word."

Ian closed his eyes. "Janet was my auntie, though two years younger, in truth. Ruairi married her to lay his hands on her dowry, which included fifty acres of MacKenzie grazing land."

"MacKenzie? That would be on the mainland, no?"

"Aye, and only a few hours sailing in a galley. The trade it opened for the Lewis Clan brought riches—further strengthening Ruairi's wealth." Ian shook his head. "He cared nothing for the lass. He'd beat her for the smallest trifle."

Merrin shuddered and clasped her hand over the scarf around her neck. "It must have been awful for her."

"I couldn't sit by and watch. Janet is too frail, she'd nay last another year."

"Where is she now?"

"Safe." He didn't want to say where, though Ruairi's henchman, Rewan MacLeod, already knew. That didn't matter. Once Ian delivered Janet into the arms of the MacKenzie, Rewan wouldn't have been able to touch her.

"Ye took her back to her kin?"

How did Merrin guess that? "Aye."

"And why didn't ye stay with them—spare yourself a musket ball?"

"I created a diversion. Ruairi's men chased me while Janet's brother spirited her inside the MacKenzie keep." Ian shook his head. "Ye must no' speak of this to anyone, for if ye do, Ruairi will send his henchman after me. They'll never stop. No' until I'm dead."

Merrin placed her hand on Ian's shoulder, a mere friendly gesture. Ian's heart shouldn't have hammered in his chest, but it did. Before he thought, he reached up and covered it with his much larger palm. Their gazes met. Ian could not mistake the yearning in her eyes, certain the same longings reflected in his own. He choked back his urge to pull her in his embrace. It was madness to allow his heart to yen for a lass in a few brief moments.

But Merrin made him feel like he was the only man in the room, which he was quite literally. Still, Ian's chest swelled, more like she regarded him to be the only man in the *world*—a king.

Her tongue slipped out and dabbed her top lip, then her gaze dropped to his mouth. Ian suddenly had an overwhelming urge to kiss her. He reached up with his free hand and cupped her face. "I haven't thanked ye for rescuing me."

She drew in a ragged breath. "Ye do no' need to. I'm just relieved Ye're alive."

He stared at her pink lips, slightly parted. Heaven help him. He gently tugged her toward his mouth and lightly brushed his lips across hers.

Merrin jumped back. Her fists flew under her chin, her eyes wide as saucers. "What was that?"

"Do no' tell me a lass as bonny as ye has never been kissed?"

Her face turning a brilliant shade of scarlet, she darted to the hearth and picked up her mixing spoon. Ian watched her. Keeping her back to him, Merrin nervously stirred an enormous kettle sitting atop an iron grill.

Bloody hell, no one has kissed the lass. Ian clenched his fists. He could not take advantage of an innocent woman, no matter how beautiful. "Where's your father?" It came out gruff, but so it should have. Kissing an innocent? He should be flogged.

"Gone to Brochel to fetch stores. He'll be back soon." She kept her face turned toward the hearth.

"I'm sorry."

She stopped stirring. "For what?" Her backside was every bit as lovely as her front.

Ian moaned. "I'm sorry I kissed ye. I lost me head staring into your bonny eyes."

His words were practically more than Merrin could bear. Had Ian really said her eyes were bonny? She'd nearly swooned when his lips touched hers. When he grasped her hand and stared into her eyes, her heart had fluttered as if propelled by wings. She tried, but she couldn't look away.

Merrin mustn't encourage him. If he saw her mark, he'd flee before he was completely healed. She would keep it covered and avoid kissing him again. But how marvelous was the mere caress of his lips. She pressed her fingers to her mouth. It still tingled.

She stirred the pottage one more time and dished up two bowls, Gar coming to life, instantly at her heel. If Ian was bold enough to kiss her, he was certainly well enough to keep down a few bites of pottage.

She skirted around the table with Gar drooling behind. Still a bit shaken, she didn't look Ian in the face until he moaned. His eyes were closed and beads of sweat dribbled from his forehead. That kiss must have sapped him of all his strength.

Merrin glanced at Gar. "May as well not waste it." The dog wagged his tail and trotted to his bowl by the door. She shoveled in Ian's portion. "What a strange day this has been."

When the sunlight dimmed, Merrin lit the candles and reclined in the rocker. She watched Ian sleep. If only she could find a man like him, she wouldn't be alone when Niall passed. She'd take fine care of a husband. Around and around, she caressed the back of her hand. A young man like Ian might never touch her again. She would savor the memory of this day and lock it in her heart. So much had been revealed in a few short moments, Merrin wondered if Niall had left her alone for her own education. Her father would do something like that. Life's lessons come from experience, he'd say.

On the morrow Niall would return, and her fascination with Ian would become a distant memory. Of that she was absolutely certain.

Chapter Five

W hen Merrin came in from collecting the eggs, she found Ian sitting on the edge of his pallet, the plaid wrapped around his waist, his well-muscled chest bare. She could scarcely breathe. All night she'd tried to block the images of his hard body from her mind. She'd bathed every inch of that masculine flesh. Doing so had stirred a yearning so powerful, her insides twisted with pain. When she'd finally left the rocking chair and sought her bed, it took forever to drift off. Each time she closed her eyes, she saw his rock-hard chest, or a sturdy thigh, a thick arm. Thick? Of course her mind would then conjure up his undeniably fascinating manhood. Heaven help her, it would haunt her forever.

Ian's beard had grown thicker during the night. The dark stubble contrasted with his flaxen tresses. He hunched over, his breathing labored.

Merrin set her basket on the table and raced to him. "Are ye ill?"

"I need to rise from this pallet and build me strength."

She laid her palm against his forehead. "Ye're still a bit fevered. 'Tis best ye let your body rest."

"Nay. My presence here is putting ye in danger. I should be on me way."

Merrin pursed her lips and gazed at him intently. He couldn't leave. Not when he was only starting to mend—not when she'd already grown accustomed to tending him. "Oh really, now?" She pulled the corners of her mouth down in her best disagreeable frown. "Aside from the fact that ye wouldn't make it to the door, where would ye go?" Merrin snapped her fists to her hips for added sternness. "Or is it ye do no' like me hospitality?"

Ian reached up for her hands and clasped them. "Of course I'll forever be grateful that ye came to me rescue. I would have no other hands but yours tending me."

Merrin's heart fluttered. His rough, warm palm cradled her much smaller hands protectively. Her gaze fell to his lips. Oh, to feel them brush against hers one more time. She couldn't allow him to leave. Not when he was this weak. He'd succumb to the fever or worse. "There's no hurry for ye to leave." Her voice was but a whisper. "Come. I'll serve ye some eggs and sausages."

His heartbeat thundered beneath her fingers, his skin warm to the touch. The fever had nearly broken. If only she could run her hands over the banded muscles in his chest. But he wouldn't want that. He was in love with Janet. A man like Ian MacLeod would never feel anything for a lowborn woman who bore the mark of the devil. Merrin tightened her grip on his hand and gave him a gentle tug. "Let me help ye to the table."

Ian frowned. "I hate this weakness."

"Aye, but Ye're strong. 'Tis amazing Ye're sitting up so soon after Da carved out the musket ball."

Merrin braced herself and pulled. Ian grunted. The color drained from his face as he stood. Merrin threw his arm over her shoulder and stepped into him for support. Goodness, he was heavy, and ever so tall—at least a hand, possibly two taller than she. "Ye think ye can make it to the chair?" Though it was only a few steps away, she wasn't certain he'd be able to do it.

Anger flashed across his eyes. "Of course I can make it. 'Tis I who should be holding a chair for ye."

"Is it, now? Well, excuse me." Merrin stood back and watched Ian stagger to the chair. He practically fell into it with an anguished bellow. "I'll need to change your dressing. That'll help your pain."

"Did I say I was in pain?"

"Nay, but ye cannot hide it from me, so ye may as well not even try. Ye're as bull-headed as me da."

"I'm not overly fond of being incapacitated. Normally, I wake early and spar with the guard. This hole in me back feels as big as a fist. Did your da use a butcher's knife to cut it out?"

Merrin picked up a trencher of food she'd prepared earlier and placed it in front of him along with a cup of ale. "He used a sharp dagger, but then he stanched the blood with a scorching poker."

Ian glanced at the tools hanging from the hearth. Among them was the blunt-tipped implement. "That would be right."

Merrin sat beside him and stabbed a sausage with her eating knife. "At least Ye're no' dead."

Ian took a bite then emitted a satisfied moan. His eyes rolled back, and he took a drink of ale. "Och, that's what I needed for certain." He crammed a whole sausage in his mouth. The juice dribbled from the corner of his lips.

Merrin stared.

"I'm starved." Ian wiped his lips with the back of his arm. "This tastes like manna from heaven. Forgive me lack of manners. I cannot help meself."

Merrin smiled. "I suppose I'm the one who starved ye. I had some pottage for ye last eve, but ye fell asleep afore I could feed it to ye."

Ian cleaned his plate and drained his tankard. Firmly placing it on the table, he drew in a deep breath, as if coming up for air. "Thank ye for taking care of me. I'm sorry I was a bear. My hunger got the better of me temper."

Heat spread across Merrin's cheeks. "Ye're welcome. I become a bit ornery when I'm hungry as well."

He reached out and brushed his finger across her cheek. "How did I come to be rescued by a beautiful, selfless woman such as ye?"

Merrin shook her head, her insides turning to mush. All he had to do was touch her and her entire body tingled, ached for more. Ian smiled and brushed a lock of hair from her face, his smile becoming thoughtful when he tugged on her scarf. Merrin grabbed for it, but in a flash, Ian pulled the cloth away.

She could barely breathe as she wrapped her trembling fingers around her neck. Merrin pushed up from the chair. Ian's brows drew together. The look of horror in his eyes. Now he knew the truth. She would always be a monster. The room closed around her. Merrin ran for the door, tears stinging her eyes. He'd seen her mark. Now he'd take his things and leave for certain. He'd not wait until he was healed—he'd flee from Fladda, run anywhere to wash her filth away.

Merrin ran for the open lea. Tears streamed down her cheek and her sobs grew louder. How pathetic her life was. How utterly meaningless. She dropped to her knees, covering her face with her hands. "God, why am I to be eternally tormented? Why didn't I die instead of Ma? She was beautiful and flawless, yet ye took her and left me here to rot on this miserable island."

Gar whined and pushed up against her. Merrin shoved the dog away and crouched into a ball. She could not go back to the cottage. She had no cloak, no scarf to cover the mark. Ian would surely cower if he laid eyes on her again.

Her body shook with sobs. Merrin rocked herself, giving into the pain and torture of twenty years living a secret life of an ogre. Gar licked her face and she batted him away. The dog leaned against her, refusing to go. He curled up beside Merrin's leg—a dog's warmth, the only comfort to her unbearable shame.

Bewildered, Ian watched Merrin's smile transform into a grimace of unbridled panic. He'd barely caught sight of the dark pink birthmark she hid beneath her ridiculous scarf. She didn't allow him enough time to truly examine it, but from what he saw, the scar did nothing to detract from her beauty.

Ian sighed and cast his gaze to the rafters. With old Ruairi and his henchman Rewan after him, he already had more trouble than he needed—not to mention a gaping musket hole in his back. *Why must I always happen upon bonny women in desperate need of being rescued?*

He leaned heavily on the table and stood. His legs trembled, but he couldn't crawl back to his pallet when Merrin was so obviously upset. The hole in his back stretched with his movement, jabbing him like someone had taken an eating knife and carved out a kidney. However, Ian was not new to pain. A Scots warrior didn't live long without experiencing a blade slicing through his flesh. A man must grow impervious to pain, lest it control him.

After discarding the plaid from his waist, he pulled his shirt from the peg and yanked it over his head. Growing a bit stronger, he grabbed his kilt and wrapped it around his waist. He found his belt and dirk alongside the pallet and fastened them a good two inches below his wound.

Ian picked up Merrin's scarf and blinked his eyes to clear his vision. A soft blue-and-red plaid with a streak of yellow. He guessed she'd woven it herself. So many things about this woman confused him. That she had a good heart was for certain. No black-hearted woman would have tended him for two days with such selfless affection.

He swallowed back a heave as he headed for the door, the pain close to overwhelming. *Weak milk-livered sop, I've been abed for near two days, I can bloody well make it to the door.* Grasping the latch, he hoped Merrin hadn't gone far, else he might fall on his face before he found her. He hated weakness in a man, and detested it even more when he was the sorry blighter with a trembling hand. Ian gritted his teeth and pushed outside. The soil was sandy, and after he'd made an errant trip to the chicken coop, it wasn't difficult to pick up the lass's tracks.

Atop the hill, Merrin looked frail, crouched in a ball. The wind flapped her skirts while wisps of chestnut hair spiraled in every direction. Even Gar appeared worried, his head resting between his front paws, yet the dog's eyes scanned the horizon. His big ears pricked and his tail beat against Merrin's hip as Ian approached.

"Go away," she shouted without looking up. The agony in her voice tore at Ian's heart.

He stopped in his tracks, wringing her scarf between his hands. He swayed in place, his knees nearly buckling. Merrin ignored him. Her staccato breathing reflected her difficulty in gathering her wits.

Ian shook his head against the dizziness. With two more staggering steps, he dropped to his knees and rested his palm on Merrin's back. "I cannot bear to see ye cry."

Uneven breaths shuddered through her back and he rubbed his hand in a circle to soothe her.

"I'm a monster."

Never before had Ian heard such torment in a woman's voice. This lassie had nothing to be ashamed of. Most women would give their firstborn to possess a morsel of her loveliness. Ian's tongue twisted in knots. What could he say to ease her burden? "Ye're a fine woman, of that I can attest with all honesty."

Her breathing stopped. "Are ye not afraid of me?"

"Why on earth would I fear the likes of you?"

She jolted upright and pointed to her neck, her eyes filled with anguish. "Because of this."

A distant memory triggered in the back of Ian's mind. He was standing beside his brother, Alexander, looking across the *caol* toward a small stone cottage. His father placed a hand on each lad's shoulder. *Ye mustn't ever cross the caol onto Fladda. A witch who bears the mark of the devil lives there. As long as we leave her be, no harm will come to the clan.* Neither Ian nor Alexander ever disobeyed him—the risk of being flogged was as great as putting their kin in peril.

Ian recalled hiding on a hill across from the islet, hoping to spy the witch in action. He must have been eleven or twelve at the time when he saw lass of no more than seven or eight. It had puzzled him to espy a child.

His mind clicked. With a gasp, Ian stared Merrin in the eye.

The lass he'd seen *had* been her.

Merrin *was* the witch to whom his father had referred.

Merrin scowled and snatched the scarf from Ian's hand. "Ye fear me. I see it in your eyes."

Ian's gut clenched and he looked away. He didn't believe her to be touched by the devil. Surely there must be a mistake. "I ken a wives' tale that I cannot believe is true."

Merrin wrapped the scarf around her neck and tied it so taut, Ian feared she'd choke. "Aye? Are ye sure about that? I sent a band of pirates running for their lives not more than a month ago."

Ian laughed, the pressure of which strained against his wound, sending stars across his vision. With a grunt he pressed his palms into the mossy earth to steady himself

"Ye laugh, but 'tis true."

The pain easing, Ian brushed his fingertips across her cheek, soft as rose petals. His hand lingered, unwilling to pull away. He cupped her lovely face and savored her warmth. "Now tell me, lass. How could a wisp of a woman take on a band of marauding pirates?"

"They came ashore, hellbent on mischief, but I faced them and tore the scarf from me neck." Merrin pulled it away and brushed aside her tresses, giving Ian a good look at the mottled, raspberry-colored mark. It fanned out from her ear and spread down one side of her slender throat, ending just above her shoulder. "I stood me ground and shouted, 'If ye come closer, I'll cast a spell of the pox on ye and your spawn, so help me God.'"

Ian frowned against his urge to emit a hearty laugh. "I can see where they might feel some trepidation upon hearing such a bold tongue."

"Aye. They turned tail and ran."

Ian's heart squeezed. "'Tis perhaps a good thing. The pirates from Rona are ruthless. They could have stolen everything ye own, or worse." Ian didn't want to frighten her, but he'd fought the bastards hiding out on the small island to the north. He had no doubt if Merrin hadn't scared them away, she'd be dead, most likely raped first. "And why does your da leave ye alone when there're pirates about?"

Sadness darkened her eyes and she shuttered them with long, dark lashes. "He kens they will no' touch me. Aside from that once, no one ever sets foot on this island." She tossed the scarf around her neck, loosely this time. "Ye say Ye're putting me in danger? I ken Fladda is the safest place ye can be. Men are afraid of this land because of me birthmark. They call it the mark of the devil." Merrin's voice strained with her last words, as if she hated herself as well as the spiteful moniker.

"Nay, lass. 'Tis just a spot of red skin."

She brushed her hands across her eyes. "Aye? Tell that to the rest of the world."

"Have ye ever done anything witch-like? Can ye fly or cast a spell?"

"Of course not. Me da has the cottage surrounded with charms to keep the bogles and fairies at bay."

"Have ye ever seen the fairy folk or a true witch?"

"Nay, I doubt they would dare set foot on Fladda either."

"I haven't seen them, no' once in me life. I doubt they're real."

"If they're no', I've spent a lifetime of shame for naught."

Ian rubbed the fringe of her scarf between his fingers. "Mayhap ye have."

Wide-eyed, Merrin stared at him. When she blinked, a tear spilled down her cheek. She briskly swiped it away and cleared her throat. "Ye need to go back to the cottage. Ye shouldna come after me. Your color is pale as your shirt."

"Do no' mind the likes of me. I'll not get back to rights if I do no' push meself."

With an absent shove, Merrin roused Gar from a nap, then stood and offered her hand. "Ye need to build your strength afore ye set out. Will ye stay now that ye ken me secret?"

"Aye. As long as I'm no' a danger to ye."

She smiled for the first time—a brilliant, white-toothed grin that lit up her face as if the sun had burst from behind the stormy clouds. "Did ye forget already? I'm the dangerous one here. Ye could be cursed for life just for looking at me."

Ian grasped her hand and let her pull him to his feet. "I guess I'll take me chances, then."

He slung his arm over Merrin's shoulder and together they hobbled back to the cottage with Gar beside them. Ian's energy sapped, he no sooner could have escaped the island even if she attempted to cast a spell to rob him of his soul.

Chapter Six

N iall still hadn't returned when Merrin fluffed a pillow behind Ian's back. "Is this comfortable enough?"

Ian gingerly reclined. "Ta. 'Tis good."

Merrin ran the dagger in a circular pattern on the sharpening stone. "Are ye sure ye want a shave now? 'Twill only grow back in a day or two."

"Aye. I cannot stand the itching."

"Very well." She rubbed her thumb across the edge to test its sharpness. "But I think the dark stubble makes ye look dangerous."

He chuckled and grasped her free hand. "I wouldn't think ye would care for a man who looks like a pirate."

Merrin's insides fluttered out of control and she pulled her hand away. "I wouldn't say a pirate." Ian was far too handsome to be thrown in with an unsavory lot. His eyes bored through to her heart, and that dark beard contrasting with his flaxen hair practically made her so lightheaded, she may very well have gone daft. Perhaps a good shaving was what he needed to stop her insides from tricking her into thinking he had feelings for her. Ian would take his leave as soon as he was able. He'd set out to rejoin Janet, the woman he'd risked his life to save.

Ian arched his brow at her. "Are ye apprehensive about cutting me?"

"Nay, just thinking is all."

He raised his chin. "Go ahead, lass. 'Tis itching like a bad rash."

Merrin started at his upper jaw and ran the blade in a straight line to his chin. "Me da never complains of the itching."

"Aye, that's most likely because his beard is long. Once it grows out, the discomfort stops."

Merrin examined the trail of reddened skin she'd made and prepared the blade for another swipe. Ian kept his chin steady as a statue while she scraped away the stubble. Warm breath from his nostrils caressed her fingers when she shaved away his moustache. Silently, he watched her with those pale blue eyes. His gaze was hypnotizing as well as trusting. Merrin didn't understand why he was different, why he hadn't fled when he learned her secret. Ian showed no fear at all. Not that she was to be feared. She knew in her heart she was good. Even Niall and Friar Pat believed in her virtue. But for some reason, God chose to mark her—or else it was a mark of shame that had appeared upon her mother's death. Believing she had to bear it for her mother made the humiliation easier for Merrin to accept. If it had helped her mother's lot in any way, she would wear the mark without a qualm.

Ian's long, dark lashes rose. "Ye're awfully quiet."

"I do no' want to cut ye."

"Your hands are much gentler than me own."

"Good." Merrin took one last swipe and stood back to examine her work. "I think Ye're shaved clean."

She doused a cloth in the basin and cleansed his face. Merciful fairy feathers, Ian was more beautiful without the beard. Heaven help her, the fluttering in her stomach swelled into her breasts. She glanced down to ensure they were still in their proper place, terrified her body would give her feelings away.

Ian slid a warm hand around the back of her neck and gently rubbed. "Ye're blushing."

Merrin slapped both hands to her inflamed cheeks. "Am I?" Why had Niall not returned? She had no idea how to face Ian. He was in love with another woman. A man as bonny as Ian MacLeod would never, ever look fondly upon her.

She tried to pull away from his grasp, but Ian slid his other hand to her shoulder and drew her toward him until she perched upon his lap. Merrin's eyes fell to his lips. His tongue slipped out and moistened them, his eyes focused on her mouth. Her head spun as she realized he was moving closer to kiss her again.

Merrin couldn't pull away. She wanted this too much. Every inch of her skin alive, trembling, the only thing that existed was Ian. Her senses filled with his spicy scent. He touched his lips to hers, but not like he had before. This time he lingered. His tongue probed inside her mouth as his lips pressed more urgently. Her shoulders tensed. Merrin had no idea how to react, except she wanted this, wanted him to show her how a man courted a woman—if that was what this was called. Ian caressed the tip of her tongue with gentle strokes. With an exhale, she gave into him and mimicked his kiss, their tongues entwining together in a delicious dance.

Merrin kept her eyes closed as his lips left hers. She wanted to savor the moment, commit it to memory for the rest of her life, positive this would be the most wonderful sensation she would ever experience.

Ian gently pulled away and rested his forehead against hers. "Apologies. I shouldna been so bold."

She snapped her eyes open. Her spirits dove. "No. Ye shouldna." Merrin forced herself to stand on wobbly legs. "No' when Ye're in love with another."

Gar sprang from his mat and launched into a barking cacophony before Ian could explain. And what was he doing, anyway? He'd kissed her—a virgin, an innocent. Boar's ballocks, she'd done nothing but show him kindness, and he'd taken advantage. He should be hung by his thumbs for kissing her. Ian couldn't fall for a woman marked by the devil. He'd stupidly fallen in love with Ruairi's wife, and that had all but ended in Ian's ruination. How could he return to Brochel and ask Alexander for a place at his table with a witch on his arm, no matter how endearing?

Of course Ian didn't believe Merrin to be a witch of any sort—aside from a temptress. She'd done nothing to make him kiss her—nothing except smell like primrose, her smile endearing as a fairy's. Perhaps she was enchanted—enchanting, certainly. Ian ran his fingers through his hair. Women were his weakness. He'd become a warrior, made his body hard. Few men could best him in a fight, but a beautiful woman could bring him to his knees with a look.

He ground his fist into his palm. None of his worries mattered. It was best Merrin thought him in love with another.

Footsteps crunched up the path. Merrin snatched the dog's rope collar and gave it a yank. "Shut up ye wily hound, 'tis only Da."

Niall pushed through the cottage door. He stopped for a moment, his eyes darting from Merrin to Ian and back to Merrin. "I thought he'd be abed for at least another two days—if he rose at all."

Ian wanted to claim the bath Niall ordered on his behalf had been a miraculous cure, but that would incite a father's ire for certain. Ian had no idea how he'd stayed upright for so long with his head spinning from the stabbing pain in his back.

Merrin's cheeks flushed red. "Ian's very weak."

Niall took a seat across from him and frowned. "Ian, is it? What clan are ye from?"

"MacLeod of Raasay. Sir, I want to thank—"

"That's an outright lie."

The wound in Ian's back throbbed with his clenched gut, but he held up a hand and explained who he was. Merrin shook her head. Ian ignored her. He couldn't see lying about his identity. It would come out sooner or later. "Me father was Calum MacLeod. I've been away for me fostering."

"Ian, is it?" Niall repeated with a tad more respect in his voice. He squinted his eyes, then lifted a brow as if remembering something. "How did ye end up with a musket ball in your back?"

Ian's head pounded. The pain drained him more than facing his demons. "I spirited a lady away from a tyrant and created a diversion for her escape. I'd nearly made it to Raasay when the shot hit me."

"A tyrant, ye say?" Niall's eyes narrowed. "Do no' tell me ye stole a man's woman."

Ian propped his elbows on the table and rested his head in his hands. He rubbed his face and looked up. "I cannot lie to ye." Sweat bled from his brow and dripped to the table. He wouldn't be able to sit upright much longer.

Merrin rushed to him with a cloth and dabbed his temples. "Stop your badgering, Da. Can ye not see that he's too ill to answer your questions? Leave him be. At least until his strength returns."

Niall slid into a wooden chair. "I've only one more question to ask."

Ian gazed across the table expectantly. Once he answered, Niall would be a fool not to put him out. Ian needed another sennight to regain his strength. He didn't want to confront his brother until he was a whole man, could prove his worth with a sword. If he crawled to Alexander now, the laird might take him in, but only through pity. And once Alex learned of the shame he'd brought upon the clan, his brother would shun him for certain—especially if Ian was too weak to prove his value to the clan. Any Highland laird would spurn a man who had crossed his ally, even if he was a wounded brother.

Merrin placed a pitcher of ale on the table. Niall's glare snapped to his daughter's neck. "Where's your scarf?"

Merrin clapped her hand over her mark, the corners of her mouth drawn down in a cringe. "He kens, Da." She backed away as if she feared her father would launch himself over the table and strike.

Niall stood, wrapping his fingers around his dagger. "Do ye fear her?"

Ian slowly spread his palms to his sides and kept his voice even. "How could I fear the hands of a maid who nursed me from death's door?"

Niall didn't draw his knife, didn't follow through with the challenge, but his hand remained fixed on the hilt. "Were ye sent by the fairy folk? Do no' lie to me."

"Nay." Ian would have laughed if it were not for the stern countenance staring at him from across the table. The only way to handle a superstitious man was to play his game. "I doubt the King of the Fairies would be so bold as to shoot me in the back and risk me death by tossing me into the sea."

Niall paused and squinted. Ian didn't move, regarding him intently. The older man's grip eased.

A relieved breath slipped through Ian's lips.

Merrin set a trencher with a roasted chicken on the table. "All this talk of fairy folk is hogwash. Ian's a man of flesh and blood, just like ye or Friar Pat." She sat in the chair beside Ian. "We all need some food in our bellies afore we go completely daft."

Niall resumed his seat, reached for a pitcher and poured three tankards of ale. "Ye have that right, lassie."

Ian accepted the tankard and drank. Would Niall continue with his questioning?

Merrin used an eating knife to cut a leg and thigh quarter and placed it on Ian's plate. She gave him a sly wink—Ian's heart skipped a beat.

"What news from Brochel, Da?"

Niall cut off a bit of breast meat. "Looks like there'll be a good harvest come fall." He popped a morsel in his mouth. "Me tincture set the sick to rights straight away."

"That's good."

"The laird was mighty grateful." He shoved another bite in his mouth and regarded Ian. "He's your brother, no?"

"Aye. Though I haven't seen him since I was four and ten."

Niall eyed him. "Ye have the look of your mother."

"Do I still?" Ian couldn't hold back his smile. When he was a lad, the women at Brochel Castle always remarked how lucky he was to inherit his mother's fair hair. Surely he'd had no problem attracting women—it was just that they never ceased to bring parcels of trouble with them.

Merrin reached for her tankard and examined Ian over the top of it. "I do no' think he looks at all feminine."

Niall chewed with his mouth open. "'Twas not what I meant. He's a brawny man, all right, but he has the coloring of Lady Anne. By the shape of his features, I can tell they're kin."

Merrin's eyebrows arched. "How exciting, to be the son of a highborn English woman, and your father, the most feared laird on all the seas."

Ian tossed his head back and laughed. "Me ma is certainly a woman of correct manners, though I believe ye've been deceived about me da's reputation."

Niall's thick brows drew together. "Your da was called the Robin Hood of Raasay. I remember Brochel was but a rundown village before he came. And he built his empire on account of his own strength."

"That he did." Ian smiled appreciatively. "I simply meant there are many powerful lairds in the Hebrides. To say my father was the *most* feared is a wee bit presumptuous."

Niall shoved the rest of the chicken breast in his mouth and washed it down with ale. He slammed the tankard on the table and wiped his mouth with his shirt sleeve. "I've got to check on me herbs. But first, ye still haven't told me who shot ye in the back."

Ian looked him in the eye, his chest tight, the throbbing in his back spreading up his neck. "Rewan. Henchman for Clan MacLeod of Lewis. I spirited the chieftain's wife back to her kin."

Niall placed both palms on the table. "Ye mean to tell me ye crossed Ruairi?"

"Aye." Ian swallowed his urge to heave. "And I'd do it again to spare that woman from his lash."

The color drained from Niall's face. "Heaven help us all."

Chapter Seven

M errin tiptoed across the floor, careful not to wake Ian. She'd hardly slept, terrified about what Niall would do now he'd uncovered the reason Ian had been shot. Rather than lock horns, her father had pressed his palms to his temples and trod off to his workshop.

She could have followed him, but decided it would be best to let Niall work through the situation alone. He was no fool. Ian was safer on Fladda than anywhere in the Hebrides. Scarcely a soul knew of the island's existence, and of the handful who did, only a small number knew it to be inhabited.

Niall told her stories near every night, and he'd often refer to the tales he'd heard at Brochel, tales of Ruairi's tyranny. She knew he would not be surprised Ruairi turned wife beater. Merrin opened the door and shuddered. Doubtless, Niall would fear retribution for harboring a fugitive running from the tyrant. That he'd allowed Ian to stay in the cottage another night was a good sign. Merrin only wondered what her father would do come morning. Niall rarely made rash decisions, but once he fixed his mind on something, his word was final. He'd returned not so quietly in the wee hours—at least that would keep him abed late this morn.

Gar followed her out the door and to the coop. She snatched up a basket and tossed out some grain for the chickens. Most of the hens hopped from their nesting boxes, save one. "Are ye growing cluckie again, Lucy?"

Merrin reached her hand under the hen. Lucy rewarded her with a vicious peck. "You'll no' be threatening me." Merrin ignored the sting, gave the bird a shove and ran her fingers across two warm eggs. "So ye think ye want to have a go at being a mama again?"

The bird fluffed her feathers and settled back over the nest.

Merrin took an egg from her basket and rested it beside Lucy. "If Ye're going to set, ye may as well have another to keep warm." If the hen was still nesting on the morrow, Merrin would slip a couple more eggs beneath her.

The chickens scattered and squawked as Merrin traipsed about the yard. She stopped at the gate. Yes, she couldn't sleep last night because she worried about Niall's reaction to Ian's plight. But the one thing that consumed her mind—had her heart aflutter—was Ian's second kiss. Nothing else had existed when his eyes lowered to her lips. In her limited experience of the world, she'd never seen a man look so hungry. Even Gar did not stare at her with such intensity, so much *desire*.

And then when their lips met, Merrin could no longer keep her eyes open. Fire ran through her body and out the tips of her breasts as his tongue caressed her mouth. Every inch of her flesh wanted to touch him, but she'd merely placed a trembling hand on his shoulder.

What she wouldn't do to kiss him again, to feel the need burning in her body so intensely. If only. Merrin toyed with the eggs in her basket. Must she constantly remind herself that Ian loved another? He hadn't denied it. The turmoil between elation and anger had battled in her mind until the cock crowed at first light. If only she could face Ian and ask him if there might be any way a man could love a marked lass, she would at least know if there was any chance for her to find love. Mayhap there would be another, unattached man out there who would not fear her.

She needed to talk to Ian. Possibly he would see her differently than Da. Niall had been so adamant she not be seen by anyone, she'd always believed the world would shun her. Honestly, the only people she knew were three men. Two old, and one so bonny he made her heart squeeze with longing. If only she could go to Brochel and watch behind a tapestry. How did other women act when a man looked at her as if he'd been starved for a month? What would it be like to see children running about, laughing and playing? Yes, Niall had shared a great many stories with her—Friar Pat, too. But Merrin wanted to see these things for herself.

Her heart ached to belong.

Merrin was so wound up in her thoughts, she barely caught herself before she pulled down the latch on the cottage door. Gar crashed into the back of her legs and the eggs nearly went flying. Merrin gave the dog a sideways look. "'Tis easy for you to curl up beside the man and sleep. Next thing I know, ye'll be following him about instead of me."

Gar whined and brushed up against her.

"Nay." She gave him a scratch behind the ears. "Ye'd never leave me, would ye, boy?"

Gar's tail thumped her backside. Merrin grasped the latch. "I dunna ken what I'd do without ye." She opened the door a crack and arched a brow at the dog. "'Tis still dark within. Keep quiet. Do no' barrel over to Ian and lick him awake. He needs his sleep."

Snorting, Gar pushed the door wide, bounded across the floor and promptly stuck his nose in the poor man's face.

"Get back, ye mongrel," Ian groused, swiping a hand over his face.

Blast Him. "Gar, come behind." The dog circled twice and plopped beside Ian. Irritated with the dog's disobedience, Merrin set the basket on the table and took to lighting the candles. "I told him to leave ye alone."

She couldn't look Ian in the eye. Not after thinking about his kiss all night. If she got a glimpse of those lips, she might throw herself upon him and demand another. "If ye go back to sleep, he'll no' bother ye again."

The straw rustled. "Nay. I need to rebuild me strength."

Merrin forgot to avert her eyes. The plaid slipped from Ian's chest as he sat up. Why the man had decided to remove his shirt to sleep was yet another matter. Merrin stared. "How are ye feeling this morn?"

"Hungry. Ye got anything to eat in that basket?" Ian flashed a grin that made her knees buckle.

"How about some eggs and sausages? It will no' take but a moment to whip some up."

Ian reached for his shirt. "Thank ye kindly, ta." He pulled it over his head with a pained grunt.

An egg dropped from Merrin's hand. She darted across the floor with a startled hitch to her step. "Are ye all right?" She slapped her palm against his forehead. "Has the fever returned?"

Ian grasped her hand and grinned. "I let out wee grunt and Ye're thinking I'm on death's door?" He softly kissed her fingers. "I'm just a bit stiff, lass, but improved from yesterday."

Merrin stared at the thick, callused fingers surrounding hers. She could barely breathe. His lips caressing her fingers was such a simple gesture, but the heat spreading through her body disagreed. She gasped, lifting her gaze to his mouth. Throwing herself atop him and kissing him raw was a definite possibility.

Before she could act on her wayward thoughts, Ian cleared his throat and released her hand. "Forgive me, Merrin. I mustn't take liberties."

"Ye mustn't," Merrin croaked, though her hand yenned to feel those rough pads protectively encircle hers again. She dared look up. Ian's eyes were dark. His brows knit as if in pain. "I do no' believe Ye're as fit as ye might think. I can see it in your eyes."

"'Tis nothing. Only..."

Merrin's heart skipped a beat. Could she hope? "Aye?"

Ian shook his head. "I'm just hungry is all."

No. Of course he mustn't grasp her hands or kiss them. He must heal quickly so he can go back to his life, back to *her*.

Ian bit the inside of his cheek. He needed to act with more restraint. Why on earth could he not keep his errant hands off the lass? Christ, the way she'd stared at his bare chest lit a fire in his groin so painful he needed to walk outside and throw himself in the sound. Ian could sniff a woman's interest across a crowded hall. Merrin might be innocent, but she was ripe as a butterfly orchid in full bloom. Her eyes could no sooner hide her desires as a child could hide his excitement before plunging into a plum pudding. Her innocence made the allure all the more arousing. What Ian would give for a chance to escort a woman such as Merrin through the wilderness of passion. His mind boggled.

Ian balled his fists. Why did he have to be rescued by *a bana-bhuidseach*—Merrin was a witch all right. A stealer of men's hearts, hidden from the world so men would have ease from their lust.

"*Bana.*" That was a good pet name for her.

"What?"

Ian looked up. "Did I say something?"

"Aye." Merrin held up the wooden spoon. "Ye said *Bana.*"

"'Tis because ye are enchanting. I'll call ye *Bana.*"

Merrin turned the crackling sausages, keeping her lovely backside toward him. "I do no' take kindly to your teasing."

"But ye are a temptress."

"How can ye say that? I've done nothing."

"You do no' need to *do* anything. Ye just are." Ian pushed aside the bedclothes. He should have kept his sorry mouth shut. Merrin obviously rued the stigma of being marked. He had no business teasing her about it. And he couldn't lead her on any more than he'd already done. No. The journey down the path of passion would have to wait for another time, and another, less innocent temptress who, no doubt, would cross his path.

He stretched his arms over his head. Stars crossed his vision. A pained grunt bellowed from the depths of his gut. Mother Mary, would the hole in his back never cease to claim his wits? Ian had been injured before, but this had him laid up like none other.

Merrin whirled around. Ian held up his hand. "Do no' worry yourself. I'm coming good."

"Mayhap ye should have some poppy juice to take the edge off your pain."

Ian frowned. "That rubbish knocks me out cold. 'Tis the last thing I need to gain me strength."

"Ye do no' need to be up and around to heal."

"I do." Ian clenched his teeth and used the chair to pull himself up. "I cannot stay here much longer. Sooner or later they'll come looking for me."

Merrin eyed him. "Ye'd better sit in that chair if ye must use it for a prop."

"I'll be right once I have some food in me belly."

"Ye'll be right once ye give your wound time to heal."

Niall's bedroom door opened as Ian gingerly slid into the chair. The older man scratched his belly and gave Ian an appraising once-over. "Sitting at the table's a good sign. Ye'll be able to join your kin soon."

Merrin plopped a trencher of sausages and scrambled eggs in front of Ian. "He's pushing himself too hard if ye ask me. Turned white as egg shells when he stood."

Ian reached for an eating knife. "I want to offer my brother me sword. Prove me worth."

Across the table, Niall pulled out a chair. "Are ye afraid of retribution?"

"Aye, and Alexander will no' take me actions lightly. I need all me wits when I face him."

Merrin served up Niall's fare and sat beside Ian. "Ye see? He needs his strength afore he traipses back to Brochel. Ruairi may even have spies there already." She stabbed a sausage with her knife and bit it in half.

Ian's gut clenched. He'd need to be on his guard when he went to Brochel. The two MacLeod clans were blood kin. When Ian showed his face, word would slip back to Ruairi in a day.

Niall used his fingers to sprinkle a pinch of salt over his eggs. "Merrin, ye have a point. But I do no' want word slipping out that Ian's here. Ruairi's henchman would burn us out for certain."

Merrin nodded rapidly. "All the more reason for Ian to stay indoors and turn his mind to healing."

"Nay. I need me strength, and I will no' hide from me enemies. If ye have a sword, I'd be grateful for the use of it. Practice is the only way to rebuild me dwindling muscles." Ian pushed away the pain and sat up straight. "Me brother will be more forgiving if I can prove meself worthy to sit at the high table. Any chieftain cannot abide a weakling."

Niall scratched his beard and narrowed his eyes. "I've an old sword and a post. Ye are welcome to it, but keep yourself hidden. I want no ships spotting a warrior practicing in me paddock."

"Thank ye."

"I wove a woolen kilt of natural and woad-blue plaid for Da." Merrin eyed her father. "It would attract far less attention than Ian's red."

Niall chuckled. "Mayhap ye should grow your beard. Any spyglass would pick up the sheen of your bonny face a mile away."

Ian ran his hand across the morning's stubble. Niall was right, of course. Ian hated facial hair, and everyone on the Isle of Lewis knew it.

Chapter Eight

R ewan MacLeod stood on the deck of the galley and watched the grey stone walls of Stornoway Castle grow from a small speck on the Isle of Lewis into the great fortress he admired, presiding over all the Hebrides, and home to his clan, the feared MacLeods of Lewis. Rewan prayed his aging chieftain would be satisfied with his efforts.

He'd killed Ian—"Raasay" the traitor. He'd always called him Raasay to remind the smug bastard he wasn't one of the MacLeods of Lewis. He might be a MacLeod, but didn't hail from Rewan's mighty island. He was only the nephew of the chieftain, though now a disowned one. Days of scanning the shores along the sound turned up no body, but Rewan's new musket hadn't missed its mark. One day, he'd see Raasay, the second son of Calum, in hell.

Rewan's uneasiness crept up his spine. His orders had been to kill them both, but the MacKenzie fortress was impenetrable to his small band. If old Ruairi wanted Janet, he'd need to send an army—which he might decide to do.

With Alick, his man-at-arms, by his side, Rewan marched through the heavy wooden doors of Stornoway's great hall, lined with rich tapestries woven in Venice. A log fire crackled in the chamber's immense hearth. Ruairi sat upon the dais in his leather upholstered chair, taking his nooning. The old chieftain beckoned Rewan forward. "Me henchman returns. I was beginning to wonder if ye'd failed me."

Rewan motioned for Alick to stay a few paces behind, then knelt before the dais. "'Tis good to be home, m'laird."

"'Tis a good sign ye've seen fit to again set foot on Lewis." Ruairi motioned for him to stand. "Tell me, are they both dead?"

"We buried a lead ball in Ian's back when he fled in a skiff—sank it, we did. But he led us away from Lady Janet—"

Food spewed from the chieftain's mouth, hitting Rewan's boots. "Do not utter her name." Ruairi chopped a gnarled hand through the air. "Ever."

"Apologies, m'laird. The woman reached the MacKenzie keep afore we could catch her."

Ruairi shrugged and picked his teeth with his little fingernail. "I've divorced her—she's ruined and dead to me."

Rewan's eyes bulged. Why had he spent the past few sennights chasing after the wench with orders not to return until she was caught or dead?

Ruairi leaned forward, a sneer etching his wrinkled face. "But I want me bloody backstabbing nephew's head. I took the bastard in and fostered him for near ten year', and this is how he repays me kindness?"

"He drowned, m'laird."

"What proof have ye?" The old chieftain wasn't going to let up.

"Me own musket ball hit him in the back. The skiff sank. We went after him through driving rain and wind—searched the shores for days. We had no chance to recover the corpse."

"Then how do ye ken he's dead?"

Rewan spread his palms to his sides. Yes, it was dark and pissing down rain and he couldn't see a thing, but that only made Raasay's likelihood of survival all the more unlikely. "He couldna survived."

"Aye." Alick stepped beside Rewan and bowed. "Ian MacLeod's dead, as sure as I breathe."

"Did I grant ye leave to speak?" Ruairi pounded his fist on the table. "I cannot believe ye returned with no proof. I want the bastard's head, his bones, his dirk. No one steals away with me wife." He pointed toward the heavy oak doors. "Go and do not return until ye can show me proof Ian MacLeod is dead."

Rewan bowed at the waist. "Aye, m'laird. I'll see it done."

He couldn't storm out of the hall fast enough. For the love of God, Rewan had spent the past few sleepless nights tormented about his failure to bring back Janet's head. Christ, he'd spent days trying to break into the MacKenzie fortress. With a stroke of a pen, Ruairi had cast aside his bloodlust for his wayward young bride?

Rewan lost over half his men—and now he'd be chasing after a ghost? Ian MacLeod's body would have been fodder for sharks by now.

Alick followed him to the courtyard, his stocky legs skipping to keep up. "How the hell are we going to find him?"

Rewan ground his back molars. "With a bit of luck, he washed up on the shore of Raasay. We'll start at Brochel."

Alick pulled his helm from his balding head. "I was looking forward to being home."

"Me as well." Rewan rubbed his crotch. "I need a good rut afore we sail. Tell the men we leave at dawn on the morrow."

Dressed in the unpretentious kilt woven by Merrin's deft fingers, Ian managed to stagger outside with Niall's two-handed sword. Blunt and showing a fair bit of rust, the weapon couldn't have been used in a quarter-century or more. Not that Niall looked remotely like he'd been a warrior at any time in his life.

Ian found a lone fencepost where he could spar. Per Niall's request, it was hidden from the water's view, near the cottage. Holding the claymore over his head, he addressed the post and slowly lowered the blade until it touched the sturdy wood. His arms trembled. He clenched his forearms until the trembling stopped. Closing his eyes, he blocked the throbbing pain in his back. He would massacre this post if it killed him.

Bellowing his war cry, he spun in place and slammed the blade into the column with every thread of force his sinews could deliver. Pain shot through his shoulders. The sturdy post gave not an inch. The force of the hit reverberated through his arms, across his shoulders, up his neck and shook his head until his brain rattled.

Ian looked over his shoulder. Thank God no one had seen that. What an idiot. The blasted blade was duller than a stone. He should have warmed up with a sparring pattern before he tried the smash the hell out of the solid oak pole most likely driven six feet into the ground. For all Ian knew, the bloody thing was petrified to rock.

Sucking in a few deep breaths, Ian cleared his head and again challenged the post. With both hands, he struck the column from side to side. Initially his muscles burned, but Ian worked through it. He would not allow a piece of wood to best him. As he worked, his legs trembled. Bloody hell, he was as weak as an old man.

Merrin appeared in the next paddock wheeling a barrow of hay. She upended the cart and whistled. An old sorrel nag sauntered up from the wood and dipped its head to the mound of fodder. Merrin stepped in and ran her hand along the old fella's neck. Her voice carried on the wind. "That's a good lad, Tam. If ye eat all your hay, I might bring out some grain for ye later."

Ian's heart skipped a beat when Merrin looked at him. He quickly addressed the post. She waved. He gave her a nod and lunged, displaying his most deadly "kill" maneuver. Nearly blinded by pain, he tightened his abdominals to keep his hands from shaking. Out of the corner of his eye, he watched her wheel the barrow back toward the workshop while he swung his sword in his warm-up routine—the one he should have started with in the first place.

After catching sight of Merrin, he put everything he had into it—reaching high, thrusting his blade down while dropping to one knee. Merrin stopped before she reached the shed. Ian leveled the sword at the pole. The damned petrified piece of oak didn't stand a chance. Ian started slowly to avoid a repeat of his first attempt to kill it. With Merrin's eyes on him, he would show her exactly what a well-trained warrior could do with a sword in his hand, even if he was injured.

He swallowed down the bile as his back tortured him for ignoring it. But Merrin was watching. He'd not be bested by a mere post. Ian swung from side to side. He darted and lunged, wielding the claymore with expert finesse. He grew stronger and more self-assured. He planted his foot. Holding the sword low, he spun with an upward slice. The tip of the post sailed through the air.

He stopped and chuckled. *I knew I'd win.* Ian wiped his sweat with his sleeve and looked to where he'd last seen Merrin. She was gone. The hole in his back needled him like a corkscrew. He brushed his hand over the bandage. Blood soaked through it. Suddenly his arms were so heavy, he couldn't take another swing.

Sucking in deep breaths of air, Ian leaned on the sword. He thanked God Rewan MacLeod wasn't after him now. He'd never be able to stand up to that bear of a man in his current state. Merrin had been right. Ian needed to allow his body some time to heal.

First he'd sharpen the blade. It didn't take a man of iron to hone a sword, and this one needed a good sharpening for certain.

Neither Niall nor Merrin were in the cottage when Ian placed the weapon on the table. He used the metal file to rasp away the rust and expose the blade's edge. He found a jug of whale oil on the shelf and dribbled some on the whetstone. He passed the blade back and forth, using a uniform stroke. Like anything worthwhile, it didn't pay to rush a sharpening job. The blade would reveal itself, shining like new when it was ready, and only the blade could disclose when it was sharpened.

The edge flickered in the light and Ian reached for a cloth, running it along the shaft appreciatively. He tested the blade with his thumb. *Nearly there.* "Ye're a fine old weapon, are ye not?"

Merrin's voice carried in through the window. "What harm is there? He should stay as long as he likes."

"He needs to be with his own kind," Niall argued. "Aside from being a fugitive, he's highborn, not meant for the likes of us."

"He's wounded. Let him return to his kin when he's able. He said himself, he needs to prove his worth to be accepted."

"I think ye've become infatuated with him."

Ian's stomach turned upside down. How could Niall be so perceptive in such a short amount of time? Surely he wouldn't have sensed Ian's attraction to his daughter. Not when Ian was doing so much to dissuade her affections—aside from kissing her, of course. But Niall hadn't been there when it happened—twice.

"Och. Ye're always trying to find ways to keep me hidden. So what if I like him? He'll be gone soon enough and I'll be back to me lonely life with Gar on me heels, cooking and cleaning until ye need me no more."

Ian exhaled. Thank heavens she harbored no false hope. That was for the best. He had far too much at risk to entertain an affair of any kind.

"I just do no' want to see ye hurt," Niall said.

"Aye? There ye stand running to Brochel every Wednesday and rubbing elbows at the castle. Can I not have a friend, just this once?" Ian froze while no one said a word. "He's no' afraid of me, Da. And he's near me age. Please." Her tone had gone pleading and soft as a whisper. "Do no' send him away afore he's ready."

Ian's heart twisted into a knot. Christ strike him dead on the spot. Poor Merrin. Poor, giving, *selfless* Merrin thought herself a demon, a marked woman. Nothing could be further from the truth. She was pure and delightful, beautiful—strikingly so. Ian should know. He hadn't been able to think of much else since he'd been on Fladda.

And why couldn't Niall see past all the superstitious hogwash at Brochel? Why had he stayed on Fladda where Merrin had no chance of finding a husband? Surely Alexander, his brother, laird of Raasay would understand...

The door creaked open. Merrin stepped inside and brushed her tresses away from her face. "Ian." She blushed scarlet. "I thought ye'd still be out in the paddock."

Servants were clearing the dishes from the afternoon meal when the ram's horn blew, announcing a ship sailing into Brochel Cove. Not as agile as he once was, Friar Pat called to the sentry up on the battlement rather than climb the tower's winding stairs. "Can ye see their pennant?"

The guard cupped his hands around his mouth. "MacLeod of Lewis."

Had old Ruairi seen fit to pay his nephew a visit? Pat doubted that, but ambled down the hill to the beach. In his great many years, one thing the friar learned well—a holy man's presence always helped to ensure the crazy Scots kept their swords in their scabbards—at least until the parley had been uttered. But Friar Pat didn't anticipate any posturing with an ally ship sailing into the bay. Nonetheless, he'd stand beside the laird and welcome the guests, as he had done for over forty years.

Alexander and his henchman, Sir Bran, nodded as Friar Pat waddled in beside them. "Have ye any reason to expect a visit from Lewis men?"

Alexander looked to Bran and shrugged. "We've both come up with nothing."

Friar Pat fondly recalled Sir Bran as a lad. He'd been a gawky cabin boy for Calum MacLeod, but no more. The man was a beast—solid as a ship's hull. He formed a daunting picture standing on the shore beside Laird Alexander, a strapping figure of a man himself with his red hair and beard. Friar Pat was often reminded how fortunate he was to be a servant to Clan MacLeod of Raasay.

The galley moored. Sir Rewan MacLeod splashed through the surf and Bran stepped forward with a mighty laugh. "I cannot believe Ye're still alive, ye old roustabout."

The two henchmen embraced as if they were long lost brothers. Rewan slapped Bran's back. "And how is your lady wife?"

"Enya's busy as a hen with a dozen chicks underfoot."

"A dozen?"

Bran grinned, standing proud as an eight-point stag. "Aye."

"Where do ye keep them all?"

Bran gestured up the hill with his thumb. "Built onto me cottage near five year' ago."

Rewan pulled his bonnet from his dark locks. "Five year'? Has it been that long?"

"Longer, I'd reckon."

Alexander stepped forward and offered his hand. "Sir Bran, ye can chatter with Uncle Ruairi's henchman all ye like, but first I'd like to ken what brings him to Brochel."

Sir Rewan turned his attention to the Raasay chieftain and shook his hand. "I'm looking for your brother."

Friar Pat stared. Then he sucked in a gasp.

"Isn't he on Lewis?" Alexander asked.

Rewan's gazed focused on the friar. "Nay. He's not."

Friar Pat's palms moistened as he fingered the large wooden cross he wore over his brown robes. *The man in Niall's cottage must be Ian. Heaven help me feeble mind, I even commented about the likeness to his father. Why hadn't I realized it at the time?*

Alexander shook his head. "We've not seen him on Raasay since he left for his fostering."

"He absconded with Lady Janet—took her back to her MacKenzie kin, and then he ran." Rewan continued to leer at Pat and inclined his thumb toward the castle. "M'laird, do ye mind if we have a word in private? There's more I wish to say, but 'tis for your ears only."

Alexander agreed and Pat took a step back, right into Sir Bran.

The big henchman waited beside Pat until Rewan and Alexander started up the hill. "Is something amiss? Ye look like ye swallowed a bitter brew."

"I ken where Alexander's brother is, and once Rewan explains his men shot Ian in the back, Alexander will ken too."

Bran grasped the friar's shoulders. "Ye mean Ian is the scrapper who washed up on Fladda?"

"Aye. I've only just realized."

Bran's gaze darted to the men climbing the hill. "Och, for the love of Christ."

Friar Pat shook his finger. "Do not take the name of the Lord in vain, not even at a time like this."

Bran pointed at a skiff. "Go quickly and warn him. I'll see what I can do. Mayhap I can convince Rewan to a few tots of whisky and to stay the night."

"I hope the lad's conscious. Last time I saw him, he was dreaming with the angels." Friar Pat stepped in the skiff while Bran pushed him into the bay. "Do what ye can and do no' let on where I am. If Rewan asks, tell him I've had a bout of rheumatism...that wouldn't be far from the truth."

Chapter Nine

Merrin grasped the pot of honey poultice. "Pull up your shirt."

Seated at the table, Ian looked up from sharpening his dirk. "No' again?"

He'd done such a fine job on Niall's old sword, Merrin leaned in and admired his handiwork. "Friar Pat told me to apply the salve morning and night, lest infection set in."

"Infection? Och, all right. I do no' want the fever to come back."

The brawny Highlander surely wouldn't care to spend a sennight or more on that straw pallet delirious with chills. "There's a smart lad. Is it paining ye much?"

Ian set the dirk aside and tugged the hem of his shirt out from under his kilt. "I should say nay, but I can still feel your da's poker singeing me flesh."

"It will heal if ye give it time." Merrin eyed his weapon, hewn so smooth, she could see her reflection. "I've never seen a dirk so fancy. Are those real stones in the hilt?"

Ian turned the silver handle over. "Aye. Me da gave it to me after he returned from one of his privateering voyages. Said he'd taken it from a Spanish captain."

She looked closer. The stones sparkled and reflected the candle-light like nothing she'd ever seen. "You've had it since ye were a lad?"

Ian nodded. "A warrior needs to learn to use a dirk afore he can master a sword."

Though she'd become accustomed to being close to him, her insides still stirred when she caught his scent. All she needed to do was raise her chin and his lips would be eye level. Her palms perspired, her heart fluttered. Rather than completely embarrass herself, Merrin chose to admire his hands. His fingers were at least twice as thick as hers, but he cleaned his dirk with gentleness, obviously taking care of a fine piece that not only served as a weapon, but a precious heirloom.

Her gaze traveled up his arms. He'd rolled his sleeves to his elbows. The muscles in his forearms rippled as he worked the blade in a circular pattern on the whetstone. She lifted her hand to touch him, feel his power, but gripped her fingers in a fist. He wouldn't want her placing her hands all over him. What was she thinking?

Merrin stepped back and grasped the hem of his shirt. Her breath quickened. She admonished herself for such foolishness. She'd tended his wound countless times since he'd arrived. But that was before Merrin decided to take some hay to Tam this morning. Of course the horse didn't need hay in summer when the grass in the paddock was practically knee high, but it had been such a wonderful idea to snatch a good peek at Ian in full daylight without his shirt, those inhumanly strong muscles bulging while he swung his sword at the post. As long as she could remember, Niall's old sword had done nothing but rust by the cottage door.

But Ian brought it back to life. He wielded it like he'd been born to be a warrior. No wonder he took Janet from the tyrant and delivered her back to her loving family. A man with a physique like Ian's who could make a blade hiss through the air and dance with it as if Mother Nature were whistling a tune on the wind. With a musket-shot hole in his back? Well, he most likely could do anything he pleased.

Ian looked like a god sparring with the pole. Even with his wound, he was impressive—fearsome. Power like his didn't come from sitting in a chair. He'd been bred to be a warrior, trained since he was a wee laddie—and the fancy dirk he was sharpening proved it.

Merrin steeled her nerves. "It would be easier if ye took off your shirt since Ye're no' lying down." She bit her lip. Had she been too bold? What harm was there in ogling his muscular back?

Ian didn't blink. "All right." He set the dirk down, and in one move the shirt was over his head and tossed on the table.

Merrin knew it was rude to stare, *but holy fairy feathers and bogle's breath and throw in some pixies as well.* The day's exercise had strengthened him. Veins stood proud on his chest, which rose and fell with each breath.

"Merrin?"

She tapped her tongue to her lip and stared at his masculine flesh. "A-Aye?"

"Did ye want to dress me wound?"

She snapped her mouth closed and met his gaze. Blast those pixies, he was grinning at her with a spritely twinkle in his eye. She glanced around at his bandages. "Oh. Yes." She pulled away the dressing and examined Ian's wound. That sobered her up. Though still seeping and red, the gaping hole was closing. "Sorry Da hurt ye carving the musket ball out and cauterizing it, but 'tis better than a slow death."

She'd only touched him lightly, but Ian flinched. "Aye. I'm grateful."

"We'll see ye fixed up and ye can be on your way." She glopped the poultice on her fingers, but hesitated. She didn't like *that* idea in the least. Ian would be heading for Brochel soon—if only he'd not forget about her when he did. "I wish I could see the castle one day—ye ken, go there without the fear of being shunned...or burned." She smoothed the ointment onto his back.

Ian hissed and arched. "Mayhap I could escort ye once I've made me place beside Alexander."

Merrin's heartbeat raced. "Do ye mean it? I could hide behind a curtain. I just want to see all the finery."

The corner of Ian's mouth turned up with a puzzled quirk. "Ye shouldn't have to hide your bonny face."

Merrin brushed her fingers across her mark. "I cannot risk being seen. Some still blame me for Mother's death."

"No one need know who ye are."

Merrin gaped at him. All her life she'd dreamt about going to the castle, eating in the great hall and dancing into the wee hours. "Do not toy with me."

Ian reached for her hand. Heavens, why did his touch always send her pulse aflutter? He studied her fingers—heaven help her, his chest still rose and fell with every breath. "I may have a number of inequities, but when I give me word, I honor it." He closed his eyes and caressed his lips across her palm. "When I am able, ye'll see Brochel and I'll ensure no harm comes to ye."

Merrin threw her arms around Ian's neck and squeezed. "Ah, Ian, I cannot believe that ye came to us. Thank the heavens ye did no' die."

Ian's warm hands ran down the length of her back. He chuckled. "'Tis no' proper for a young maid to throw her arms around a man's neck. Especially when he's half dressed." Making no move away, he grasped her waist, his eyes lowering to her lips. "It makes a man want to do...so many things."

The tingling sensation churning in her bosoms felt so inexplicably good. His powerful, naked chest pressed against her breasts. How did that happen? She couldn't recall, but he definitely was going to kiss her again. She moistened her lips and leaned closer.

"I cannot resist ye." His voice was but a low whisper.

The last thing she wanted was for him to resist her. True, he would soon take his leave, but at this moment, Ian was in her cottage and in her arms. All restraint cast aside, this was her chance to connect with a living, breathing, unbelievably handsome man. "Ye do no' need to. I want to experience life, Ian. I may never have a chance again."

With a slight tilt of his head, he slid a hand up the back of her neck. His fingers threaded through her hair. Ever so softly, he touched his lips to hers. Merrin closed her eyes and melted into him, his taste spicy, exotic. She tried to imitate his motion, circling her tongue. Her body on fire, she rubbed her breasts against him, melting.

A deep moan slipped from Ian's throat. He gently sucked. Merrin's breasts ached so, she thought they'd burst. Something deep within screamed for more. She wanted her whole body to touch him. It would be ever so bold to swing her leg across his lap...she'd do it if it weren't for the heavy skirts of her kirtle and the fact that Niall was only steps away in his workshop.

Ian traced his finger from the tip of her head down to the neckline of her bodice. She threw her head back at the heavenly tingling.

Voices.

Urgent tones.

Merrin jerked away, her eyes darting to Ian. He already had the sword in his hand. His face stone hard, wary.

Merrin silently wrapped the scarf around her neck and listened. Ian put his finger to his lips. She nodded. He carefully limped to the door, blade at the ready.

Ian reached for the latch but the door opened. Friar Pat's eyes bulged. "Ian?"

"Och, friar, ye gave us a fright." Ian lowered his sword and pulled the holy man into an embrace. "I'm so glad to see ye, old friend."

The friar slapped Ian on the back, the poor warrior bellowing a pained grunt.

"I've come to warn ye." Pat looked to Merrin and back at Ian, then over his shoulder as Niall crossed the threshold. "Rewan is on Raasay, looking for ye—or your remains."

Ian stepped back. "Holy bloody hell."

Pat's head bobbed. "Aye, me sentiments exactly."

Ian slid the sword into its scabbard and plucked his dirk from the table, slipping it into his belt. "I must away."

"Nay." Merrin rushed forward, grasping the sleeve of Friar Pat's robe. "He's too weak to flee."

Gar hopped up from his bed and slipped his body between Merrin and the friar, his wagging tail beating against her leg.

Niall crossed to the table. "'Tis time Ian took his leave. We've nursed him long enough."

The room spun and Merrin pushed Gar away. Ian couldn't leave now. He'd die. The henchman and his men would track him down and kill him. Besides, she wasn't ready to say goodbye. Merrin yanked her cloak from the wall and grabbed a satchel. "I cannot let him go alone." Gar rubbed against her thighs and whined.

Niall grasped her arm. "Nay, Merrin."

Friar Pat placed a weathered hand on Niall's shoulder. "She's right. Ye all must leave."

A loaf of bread in hand, Ian stopped. "Ye must be joking."

The friar steepled his hands under his chin. "Ye ken Rewan will burn this place and kill them if he discovers they've helped ye."

Niall threw up his hands. "Ballocks to that."

After tripping over her dog for the third time, Merrin grabbed the oatcakes and sausages, shoving them into her satchel. "We must go, Da." She shook her finger under his nose. "Ye see? 'Tis the only way." She turned to Ian. "Pack the poultice and the bandages."

"Bloody bogle's breath," Niall said, sliding his dirk into his belt. "I kent helping a man with a musket hole in his back would bring nothing but misery."

Gar paced back and forth in front of the door, yowling like he'd been skewered. Pat held a satchel while Ian filled it with medicine and more food. "Ian is our son," the friar said. "We cannot turn our backs on him."

"He's no bloody son of mine," Niall groused, doing nothing to help.

Merrin ensured her scarf was secure around her neck, then fastened her cloak. "Are we ready?"

Ian gave her a firm nod and Niall looked like he could kill a bull. A spike of fear shot up Merrin's spine. She was about to leave Fladda, something she'd never done—not even once. She was fleeing with an old man, and another so weak, yesterday after he'd found her crying, he had barely made it back to the cottage without collapsing. Now they were running from the most notorious chieftain in the Hebrides and his feared henchman, Rewan MacLeod.

Ian had experienced Rewan's ruthlessness firsthand. He'd worked for the taskmaster—sparred with him every morning from the time he was ten and four. Rewan had taken every opportunity to show him his birth as a second son meant nothing. Ian needed to prove himself or live in a cesspool of shame—a lesson ingrained by his uncle.

True, when he did as told and kept his mouth shut, Ian had little issue with the henchman. But it was Rewan's job to protect and carry out old Ruairi's orders, and Rewan took his role of henchman seriously. Rewan's viewpoint? Nothing his laird demanded was outrageous. Nothing. Unconditional loyalty and ruthlessness kept him by Ruairi's side for the past thirty-odd years.

Heading to the skiff, Ian strapped the claymore to his back, right shoulder to left hip, to avoid contact with his wound. "Have ye got a bow and arrows?"

Niall turned toward the cottage. "I've a bow. Not sure about the arrows."

"It'll be handy if we need to fell a deer."

"You go ahead. I'll fetch it."

Bile burned Ian's gullet as they hastened to the skiff with Friar Pat mumbling prayers behind them.

Merrin pointed to the boat and clapped her hands. "Gar, jump in."

Ian stopped on the shore. "Ye do no' mean to bring the dog?"

"And leave him here to fend for himself?" Merrin climbed in and threw her arms around the deerhound's neck. "I'm no' leaving without him."

Niall caught up, bow in hand—only one arrow. "Your damned dog could give us away."

She clamped her grip on Gar tighter. "He's coming or I'll stay here and face Rewan alone."

Ian nudged Niall's shoulder. "There's nay time to argue. Climb in the skiff."

Pat lumbered up, leaning on his walking stick. "Where will ye go?"

Ian grasped the oars and glanced back at Niall. "Skye?"

The old man spread his palms. "Do ye think the MacKenzie will take us in?"

Ian frowned. "'Tis the first place Rewan will look."

Niall pointed across the sound. "There's a place we can hide the skiff in Bearreraig Bay. 'Tis about the only close cove we can row ashore that's not a sheer cliff."

Merrin pulled her cloak taut around her neck. "Are there many people there?"

"Not near Bearreraig Bay, but if we go north, we'll meet the MacQueens and south the MacKinnons."

Ian nodded. "Not to mention the cutthroat MacDonalds and the Nicolsons in the middle."

Friar Pat pointed southwest. "If ye can make it to the western part of the island, Alexander is friendly with the Dunvegan MacLeods."

Ian splashed the oars in the water. "Ruairi is friendly with them as well—they're kin. 'Tis best we find an inconspicuous place to hide."

Merrin clutched the satchel on her lap with one hand and held on to Gar with the other. "Aye, lest they see me."

Sitting beside her, Niall clutched her elbow. "Keep your mark covered at all times, lass. Ye never ken when someone will happen upon us." The old man's ill temper was cooling down. If they didn't work together, they could all end up dead. The man had protected his daughter for years. *His survivor instinct must be strong.*

Friar Pat leaned into the hull and pushed the skiff into the surf. Ian ground his teeth and worked the oars. He didn't have to reach his hand back to see if he was bleeding. Warm blood pooled in the waistband of his kilt. Pain didn't matter. He'd gotten Merrin and Niall into this mess, and by God, he'd ensure they didn't lose more than they already had.

"Once Rewan finds Fladda abandoned, he'll move on toward MacKenzie land for certain." Ian tried to sound reassuring. After all, that was where the two had last met. Fleeing to Skye on the other side of the sound was a much better option—one that Rewan wouldn't expect.

"Ye reckon?" Niall asked.

"Aye. Then I'll take ye back to Fladda and be on me way. Ye shouldn't need to be gone from your home long."

Niall glanced over his shoulder at the tiny isle as they rowed away. "Providing there's a home to return to, God willing."

Merrin got Gar to lie at her feet. "Ian, ye look like Ye're about to fall from your perch. We'll stay beside ye until Ye're strong enough to go off on your own."

Was his weakness that obvious? He must show her differently. He was deep in this, but Merrin and Niall were innocent. He could not see them ruined. "Rowing helps build me strength. I can feel it coming back." Aside from a wave of queasiness, the pain Ian's back had numbed a bit with exertion.

Niall studied him with knit brows. "Your color's gone pale. Let me take the oars."

Ian glanced over his shoulder. They'd crossed about a quarter of the way, but he couldn't abide having an old man take over his responsibility. "I'll keep on. If I cannot make it, I'll have ye give me a spell."

Merrin shook her head. "Ye're a stubborn man."

"I'm a MacLeod. 'Tis in me breeding."

But Ian knew his body had limits. His strength sapped, he prayed he could at least make it across the sound. Blast it all, he should have taken the skiff and set out on his own yesterday. He could have lain in the hull and drifted until he hit a shore. Any shore would do, as long as no one recognized him. He'd be able to hide his injury now the lead ball had been removed.

He hated bringing Merrin and her father into his problems. He regretted the day he met Janet MacKenzie. But he'd never apologize for helping the lass. No woman deserved abuse. Not even one who would use him for her own gain.

Ian's mother, Lady Anne, had been put on a pedestal by his father—where she ought to be. He wished he could see her now, carrying her head high, teaching him about everything, from etiquette to languages to falconing. Ian never did like etiquette, but as a man, he realized it had its place. His shoulders tensed. Etiquette was something old Ruairi never learned in all his years.

Once behind closed doors in the laird's solar, Rewan accepted a cup of whisky from Alexander's hand. Though broad in the shoulders, the laird was shorter than his father had been.

Alexander poured for himself, but did not lift his cup. His fiery eyebrows drew together. "What's this you say about Ian absconding with Janet MacKenzie?"

Rewan swirled the amber liquid thoughtfully. He'd never been fond of the way Ruairi treated his young bride, but it wasn't Rewan's place to question the chieftain of his clan. That aside, his brother Ian had broken the Highland code of trust and clan loyalty when he spirited Janet away in a galley. The pair could have even been lovers. *Bloody oath, that's certainly the way it appeared.*

Alexander cleared his throat. "Ye're awful quiet for a man who wanted a private audience."

Rewan snapped his gaze up. The intensity of Alexander's blue eyes charged the air with unspoken challenge and made Rewan's fingers ache to touch the hilt of his dirk, but that would be a mistake. "Gathering me thoughts, m'laird." Rewan shifted in his seat. "We tracked Ian to MacKenzie land. He delivered Janet into the hands of her kin, then gave us chase."

Alexander sat at the head of the table. "It doesn't surprise me that me brother would be mixed up with a lass as bonny as Lady Janet, but I've difficulty understanding why he would forsake his oath of fealty to our uncle."

Rewan knew this question was coming. He'd like to know the answer himself. "I dunna ken, but he did." It was a limp reply, but one that might purchase some time and enable him to dig deeper.

"So why are ye here?"

Rewan tossed back his whisky and wiped his mouth with his hand. "Have ye seen him?"

Alexander fingered his silver brooch, which sported a chunk of amber in the center. "Nay, he's not here. Have ye tried the MacKenzie? Mayhap he doubled back."

Rewan set his cup on the table. "He's no' with them." The laird had responded without hesitation. *He truly must have no idea where his brother is—unless he's a talented player.* Rewan sat forward. "Last I saw him, he was rowing a skiff across the Inner Sound. Across to Raasay."

Alexander's eyes narrowed. "Ian is here?"

"He did not wash up on your shore?"

"Wash up?" Alexander pounded his fist on the table. "Are ye telling me he's dead?"

Rewan held both palms up. "Or injured."

Alexander passed his hands over his face and squinted sideways. "Exactly why would me brother be dead or injured?"

Rewan's pulse hammered beneath his skin. His fingers twitched close to his dirk—he didn't want a fight with kin, but if Alexander was anything like Ruairi, he'd be quick to anger. "He could have been hit by a musket ball."

Alexander stood and moved to the window. The door opened and Sir Bran stepped inside. The laird turned. "Sir Bran, have ye heard anything about a man with a musket shot in his back?"

Rewan's gut clenched. He'd not said anything about where he'd shot the bastard.

Bran scratched his dark beard, keeping his gaze lowered. "Och. No blighter with a musket wound around these parts." He pointed to the flagon. "Do ye mind if I pour meself a tot and join ye?"

Alexander rolled his hand. "Please do."

The two men locked eyes—only for a heartbeat, but Rewan caught it. Something was afoot and he would dig to the bottom of it.

Bran sat in the chair beside him. "Are ye planning to stay the night, old friend? I put in an order with the kitchen for ye and your men."

Rewan cracked his knuckles. He liked Sir Bran, but he didn't care to be hoodwinked and deceived. His teeth clenched so tight, they hurt. "I did not say where Ian was shot."

Bran and Alexander again exchanged unreadable looks, but Rewan knew their meeting of the eyes communicated more than a hundred words.

Rewan pulled on his thumbs, the room echoing with popping sounds. "Neither did I like the way your shifty friar welcomed me on the beach."

Bran's hand slipped beneath the table. "Do no' be backbiting the friar."

"He kens were Ian is—be it dead or alive." Rewan slid his fingers over the leather-sheathed handle of his dirk. "I think ye do too."

Alexander held up both hands—void of weapons. "Calm yourself, Rewan. This is the first we've heard of me brother possibly washing ashore." His fists clenched and lowered. "And Uncle Ruairi did no' see fit to send me a missive about me own brother?"

Rewan panned his eyes across Bran's shoulders. The man's shirt nearly split at the seams, and Rewan was well aware only solid muscle lay beneath the linen. He'd sparred with Bran before, and though Rewan might be able to best him, he'd be in a world of hurt if he failed. No. Ian MacLeod was alive and nearby. Rewan would discover where before the sun set. No need to cause a stir here—at least not yet.

Rewan stood and bowed. "Thank ye for the offer of hospitality, m'laird, but I must be on me way."

Bran offered his hand, but Rewan brushed past it and hurried down the tower stairs.

His men were scattered across the great hall, tankards of ale in their hands. Rewan eyed Alick and slid onto the bench beside him. He pressed his lips to Alick's ear. "Have ye seen that meddling friar?"

"He headed north in a skiff right after ye took your leave with the laird."

"Assemble the men in the galley at once. Me guess is we'll find that backstabbing Ian MacLeod a wee jaunt up the coast."

Chapter Ten

F riar Pat watched Ian row the skiff into the sound, staring at the backs of his dear friend Niall and his precious daughter. "Dear Lord Jesus, bless those poor souls and keep them safe from harm's door."

Pat wasted no time launching his own skiff. Rewan's leering gaze emblazoned an ugly image on his mind. As soon as the henchman discovered an injured man had been cared for on Fladda, he'd put the pieces together. Back on Brochel Beach, Pat's gasp had all but given Ian away. Heaven help him, if only he'd realized who Ian was when he'd first laid eyes on the lad, he would have stifled his reaction.

He hoped to heaven Bran was successful at keeping Rewan overnight. But Pat wasn't taking any chances. He'd already made one major mistake. He couldn't make another.

The fastest route back to Brochel was to row around the north tip of Raasay. He'd take an alternate route this day. If Bran failed and Rewan did set sail for Fladda, he'd use the north route for certain. Friar Pat rowed his skiff south. It didn't take long to paddle into Loch Arnish where the curve of the bay would hide him from being spotted by Rewan's galley.

Pat steered the boat to the far end of the loch and pulled the skiff into the brush. Working quickly, he broke branches of heather and spread them over the hull to ensure the little boat could not be detected from the sea. He wheezed heavily and hurried up the hill. The journey back to the castle wasn't but a couple of miles. Nonetheless, he'd be battling steep and treacherous terrain—*not so easy for a fat old friar with rheumatism.*

He needed to haste back to the castle quickly before anyone noticed him missing. Sir Bran would only be able to cover so long, and the less the others knew of Ian's plight, the better. All keeps had their spies, and if anyone discovered the friar knew the whereabouts of Ian MacLeod, Ruairi would be notified in less than a day.

When the friar finally huffed over the ridge where he could peer down to Brochel Bay, his stomach sank to his toes. Rewan's galley had sailed.

Heal quickly, my son, for hell has just made chase.

Merrin watched a bead of sweat trickle from Ian's brow. He was hurting. She had no idea why he wouldn't let Niall row the skiff. Niall might be older, but a musket ball hadn't been carved from his back three days past.

The fact that Ian managed to stay upright was nothing short of a miracle. She prayed they'd be able to find a quiet place to hide on Skye, somewhere they wouldn't be seen. She'd spent many a day gazing across the sound at the big island. At least from what she could see from Fladda, Skye had no permanent residents—no cottages or fences of any sort. If Rewan sailed the opposite direction to the mainland, they'd be hidden for certain and it would give Ian time to heal.

Ian's rowing clapped the waves in a steady rhythm. The steep cliffs of Skye loomed nearer.

Niall pointed to the northwest. "Steer the boat into the cove. We're nearly there."

Ian glanced over his shoulder. His cheeks puffed with air, which he released slowly. Thank heavens. They'd nearly crossed the sound. Ian truly must be made of iron.

Gar splashed over the side as they tugged the boat onto the stony beach. Niall and Ian maneuvered the heavy wooden hull behind a pile of boulders to hide it from view by sea.

Then Da pointed to the smooth, wide line the skiff made in the stones and sand. "Cover our tracks."

Merrin picked up a stick of driftwood and raked it over their trail.

Ian pointed to a grove of trees on the cliff above. "Is there a quick way up there? The wood can give us cover, and we'll have a clear view of any seafaring vessels."

"Aye." Niall headed up an overgrown path and beckoned them. "Come."

Gar bounded ahead, but stopped and turned when the path seemed to end. Niall pushed aside the brush. "'Tis only an old game trail."

"That's even better." Ian picked up a sturdy stick and leaned on it. "A concealed path will make it harder for anyone to track us." He turned back to Merrin. "When we can, we'll use a branch to scratch out our tracks."

Merrin scanned the waters. "Do ye think they'll come this way?"

"If not now, eventually. Ruairi needs proof of me death. Rewan cannot go back to Stornoway without it."

"Ye mean he'll never stop?"

"Not till I'm dead."

"Then why are we running? Ye should have let me take the blade to your neck and had it done with," Niall barked over his shoulder.

Merrin had never seen her father in such a mood. Sure, he often groused, but what else were they to do?

Ian grumbled something imperceptible and marched ahead.

Merrin caught sight of his back and gasped. "Ye're bleeding."

Ian batted the air with his hand and kept on. "It'll stop soon enough."

"Nay, Ian, Ye're bleeding a lot. We need to rest. Ye should have let Da row the skiff."

Ian stopped, his eyes fierce. "Aye, I'm bleeding, but we'll no' stop. We'll keep going until 'tis safe for ye to return to Fladda and your lives."

Merrin clamped her mouth shut. Together, the two men would have been welcome in a camp of ogres. Let Ian walk on until he dropped if that was what he wanted. Of course then she'd be forced to tend his wounds. She and Niall would have to drag him someplace safe. Mayhap they'd find a hole in the ground so they could hide like rabbits.

"Gar, come behind." At least Merrin could tell the dog what to do. Gar dipped his head and gave her a reluctant look. She clenched her fists. "Ye do what I say, or...or else." There. Now all three mongrels had their hackles up.

Pat found Alexander and Sir Bran in the laird's solar.

Bran stood. "I'd begun to fear you'd had a run-in with Rewan. I was just about to launch a search party."

"Had to cross overland." The friar took a deep breath and eyed the flagon on the table. "I've a thirst like a mad cow."

Alexander gestured toward a tankard. "Help yourself."

"Thank ye." Pat poured the ale and caught his breath. "Ian set sail in a skiff with Niall and his daughter. They're heading toward Skye."

Alexander knocked the table with his fist. "Blast it all. We should be going after him."

Bran resumed his seat and leaned back. "We've gone over it fifty different ways. If we defend Ian, we'll incite a feud between the clans."

Pat swallowed his ale. "'Twould mean the end of us all. The Lewis guard has more than three times our numbers."

Bran nodded. "We'd lose our lands for certain. Ian's a smart lad, far more intelligent than Ruairi's henchman."

Alexander shoved his chair back and paced. "I do no' like it. Damn Uncle Ruairi to hell. Ian's me brother. I cannot turn me back on him."

Friar Pat clasped his cross. Blessed be Jesus, was the laird honestly willing to sacrifice every soul on Raasay for his brother? "Wait. Afore ye go off half-cocked, think it through." He eyed the two men. "Niall's as cunning as a fox. Ian's become a man—he's nearly as big as Bran, muscles like a gladiator, too. And, they're heading for Skye. It'll take time for Rewan to discover they're no' on Raasay or Fladda. He'd be daft to search Skye. It makes far more sense for Ian to flee to the mainland."

Bran slapped the table. "Ye've got a point. Ian will have a good head start."

Alexander stared out the window. "Where do ye think he'll go once he reaches Skye?"

Bran pulled on his black beard. "If it were me I'd go down to Portree, find a galley and sail to Ireland for a time."

Pat nodded. "It might be best for them all to make a start in a new place." *Mayhap even Merrin could find acceptance...*

Alexander turned. "Agreed. Though it galls me, we cannot risk the clan for one man. If Ian's chances of success are so great, we'll drink to him and bid him a safe journey."

All three men held up their tankards and guzzled their ale.

Friar Pat only wished he could ward off the tightness in his chest. All three souls meant a great deal to him, as did the other two hundred in his care on the Isle of Raasay. He'd be on his knees offering prayers of penance for days to come.

After they sailed around the tip of Raasay and through the narrows of Rona, a verdant isle caught Rewan's eye. He nudged Alick with his elbow. "That looks a likely place."

Alick shook his head. "I do no' think we want to go ashore there. 'Tis Eilean Fladda—word has it a witch lives on the south end with an old healer."

Rewan gave his superstitious man-at-arms a shove. "A witch, ye say?"

"Aye, not even the Rona pirates dare set foot there."

"I think Ye're spending too much time in the tavern. That sounds more like an old wives' tale to me—besides, I'm more interested in the healer part." He waved to the oarsmen. "Ashore."

The galley skimmed onto the soggy grey sand lining the shore below a steep incline of pasture land. Standing on an oarsman's bench, Rewan made out the top of a thatched roof. He climbed over the side and his boots sank into wet sand. Two of his six men stayed behind to mind the galley. Rewan led Alick and the others up the hill. Sure enough, a lime-washed cottage perched at the top with a quaint thatched roof. He chuckled. Tufts of smoke rose from its chimney.

The same tingle he got in his gut just before engaging in a battle made Rewan's chest hairs stand on end. He widened his strides. Even if Raasay had died, he might find proof right here and now. He grasped his hilt and drew his sword from the scabbard on his back. In a few minutes, he'd either be fighting with the only man on Lewis who could best him, or he might be on his way to Stornoway and his woman.

As they encircled the cottage door, Rewan signaled for his men to ready their weapons. Alick raised his fist to knock and glanced back for a nod. Rewan dipped his chin once. Alick pounded with such force, the deep rattle could most likely be heard across the entire isle. They waited. Nothing.

Rewan heard not a single footstep. "Kick it in."

Alick slid his hand to the latch. It clicked. He glanced back at Rewan and shrugged.

Rewan raised his sword, making eye contact with the other men. With a quick nod, they bellowed their war cry, charging into the tiny cottage. Rewan spun in a circle. The fire in the hearth crackled. A pallet of straw lay on the floor. It looked like the old healer had a visitor.

Alick opened a door, revealing an empty bedroom. It took Rewan no time to discover the inhabitants of the cottage were nowhere to be found. He sent two men to scour the isle while he knelt alongside the pallet. He threw back the plaid. Bloodstains pooled on linen sheets, lower right side of the back—exactly where Rewan reckoned he'd shot Ian MacLeod. "Ye've eluded me again, have ye now, Raasay?"

Alick moved in behind him.

Rewan pointed. "Looks like we've just missed him."

"By the state of the fire, they haven't been gone long." Alick stepped up to the hearth and pulled a red-and-black kilt from a peg. "This looks like Ian's plaid."

Rewan jumped up and examined it. Bloody oath, it was his. "Ballocks. Someone must have warned them."

Alick rubbed the wool between his fingers. "That pesky friar."

"Aye." Rewan snatched the plaid and paced around the table. That damned Raasay would never die. He'd soon be chasing the phantom bastard all over the Highlands—and worse, he even liked the wayward barnacle before he'd gone off with Ruairi's wife. This was a bitter task. One he'd prefer to be free of. But what choice did he have? If he failed to carry out Ruairi's orders, he'd be cast out of Stornoway. After so many years of loyal service, he'd be handed his bonnet with no place to go. Not many rogue warriors survived without a clan.

"What next?" Alick's question snapped Rewan from his thoughts.

He threw the kilt into the fire. "Burn it."

Before the wool could catch fire, Alick snatched the plaid from the flames and shook it. "Ruairi wants evidence, no?"

Rewan growled. He should have thought of that. "Keep it—but we *will* track the bastard down. I've no doubt Ruairi would enjoy a hanging from the Stornoway gallows."

Alick walked around the outside of the cottage with a torch, setting the thatched roof alight. Rewan stood back and watched, his arms folded. No one would harbor a man who crossed his chieftain and not suffer the consequences.

The two men he'd sent to scour the tiny isle approached. "No sign of a soul," one said.

Rewan pointed to the ship. "Go ready the galley."

The flames grew and crackled across the timbers. Rewan picked up a burning ember and took it to the lean-to with drying herbs hanging from the eaves.

He held the burning stick up, but a gentle tinkling of bells stopped him. He turned toward the soft music and stared. Metallic bells flickered, catching the sun in a kaleidoscope of colors. Entranced, he stepped toward them. *Tink, tink.* The bells were so soft, reminiscent of his mother's lullabies.

Alick stepped in beside him. "Everything in the cottage will burn, save the stone walls." With a gasp, he shuffled backward and pointed. "'Tis bad luck to burn a witch's lair."

Rewan glanced away from the lulling bells. "What the bloody hell are ye talking about?"

Alick pointed to the mortar and pestle on the table and shook his finger. "She's probably put a curse on it—we'll all meet our end if we burn it."

Rewan tossed his torch into the grass. Not that he was superstitious. It was just those damned bells. "Sometimes I think Ye're touched in the head."

Alick gaped, his eyes wide. "I ken what I'm saying. Burning the cottage is one thing, but I do no' think we should test our luck and burn her workshop as well."

Rewan headed back to the galley. "Never mind that rickety old shack. The wind will blow it down soon enough." Alick trotted beside him and Rewan threw one last glance over his shoulder. *Tink, tink.* Those blasted bells were mighty annoying.

"Where to next, sir?"

From the top of the hill, Rewan looked across to the mainland. Ian wouldn't flee to the MacKenzie, the first place anyone would look. The Isle of Raasay was far too obvious as well. What would be the most unlikely place he'd run?

Climbing the steep slope, Merrin's worn boots provided little support. Her ankle twisted but she clenched her teeth and didn't stop. She kept an eye on the wet bloodstain on Ian's shirt. It seeped the linen through, though it was no use trying to force him to stop to apply fresh bandages. The man would push on until he dropped. A lot of good that would do them—on the run from Chieftain Ruairi's men, dragging an unconscious Highlander through the wood.

All her life she'd dreamt of taking a holiday from Fladda. However, never once did she consider she'd be running for her life. With all Niall's talk about bogles and fairies, any running she thought she'd be doing was from fae folk.

Once they reached the plateau above the sheer cliffs of Skye, the going was easier, though her ankle popped now and again. Gar dipped his head and maintained an easy amble at her side. With

Ian leaning heavily on his walking stick, Niall led them north-wards, staying close to the cliff face.

Merrin glanced at the outline of Fladda before they entered a copse of trees. It looked so small from across the sound, but her heart tugged. They hadn't been gone a whole afternoon and she missed it. She stopped dead in her tracks. "Da, who will feed the chickens?"

"I opened the coop when I went to fetch the bow from me work-shop. They can live on bugs and grubs until we return."

"I hope the sheep will be all right—and Tam."

"Do no' worry your head. They've enough grass to eat until the first snow, and the pond is full—they will no' even miss us."

Merrin's chest tightened. Fladda seemed so close, yet she won-dered where she'd sleep this night. Not on her feather bed, that was for certain. She bit her bottom lip. Now that she was away, Fladda didn't seem such a dreary place.

As Ian led them farther from the shore, the forest grew thicker. Merrin could no longer hear the roar of the surf. The silence was almost deafening. Having spent her entire life on Fladda, the rum-ble of the ocean never stopped. Birds called louder. Their footfalls crunched more noisily than ever. She tested her voice and sang a line from a ballad Niall had taught her.

Ian glanced back and smiled. "Are ye feeling good, Miss Merrin?"

"Odd, I'd say. I've never heard things so quiet before."

"Ye have a lovely bell-like tone to your voice."

Merrin skipped a step. Niall often asked her to sing, but never said she sounded like a bell.

They'd been walking for some time when the trees opened to open moorland, spread flat atop the cliff. In the distance, the sun glimmered on the smooth surface of the sound. Merrin patted Gar's head. "Come, boy, let's have a look at our island. I'll bet 'tis even smaller from here."

She ran ahead with the dog. The deep blue water of Raasay Sound came into view, as did black smoke billowing into the sky.

Merrin stopped short. Suddenly, her gut twisted as if she was going to be sick. It had to be Fladda. They hadn't walked *that* far. Her eyes darted to the south. She could still see Dùn Caan peeking over the hills on Raasay. Tears sprang to her eyes. The black smoke filling the air billowed from no other place but her home.

"Nooooooo!"

Merrin flailed her arms as if she could put out the flames from across the sound. She staggered forward, her insides grating, hollow.

"Stop!" Ian grasped her arm and yanked her back.

Merrin whipped around to face him. "Do not touch me."

He pointed downward. "Ye were about to plunge to your death, ye daft woman."

Merrin looked down and jolted into Ian's chest. She drew her fists up and pushed him away. "Me home is burning." She paced in a circle, willing herself look again. "Please, God, no!" She dropped to her knees. "All our things—Ma's things." She pounded her fists into the earth. "Stop them!"

Ian knelt beside her and placed a hand on her back. "I'm sorry, lass."

"Sorry? Make them stop." She couldn't hit anything hard enough. Why weren't they heading back? She lumbered to her feet, tripping over her skirts. Ian tried to help, but she slapped his hand away. "Are the pair of ye just going to stand there?"

Niall's grim frown spoke a hundred words. He stood motionless.

Merrin had to do something. Her loom, her rocking chair, the feather bed she'd just made. It couldn't all be lost. Tears stung her eyes and streamed down her face. She hiked up her skirts and ran back toward the trail they'd climbed. She'd take the skiff herself and confront those evil, mean-hearted men.

"Merrin!" Niall called after her.

Ian sprinted to her side. His hand latched on to her shoulder. In two bounds he stopped her, both hands shaking her shoulders. "Ye cannot go back. Not now. They'll kill ye."

Merrin stared at him in disbelief. She opened her mouth to argue. The only thing that came out was a high-pitched wail.

She pushed away and tried to choke back her tears, but everything she'd ever owned, ever loved, was going up in a whirlwind of blackness.

Niall caught up and cradled Merrin in his embrace. Desperately, she tried to find her voice. She twisted out of her father's arms and yanked off her scarf. Thrusting up her finger, she pointed to her neck. "I have no place to go. N-no place is safe for me now."

"There, there, lassie." Niall tugged the scarf from her hands, keeping his voice soothing, like he did when she was a wee bairn. "The roof and the fine things might burn, but they can be replaced. The cottage is made of stone and it will withstand a fire. When this is over we'll go back and start anew."

Merrin tried to blink away her tears—tried to will her inner strength to return. This was no time to lose her head, but she could not allay her ragged breaths. "G-Gar. C-come." She marched onward, wiping her arm across her face.

Ian fell in step beside her. He reached for her hand, but she snapped it away. "Merrin. Ye have me word. I will make this right with me own hands."

Ian should have fled the day he gained consciousness. Every moment he'd stayed in the cottage had put them in danger. If they weren't poor enough already, they'd now lost everything. A rock the size of a leg of lamb took up residence in Ian's gut. Merrin was emotionally exhausted and Niall couldn't hide his ashen face when he tried to console her.

Their home was ruined, up in smoke. Rewan always burned and ransacked until nothing was left. Hopefully the bastard would leave the livestock alone, else there'd be no food for them at all come winter.

Ian clenched his fists and closed his eyes. He had to make this up to her. But how? Blindly, he'd promised to make it right. He had not much more than a few shillings to his name and a hole in his back. Damn it all. None of his miserable lot in life mattered. Once he healed, he vowed he'd help them rebuild—if Rewan didn't track them down and kill him first.

Ian's entire body tensed. Rewan would have no qualms about killing a healer and his daughter. In no manner could Ian allow that to happen.

What would Rewan do to them if they parted ways? Would they escape retribution? Could Ian find a sanctuary where Merrin and Niall could stay until this mess was over? There was no MacKenzie clan to protect these poor souls who'd taken him in, shown him selfless kindness. If Ian left them, he'd have no way to ensure their safety. But then he wasn't exactly ready to face Rewan sword to sword. Not yet.

Could he create a diversion? Could he lead Rewan and his men away like he had for Janet? The risks would be great.

Ian opened his eyes. God on the cross, if things didn't grow worse. His entire body tensed when he caught sight of Rewan's galley. He'd made a reasonably sound judgment and even that had failed him. "Niall." He tried not to sound too alarmed. "Is there a place we can hide?"

The older man followed Ian's gaze. "God's teeth. Have they not done enough?"

"What?" Merrin asked.

Ian pointed. "Rewan's galley is sailing directly for Skye."

"Tell me it isn't so." Merrin stomped toward the water. "I thought you said he'd head for MacKenzie lands?"

Ian locked eyes with Niall. There was nothing they could do about it now. Soon Rewan would find the skiff down below and sniff out their trail. "We must move fast."

Niall's jaw ticked. "I do no' like our odds."

Ian spread his arms wide, looking west. "Ye ken this land better than anyone. Think."

Niall took off his bonnet and scratched his head. "There's a place, but it would be madness to go there."

Ian grasped Niall's shoulders and gave a firm shake. "We've a woman, a wounded warrior, an old man and a dog. We've no horse. We've no allies. Now pull your worries out of your arse and make haste. There's no more time for chat."

Niall shot an apprehensive grimace toward Merrin and then handed her the scarf. "Come."

Merrin hurried beside him, tying the cloth around her neck. "Where are we heading, Da?"

"The only place I ken where we'll be assured of sanctuary." He grasped her hand and pulled her close. "Fairy Glen."

Chapter Eleven

M errin almost choked. She'd gone completely numb from watching her home go up in smoke, and then her father uttered the forbidden words. Long ago he'd made her vow never to mention *Fairy Glen*. He'd spent all his life trying to keep the fairies and bogles from stealing her away, and now they were heading straight for the legendary glen. *What in heaven's name is he thinking?*

Gar trotted alongside her, his expression alert, protective, as if the dog knew something was afoot. Merrin reached up and touched her scarf. What would happen now? Surely there would be no sleeping in Fairy Glen. They wouldn't be able to stay there for long. Merciful Father—what if...what if *they* tried to claim her? She'd be better off dead.

Ian's pained hitch clapped the ground behind her with rapid steps. The man's ability to endure pain boggled her mind. In addition, never in her life had she seen her father move so fast or with such determination. A sharp ache in her side jabbed with every step. Merrin ground her teeth. She'd not complain. They had no choice but to move quickly.

Niall stopped and pointed to the brook. "They'll not be able to follow our tracks if we wade upstream."

Merrin grasped her skirts and glanced back to Ian. He'd see her ankles.

His gaze dipped to her hem. "Your father's right."

For everything holy, Ian had probably seen hundreds of ankles. Hers were most likely hideous compared to Lady Janet's—and he could take his ogling eyes and look the other way if she offended him.

Her reasoning did nothing to allay the rush of heat to her cheeks. "If it cannot be helped." She tugged her kirtle to her knees and carefully stepped into the stream. Ice-cold water filled her boots. "Merciful mercy, 'tis colder than..."

"A witch's teat?" Ian suggested behind her, playfully tugging on her hair.

She shot him a frown. "I was going to say snow on Hogmanay." How could he jest about witches at this time? Would he be so bold with Lady Janet?

Ian splashed into the water. "Bloody hell. Ye weren't wrong there."

Gar took a running leap. A spray of water drenched the front of Merrin's kirtle. "Och, ye mangy mutt, did ye have to barrel in like a mad bull?"

Gar wagged his tail and bounded ahead of Niall.

Ian lumbered beside her, leaning heavily on his walking stick. "Are ye all right?"

"Better than the likes of ye, I'd reckon."

Ashen, he couldn't hide his pain from Merrin. Still, his eyes slipped to the white linen shift that puckered above her scooped neckline. The wet cloth clung to her breasts, showing far more than was proper. Yes, even Merrin knew something about being proper, thanks to Friar Pat's lessons. She looked like a harlot. *Curses, curses, curses.*

She glared back at him. Was that a blush she saw in his cheeks? It should be—*a witch's teat*—how could he even think that?

Ian swiped a hand across his eyes. "Apologies. It'll be dry soon."

By the time Niall stepped out of the water, Merrin could no longer feel her toes—or her feet. Gar swirled his wet dog body around her and shook. Merrin skittered away. Her toe caught on a rock, sending her stumbling backwards. Her arms flung out. Her mouth opened to scream. Unable to stop, she closed her eyes to an inevitable icy drenching.

Two large, very strong hands plucked her from midair. Fighting against the forces of gravity, they levered her upward. In the blink of an eye, Ian held her cradled to his chest. His heart thudded against her arm. His body was so incredibly warm and he smelled so good, decidedly male—intoxicatingly so. She rested her head on his chest and inhaled. *Heaven.*

"Are ye hurt?" His deep voice vibrated.

Merrin met his pale blue gaze. Only Ian could manage to completely jumble her mind merely by looking at her. "How...how did ye do that?"

Ian dipped his head, his lips ever so close. But she was mad at him, was she not? He lowered his lids, his eyes shuttered by lashes so long they had no business being on a man. Would he kiss her right in front of Niall? Though the thought mortified her, the flutterings inside went for a merry romp. She raised her chin and pursed her lips. Mayhap one wee kiss?

Ian grinned. "I couldn't allow ye to fall. It would take forever for that woolen kirtle and cloak to dry without a fire."

Niall marched in. "That's the second time I've seen ye put your hands on me daughter." He tugged Merrin's arm. "Ye should have listened to me and left the dog."

She folded her hands into her chest. "I couldn't do that."

With an agonizing grunt, Ian set Merrin on her feet. Somehow, her arms ended up around his neck. Ignoring her father's frown, she gave Ian's cheek a peck. Bless it, she couldn't stay mad at him. "Ye're right. I could have caught me death had I fallen in. Thank you."

Merrin ran her fingers down the length of his arm. *Saints preserve me, he's got bands of iron for arms—so thick and strong.* Ian caught her hand and squeezed before he let her go. A corner of his mouth ticked up.

Niall stepped between them. "Come. We're nearly there."

Merrin hurried along. Single file, they made their way through a dense forest. Niall led, Merrin followed, Gar stayed on her heels and Ian took up the rear. Her lips burned. Ian's stubble had grown in. She liked the roughness of it—how his coarse skin contrasted with her soft. If only she could run kisses along his jaw line. But this was not the time.

She glanced back. The sallow pall in his cheeks had returned. "Are ye hurting?"

Ian tossed aside his walking stick. "A man grows accustomed to it after a time." He still had a hitch to his step. Merrin thought it foolish of him to forgo the crutch so soon—besides, heroically saving her from a drenching would have caused unimaginable pain. Ian swiped the sweat from his brow. *Stubborn Highlander.*

Roaring water filled the air when Niall held up his hand and stopped. "We must ask permission of the fairies before we enter."

Merrin swallowed the lump in her throat and peered under the thorny yellow gorse. Beside her foot was a clump of primrose in full bloom. No fairies at her feet, thank heavens.

"Oberon, King of the Fairies, we seek sanctuary from Ruairi's evil henchman. Please allow us entry into this spiritual place." Niall turned to them. "Wait here."

Ian scoffed. "He really believes this malarkey?"

His breath brushed her ear. Merrin didn't need to turn around to know he was close enough to touch. All she needed to do was lean back a tad, and his warmth would soothe her. She inclined her chin. "Aye." What else could she say? All her life, her father had held on to the old ways. He'd ensured their cottage had every magical deterrent known—all because of her mark.

Ian's hand slid into the curve of her waist. Worries of her father's superstitions melted. Shivers of pleasure coursed across Merrin's skin. How could she still react to him with such strong feelings? She should shun him and never speak to him again. They took Ian in and look what had happened. But it didn't seem to matter to her heart. Ian's touch not only made shivers course across her flesh, it filled her with confidence and power. True, she'd never seen the slightest sign magical folk existed, but her father believed it so fervently, she hadn't doubted.

She smiled up at him. "I'll never let them take me. Mark of the devil or no."

"That's my lass. Ye're a strong-willed fighter. No meddling sprite stands a chance against you."

Though there was humor in Ian's voice, the only thing Merrin could focus on were the words "my lass." Surely he hadn't meant she was his. Surely he meant something like "good lass." She stole a glance at him. He grinned. Merrin's knees wobbled. *Holy fairy feathers, why does he have to be so handsome? Why couldn't a haggard old man have washed ashore?*

Ian's released his hand as Niall trudged back up the path. "'Tis clear. Come."

Merrin stepped lightly as she peered through the moss that hung from the trees. Her breath caught. If magic did exist, this place undoubtedly was enchanted.

Niall pointed to a gap at the root of a tree. "Keep your voices down. That's a fairy house."

Merrin bent closer to study it. Strewn with moss, the dark, cavernous hole led beneath the root of the tree. It didn't seem very inviting, nor could she imagine fairy folk trying to pull her through a burrow no bigger than her head. She simply wouldn't fit. *Odd.*

Ian grasped her elbow and encouraged her along. Green surrounded them. The rushing water sang a soothing tune that took her sorrow and washed it away. Up ahead, a waterfall cascaded into a pool. Gar bounded to the edge and lapped greedily. Merrin stepped beside him and ran her fingers over the dog's damp, wiry fur. She took in a deep breath. The fresh air spread through her body like a fast-acting tonic. If nothing else, the tranquility of this place eased her mind.

She pointed at dark shadows moving beneath the water's surface. "Look. The water's so clear, ye can see the fish."

Gar's ears pricked up. He looked hungrily at the darting trout and wagged his tail. Everyone else completely ignored her.

Ian turned full circle. "This doesn't look like a good place to hide. 'Tis wide open once ye clear the trees."

Niall pointed to a flat-topped crag. "There—the Castle of the Fairies."

Ian scoffed. "The way ye carry on about the fairy folk, I'm beginning to think Ye're daft."

"Wheesht." Niall pressed his finger to his lips while his eyes darted side to side. "Keep your voice down, else Merrin will be in more danger than she already is."

Ian folded his arms. "Very well. Ye want us to climb that rock? We may as well flash a beacon."

"Nay, nay. If ye lie flat, no one will ken we're here."

Ian scratched his chin and frowned. "Hell of a shelter ye've brought us to."

Merrin tugged his hand. "Come. 'Tis growing dark."

"Aye." Niall led them up a strip of grass that cut through the middle of the flat-topped rock. "Ye'll see. There's no place safer on all of Skye."

"Unless it rains," Ian grumbled.

A thorny bramble snagged the hem of Merrin's cloak as she climbed. Bending down to release it, a thorn pierced her thumb. She jerked back, but the nasty vine swiped under her dress and across her leg. "Ouch." The vine then grew a mind of its own and grabbed her kirtle as well.

Ian grasped her hand. "It's bleeding." He covered her thumb with his mouth. His tongue moved across her flesh smoothly, his eyes closed as if he were kissing her. She could have swooned. Her lips parted and her breathing became labored while she watched him tend her thumb as if she were a princess. His cool mouth soothed the sting—actually, there was no longer a sting on her leg either. She could have floated to the top of the butte.

Merrin stared at Ian's rugged profile, imagining he was kissing her mouth and not her silly thumb. But he took so much care with such a trifle as a pricked finger. Niall had never shown her that kind of tenderness. As a man, Ian was different from her father in so many ways. She never imagined a man could be so *desirable*. It almost frightened her.

Ian grinned and stood straight. "Put pressure on your thumb and I'll release your skirts...if ye'll allow me."

Merrin pinched her thumb with her forefinger and nodded. "But I do no' think ye should lick me leg." Heaven help her reaction if he did. Besides, Niall would skewer him.

With a chuckle, Ian knelt. Carefully, he released the thorns from her gown and cloak. Merrin considered stopping him when he lifted her hem and peered at the scrape just above her ankle. "We'll need to cleanse your leg when we reach the top." But he was tending her, not ogling her. That had to make it acceptable—she thought.

When his fingers brushed her calf, Merrin gasped, her heart thumping like Gar's paw when he scratched. His hardened calluses stroked roughly against her tender skin, his touch gentle yet powerful. For some strange reason, she suddenly craved him to run those strong hands further up her leg, caress her thigh. She closed her eyes and moaned.

Niall called over his shoulder. "What's got ye dallying?"

She jumped only a fraction, but the jolt from her heart made it seem like she'd hopped fifty feet. She smoothed her skirts. "Just got snagged by a bramble." Her voice sounded far too chipper. What on earth was wrong with her? She cleared her throat and lowered her tone. "We're right to go now."

"A bramble?" Niall scurried to her side. "That gives me an idea."

Merrin puzzled. "What?"

"You and Ian keep going. I saw a clump of petty morel under a group of ferns—'tis fairly rare this far north. Mayhap the fairies are on our side."

Ian planted his fists on his hips. "Are ye serious? Rewan and his men are probably right behind us. Do no' risk being caught for the sake of a few berries."

Niall held up a finger. "Ah, but ye do no' understand. A salve made of the plant and berry soothes inflamed joints, but the juice of the berry will bring on drowsiness and a pounding headache if it mixes with your blood—'twill even cause vomiting."

Ian narrowed his eyes. "Go on."

"Ye see, if I rearrange the brambles across the path and drip juice from the berries on them, it will only take a small scrape to slow a man down."

"How fast does it take hold?"

"If it mixes with the blood?" Niall twisted his face. "Not long."

Ian smirked. "Aye, so after they slit our throats, their heads will be pounding?"

"Ye got a better idea?" Niall brushed past him. "Merrin, sprinkle oats in a circle atop the Castle of the Fairies."

She clutched her fingers around the satchel strap. "But we need the oats for eating."

"Do no' argue with me, lass. I ken what I'm on about."

She watched Niall patter down the path and then turned to Ian. "Sometimes I think he's losing his mind."

"He's a superstitious fellow, but he means well."

"Aye, he protects me sure enough."

Ian continued up the path. "He may no' be a warrior, but he's smart. I never would've thought about putting poison on bramble vines."

"Da kens everything about healing and herbs." Many a time Friar Pat had told Merrin her father was the most talented healer he knew.

"'Tis a valued skill. Have ye learned much yourself?"

"Aye, I help him most days—learned a lot, though I'm no' as knowledgeable as he. Not yet, anyway."

"Did ye ken about the petty morel?"

"I did, though never considered using it for a trap." Merrin grasped her satchel cord and pulled it tighter over her shoulder. "Come, I need to apply a new dressing to your wound while we still have some light."

Merrin heaved a big sigh when she slid the satchel from her shoulder. Ian took it and rested the bag beside the two he carried. Gar flopped down alongside them in a heap. Ian clasped his hand to his forehead and groaned. "I cannot apologize enough. I'd set out on me own if I thought Rewan would leave ye alone."

Merrin tugged his hand in a silent command to sit. "What's done is done. It cannot be helped. Da and I are in this with ye now. We'll see it through together." Merrin blinked. She could no sooner think of Ian heading out on his own that she could handing him over to Rewan and his band of murderers.

Ian removed the claymore from his back. "You've lost your home because of me."

A hollow void filled her chest.

Her home. Gone.

She'd tried to block it from her mind. What would she do? She and Niall could rebuild, but with what? That didn't frighten her as much as the prospect of what might happen when they ran into strangers. She fumbled inside the satchel. "Blast it all, I ken your salve's in here."

Ian placed a calming hand atop hers. "Let me have a look."

Merrin handed over the leather bag. Ian reached in and effort-lessly pulled out the stoppered pot. "Is this what Ye're looking for?"

"Ye ken it is." Merrin took it.

"What about your leg?"

Heaven help her, she couldn't allow Ian to touch her leg again. What if Niall came up and saw her exposed to the knee with eyes rolling to the back of her head? What if she lost all sense of pro-priety and actually asked Ian to run his fingers up her thigh? The fact that she'd even thought about how delightful his touch would feel made her swallow hard. Was she wanton? Were the fairy folk playing tricks on her mind? Could they do that? "It does no' hurt in the slightest." She cleared her throat. "Now pull up your shirt."

"I should be making arrows. One will no' help us."

Merrin glanced around the crag. There was nary a tree within a hundred paces. "We should have collected sticks when we were in the forest."

Ian tugged his shirt from his waistband. "Aye, we must make it a priority on the morrow."

Merrin shuddered. His bandage was saturated with blood. "Ye should still be abed the way this is bleeding."

"'Tis hardly paining me."

Merrin glopped salve on her fingers and rubbed. "Ye expect me to believe that?"

Ian winced. "It grows a bit better every day. There's no use whining over it."

Merrin applied a fresh bandage. Her nose lightly touched the exposed part of his back as she reached around and unwound the roll of cloth. The way her head swooned, she had to be starving. But his warmth drew her in. She rested her cheek against his back and closed her eyes. She could rest like that for hours. The stress of the day fled.

Ian grasped her hand. "Let me do it."

Merrin sat up and tightened her fist around the roll of linen. "I can." She unrolled the bandage and tied it off, completely aware he watched her every movement. She liked his attention—liked it too much. Her thighs shuddered. Blast her wandering mind.

Merrin met his gaze. His pale eyes turned dark, his lids heavy. *He must be awfully hungry as well.*

He ran his finger along the inside of her shift—the part that ruffled along the neckline of her bodice. "'Tis nearly dry."

Merrin shivered. She should pull away, but something deep inside screamed, *more*.

Chapter Twelve

Ian thought he could resist Merrin, until the back of his finger caressed her breasts. Merciful Lord of lords, her pliable flesh rendered him a complete and utter lovesick fool. Of course he wasn't *in love*, but for everything holy, he could not deny his infatuation. Sooner or later a woman always managed to seize his heart, and Merrin had worked her magic tenfold—in record time.

Ian slid his finger back along her feminine ruffle. Silken skin made the ache under his kilt throb. With a guttural moan, he closed his eyes and inhaled her intoxicating scent.

He completely lost his mind when Merrin was around, but today had him behaving like an adolescent lad. When Gar splashed her shift, it was all he could do not to stare at the paper-thin fabric that clung to the tops of her breasts. He continually glanced sideways, willing her bodice to slip down just an inch and expose delectable pink nipples. If Niall hadn't been there, Ian would have unlaced her kirtle and tore it off the lass.

On second thought, it was by the grace of God Niall had been there. Ian absolutely could not allow himself carnal knowledge of such a sweet, innocent maid. The fact that he ogled her continually had him practically knotted up with self-loathing, though he couldn't quite go that far.

The one thing that did have him feeling like an enormous arse was the sight of black smoke billowing from Fladda. Christ. That was enough to snap his eyes away from Merrin's forbidden fruit.

He yanked his finger from Merrin's bodice and balled his fist.

Merrin's breath caught.

Ian looked at her. Damn. Her eyes took on the color of the darkening sky.

She grasped his fist with trembling hands. "Why can I not resist your touch?"

He leaned in, transfixed, mind numb—again. "Mayhap the same reason that I cannot seem to keep me hands to meself."

She gave him a puzzled stare and then sat up, her eyes bright. "I think we have a common fondness for one another."

She thinks? Ian grinned. "That we do." He brushed his finger across her petal-soft cheek. "I cannot believe Ye're speaking to me at all."

She fluttered her lashes. Had she no clue what that did to a man? "Why?" she asked.

"I'm the reason ye lost your home."

Merrin's smile fell. She reached for her satchel and pulled out a leather bag. "I cannot think about that now." She untied the bag's thong and filled her hand with oats. "I've got to spread this around to keep the bogles and fairies at bay."

Ian wanted to shake her. *Fairies? Bah.* "That's good food Ye're wasting."

She stood and grimaced. "Da will be awful sore if I do no' do it." She shoved in her fist for another handful. "Besides, I need something else to keep me mind occupied."

He knew exactly what she meant. But it didn't help having her stoop over, giving him an eyeful of shapely hips. In two steps, he could be across the plateau and fill his hands with them.

The dog darted to Merrin's heels, lapping up the oats as fast as she scattered them. She spun around and thwacked him atop the head. "Gar! 'Tis no' for you, ye thieving hound." She pushed him toward Ian and shook her finger. "Ye'll have your supper with the rest of us, but do no' eat the oats."

The dog's ears flattened. He tucked his tail and plopped on his haunches. Ian ran his hand over Gar's wiry fur. Whining, the big deerhound leaned into him. Ian had even upset this poor mongrel's life. Forlorn, they both watched Merrin, wanting things that were forbidden.

Their lot would have been better all around if Rewan had killed Ian in the first place. He watched Merrin kneel down and carefully drizzle her oats, conserving as much of the precious food as possible. Ian couldn't remember ever feeling this lousy. No one cared whether he lived or died—well, died, mayhap. He'd brought Merrin into this mess and there he sat, the pain in his back sapping his strength, rendering him useless with a sword. He might as well walk up to Rewan with his hands in the air and take his execution like a self-respecting condemned man.

"I wish she'd never found me—let me body wash out to sea," he mumbled to Gar. "Then none of this would have happened."

Merrin stopped. "I cannot even think of it," she whispered. Her shoulders curled over. "That would be even worse..." Her breath caught—she looked at Ian, torment in her eyes. She dropped the bag and pressed her palms to her face.

A sorrowful wail erupted from the depths of her soul. It pierced through Ian's skin and seized his gut. Merrin doubled over, her body shaking, racked by uncontrollable sobs.

Crying. A woman's tears made him crumble—and this time he'd caused Merrin's. He was such an idiot. She'd heard his senseless mumblings. Ian sprang up and closed the distance, then drew Merrin into his arms. "I'm sorry. I was only wallowing in me own self-pity." He nuzzled into her neck.

Cords stood prone on her neck. Her sobbing turned into stuttered wails. "I...I...dunna ken what will become of me..." Merrin's mouth drew down with a painful wail that shot an arrow straight through Ian's heart. Her eyes filled with more anguish than he'd ever seen in one human being.

His heart twisting, Ian kissed her hair and dabbed her eyes with the tips of his fingers. "There, there, Merrin." Her name rolled off his tongue like butter. He had to stay alive, if only to protect her. God, he couldn't stand to see her in so much tormented pain. "I promise I'll help ye. I'll never see ye abandoned."

She grasped his fingers and held them tightly under her chin. A lone tear slid down her cheek as she tried to catch her breath. "Oh, Ian. Ye promise? I can cook and clean for ye. Ye will no' ever regret having me whilst I'm in your care."

Ian squeezed her in his embrace. Her breathing still shuddered. "Easy now. Ye've nothing to worry about." He smoothed his hand over her thick tresses. "Everything will be all right. Ye'll see."

Ian closed his eyes. He'd just promised he'd not abandon her. He prayed he could keep that vow. So many odds were against him. He could be dead by sunrise. But on one thing he was firm—whilst he breathed, he would see to her safety. He could not leave Merrin or Niall to fend for themselves now their home was burned. Once he found a place where they could build anew, he'd see them settled and then he'd be on his way. He'd ensure they would never pay for his sins again.

Merrin leaned into him, inhaling a deep, trembling breath. Her gentle hands found their way around Ian's back. She pressed her breasts against him—those full, alluring breasts that forever teased him above her bodice. She smelled of peat smoke and wildflowers. Ian slid his hands down her spine to the feminine curves at her waist. Hungry desire radiated throughout his body—over every inch of flesh and deep inside. Longing inflamed his heart and shot straight to his groin.

Merrin possessed every desirable trait in a woman. Forget the tears, all she had to do was meet his gaze and he'd give her the world. He wanted to show her pleasure, take her to places of passion and watch her blossom as she experienced all that womanhood had to offer.

His hand slid to her buttock.

Merrin moaned and pressed against his rock-hard erection.

Ian filled his hand with female flesh, so soft, so pliable his knees shuddered. He loved how her hips flared from her tiny waist. He loved the delectable breasts that pushed against him. His pulse quickened as he swirled his tongued down her long, slender neck.

Gar stirred and whined behind them.

"Remove your hands from me daughter."

Niall's words crept across Ian's nape like a slithering garter snake. God, could he be any more of an idiot? Telling Merrin that he'd always be there for her, and now caught with his lips racing down the lass's neck and his fingers kneading her arse? Releasing his hands, Ian forced a smile and chuckled.

Merrin stepped back and beckoned Gar to her side with a snap of her fingers.

Niall sauntered toward them, thin-lipped, eyes narrowed. "I leave the two of ye alone for a shake of a lamb's tail, and ye wind up in each other's arms?"

Ian bit the inside of his cheek. He deserved all Niall could dish out and more. He'd just taken advantage of the poor lass—even gave her false hope. "I…"

Merrin fisted her hips. "For goodness' sakes, Da, he was only lending me a shoulder to cry on."

Niall shot a suspecting glance between them.

Ian spread his palms, feigning his most innocent face—the one he always had used on his mother. "Merrin just lost everything. But Ye're right, I shouldn't take such liberties. 'Twill no' happen again, sir."

Merrin's elbow darted into Ian's ribs. Ian gave her a quick grimace. What else could he have said to calm the old man's ire? But Niall was more than right. Ian couldn't be trusted to be alone with his daughter. She posed more temptation than Eve in the Garden of Eden.

Niall fished in his satchel and retrieved the leftovers from last night's feast of boiled chicken. "We'll eat this—cannot take a chance on building a fire with Rewan and his men so close on our heels."

"Agreed." Ian sat beside him. "Did ye find the petty morel?"

"Aye, and spread the brambles over the path—covered our tracks as well."

Ian tore off a piece of breast and offered it to Merrin. "Excellent."

She smiled and plucked the meat from his fingers. "I hope ye washed your hands, Da."

"Of course I did. Who taught ye the healer's trade?"

Merrin took a bite, then tossed a morsel of meat to Gar. "Will the poison kill them if they're hit with a heavy dose?"

Niall reclined against a large rock. "Not likely, unless there's a sensitivity. But it will make a man sick and sleepy for a time."

"How long?" Ian asked.

Niall un-stoppered his flask. "A day, two at most." He took a swig of whisky and passed it to Ian.

The liquid slid down his gullet with the welcomed burning sensation to which he'd become accustomed over the years. It warmed his insides. A day or two would give them a chance to flee, but Rewan would quickly be on their heels—and the blasted poison had to work. They needed to find horses or a boat...and most definitely a miracle.

Ian shivered. Droplets splattered on his face. Had the fever returned? A warm tongue slurped his ear. The stench of wet dog invaded his nostrils.

Ian swiped a hand across his ear and his eyes flew open. "What the devil, Gar?" The dog lay beside him, slapping his tail against Ian's thigh. Wet. Ian had no fever—everything was soaked clean through. If there was one thing Ian could count on in the Hebrides, it was rain.

Thick mist curled around him, translucent white in color. *It must be dawn.* Ian looked to his right. Niall's snore caught in the back of the healer's throat and garbled there as if it were alive. Next to the old man, Merrin curled with her backside touching her father, his thin plaid over their shoulders. Ian moaned. He'd give his morning meal to have Merrin press her bottom against him like that.

Stretching, Ian sat up. The wound in his back stabbed at him, complaining from the moss-covered rock he'd used as a bed. He flexed his arms and his elbows cracked. The rain had left him stiff, sore and miserable. Niall's idea of sanctuary lacked every comfort known to man. Today, Ian would scout around and see if he could find a place that would keep them out of the weather at the very least.

Ian grasped the back of his neck and rolled his head. From the creaks and pops, it was stiffer than his arms.

With a low growl, Gar sprang to his feet. Ian reached out to grab him, but Gar lunged forward with ferocious snarls and barks. Ian started to stand, but stopped on his knees. If Rewan was there, the henchman would see Ian if he stood. He wrapped his fingers around the hilt of his sword, dropped to his belly and slithered to the edge of the crag.

"Gar, come behind," he said in a commanding whisper.

The dog obeyed. Unfortunately, the damage was done. Anyone within a mile would have heard him.

Slowly, Ian slipped his head over the rock's edge and peered down. Below the mist coming through the trees like ghosts, Rewan's men crept forward, swords drawn. Worse, every eye was focused on the bloody Castle of the Fairies. Any fae magic Niall conjured up must have vanished. They'd completely exhausted their fairy welcome.

And why the hell was Rewan up before dawn? Didn't the bastard sleep? Ian had no time to ponder answers to his questions. He shoved back from the ridge. Merrin and Niall crouched together, staring at him expectantly.

Ian swallowed. "If they didn't know where we were hiding, they do now."

Niall glared. "That bloody dog."

Ian scooted beside them and kept his voice to an intense whisper. "We've little time. With any luck, the trap of brambles will slow them down. But I hold no illusions it will stop them completely. We must scuttle down the far side."

"Are you mad?" Niall's face turned tomato red. "'Tis as steep as kilt rock."

Ian thrust his finger toward the dirt. "'Tis that or face Rewan's men in the wet on this stony crag right here."

Merrin grabbed Gar's collar and pulled the soggy deerhound against her body. "Will they kill us?"

"No doubt they will." Ian looked Niall in the eye. "Take Merrin and go now. Slide down on your arse and ye'll live."

Ian reached for the bow and single arrow. If he hadn't been so friendly with Merrin last night, he would have made a couple more. Bloody lovesick laddie, would he ever learn? Probably not before he met his end.

Merrin grasped his arm. "Ye're no' planning to stay here and fight?"

"That's exactly what I should be doing." Ian inclined his head to the back of the crag. "I'll do what I can to stall them. Then I'll follow. Now go."

She gave him a squeeze. "Do no' forget your promise."

Ian clipped a nod. Of course he wouldn't forget. He was making promises he knew he couldn't keep, but by his oath he'd do his best to honor them while he still breathed.

He watched Niall and Merrin disappear over the edge of the cliff while he collected a pile of stones. Gar paced back and forth and finally took a leap. Ian pulled a leather slingshot out of his sporran. He hadn't used it in years, but at one time he'd been accurate. He prayed he hadn't lost his skill.

Ian again peered over the ledge. In minutes, the men would hit the brambles—close enough for an arrow and a rock. Fortunately, the path up the Castle of the Fairies tapered into a narrow passage—a fat man wouldn't make it through. One or two fallen men would block it—for a time. At least Merrin and Niall would have a fair chance at escape.

Ian took shallow breaths while he waited—his heart thundering in his ears like it did before a battle. The first man howled when he hit the brambles. Ian stood with the bow and let the arrow fly into the heart of the second warrior. Snatching up the slingshot, he loaded a rock. With two swings around his head, he released. He didn't wait to see if he hit his mark. He loaded another rock, and another. The men below bellowed with pain. Ian couldn't tell who'd been hit and who'd been snagged by poison brambles, but their bodies were embroiled in mayhem.

Ian grabbed the sword and slid it into the scabbard on his back. He ran to the nether ridge and took a blind leap. Midair, he marked his landing spot—a thick clump of moss. He prayed he wouldn't meet solid rock beneath.

His knees jarred hard, but stars crossed his vision when his back absorbed the shock. His wound must have opened and torn a gargantuan hole. At least that was what Ian imagined as his feet pummeled down the steep slope.

Either he was functioning on raw fear, or his strength was coming back despite the odds. He raced for the trees, running every bit as fast as he had the night Rewan MacLeod shot him in the back.

Before he reached Merrin, the earsplitting blast of a musket boomed behind him. Ian didn't turn around, fully aware he was out of range. Rewan's gun had fired a warning. One that ran cold through Ian's blood.

Chapter Thirteen

M errin came to a skidding stop after the musket blast echoed through the air. "Ian!" Her heart raced.

Niall grasped her hand and tugged. "Ye cannot worry about him now." Her father's quick inhales wheezed. "We must continue on."

Gar trotted in a circle and yelped.

"And your bloody dog needs to keep his mouth shut."

"Wheesht, Gar." Merrin clamped her fingers around his collar and they carried on their steady trot along a narrow game trail. Her feet stung with savage blisters. "Do ye ken where we're going?"

"Southwest."

"Is there anything there?"

"Just hills, lochs and valleys."

Merrin threw a quick glance over her shoulder. The grassy landscape was sparsely forested. Hills sprang up in every direction. Ian was nowhere in sight. Had he been shot? Sucking in a gasp of air, she willed herself not to consider it.

Perspiration beaded her forehead, yet her body shivered from the cold, damp clothes sticking to her flesh. She swiped her arm across her face. Her legs burned from so much abuse.

Gar yanked on her hand and whined. "No, ye must come."

But the dog insisted. Straightening his legs, he dug in his paws and resisted her pull on his collar. Merrin hesitated and Gar tugged her back along the trail with soft whimpers, as if he knew he shouldn't bark. Merrin followed a few paces and cast her gaze to the top of the hill behind. Ian barreled into view with a noticeable limp.

She clasped her hands over her heart and raced to him, her heavy muscles suddenly feather light, blisters forgotten.

Ian covered twice the distance and opened his arms.

"I heard the musket shot." Merrin's toe caught on a rock and she stumbled into him. His arms flung around her with a soft grunt. "Are ye hurt?"

"Nay." Ian ran his fingers up her back then grasped her shoulders. Holding her at arm's length, he looked past her ear and tilted his chin up.

Niall's watching.

Ian's handsome gaze switched back to hers. "We need to keep moving—find a place where we can build a fire and dry our clothing."

Too relieved and overwhelmed to reply, she nodded and motioned for Gar to follow.

Ian took her hand and led her down the hill. Niall waited with his fists on his hips. "Did we stop them?"

"Aye, but I dunna ken for how long."

Niall pulled Merrin to his side. "Mayhap we have a day, two at most."

Ian scratched his head. His gazed shifted between the two. "We're on MacDonald land. We'll find no sympathy here. I want to head southwest. We'll surely find sanctuary at Eilean Donan Castle."

"'Tis a MacKenzie keep, no?"

"Aye, but governed by the MacRaes. If they've had word of Janet's escape, they'll take us in for certain."

Merrin touched the scarf at her neck. "Even with me mark?"

Ian's lips thinned. "I think so—'tis worth a try, especially since it appears Rewan's after me and not the MacKenzie."

She knit her brows. Ian could have no idea if they'd accept her or offer sanctuary. Could he? What would they do if the MacRae turned them out? Merrin pulled Gar close and ran her fingers through his coat. How long could she keep her mark a secret in a castle filled with curious and suspicious people?

Ian marched on course due south. "We'll stay away from the coast for a bit—to give Rewan's galley a wide berth. Doubtless he's left a man or two to mind it."

"What do ye think he'll do next?" Niall asked, following.

Ian quickened his step. "I wish I bloody knew. One thing's for certain. We cannot underestimate him."

Rewan surveyed the mess. Two men lay unconscious, their heads bleeding, bludgeoned by mere pebbles. One man lay dead with an arrow stuck in his heart, and two more were puking their guts out, complaining of stinging scratches from paltry bramble thorns.

Alick wrung his hands like a woman. "'Tis the work of the fairies for certain. Do ye ken where we are?"

Rewan frowned. He could have slipped his fingers around Alick's thick neck and strangled the superstitious fool. This was no magic. Raasay was up to his tricks, and now he had an herbalist to help him.

"This is Fairy Glen, mark me words." Alick pointed to the impressions in the moss where that onion-eyed varlet and his accomplices had slept. "This is the Castle of the Fairies. We should take the men out the way we came."

"Are ye aiming to heft them on your back, then?"

Alick twisted his mouth closed.

Rewan kicked a rock. Bloody hog's breath, his toe throbbed. "We should have sailed around to Dunvegan and asked for a lend of the chieftain's horses. Ballocks. Leave it to conniving Raasay to find a way to slip through a half-dozen well-trained Highlanders yet again."

Alick shrugged. "So what's your plan?"

"We'll hide here until these miserable sops can walk, then we'll sail the galley round to Dunvegan for the bloody horses—send out spies. Ian will no' venture far with a woman and an old codger in tow." He pointed to the dead man. "And ye can bury him while we're waiting."

Rewan rubbed his shoulder and winced. One of those damned stones had broken the flesh. Blood pooled on his shirt. He could kill Ian for that alone.

The one thing prickling the back of his neck was that Raasay had taken up with a healer. Though Rewan mistakenly thought Niall hailed from Brochel, the older man had a reputation for his skills with potions and tinctures, even in Stornoway. Brambles that made men puke their guts out? Rewan had no doubt wizardry was involved—and hiding in the Castle of the Fairies confirmed it.

Rewan would not succumb to sorcery of any sort. He'd find Ian MacLeod, and he vowed the bastard would not keep him from his woman much longer.

Cold and hungry, Merrin hoped they were going to stop and build a fire, but Ian pushed them on. By the time they reached the eastern shore, her clothing had mostly dried, but her feet were raw. The blisters burned, screaming for her to stop. She could have walked around Fladda more than a hundred times by now. If they didn't rest soon, she'd be useless on the morrow.

Ian pointed toward the beach. "Look. A skiff."

"Praise the good Lord." Merrin clapped her hands and cast her gaze to the puffy clouds sailing above.

Niall patted her shoulder. "Come. There's no time to waste."

Though it was a small skiff, Merrin breathed a sigh of relief. At last they would be able to rest their feet whilst moving swiftly. The prospect of seeing a castle excited her. She'd keep the scarf tight and tucked into her bodice so the ends wouldn't accidently catch on something, especially a curious person's fingers. She'd learned her lesson at the cottage with Ian.

He unstrapped the sword from his back and placed it in the boat. "Only one oar."

Niall clambered over the side. "'Tis better than none. We should be right if we stick to the shoreline."

Ian helped Merrin step in and she patted the wooden bench beside her. "Gar." In one leap the dog nuzzled next to her, tail wagging. "Ye wouldn't complain about catching a ride, would ye, laddie?"

Ian shoved the boat into the surf, baring his teeth, face straining. Then he jumped over the side and manned the helm as if he'd never had a hole in his back. He grunted as he paddled the oar from side to side. The movement had to be causing pain, though it was no use trying to convince him to let Niall do it.

Ian paused for a moment. "Keep a look out for Rewan's galley. It'll be flying the Lewis pennant."

Merrin scanned the waters around them. Her gaze stopped at her island. Fladda sat abandoned, looming off the coast of Raasay. It looked foreign from this viewpoint—nothing like the home where she'd spent her entire life.

She couldn't see the cottage, or what was left of it. That was probably for the best. Only spindly birch and heather dotted the slope, interspersed with the occasional clump of yellow gorse.

Gar stirred, leaning his heavy body against her arm.

"Bloody miserable piece of worthless driftwood." Niall's venomous curse snapped Merrin from her thoughts.

Icy-cold water sloshed over the toes of her boots.

"Start bailing," Ian shouted, rowing harder.

Merrin spread her palms. "With what?"

"Your hands."

Niall and Merrin went to work, ladling handfuls out of the boat. Not long and her fingers went numb. She glanced at her feet. The water had risen to her ankles.

She grabbed her satchel and dumped the contents into the hull. Niall gasped. "Our food."

"Bloody will no' do us any good if we capsize."

Niall gaped at her brash use of a vulgar tongue. She'd never in all her days uttered a "bloody" before. Not once. But this desperate situation demanded far more than a mere "merciful fairy feathers."

Merrin worked to scoop the satchel through the water and dump it overboard. Niall stopped and did the same with his satchel. They managed to keep the water from rising higher, but Merrin couldn't maintain this pace much longer.

Ian looked directly at her. His rowing continued at the same rapid pace. "Ye're keeping up well."

Merrin's heart sped—mercy, he could motivate any lass with a look. His compliment gave her renewed strength. He even smiled through gritted teeth.

"There's no way we'll make it past Portree before we sink." Ian inclined his chin toward a point jutting into the sea. "We can cast ashore there where we'll not be seen by the townsfolk."

Niall glanced at Merrin's neck. "Tie your scarf tight. The last thing we need is a whole village after us."

She smoothed her hand across the woolen fabric. If only there was a better way to conceal her mark. Even Ian had grown sus- picious back at the cottage when he saw her wearing the scrap of wool—who wears a scarf around their neck in July?

Ian's luck couldn't have been much worse. The elation of finding an abandoned skiff was dampened by the fact the pitch no longer sealed the boat's seams. Merrin's skirts were soaked clear up to her knees. The poor lass would catch her death if he didn't find a way for her to dry out.

With any luck—forget the luck—Ian prayed it would take Re- wan a good long time before he sniffed out their trail. Ian rowed the skiff onto the sand bank and helped Merrin disembark.

Niall scowled and splashed to the shore. Ian couldn't blame him. He'd be madder than a honeybee if he took a stranger in, healed him and then lost his home in the process. If Ian could lead them to Eilean Donan, the MacKenzie would help. *Right?* He prayed again. Unfortunately, he feared he hadn't built up enough inventory of good deeds for the Holy Father to pay him much mind.

Ian latched on to the hull. "Niall, help me carry the boat into the trees. I'll not have it sitting on the beach as if it were a waving torch for Rewan."

Merrin pointed up the craggy bluff. "Is that a cottage?"

Ian followed her finger. "It looks like something—mayhap too small to be a cottage."

"Let's hope 'tis not." Niall picked up the back end of the boat. "A shelter we could use. Meddling folk, no."

Ian squinted through the trees. The shack certainly appeared abandoned. "Let's heft the skiff up there. 'Tis not much further than the tree line."

Niall's face strained red beneath the boat's weight, but he nodded.

The hole in Ian's back punished him for ignoring it. He ground his teeth. The blasted useless, unseaworthy vessel weighed at least twenty-one stone.

Merrin limped ahead with Gar on her heels. She hadn't complained, but she walked gingerly like she curled her toes inside her boots. Ian had run them both hard all day. He'd had no choice. Life was worth more than a pair of sore feet. They'd all need to swallow their aches and pains and keep going.

Ian scanned the trees. A rabbit scurrying in the shadows was the only sign of life. Merrin disappeared around the corner of the building. Derelict, stones were missing from the walls, but it had a thatched roof—in places.

Ian rested the skiff beside the shack. "We can use this for firewood."

"Aye, if we can find an axe."

Merrin poked her head around the wall. "It looks abandoned."

"I'll say." Ian pulled a piece of rotten thatch from the sagging roof. "But it will do until we can find another boat."

Niall kicked the skiff. "I think we might be able to patch this. I can make pitch from branches of these juniper trees."

Ian liked the old healer more and more. He certainly had a number of skills. "Patching the seams would help. But we wouldn't be able to outrun a galley."

"Aye, but it would take us down the coast. Especially if we traveled at night."

Ian couldn't argue. "Good thinking."

Merrin popped around the corner and tugged them both into the musty shack. Aside from moss and ferns sprouting out the dirt floor and daylight peeking through the roof, it would suffice. Mayhap they could hide there for a day or two and repair the boat.

Niall walked to the far corner and picked up a broken clay pot. "I think I can use these larger potsherds to make the pitch."

"Are ye going to fix the boat?" Merrin asked.

Niall reached for another piece of pottery and held it to the light. "Aye."

Ian tapped the discarded rubbish that littered the floor with his toe. "How long do ye think it will take?"

"I need at least a day to leach out enough resin to make it worthwhile, then it'll take three days for the pitch to set."

"Three days? That's madness."

"Do ye want it to work?"

"Aye, but I do no' want Rewan to come and slit our throats in the meantime. It only needs to take us as far as Eilean Donan. We're no' trying to make it seaworthy for a decade." Ian walked to the doorway. "I'm going to find shafts and feathers for arrows and set a rabbit snare or two."

"I'll go with ye—I can set the snares." Merrin patted the dog's head. "Gar, stay." Then she bent down and unlaced her boots.

"What are ye doing?"

"Me blisters are killing me. Anyway, I go without shoes on Fladda on sunny days. Not to worry, I'll be better off without them."

"Until ye tread on a thistle."

She cast her boots aside and smiled like a mischievous sprite. "I'll be careful."

Ian scavenged for straight branches and feathers, trying to avoid eye contact with Merrin. He'd acted like a complete fool when he ran over the hill and saw her running toward him. It wasn't as if they'd been separated for long, but he'd opened his arms and wrapped her in his embrace as if he'd been missing her for ages. Worse, all tension melted when she gripped his back and rested her head upon his chest. If Ruairi's henchman hadn't been after them, he could have easily led her to the tall grass and...Ian took a deep breath and stopped his line of thought.

Merrin should have stayed with Niall and tended her blisters. Damn. If Ian didn't have enough to worry about, every time Merrin came within an arm's length, her delicious feminine fragrance sent him mindless. It was as if her scent had an invisible string attached to his cock, and up it would go. Ballocks, he was hopeless around women. He had been all his life. But Merrin topped his list for most alluring *and* most forbidden. Mayhap that was why he couldn't resist her. He never could buck a challenge.

He picked up a feather and slipped it into his sporran. Ten paces ahead, Merrin bent down to secure a sapling as a trigger for her snare. Her backside made a delectable sight—narrow waist, rounded hips. Ian closed his eyes and imagined her without her skirts. In the blink of an eye, he crossed the distance between them.

She stood and smiled—that beautiful, innocent, lovely grin. "I think that'll do."

Ian glanced down for an instant. She'd used a thong from her satchel and had the trap set just outside a rabbit hole. Ian's hand strayed to her waist. "Where did you learn to do that?"

"Me da, of course. There are plenty of rabbits on Fladda."

She stepped into him, and Ian closed the distance. He slid his palms to her back, his gaze on her plump, raspberry-colored lips. Merrin boldly smoothed her hands up Ian's chest.

Heaven help him, it felt good.

Before he could exhale, his cock went from somewhat flaccid to rock hard. He covered Merrin's delicious mouth. She eagerly responded, her fingers running through the back of his hair. Her breasts brushed against his chest. Ian moaned. She pressed the full length of her body to his, sending him mad with desire.

Heaven showed him no mercy. The reckless man deep inside took over. All he had to do was lay her down on the moss and tug her skirts up around her hips. He ground his erection against her mons and rubbed from side to side. Her mouth showed Ian what she wanted with the sucking swirl of a tantalizing tongue. She couldn't possibly know what she was doing to him. If only he could slip out from under his kilt and pull her body closer. Even with all the layers of clothing between them, she could make him come—her relentless hips were driving him to the edge of reason. His hands slid down to her buttocks and increased the pressure.

Merrin sucked in a ragged breath. "Me body aches for this."

Oh, God, so did his. But Ian hadn't lost his mind so much he'd forgotten Niall was nearby. And this was *Merrin* in his arms—she was a treasure, not a lassie to use and cast aside. What would happen once they got out of this mess with Ruairi? Ian's duty was to stand beside his brother and support the clan. He squeezed his eyes shut and buried his face in her soft tresses. "I mustn't take your innocence." The words ripped out his heart.

She rested her head just under his chin, as if the hollow right there had been designed only for that purpose. "How else am I to learn of these things?"

"It would ruin ye."

Merrin pulled the scarf away from her neck. "Am I not ruined already? Who will love me with his?"

She had no clue of the extent of her beauty. He must make her understand. "Ah, *Bana*, there is so much to love. I've never known a woman more caring or generous."

"But ye do no' want me." She released her grip. "Not like a ram wants a ewe."

Ian tried to tug her into his embrace. "I want ye too much, but it is no' proper. I cannot..."

Merrin backed away, her eyes filled with hurt. "Ye cannot or ye will no'?" She turned and ran for the shack, Gar pattering alongside.

Chapter Fourteen

Merrin rose early and took Gar to check her snares. For heaven's sakes, the way Ian carried on last eve, one would think the shack would be besieged at any moment, yet they had a clear view of the sound, and Rewan's galley was nowhere in sight. It was obvious the trap they'd set at the Castle of the Fairies had worked. Merrin hoped Ruairi's henchman would never find them.

Yesterday, out of the corner of her eye, she'd watched Ian make his arrows while she helped Niall gather juniper branches. Ian used his dagger to shave off the wood in short, stilted strokes, mumbling curses under his breath until she couldn't take it any longer. The way he'd grumbled, it was as if she'd hurt his feelings, not the other way around.

She and Niall found dandelion leaves and bulrushes to eat, but she prayed her snares had trapped something more substantial. Getting away from the pair of them for a few moments was what she needed to clear her head. Ian had held her in his arms with such passion, and then he'd pushed her away as if he'd come to his senses and realized he couldn't be amorous with a woman like her. Why could she not look upon Ian as she did Friar Pat? A dear friend was all Laird Calum MacLeod's son could ever be.

Beside her, Gar growled and crouched. He crept forward, ears pinned. Merrin glanced over her shoulder. Perhaps she should have taken Ian's advice and let him come with her. She slid her dagger from her boot and crept behind her dog. They stepped into the clearing where she'd set the first trap. Gar launched into a snarling, yapping tirade.

Squealing, a boar the size of a large dog tried to run, but didn't go far. Its leg snatched him back, caught in Merrin's snare. Gar pounced and twisted the boar to its back, fangs clamped around the beast's neck.

Merrin gasped. "Come behind!"

Snarling, the deerhound released his death grip and backed slowly to her heel. The knife shook in her hands. She should have let Gar kill the pig. Now she'd have to do it. Inching closer, Merrin raised her dagger for a killing blow. The boar sprang to its feet and faced her, its little eyes pleading. Though she'd killed many a chicken at home and her empty stomach rumbled, Merrin couldn't bring herself to stab the helpless mongrel.

Footsteps crashed through the trees, snapping twigs, branches rustling. "Merrin!" Ian roared.

He barreled into the clearing, sword drawn. Stopping, he looked from Merrin to Gar to the pig. His panicked expression turned to a grin. "Ye caught a boar?"

Merrin lowered her dagger. "Aye, but I cannot kill it."

Ian cupped her cheek. "Ye're too kindhearted, lass. Avert your eyes and we'll feast tonight."

No matter what, Merrin couldn't stay upset with Ian. He looked so dangerous, charging through the woods to her rescue—so ruggedly male.

Niall tromped up and gasped for breath. "Thank heavens, ye snared us a big fella."

Merrin blinked, pulling her mind away from its conjuring of Ian's display of a raw warrior in motion, ready to fight for her. "Aye." She cleared her throat. "And Ian's finishing him for us."

Niall licked his lips. "Very well, I'll go throw some more wood on the fire."

Ian made quick work of gutting and cleaning the boar and then carried it back to the shack. Good thing he was there, because the carcass must have weighed at least seven stone. How Ian managed it with his wound still angry raw, she couldn't fathom, but Merrin gave up worrying about his back. The wound was gradually healing, even though he kept making it bleed.

Merrin fashioned a spit by using two Y-shaped branches and suspended the pig on a long stick between them. They all had a go at turning the beast above the fire. All the while, Ian never took his eyes off the Sound of Raasay. Once daylight faded into darkness, he gave up his search. "I think we're safe for the night at least. We'll need to keep the fire to coals."

"Good." Merrin cut a piece of meat and took a bite. The juices spread across her tongue and made her mouth water. "Mmm. Because I reckon the pork is ready."

They all dug into the meat as if they hadn't eaten in a sennight. Aside from a few soggy, smashed oatcakes, bulrushes and dandelion leaves, there had been nothing since the meal of chicken they'd had night before last. Dumping the food in the hull of the skiff to bail water forced them to live on anything they could scavenge.

"I'd bet there are clams aplenty on the beach," Niall said.

Ian rubbed his belly. "Aye, but we'd be seen for certain."

"I could go down," Niall suggested. "Rewan has no idea what I look like. No one would suspect an old man clamming on a beach."

Ian smiled, the flames dancing in his eyes. "All right. I wouldn't complain about adding clams to me diet."

Merrin dabbed her mouth with her fingers. "And crab, if ye can find it."

"Always count on a woman to make your task more difficult." Niall pulled a small wooden flute from his sporran. "Ye fancy a tune, Ian?"

"Music? Had I known we were going to have a fete, I would have brought me pipes."

Merrin gaped. "Ye play the bagpipes?"

"A second son needs to be of some use at all those gatherings."

Would Ian never cease to amaze her? "Ye mean ye've played in the castle with people dancing?"

Ian gave her a quizzical look, and then his face softened, taking on the sultry amber glow of the flames. "Aye, lass."

Niall's lyrical flute floated over the campfire and swirled around as if swaying to a dance of its own. Ian stood and sauntered to Merrin's side. Placing an arm across his waist, he bowed deeply. He shot a quick glance to Niall, who blinked his eyes with a nod. "May I have the pleasure of this dance, m'lady?"

Though no kin to nobility, for the first time in her life, Merrin felt like a princess. It didn't matter that she was sitting on logs alongside a campfire. Ian's powerful frame looked so gallant in the plaid she'd woven. As was customary, he wore the length of it draped across one shoulder. With his ermine sporran and bejeweled dirk hanging from his waist, he could have passed for a prince—if only he could be *her* prince.

Ian offered his hand. Her fingers trembled when she placed them in his callused, much larger palm. "I dunna ken if I can do this."

"Have ye danced with your da?"

"Aye."

He lowered his gazed and met her eyes. He smiled—so warm, so friendly, but more. "'Tis no different."

He pulled her close, but not quite touching. Butterflies swarmed inside her belly. "I daresay it is." Something about this night made Ian even more handsome. There had been fires in the hearth at home, but the firelight dancing across his face made him dreamy, intoxicating.

He took her hands and danced slowly to Niall's ballad. She looked down at his feet. He caught her chin with the crook of his finger and encouraged her to gaze upon his face. She relaxed into the lyrical flow of his footsteps. She floated, as if they danced upon a cloud. She could hear the soft call of the flute, though distant, like in a dream.

Merrin hummed a bit and Ian pressed his hand into the small of her back. He pushed against her right hand, which she instinctively took as a cue for a turn. When she executed it without stumbling, he did it again. Ian's eyes flashed wide and he spun her around the fire. "I like it when ye sing." His deep voice rolled like honey. "I remember your singing in the cottage. 'Twas beautiful."

Merrin knew she was blushing. Ian had a wonderful way of making her feel beautiful—though she knew she could never be.

Niall suddenly switched to a reel.

"Ha!" Ian picked up the pace with scarcely a hitch to his step and locked his elbow with hers. Together they danced in circles, laughing—just as she did back in the cottage with Da. Except it was unlike anything she'd ever experienced. Ian had not a line on his handsome face, not a grey hair in the flaxen locks that hung to his shoulders. Ian looked at her with hungry eyes, as a man would a woman he wanted for more than a simple dance.

Though she didn't always understand Ian's actions and how they sometimes conflicted with his words, Merrin allowed herself to enjoy every moment. She desperately wanted to experience everything, and forced herself not to ponder upon the future. Her time was now. No, Ian would not be swinging her in a reel forever, but she would take all she could reap and lock it away. She'd savor it for the lifetime of loneliness—which, no doubt, would return.

Ian lay awake listening to the rush of the waves melodically rolling onto the shore below. Nights were the worst, listening to Niall snore whilst Merrin slept on the other side of her father. Ian's fingers itched to run through her hair, to explore every inch of her supple flesh.

She'd been so full of life when they danced. Her face glowed with the excited anticipation of a child seeing and doing things for the first time, yet she was nothing of the sort. An attractive and alluring woman full grown, dressed in a gown of silk, Merrin would be the center of attention at any gathering in the Highlands. And when she hummed, her voice confident and tantalizingly sweet, Ian's loins stirred to life. If things were different, he'd ask Niall for permission to court the lass. Yes, him, the lover of all women, wanted only one.

Ian groaned. He always desired that which he could not have.

He stared at the patchy ceiling. He needed to focus his mind on how he would get Rewan off his trail. He could try to enlist the help of the MacRaes, who bore arms at Eilean Donan for the MacKenzies, but that would be unlikely. Why would they stick their necks out for a chieftain's second son, a healer and his daughter? Though being the son of a chieftain had its pull, Ian doubted he could convince an army to stand beside him and fend off Rewan and his men. The possibility turned over in his mind—he wouldn't discount it, not yet.

Asking for transport might be a better idea. He'd need to think of a place he could take Merrin where she'd find acceptance. Perhaps they could steal away to the Americas—news had reached the Hebrides the new continent had land aplenty. Ireland, Wales, mayhap the Americas. There were numerous options, but the one Ian prayed for the most was to return to Raasay. He knew the land and belonged to the clan. He wouldn't set sail for a foreign shore unless there was no other option.

A sharp jab shot through his wound and Ian grunted at the discomfort. Though the pain in his back had lessened, it still weakened him, no matter how much he tried to ignore it.

Ian tried to close his eyes and clear his mind. The only thing he was sure about was they needed to keep moving. Staying put wasn't taking them any closer to Eilean Donan or safety. He'd give Niall a day, then his pitch had better work.

Merrin opened her eyes. Light streamed in from the window and the section of caved-in roof. A nasty rock jutted into her hip. It felt like she'd grown another appendage. She must have slept upon it near all night. She sat up and rubbed her backside, willing some feeling to return.

Merrin swiped a hand across her eyes. Neither Ian nor Niall were where they'd bedded down for the night. *Even Gar must be outside.* A thud resonated in through the window, followed by a grunt and another thud. Merrin stretched and crept to the doorway.

Her heart fluttered. Any sleepy cobwebs her head may have had when she opened her eyes completely dissolved at the sight of Ian half naked, swinging the claymore in a deadly battle with a tree. *Chiseled perfection.*

Gar slept, curled under a sycamore a safe distance away, but Ian had cut the limbs from the hearty oak. The tree shuddered with each pummeling blow. The muscles in Ian's back rippled and bulged. The sword hissed through the air in a deadly but graceful rhythm.

Merrin glanced at Ian's bandage. It seeped with blood, yet he seemed not to be affected by any pain. Doubtless it needled him, but with Rewan MacLeod out there somewhere, Ian had no choice but to push himself.

Pulling her gaze away, Merrin spotted Niall on the beach, bent over with a satchel in his hand. He scooped through the sand and picked something up, then tossed it into his satchel—a clam for certain.

Ian's breathing increased with the speed of his sword. He thrust at the tree, side to side while his feet danced, keeping tempo. Ian spun and sliced the claymore into the trunk. A clap rang out across the clearing.

Ian dropped to his knee. "Arraugh!"

Merrin ran and dropped beside him. "Ian! Are ye hurt?"

One corner of his mouth grimaced and he held up a palm. "Do no' worry. The hard wood of this oak is a fair bit less forgiving than the flesh of a man."

Merrin cringed. "I do no' think I'd like to see your blade in a fight against another man. He'd be bested for certain."

Ian stood and helped her up. "I've trained beside Ruairi's men. They're all skilled with a blade, and daily practice builds hardened warriors."

Merrin fanned herself. Ian's glistening chest rose and fell with his breath. She imagined a courtyard filled with shirtless Highlanders and forgot to breathe.

"Merrin?"

Her gaze shot up to his eyes. "Aye?"

"Did ye break your fast?"

"Nay." She cleared her throat. "Why did Da no' wake me? I've never slept this late."

"I thought ye needed rest." Ian planted the tip of his sword in the dirt and leaned on the pommel. "Besides, ye looked too peaceful to disturb."

Merrin snuck her hand to her backside and pinched. No, she wasn't dreaming. Yet another day had come and Ian was still there paying her compliments. How could a young man be so daft? But she enjoyed his attention. So much so, she wasn't about to discourage it. Her gaze slipped down the length of his body and back up again. She'd lost everything, and right now she couldn't bear the thought of losing Ian. "When do ye think ye'll see Janet again?" she blurted. She could have kicked herself.

Ian pulled up his sword and addressed the tree. "I dunna ken. I haven't really thought about it."

Merrin puzzled. She assumed he thought about Janet a great deal. "What will ye do when ye see her?"

Ian slashed at the oak. "I might not ever."

"But what if ye did?"

"I guess..." He lunged in with a downward thrust. "Things would be different."

"How so?"

He grunted and stretched his spine. Clearly, sparring caused him pain. "She'd be back in her father's care, for one."

"Would ye dance with her?"

He pointed the sword at the blasted tree, not looking her way once. "Mayhap—if there was a gathering. That's what people do at gatherings."

Merrin's chest burned. Of course she was painfully aware of what people did at gatherings. Dancing with Ian last night only strengthened her desire to be a part of it—to go to Brochel Castle and dance into the wee hours. But the image of Ian dancing with anyone but her tore Merrin's insides into tiny pieces and set them afire.

She turned and ran. Tears streamed down her face. She couldn't let Ian see her cry again—besides, she was the one being completely daft. He mustn't know how deep her feelings had become. Merrin clenched her fists until her nails cut into her palms. The son of a chieftain, Ian could go anywhere or do anything he wanted once he resolved this mess with Ruairi. She could never be more to him than a bit of amusement. Why did she melt into his arms every time he touched her? Why did she let herself swoon when he looked into her eyes? She must find the strength to resist him.

Barely able to catch her breath, she stopped beside a clear running brook and rested her hands on her knees. Dipping her head, she shook the anguish from her mind. She must close her heart to Ian. That would be the only way for her to maintain her sanity.

The water tinkling over the stones brought a soothing melody. She hadn't had a bath in days and days. Merrin untied her laces and pointed to Gar. "Stay." Cleansing the grime from the trail might help wash away more than dirt.

Ian finished sparring with the tree and stood still. Aside from the breeze rustling the leaves above and the call of a willow warbler, an eerie silence spread through the clearing. Merrin had just been there. Where had she gone? He checked the shack and found it empty. Ian peered down to the beach. Niall was still alone, hunting clams.

Ian didn't like it when Merrin set out alone. Even with Gar at her side, it was dangerous. Rewan wasn't the only predator they had to worry about.

He spotted Merrin's freshest set of footprints and followed the trail. The last conversation they'd had, she'd asked about Janet and dancing. Had he upset her? As far as Ian knew, they were having a casual conversation about dancing at a gathering. Ian stopped and looked toward the sky. Was Merrin jealous of Janet? Wispy clouds sailed above. Ian exhaled. He hadn't thought much about Janet of late. Funny. At one time he'd thought of her often.

A splash of water caught his attention.

Ian headed through the brush until he passed a break in the thicket. His mind registered something unnatural at the fringes of his vision. He backed up and peered through the gap. His heart stuttered, completely knocked from its rhythm.

May God have mercy on my soul.

Ian should have pulled his gaze away, but how could he hide his eyes from a glimpse of perfection? Merrin's long, dark tresses contrasted with the smoothest, creamiest skin he'd ever seen. Completely naked, she stood knee deep in the stream, scooping water with her hands, quickly splashing it against her body.

She grasped her locks and pulled them to her nape, tying them in a knot. A rush of heat swelled beneath Ian's sporran. A completely naked, unobstructed goddess bathed twenty paces from him.

Ian stretched his fingers, longing to cup her exquisitely formed breasts. Succulent pink buds stood proud, made rosier by the cold water. Ian's gaze trailed to her waist—it was even smaller than he'd imagined. Would his fingers meet if he wrapped them around her? Merrin's hips flared in a captivating arc. Ian's breathing sped. Her dark mound of hair formed a perfect triangle, as if her womanhood was wrapped in a package of silk, waiting for him to open her treasures.

Tapping his tongue to his upper lip, he had an overwhelming urge to taste her. He not only lengthened under his kilt, a painful erection pushed into his sporran. He slid his fingers beneath his hem and wrapped them around his cock. He moaned with his need for release.

Gar's ears pricked.

Damn.

The dog jumped up and barked. Ian eased his grip and crouched behind the thicket. Gar bounded up to him and licked his face.

"What are ye doing here, big fella?" Ian said it loud enough for Merrin to hear. She mustn't think he'd been standing there gawking at her lusciously naked body.

"Ian?" Merrin nervously called.

"Aye." He popped his head through the gap. "I was wondering where ye got to."

She had her cloak wrapped around her shoulders, pulled tight across that bewitching body. "I needed a bath, but with no soap 'twas nothing more than a rinse off." Her voice warbled. "I-I must dress."

Ian covered his eyes. "I'll wait here with Gar, then."

"No. Ye'd best go back...Gar, come."

The dog obediently trotted to her side. Merrin gave Ian a curt nod.

He hesitated.

She flicked her hand. "Go on, then."

"If Ye're not back at the shack in two shakes of a lamb's tail, I'll be coming right after ye."

Dismissed, Ian marched on. Heaven help him, he was going to hell. No man should desire a woman so fervently without first bending his knee.

"Sir Rewan from Lewis, m'laird," the man-at-arms announced.

Roderick, the newly appointed chieftain of Dunvegan, stood and offered his hand. "Rewan? What business does Ruairi's henchman have on my island?" He went pale. "Do no' tell me something's amiss with the old laird."

"Nothing like that." Rewan removed his feathered bonnet. "Surely ye've received word of his issues with his former wife, Janet?"

"Ah, yes. Her, shall we say, departure from Lewis was mentioned in his last missive."

Rewan eyed the jug of whisky on the sideboard. "Do ye mind if I pour meself a tot?"

Roderick rolled his hand through the air. "By all means, pour one for me as well. Ye must be parched after your journey."

"Aye." Rewan licked his lips and un-stoppered the vessel. "Ian MacLeod was Lady Janet's accomplice."

"Calum's son?" Roderick met him at the sideboard and nodded to a second cup. "What business had he with Ruairi's young wife?"

Rewan filled the two silver cups and handed one to the chieftain. "We thought he aimed to pursue Janet's divorce and marry her, until he left the woman with her kin. Presently, he's on the run—but no' without pain. Me musket managed to lodge a bit of lead in his back."

"So is that why Ye're here? Ye're looking for Ian?"

He swirled the whisky in his cup and took a sip. Rewan nearly moaned at the smooth taste of it. Oh, how he missed home and his nightly tots, almost more than his nightly tups. "Aye. He's on the run with an old healer and his daughter."

Roderick tossed his drink back. "He's no' been here."

"We caught up with him at Fairy Glen, but they laid a trap for us. I do no' understand it—me men were just scratched by brambles, but a pair were so sick, they couldn't march for two days."

Roderick ambled to the table. "Ye said Ian took up with a healer?"

"Aye, and his daughter."

"And what kind of wizardry does this healer possess?"

"M'laird?"

Roderick narrowed his eyes. "Anyone who enters Fairy Glen and uses magic must be a wizard of the worst sort."

Rewan clenched his fingers around his cup. He never believed in such hogwash. But he had no explanation for what happened. A grove of brambles most certainly shouldn't have caused sickness. "It could have been poison of some sort." He drained his drink and wiped his mouth on his sleeve. "I need some horses, and a few men. I've only five warriors to man the galley. I'd like to chase them overland as well as by sea."

Roderick sat in his wide upholstered chair. "A few horses I can spare, but I do no' care to have me men chasing after a man who's sold his soul to the King of the Fairies."

"They did no' stay in Fairy Glen for long. Mayhap he used up his welcome." Rewan placed his palms on the table and leaned across. "I need a few fighting men to avenge Ruairi's name. Surely ye can sympathize with me chieftain's broken heart."

Roderick laughed. "Word has it Ruairi is already divorced. I received an invite to his wedding only yesterday. The old codger's heart heals quickly."

"Mayhap, but I've been tasked with bringing Ian MacLeod to justice." Rewan folded his arms. "Will ye help me or nay?"

Roderick flicked his hand. "Very well. Take the horses and three volunteers. I'd like to help more, but 'tis all I can spare."

Chapter Fifteen

Ian used a clump of dried grass to apply yet another coat of pitch to the boat. It had been three days and Niall insisted on yet one more application of this hideous, sticky goo. They needed to be on their way. If they stayed longer, they'd be found by a local crofter, or worse, spotted by Rewan himself.

Ian had no doubt Ruairi's henchman would come after him with vengeance. The man didn't take kindly to any sort of deception. The fact Rewan's galley had not yet sailed down the sound worried Ian more. That meant he'd most likely gone for reinforcements. The bastard might just sail down the sound with an armada of sea galleys.

Niall dunked his makeshift brush into the pitch. "What's your plan once we have this heap of rotten wood seaworthy?"

Ian rocked back on his haunches. "I'm still planning to ask for support at Eilean Donan Castle."

"Ye reckon they'll give it?"

"Mayhap no' at first. They'll probably want to send word to the chieftain—Janet's da." Ian filled in yet another gap. "But they'll take us in, at least until he replies. Being the son of a laird has some advantages."

"And what if the chieftain decides Ye're no' worth his effort?"

"I'll ask the MacRae to give ye and Merrin shelter until I can convince me brother to help us."

Niall looked up and frowned. "Ye cannot take Merrin to Raasay. Too many fear her there. Even after all these years, I watch me back whenever I visit."

"I ken."

"Do ye?" Niall grasped Ian's arm. "They'd burn her."

"But near twenty year' has passed since—"

Niall jabbed his finger into Ian's chest. "Aye, but do no' under-estimate the power of fear. Some think her a witch." He shoved his thumb at his own sternum. "But I ken she's no' bad. I've done everything I can to keep fae folk at bay, but do no' misunderstand. Merrin is charmed—she's too bonny no' to be."

With a sharp nod, Ian stood. He didn't like seeing superstition in another man, though he knew it existed. He solved his problems with his sword, faced them head on. A good sparring in the court-yard might yield a few cuts, but it resolved a great many differ-ences. He walked around the hull and examined their handiwork.

Merrin was one person he could not challenge to a sparring match. She'd been such a quandary over the past two days. She'd hardly looked his way. Women could be so damned difficult to figure out. He shouldn't let her sudden coolness needle him. After all, he'd kicked himself enough times for kissing and now ogling the lass. But her silence had nearly sent him over the edge. He needed to find out what had her upset. He much preferred to have the happy, bubbly Merrin back, even if he couldn't resist her.

"I dunna ken what I'd do without her." Niall's voice cut through Ian's thoughts. "She's a good lass."

"Merrin?"

"Who else?"

It seemed they both were thinking of the blue-eyed vixen. "Aye, she's the best sort."

Niall cast his brush into the fire pit. "I would like to see her cared for. Ye ken I will no' be around forever."

Ian eyed him. If only his future were clear, he'd tell the man he would be there to protect his daughter. "I cannot make any promises—no' until this business with Ruairi is settled."

Niall picked up the container of pitch, his shoulders sagging a bit. "Aye."

Ian combed his fingers through his hair. He owed Niall and Mer-rin his life, damn it all. "If I live, ye have me word I'll see to her comfort."

"Thank ye." Niall rested the pot against the shack and gave him a wink. "I didn't leave her alone with ye back at the cottage for naught."

Ian looked to the skies and chuckled. The old man certainly had some unorthodox ways about him.

"Besides, ye were too weak to do much damage."

Ian stepped back. "Have ye forgotten what it's like to be a young buck?"

Niall's eyebrows shot up and down. "Never. But your protection for Merrin is all I can ask." He thwacked Ian on the shoulder. "It puts me mind at ease."

Ian glanced around the clearing. "Where *is* Merrin? She and Gar should be back by now." She'd set out to check her traps some time ago.

Niall turned full circle. "Blast the wandering lass."

"Do no' worry, she's probably found a meadow of daisies. I'll go fetch her."

Ian wasn't far from wrong. He found Merrin asleep beneath a hazelnut tree, Gar curled up at her feet. Ian plucked a buttercup and sat on the mossy ground beside her. The deerhound pricked an ear, half opened one eye and drifted back into slumber.

Merrin lay on her back with her head turned to the side, facing Ian. In the shade, her skin looked as soft as spun silk, her lips pink, pursed together in a perfect bow. One errant lock of hair draped across her nose, and it puffed slightly with each breath.

Ian's chest swelled. He could sit there all day and watch her sleep. He brushed her cheek with the buttercup. She stirred. Her hand lightly swept the flower away.

"Beautiful *Bana*," he whispered.

With a sigh, Merrin rolled to her side. Ian loved how her tiny waist curved up to a perfectly rounded hip. He put the flower in his teeth and ran his finger from her shoulder to the top of that curve.

"Are ye teasing me, now?"

He glanced down, grasping the flower's stem between his fingers. "I wouldn't tease the likes of you."

Her blueberry eyes watched him, half cast and half awake. She shuttered those lovely blues and drew her arms against her torso.

"Merrin?"

"Aye." Her voice was exquisitely dreamy.

"Ye've been quiet these past few days."

"Mm hmm."

"Are ye upset with me?"

She rose up on her elbow, eyes suddenly wide. "Now what makes ye ask that?"

Ian dipped his chin, a bit disappointed he'd roused her so. "Ye've hardly said a word to me."

She looked sideways. "So what of it?"

Ian twirled the buttercup between his fingers. "I thought a...a fondness had grown between us."

She pulled herself to a sitting position and faced him. "A *fondness*? And where will your affection be when ye return to *her*?"

Ian knit his brow, and then it dawned on him. *Janet. What would* he do if he saw her again? They'd said their goodbyes, agreed that she needed to start a new life with her kin. He glanced at Merrin, who stared at him expectantly. *Beautiful, innocent Merrin.* His heart squeezed. If only he could tell her how he felt. "I doubt I ever will." He brushed her lips with the buttercup. "I've missed kissing you."

He caught her subtle gasp. "Ian, ye shouldn't say that."

He reached out and pulled her onto his lap, ignoring the dull stab in his back. "Mayhap Ye're right, but 'tis how I feel."

Her eyes dipped to his lips and the color in her cheeks blossomed. He needed no more encouragement. Merrin's soft buttocks pressed against his manhood. His hips grew a mind of their own and ground against her. Deliberately, he dipped his head. He closed his eyes and savored her, letting his tongue express the feelings he longed to utter.

Merrin turned to sweet cream butter in his arms. She placed her hands on his cheeks and returned his kiss. The first hungry lick of her tongue took his breath away. The honeyed taste of her mouth, so silken and warm, made Ian want more—all of her. Merrin's bottom gently rocked against his groin, sending him into euphoric agony. Ian's excitement coursed across his skin as if a million butterflies swarmed around them.

His hand slipped up her bodice until his fingers wrapped around the ties of her kirtle. In one tug he loosened the bow and made quick work of freeing her laces. She eased her kiss. Ian ran his free hand up to her neck, preventing her from pulling away. He increased the depth of his kiss, demanding that she return it in kind.

He grasped the lace bow at the top of her shift and released it. Pressing his fingers through the top of her stays, at last he found a full, lusciously ripe breast. Just as he'd imagined at the stream, it filled his hand. Her nipple jutted against his palm. He had to taste her.

Merrin shifted in his lap, his cock rigid, aching beneath her alluring bottom. He trailed kisses along her neck until his lips arrived at her heaving cleavage. God, she defined perfection. He gently pulled her nipple above her stays and suckled.

The long, slow moan that vibrated from her throat attacked Ian's loins with vicious need. He tilted his hips into her buttocks. She rocked languidly against him. Only a few layers of cloth separated them from joining. If only Niall weren't on the other side of the grove, Ian could take his time.

He caressed the erect tip of her nipple with his tongue. "I want to see ye bare." And this time he wanted her to know he was looking.

Merrin chuckled, a low female rumble that turned his balls to fire. "Ye are a naughty Highlander, are ye not?"

"One that cannot resist you." He covered her mouth and trailed his hand down to her hem. Though he was usually confident when it came to women, Ian's fingers trembled. His cock pulsed with an aching surge when his hand slid over her boot and found exposed skin, soft, pliable under his fingers. He continued up, his breath growing heavy.

Merrin tensed. "Ian, ye mustn't."

He opened his eyes. "Let me touch ye. Please. I can show ye pleasure."

The higher his hand went, the warmer her skin grew. He slid his hand between her thighs. Her skirts billowed with his movement, blessing him with ambrosial fragrance. He nearly spilled his seed with Merrin moving against him. He groaned, picturing himself sliding into her.

Merrin buried her face in his shoulder. "Ian." Her voice strained. "Does it feel good?"

"Aye, too much so."

His fingers found a delightfully soft tuft of curls. He inched through the parting of her treasure. "Ah, *mo Bana*, tenderness between a man and a woman can never be too good. There is no finer joy."

Her breath caught with a sharp gasp.

Hot moisture met his finger. "Relax." He splayed his hand and encouraged her thighs to part. "That's it, love. Let me touch you."

"Ian?"

"'Tis all right." He caressed her tiny button with languid swirls. Her quick gasps sent a surge of throbbing heat to the tip of his cock. Expertly, he teased her to the brink of ecstasy before sliding his finger lower.

Merrin's breath came in short bursts. "I dunna ken...how much more I can stand."

He growled against her ear. "Close your eyes, *mo Bana*. I promise I'll not hurt ye."

He slipped his finger inside her warm center. Tight walls gripped him—she was so small. God, he could scarcely restrain himself from climbing over her. With a grunt of pleasure, Ian licked his lips and watched her. She was close to coming undone. He circled his finger. Merrin's hips ground against his throbbing cock. Tiny cries erupted from the back of her throat. He fingered her faster, applying the lightest friction to the spot that would send her mad.

Merrin's eyes flew open. A cry caught in her throat. Her body held tense, and then she roared. Not only did her womanhood erupt in sweet spasms, her whole body found release. Completely spent, she gasped for air, resting her head against Ian's chest. A spurt of seed spilled in his kilt. Right now he could lay her down in the moss and slide inside her, claim her for himself. But he mustn't. This was her time—Merrin's overdue chance to discover what it meant to be a woman.

He held her close and kissed her forehead. "Ye reached your release."

"I've never felt like that before. Was it magic?"

"Nay, lass—'tis far too good to be sorcery of any sort."

She shifted in his lap and slid her arms around his neck. "But 'tis not all. What of your pleasure?"

Ian clenched his bum cheeks against his own longings. "Mine comes from pleasing you."

"I do no' believe that. I've seen animals...ah...ye ken."

God, she *wanted* him to make love to her, and he was so ready to do it. Ian glanced through the woods toward the shack. "I want nothing more, but your da's most likely worried for our whereabouts."

Her face fell.

Ian cradled her chin and kissed her fully. If he couldn't tell her how much he cared for her, he'd show it.

Chapter Sixteen

M errin grasped Ian's hand tightly as he led her back to the
shack. She never wanted to let it go. Her heart swelled with
joy. The world around them floated, as if they were the only two
people on the Isle of Skye, or anywhere for that matter. A thousand questions swarmed through her mind, but she wouldn't ask
a one—she couldn't spoil the moment, it was too perfect.

Ian's fingers threaded through hers and he walked beside her,
just as if they were always meant to be together. *This must be what
it's like to have a husband—to have someone to share your life with.*

Merrin wished with all her heart their bond would last. She'd
been dreaming about him when he sat beside her. The sensation of
the flower touching her face woke her only slightly. That gesture
alone was enough to tear down her defenses. She'd tried so hard
to push Ian away, kept herself busy with gathering and preparing
food, refused to look him in the eye. But she couldn't explain her
heightened awareness or the tingles rushing through her limbs
when he appeared beside her.

She'd nearly squealed when he pulled her into his lap—considered pushing away, but it felt too good. Their kisses had gone
from the light, tempting caresses back on Fladda to deep, searching passion—but this time the urgency made her heart race. In
his arms, Merrin was bewitched, alive with desire. And then he
slipped his hand beneath her skirts. The memory of it made heat
spread across her cheeks. She'd experienced many new sensations
since Ian's arrival, but his deft fingers under her skirts took her
to an unimaginable, heart-stopping height of passion. Wantonly
grinding her buttocks against his thick column, the only thing she

could focus on was his body—the time she'd bathed him and saw him erect and exposed.

What would it be like to mate with him, to feel his manhood where he'd put his fingers? Heat flushed across her skin. Would she be able to withstand it? Would he take her to such heights her heart would stop?

Certain the warmth crawling across her skin made her blush from head to toe, Merrin released Ian's hand. She'd be mortified if Niall guessed what they'd been up to.

The shack came into sight, but nothing stirred. "Where's Da?"

Ian stopped and held his finger to his lips. Eyes darting, he crept forward. Drawing his dirk, he inclined his ear, but not a sound came from the surrounding wood.

Niall had to be nearby. She tiptoed to the tree line edge and exhaled. "There he is, on the beach."

Ian stepped beside her and sheathed his dirk. "It looks like we'll have clams for supper."

"Again?"

Ian didn't respond. His face took on a deadly edge, his jaw tense. Merrin followed his gaze. From the north, a galley skimmed the sea. Merrin froze. It flew the Lewis pennant. "Rewan?"

"Aye." His gaze darted to her face, then to the beach. "I kent we stayed too long."

Merrin gasped. They'd see Niall for certain. "What can we do?"

"Pray."

If Niall saw the galley, he didn't let on. He dropped to his knees and dug deep into the stony beach.

Merrin clamped on to Gar's collar. "He's making a good show of clamming. Do ye think he noticed them?"

"I'll bet he did. Increased his efforts, he has." Ian pulled her behind a tree. "Stay hidden. If Niall doesn't lose his head and race up here, they may not suspect him."

It seemed to take forever for the galley to pass. When it finally slipped out of sight behind the stony cliffs of Skye, Niall collected his bundle and hastened up the hill.

Merrin started to run to him, but Ian caught her by the arm. "Stay under cover of the trees. If they have one thread of suspicion, they'll double back."

Merrin nodded and tightened her grip on Gar's collar to prevent him from running to Niall. Rewan and his men had already heard him bark. Seeing a dog would only increase suspicion.

Niall huffed into the clearing. "Did ye see?"

"Aye." Ian's fists found a home on his hips. "We should be down the coast by now. Do ye think they suspected you?"

"I put on me best show to ensure they did not."

Ian glanced to the skiff. "We must leave tonight."

"But the pitch isn't cured."

"It will have to do."

Niall stepped closer to Ian and craned his neck. The two men faced each other with determined scowls.

Merrin tapped her father's elbow. "Da. We must go."

Niall stopped and ran his fingers over the pitched hull. "I do no' know..."

"Ye have a better idea?" Ian glared. "Take the pots in case we need to bail water—Merrin, pack all the food we've gathered and what remains of the pork. I'll set to work on finishing me arrows. We leave at dark."

Merrin ran to the cottage and grabbed her satchel.

A pained bellow roared from outside. *Have they found us already?* Merrin dashed to the doorway. Her heart flew to her throat. Ian crouched, doubled over. "What happened?"

He took in a deep breath, his face too pale. "'Twas just a twinge."

Merrin marched forward. "From the sound of it, I thought ye'd been shot again. I knew ye were pushing yourself too hard. Come, 'tis time I dressed your wound."

"Nay." Ian stood, his jaw set. "I need to finish me arrows."

"Ye can sit on the log and work while I tend ye." She shook her finger and stood her ground. "I'll not take your back-talking. Set your arse down."

"Merrin," Niall scolded.

"Pardon me vile tongue." She stomped her foot. "We do no' need a bellowing warrior succumbing to fever." She glared at Ian. "Or worse."

Merrin marched into the shack and grabbed the poultice. The bandages had long since been used, but he needed a fresh dressing.

Ian was on the log, whittling his arrows when she stepped outside. She stood a little taller and smoothed her hand over her hair. At least someone listened to her when she cursed and made a royal fuss. Gar trotted to her side and she gave him a scratch behind the ears while sidling up to Ian's back. "I'm glad I did no' have to strong-arm ye."

He chuckled. "That would have been amusing."

"Och, ye tease me." She pulled his shirt from his waistband.

"Only because 'tis so much fun." He glanced over his shoulder and gave her a wink. "Besides, Ye're right."

She giggled and removed his bandage. The wound seeped, with a reddened ring around it. She leaned closer and sniffed. *Not putrid, thank heavens.*

"What?"

Merrin un-stoppered the pot. "It looks angry. Ye've been pushing yourself too hard." Frowning, she ran two fingers around the inside. "And there's only enough poultice for one application."

Niall sauntered over. "No more, aye? We'll have to use salt water to cleanse it."

Ian arched his back. "That'll burn worse than a flame."

"But ye'll live." Niall patted his back. "I've heard it takes a man a near six months to recover from a musket wound—if he survives. Ye're no' even to a month yet."

Merrin pulled out her knife and lifted her skirts.

"Merrin." Niall yanked her kirtle down. "What are ye on about?"

"There are no more bandages. I aimed to cut one from me shift."

Niall knit his bushy brows and examined Ian's wound. "Wait a moment." He unsheathed his dagger. "Cedar bark will help him heal and protect the wound."

Niall crossed to a cedar tree and began carving while Merrin massaged in the poultice.

Ian picked up an arrow shaft. "You pair are a good team for a warrior to have around."

Ian stood behind a tree and looked across the sound to his island home, wondering if he'd ever set foot there again. With Brochel Castle hidden over on the east side, the island looked uninhabited. Dùn Caan presided above the land like a mighty monolith.

Twilight was approaching. The clan would be assembling in the hall, preparing for the night's feast. His mother would be above stairs, dressing, ensuring her hair was properly covered by a silk wimple. Lady Anne always had a flair for fashion.

Alexander now occupied the laird's chamber. His older brother had proceeded with an arranged marriage near two years. From the few letters he'd received, Alexander's wife Ilysa, a daughter of Laird Ross, was a good match and she'd given him an heir. Alexander had always been serious as a lad. Ian wondered if he was happy. He should be. He'd inherited the family's wealth of silver and gold whilst Ian took a few meager pieces of finery and left to serve their uncle.

Merrin ambled up behind Ian. "Do ye miss your home?"

"Aye, and me ma."

"She's a special woman, is she not?"

"None finer." Ian bit his lip. "More refined, I should say." He brushed the back of his finger against Merrin's cheek.

"Aye, but she's a real lady."

"Ye mustn't belittle your own value. Ye are more beautiful and have a loving heart, just like me ma."

She bit her bottom lip. "What was it like? Being a laird's son?"

Ian looked up and watched the trees sway and rustle against a backdrop of clouds and sky. "'Twas a life of privilege that was no' to last. At least not for me."

"It must have been marvelous—gatherings and celebrations, the music." Merrin twirled in a circle. "I can only imagine."

"There was always something going on. But as a laird's son, much was expected of me as well. I couldn't just sneak off into the shadows and play with the other lads. Me ma watched me like a hawk. 'Education is the weapon of all great men,' she'd say."

Merrin smiled and looked across to Raasay. Ian took her hand and threaded his fingers through it. He'd dearly love to take her there. The grandeur alone would make her giddy, and she'd taste rich, exotic foods imported from the corners of Europe. But his musings were a dream. He kissed the back of her hand. "Are ye ready to go once it turns dark?"

"Aye. We haven't but a few satchels among us." She glanced back at the shack. "I ken 'tis no' much, but I shall miss this musty old place."

As soon as darkness cast its shadow across the Sound of Raasay, Ian and Niall hefted the skiff down to the beach. Gar trotted ahead, laden with satchels of food that Merrin had tied to his back. Behind the boat, she followed with Niall's broken pots cradled in her arms. Ian hoped the boat would hold. It wouldn't take them long to row to Eilean Donan. With a favorable wind and calm seas, Ian thought they might make it there before dawn.

"We'll need to stay close to the shore." Ian glanced over his shoulder. "Can everyone swim?"

Merrin's eyes looked like round scallops shining in the darkness. "Ye want us to swim?"

"If we take on too much water, ye may need to."

"As a wee lass I learned to float in the *caol* with Da." Her voice vibrated with her footsteps. "But me woolen skirts are too heavy—they'll drag me under if we sink."

Ian strained to keep the boat from tipping to one side, though it was much easier to haul the blasted thing downhill—and his strength was returning. "Sit close to me once we launch the skiff. I'll help ye if we capsize."

Ian continually shifted his gaze across the sound, watching for any sign of life. He crunched onto the beach's smooth rocks then stopped short. Niall tripped over a boulder and dropped his end. Something dark moved ahead. "Sh."

The cloud cover made it all the more difficult to see. Ian squinted. Two forms moved. Gar barked and bounded after them.

"No!" Merrin yelled. "Come behind."

Gar skidded to a stop. Ian had hoped for a quiet getaway?

The dark forms squirmed toward the surf, barking—of sorts. "Seals."

Niall huffed behind him. "Let's hope they're the only creatures we encounter this night."

Ian watched them wiggle into the water. "Aye. If it were another time, I'd make Merrin a sealskin cloak. She's earned it."

Merrin stepped beside him. "Well now, mayhap I can hold ye to that someday."

Her face appeared surreal in the darkness. If only he could kiss it. "Come."

They carried the skiff to the surf and Ian shoved off, splashing through the waves until the water buoyed the boat. During their time in the shack, Niall had fashioned another oar. Ian picked them up and rowed with long, powerful strokes, facing Niall and Merrin seated on the bench across. The ease of handling two oars proved far better than managing with one. But the pain the motion caused sent stars across Ian's vision. Six months to heal from a musket shot? Ten days was already more than he could afford.

He swallowed his pain and strengthened his stroke. "Keep an eye out for sailing vessels. Even if it's not Rewan, we do no' want anyone to see us."

Niall nudged Merrin. "Watch for leaks."

She patted Gar, who'd already curled up at her feet. "I think the big fella will tell us if it gets wet."

Ian looked down. No sign of water.

They made good progress across Loch Portree, which fed into the sound. With Raasay to the east, Ian wanted nothing more than to pull ashore and ask for protection, but Merrin wasn't safe there. Besides, he couldn't bear the thought of bringing Ruairi's wrath upon his clan.

Ian groaned when they skimmed near a peninsula jutting into the water. White caps crashed into it on the other side, but still, it would be easier to row around than to carry the boat across the craggy turf.

The detour took them into deeper water. Gar stood and shook. Water droplets sprayed Ian in the face. He dropped his gaze. A good inch of water sloshed in the bottom of the boat.

"We're leaking," Merrin said.

Niall handed her one of the cracked pots. "Set to bailing. I said the pitch needed more time to cure."

Ian groaned and rowed harder. If they had a sail, they'd be twice as far by now. But nothing could be easy.

Merrin dumped a pot of water over the side. "'Tis no' too bad this time."

Now they'd navigated past the peninsula, Ian pointed the skiff toward the shore. They must row to shallower water in case the boat sprang a nasty leak.

An earsplitting clap resounded across the cove. Ice filled Ian's veins. He'd never forget that sound.

Gar whimpered and crouched.

Ian whipped around. Where the hell had the shot come from? "Holy Christ!" Ian ducked.

A flash, a clap. Merrin screamed. Musket fire lit up the outline of a galley hull that waved the MacLeod of Lewis pennant.

Ian grasped Merrin's arm. "Are ye hit?"

"Nay."

"Get down, both of ye."

Niall pulled Merrin below the skiff's rim. Arms clinging to her father, she looked up, eyes filled with horror. "What are we to do?"

Chapter Seventeen

T here was only one thing he could do before Rewan's men had a chance to reload their muskets.

Ian turned the skiff, and with two strong pulls of the oars, he set it on a course for the peninsula—deep water, no beach, no place for a boat to moor. Ian drew the claymore from his back.

Niall held up a hand. "No!"

Ian held the sword above his head, its point aimed toward the hull. "Tie the bow and arrows to your back. Merrin, take off your cloak and wrap your arms around an oar. Quickly!"

Another volley of musket fire erupted from the galley. Changing course put them with the wind, and the boat skimmed toward the rocks. The galley was slower to turn. Its sail fluttered. Musket balls slapped the water just beyond the tiny skiff. The galley's sail would soon pick up. Guaranteed, the next volley wouldn't miss.

Ian slammed his sword down. The rotten wood splintered. Gar yelped. Merrin shrieked. Ian hit the hull again and again. Icy water sloshed over his hips. Sinking, he secured the sword on his back. Losing it now would mean certain death.

Deathly cold water hit his chest. He forced in a gulp of air. Niall could fend for himself, but where was Merrin?

Ian's gaze darted, blocked by angry swells and dim light.

There. Her head bobbed alongside Niall's. Ian sprang from the sinking skiff and latched on to her arm. Good. She clutched the oar for buoyancy. Ian rolled to his back and supported her atop his body, kicking with his legs. The weight of Merrin's skirts and his claymore sapped his strength fast.

"Where's Gar?" She tried to stop, but Ian strengthened his grip and forced her onward.

"He's fine." He couldn't look for the dog. Not now. If they didn't hit the shore soon, all would be lost.

Merrin's movement slowed. "I cannot go much further." Her teeth chattered.

Ian glanced ahead. The shore's craggy outline might as well have been a mile off. A riptide snared his legs and dragged him under. Holding Merrin above him, Ian kicked harder than ever before. Merrin thrashed—he held her up. Ian's lungs burned.

His head shuddered. He needed air. His grasp on Merrin slipped. *No!*

Ian pressed his ankles together and kicked both legs together. His free hand fought the current while his other groped for Merrin. Stars crossed his vision. He clasped her hand. His arm pulled. When blackness blinded him, his head broke through the surface.

Sucking in life-giving air, he heaved Merrin up. She sputtered and gasped. "I cannot."

"Ye can!" Ian looked to the shore—still so far to go. He pulled her onward. "Kick your legs. Do no' give up."

Merrin strained, her body sinking. Ian took a quick glance around. Niall was nowhere in sight.

A wave crashed over them from behind. All momentum lost, the air whooshed from Ian's lungs. The force of the water spun him out of control. He clamped down on Merrin's hand. Her small fingers yielded under his torturous grasp.

His head hit something hard. He tugged Merrin's hand. Again his head broke the surface. Hot blood oozed into his eye. Merrin sputtered. Thank God, she still lived.

Another wave crashed over them. Ian collided with a rock. He yanked Merrin behind him. She slammed into his back. Ian heaved in a breath of air, pushing aside his pain.

He grasped the rock above. "Put your arms around me neck."

Merrin latched on to him with a choking gasp. Every sinew strained as he pulled their bodies up and peered beyond the rock. "We're nearly there."

"That wave must have pushed us."

"Aye, but it nearly killed me."

"Do ye see Gar?"

"Nay."

"Da?"

Ian's gut clenched. "'Tis too dark to see much of anything." He had to spirit her to safety before he could worry about the others. *Rewan*. Ian snapped his head around. The galley loomed in the distance, cutting through the angry swells, its sail full.

He couldn't worry about that now. Ian pulled them around the rock. His feet touched and slipped. Merrin tightened her grip. He grasped her arm. "I...cannot...breathe."

Her arms loosened "Sorry."

Ian levered them forward. Fierce wind cut through his body as they cleared the surf.

Merrin took her own weight. "'Tis so cold."

"Aye. Wring out your skirts."

"Gar," she called.

Woof. The dog bounded toward them, satchels still attached.

Ian scanned the shore for Niall. A heap lay over a rock fifty paces away.

Merrin wrapped her arms around the sopping deerhound.

Ian dashed to Niall. His eyes were closed. Ian felt for a pulse. It was faint, but Niall wasn't moving. Ian shoved his back. "Niall?" He rolled the old man to the ground and pounded on his chest.

Water spilled from Niall's mouth with a fit of coughing.

Merrin dashed to his side and dropped to her knees. "Da!"

Niall held up his head. "Merrin? I thought all was lost."

Ian snapped his gaze to the sea. A shock of light blazed, followed by the crack of a musket. "We must run. Quickly!" He pulled Niall up and grasped Merrin's hand. "Run!"

Niall raced for the trees, but Merrin lagged.

"Ye must keep up."

She yanked her hand from his. "Me gown is too heavy."

Ian looked over her shoulder. The galley was heading them off. They must head inland. Grasping his dirk, he held out the front of her kirtle and cut the laces. He shoved it off her shoulders and ripped it down past her hips.

"But—"

"Ye want to live?"

She climbed out of the dress and snatched his hand, her thin, wet shift clinging to her body like skin.

Ian sprinted, pulling her into the safety of the tree line. He tugged Merrin behind a birch, shielding her with his body. Gar circled beside them. Niall lumbered up, coughing.

The galley's sail had been furled.

Ian sucked in a breath. "They'll be coming ashore."

Merrin shivered and leaned into Ian's warmth. Her kirtle was gone. Come daylight she'd be all but naked—on the run in her thin linen shift. She'd nearly died when Ian tore off her kirtle. But he'd done right. Trying to run in a soaked woolen gown was impossible.

Niall leaned against the tree, gasping for air. "And we cannot outrun them."

Ian pulled Merrin against his body. "We cannot stay here."

Soaking up his warmth, she snapped her gaze to his face. His jaw set, he held her against him possessively, as if protecting her was his first concern. She clutched his waist, melting into him, if only for a moment.

Niall pulled down the trunk of a sapling until it touched ground. "We may not be able to outrun them, but we can use these to slow them down—trigger them like a snare."

"Aye." Ian released his hold and went to work. "You too, Merrin. Tie them down with anything ye can find."

The wind ripped through her, but she grasped an eight-foot sapling and secured it by shoving the top under a clump of thorny gorse. It might not kill a man when it snapped up, but it'd give him one miserable whack.

Ian pointed to the shore. "They're launching a skiff." He turned to Niall. "Give me the bow and arrows—take Merrin and head southeast."

Merrin grasped Ian's arm. "Ye cannot stay and let them butcher ye."

He pulled her into a tight embrace. "Go with your da. There's no time to argue."

Merrin's teeth chattered. "I love you."

He pressed his lips to her ear. "I'll find ye, I promise. Now run!"

Merrin wasn't about to let go, but Niall gave her a tug. "Come. They're nearly to the shore."

She gave Ian's hand one last squeeze. Tears stung her eyes as they ran with Gar on their heels. Her teeth chattered. She could have rolled in a snowdrift and still wouldn't feel as cold as she did right now.

"Can ye run faster?" Niall reached back and grasped her hand.

Merrin swiped up her fingers, shoving her matted hair away from her face. She pushed her legs harder. Would this night never end? Da led her alongside a stone fence. Merrin glanced over her shoulder. Through the darkness, she thought she saw men running on the thin strip of land.

God help him.

Niall pulled her to a stop. "A horse."

Merrin's heart pounded in her chest. "But what about Ian?"

"He'll find us." Niall unbuckled his belt. "And mayhap we can stop running if he does no'."

"Do no' say that." Merrin stomped her foot. The mere thought sickened her. "Never say that."

Niall clambered over the fence. "Bloody women—he'll be along, blast it anyway. I'll catch us this nag and Ian will find us."

Merrin clenched her fists. She should be beside Ian now. This was the second time she and Niall had left him to stand and fight while they ran. Gar rubbed against her, his satchel bumping her leg. Merrin bent down and unfastened them. "If Da and I can ride, the least I can do is ease your burden."

"Easy, laddie," Niall crooned over the fence.

Merrin watched her father creep to the horse, a clump of grass in one hand and his belt in the other. The bay appeared old by the relaxed way it carried his head and shoulders, not tense and spirited like a filly or a colt.

The horse raised his nose only high enough to smell the grass Niall offered. He took a step in. Niall slid his arm around the horse's neck and slipped the belt around. He led him to the fence.

Merrin climbed over. "That was easy."

"He's an old gelding, but he'll take us further than we'd manage on our own."

Merrin petted his neck. "Have they put ye out to pasture, old fella?"

"Merrin?" Niall pinched her shift. "What happened to your kirtle?"

He's only just noticed?

"Ian tore it off me."

"What?"

"I couldn't run with it—the wool weighed more than a barrow of rocks." She moved to the horse's side and placed her hands on his back. "We've wasted enough time. Give me a leg up."

Niall helped her, then led the horse to a fallen log and mounted behind her.

Merrin looked at his rein-less hands. "How are ye going to steer?"

"I'll use me knees."

A clap resounded from the water. Merrin jumped and craned her neck. The bright light of musket fire lit up the shore. She counted four, but there could be more men—most likely not everyone would have a weapon as valuable as a musket.

"Hurry, Ian!"

Ian crouched behind a tree and counted the number of men rowing ashore. *Four? Rewan must underestimate me.* Ian glanced over his shoulder. *Unless he's split his forces.* Trees and darkness blocked Ian's sight, but he listened. Only the rustle of leaves and the sound of waves crashing into the rocks—he held his breath but heard nothing more than his heartbeat. He marked Rewan's bulky outline when the men stepped ashore. He probably knew every one of them. Ian abhorred killing. That he knew the men, some by name, made it worse.

He loaded an arrow into the bow and waited. The men crept slowly. Ian steadied his breathing, willed himself into a deep calm. He eyed his target, the leading man. Too bad it wasn't Rewan.

He raised the bow even with his shoulder and pulled back the string. He waited. Nearly there. He squinted. Two more steps. Ian released. *Ballocks*. The arrow soared wide right, only clipping his target in the shoulder.

Musket balls flew past his head to the ear-splitting weapon cracks. Ian snatched another arrow and fired. This one whizzed low and caught a man's thigh. His bellow echoed between the trees—he'd most likely not rise.

Ian ran faster through the forest. A sapling snapped and a howl followed. Another snap. Ian grinned—their traps were working. Mayhap they'd foiled Rewan again.

Horse hooves pounded the earth ahead. Ian darted behind a rock and peered over. *I'll be the son of a motherless dog*. Alick led the charge—straight for him.

Had they spotted him? Ian crouched and fingered his arrow. If he fired, they'd know his position for certain. Out of the corner of his eye, he spied a pathway leading toward the other side of the peninsula. If Ian could make it to the water he might be able to swim through the shallows—at least until they realized they'd lost him. The galley would have to sail clear around that strip of land—if they could figure out where he'd gone in the dark. It just might work.

Ian bent down, half walking, half crawling. He used the rocks' shadows to conceal his movement. The trees along the path grew sparse, making each step more precarious.

"Where is the bastard?" Rewan shouted behind him.

Staying low, Ian crept through a maze of rocks, willing the water to come underfoot with every step.

"There he is!" someone yelled.

Ian didn't look back. He sprinted ahead. When the water came into view, he skidded to a stop. It beat against the cliffs fifty feet below. *Merciful bloody Mary, I'll be skewered by me own dirk*.

He took one last glance over his shoulder. Alick and his men were driving their horses through the rocks. He'd run out of luck and out of time.

Ian sucked in a deep breath and took a sprinting leap.

Chapter Eighteen

"**H**e jumped," Alick yelled from the top of the crag.

Rewan slammed his sword into the sand. "Son of a bloody, putrid English harlot." Clenching his fists, he paced while he waited for Alick and the others, praying that Ian met his end and hit the rocks below. All he'd have to do is find the carcass. If he was lucky.

Alick trotted beside him. Rewan fisted his hips. "Did ye see the bastard's body on the rocks?"

"'Twas too dark."

Rewan kicked the sand. "Ballocks."

Alick dismounted. "Me men are tired. The horses are spent. We've been driving them for days."

Rewan shook his finger. "No one rests until we find him." He paced in a circle. "We nearly had the bastard."

"The leap probably killed him." Alick folded his arms and lifted his chin. "If he's dead, we'll have much better luck finding him come dawn."

Rewan knew his man-at-arms was right, but his pride wouldn't allow him to admit it. Not when they were so bloody close. "Ye take the horses to the other side of the bay and wait." Rewan signaled to his crew. "Come with me, men. Time to sail around the point and find a corpse."

Merrin's head bobbed against Niall's back. Her eyes refused to stay open and her teeth would not cease their chattering. Beyond cold, the wind continued to punish them. Her only comfort was the bit of heat she could steal from her father's back. From the way he shivered, his discomfort matched hers.

"How much further?"

Niall sat up with a jolt, as if her words had stirred him from slumber. He pointed. "Methinks there's a chapel atop the hill yonder."

Merrin followed his finger. "Thank heavens. The wind is cutting to the bone."

The gelding slowly walked up. He hadn't done anything but walk, though he'd given their legs a much-needed spell. "Do ye think the horse can trot?"

"I've cued him for it, but he seems to have only one gait."

"Mayhap he'd be a bit more willing when he does no' have two on his back."

"I'd say he's an old nag without much life left."

Merrin ran her hand along the gelding's rump. "He's a bit thin, but he's been of good use to us, I'll say."

"That he has."

Merrin glanced around Niall's shoulder. The chapel loomed dark against the night sky—almost eerie. "It looks abandoned."

"'Tis best if it is. We do no' need anyone asking questions—and ye've lost your scarf."

Merrin's hand slipped to her neck. It *was* gone. So many times she brushed her fingers across it, the movement had become habit. But with their frantic escape, she hadn't thought of the one thing that protected her from notice. Not once. "God save us."

Niall tapped his heels against the gelding's barrel. "We're in the right place for that." After cuing the horse to a stop, he helped her down and then slid off the gelding and led him to a patch of grass.

Merrin folded her arms tightly across her chest, shivering more without Niall's heat. "Are ye just going to leave him there?"

Niall shrugged. "I've no rope to hobble him."

"Do ye think he'll be there in the morning?"

Niall pointed to a brook. "Why not? It looks like there's grass and water aplenty."

Merrin was too tired to argue, but it would be a miracle if the old fella didn't turn tail and head back to his paddock before morning.

Niall thumbed the latch on the chapel door. It clicked. Merrin rubbed the outside of her arms as they stepped inside. It was even darker. Her boots crunched—*thatch?*

Niall patted her arm. "There might be a candle on the altar."

Merrin blinked her eyes and glimpsed the outline of chairs. "Can ye see it?"

"Nay, but an altar is always at the front of a church."

"Oh." She tried to force her eyes to focus. She'd never been in a holy place before, though Friar Pat had taught her how to pray. Going to Sunday services on Raasay was forbidden, of course.

Niall's dark shadow progressed up the aisle, his footsteps echoing off the walls as if in a cave. He stopped with a sweeping sound. Merrin prayed he'd find a candle and a flint. Perhaps there was a hearth to calm the shivers coursing across her skin.

"Here we are." Niall's satisfied voice was soft, but echoed as if he'd shouted the words.

She clearly recognized the next sound. Iron on flint, followed by yellow sparks, and then a flame illuminated her father's body. Merrin gasped. A bronze cross sat atop a stone altar and on the far wall, a beautiful stained glass depicted Jesus clothed in white, holding a shepherd's staff.

"Beautiful." The nave was filled with rows of wooden chairs with seats woven with rough-hewn nettle. "The place looks like 'tis still in use."

"Aye, but 'tis our place of sanctuary for the night."

Merrin didn't see the one thing she needed most. "There's no hearth."

Niall turned full circle with the candle held high. "'Tis best we do no' build a fire anyway. The smoke might attract Rewan and his men." He put an arm around her shoulders and led her to the back corner. "At least we're out of the wind. We'll huddle here and keep each other warm."

Merrin slid down the wall and held out her hands. "Gar, come." The dog trotted into her arms and leaned up against her. He stank, but his warmth felt good. She patted the floor. "Lie down, big fella."

Sandwiched between her father and her faithful dog, Merrin closed her eyes. Her heart squeezed. *Where is Ian? Dear Lord, please help him find us.*

Ian hit the water feet first. Though he wore boots, his soles stung like he'd landed on a slab of rock, but the freezing water gushed around him and pulled him under. He fought against the tumbling motion dragging him downward. Over and over he rolled with the riptide as if he were a helpless doll. With a surge, he managed to break away from the pull, kicking with everything he had. Disoriented, he looked for the surface, but darkness surrounded him.

Overcome by his need for air, he bore down and swam with powerful strokes, praying he'd break the surface. When finally an ice-cold gale hit his face, he sucked in life-giving air, coughing and sputtering.

He treaded water to regain his wits. Spinning in a circle, he caught sight of the shore and got his bearings. His energy sapped, it was all he could do to stay afloat.

Ian fought to keep his head above water and let the current pull him across the bay. Without a boat he'd be impossible to detect, but his teeth chattered. The shore was in sight. If he stayed in the sound much longer, he'd succumb to the cold. He'd already had to shake off the blackness twice.

His muscles ached when he heaved through the water to speed his progress. His head spinning, he let his feet drift downward one more time.

Sand.

He resisted the urge to run to the beach ahead. With only his head above water, he turned full circle. No sign of Alick and his horses. Ian scanned the surface as far as he could see above the waves. His gut squeezed. Was that a galley rounding the point? Why on earth would he think the bastard would ever rest? Ian let the surf take him into the shore on his belly, just like it would a seal.

When he hit the smooth rocks on the beach, Ian glanced over his shoulder and pinpointed the galley. It turned into the bay. If he stood, they'd see him. He crawled with his elbows until he reached a giant boulder. Ian slipped behind its shadows and surveyed his options. The galley sailed past, heading deeper into the bay. Still no sign of the Rewan's mounted men, but Ian knew better than to head west with the galley near. The only other option was south. He turned to study the terrain. His gaze climbed higher, up and up. Just what he needed—a mountain. As he recalled, the cone-shaped peak was named *Glamaig*. From its summit, he'd be able to see for miles.

Ian crouched low and scurried through the heather until he reached the cover of spindly birch. With a burst of vigor, he tore through the trees. Freezing cold, up he climbed until he met only heather and brush ascending the steep slope.

Again, Ian surveyed the surrounding scene. The moon shone through a parting in the heavy blanket of cloud and glistened off the water. The mountain blocked the westerly. For that he was grateful—his teeth had nearly stopped chattering, though his damp clothing still clung to his skin. At least the exertion warmed him.

Rewan's galley had moored at the far end of the bay. The dark shadows of men walked along the beach, no doubt searching for Ian's remains. Bigger than the others, Rewan's outline hunched as he swept his sword from side to side. He kicked something—definitely not the action of a happy man. Rewan's thirst for blood would be consuming. They had no idea where Ian was. Teeth resuming their chattering, Ian continued his climb. Now he needed to locate Niall and Merrin before Rewan and his band of murdering bastards found them.

At the summit, the wind cut to the bone. He scanned the surroundings for any sign of Merrin, but it was too dark to see. If he moved on now, he'd run the risk of missing them. Ian sought shelter by sliding between two boulders and then curled into a tight ball to fight the cold. At first light, he'd find his bearings and do whatever necessary to protect Merrin.

A blinding light startled Merrin awake. Gar sprang to his feet with a bark and a ferocious snarl.

The chapel door closed. "What the devil?"

Merrin rubbed her eyes. A holy man gaped at them. He wore a brown habit, similar to Friar Pat's, and his head was shaved, except for a ring of brown at the sides.

Niall jumped to his feet. "Good morning, friar." He extended his hands, blocking the holy man from Merrin's view. "My daughter and I capsized in the night. We found an old gelding, which brought us here."

The friar tried to peek around Niall, but Da stepped into his line of sight, clearly keeping him from a closer look.

Merrin hugged Gar to her chest and hid her neck behind the dog's fur. She pulled her hair forward to further conceal it.

"Me daughter was forced to shrug out of her kirtle, lest it pull her under the sea. She needs a cloak." Niall glanced at her and held up his palm, signaling for her to stay put.

The holy man skirted around him and gave Merrin a good once-over. "I see." He beckoned with his hand and headed toward the altar. "I have another robe in the sacristy. You must be hungry as well."

"Aye, we're starving," Merrin called from her perch.

Niall whipped around and glared, shaking a scolding finger.

Holy fairy feathers, could she not say a word?

The friar stopped at a doorway. "I'll fetch the robe and then ye can follow me outside. I've plenty of oatcakes and cheese in me saddlebags."

Niall clapped his hands together reverently. "Thank ye, father."

"Ye're lucky ye caught me. I ride the circuit around these parts. I'm only here once a month." The friar came out holding up a brown robe. "This one's a bit moth-eaten—left here by the last priest, I suppose, but 'tis far better than running around in one's undergarments."

Niall took it from him. "Yes, father. 'Tis a godsend."

He hurried back to Merrin and shielded her in the corner while she put it on. A heavy, musty old thing. She sneezed.

"Bless you," the friar said, standing patiently with his back turned. "Come outside with me and I'll fetch you some food. Can you stay for Sunday service?"

Merrin counted back. Was it Sunday?

"Today?" Niall asked.

"Well, yes, the locals gather just after the noon meal."

Merrin tied the rope sash, then pulled her hair around to the side and draped it down the front. She nudged her father. "How is this?"

He turned, his eyes darting straight to her birthmark. "Good." He leaned in and whispered, "Keep it hidden."

The friar opened the door and beckoned them with a wave of his hand.

"Do ye have many worshipers out here?" Niall asked.

"Nay."

The old gelding stood beside the friar's horse. "Looks like ye found a friend, Mary Louise." He dug in his saddlebag and pulled out a brick of cheese.

Merrin's mouth watered. She eased beside Niall, smiling. A gust of wind blew her hair straight out. Her hand flew to her neck.

But the friar saw. He stared at her as if she were the devil himself.

Niall grasped the cheese and pushed Merrin behind him. "Thank ye kindly."

Gaping, the friar pointed his finger. "She has...you brought *her* into a house of God?"

Merrin cowered behind her father. He grasped her arm and headed for the gelding. "She's a good girl. 'Tis not what ye think."

The friar stood his ground, his finger shaking as if he could summon the wrath of God and damnation upon them. "Ye will be punished for this! And I allowed ye to put on hallowed vestments?" He marched up to Merrin and grasped the robe.

She clutched it tighter around her body and shook her shoulders. The old garment was doing her a lot more good than it would hanging in a musty old cupboard, feeding the moths. "Get away from me. Ye're the one who's evil."

Gar growled. In two bounds, he hurled his front paws into the friar's side. The skinny man stumbled.

Niall lunged in and gave him a final shove to the ground. "You, sir, are no man of the cloth to me." He yanked Merrin's arm. Latching onto her waist, he hurled her atop the gelding's back. After pulling the rope from the cowering friar's belt, he looped it around the horse's neck and handed her the makeshift reins. He grasped the friar's bridle.

Merrin slapped her hand over her mouth. They couldn't take a holy man's horse. "No."

Niall glared at her. "We need two."

"But he'll send his people after us."

Niall glowered at the friar, who recoiled on the ground, shaking his cowering fists beneath his chin. Niall pulled the dirk from his scabbard and then slid it against the man's neck. "If ye send a soul after us, she'll not only curse you, she'll curse each man and all their kin with the Black Death." He pushed the dirk hard against the friar's throat. "Swear it."

The friar held up two trembling palms. "Please, do no' kill me."

"I said swear it."

"I swear, I swear, just leave me be."

Niall spat on the ground beside him. "Ye're no' worth me time." He swung his leg over the mare and headed off at a brisk canter.

Merrin cued the gelding to follow. After witnessing her father's unorthodox and unbridled ire, she had a bit of trouble lifting her chin from the horse's neck and closing her mouth. The old nag surprisingly picked up a canter, as if he were a spring colt—quite changed from the night before. "Come, Gar."

Merrin had never seen her father so ferocious. Had he once been a warrior like Ian? He'd never mentioned anything the like.

The wind blew her hair back, but she didn't care. Hope surged through her blood. They would find Ian soon and together they would work out a plan to thwart Rewan. She knew it.

Chapter Nineteen

Ian opened his eyes to the call of an eagle. The sun peeked over the horizon. His stomach growled. He stretched his arms forward and winced. Everything hurt like he was a rusted jumble of hinges needing to be greased before they'd budge.

He rubbed the sleep out of his eyes and pulled himself up between the two sheltering rocks. As he suspected, he had an excellent view of the surrounding area, though he was still a good day from Eilean Donan.

Down the slope, movement caught his eye. Two people mounted on horseback, cantering away from a stone chapel with a big dog on their heels. Ian squinted. Long, dark hair fluttered with the wind. Had Merrin and Niall found horses? *Aye, and she's found a cloak as well.*

Ian marked their course. Good, they were heading south—and at a rapid pace. While panning his gaze back past the chapel, his heart gripped like a vise. Ascending the hill from the north, four mounted men rode on a course to intercept them.

He licked his chapped lips with a dry tongue. His gaze darted northwards to Rewan's galley moored in the bay. Ian didn't need a spyglass to know Rewan was one of the mounted riders. The henchman's bloodlust ran too deep for him to lie in wait on the galley. Most likely, he'd left a crew to mind the ship.

If Ian could take the galley, he'd have the vessel he needed to flee—mayhap go to Ireland and start anew. But not yet—not with Rewan on Merrin and Niall's trail.

Ian watched as Niall and Merrin slowed to a trot, a gait their horses could easily sustain. Rewan and his men stopped at the chapel. A friar ran out the doors, flailed his arms and pointed. Ian had to move fast. Dashing down the southern face of the mountain, loose gravel assisted his descent.

Ian had a clear view of Merrin and Niall rounding the rolling foothills. From the corner of his eye, Rewan's warriors galloped closer. Ian's knees burned with the unrelenting downward force. Grinding his teeth, he pulled the bow from his shoulder. Nearly to his attackers, he snatched an arrow.

Rewan's men pushed their horses into a fast gallop. Hooves pounded the earth. Ian's lungs burned. He crashed through the brush, scarcely aware of the thorny gorse clawing at his skin. In seconds, Rewan would round the tip of the butte and see them. Ian leapt onto a massive rock and planted his feet. He yanked back the bowstring and trained it on the nearest man. His fingers released.

The arrow hissed over the sound of pounding horse hooves. Ian knew the line was true. Upon impact, the warrior's body jolted and hurled through the air. Ian had another arrow lined up when the body thudded to the earth.

"Up there!" Rewan yelled.

Ian released. Not stopping to watch his arrow fly, he leapt from the rock and ran through the copse of spindly birch trees.

Merrin and Niall had stopped, blast them. "Run!"

Gar barked. Merrin locked eyes with Ian. *Ballocks, why did they stop?* "Run!" he hollered, louder.

Rewan's horse galloped around the bend with two men in its wake.

Gar's barking erupted in a snarling, growling savage bray. The dog bounded head on with the approaching horses.

"No!" Merrin screamed.

Ian barreled toward them. "Get out. Now!"

Niall pulled on Merrin's reins and slapped her horse's rump. She shrieked. Ian's heart slammed against his chest, but he couldn't race to her now. He pulled another arrow and fell in behind Gar.

The deerhound headed straight in line for a collision with Rewan's bay. Gar launched himself through the air and sank his teeth into the horse's throat. The steed careened forward. Rewan sailed. Gar held on as the horse tumbled.

Ian released another arrow, hitting his mark dead in the heart. Somersaulting backward, the warrior crashed to the dirt. Thank God some of his arrows were straight.

Growling, Gar held his grip on the horse's neck.

Rewan struggled to stand. He drew his sword from his belt. "Ye're not slipping away this time, Raasay." He beckoned with his fingers. "Come here and fight me like a man."

"Some other time." *That's a promise.* Ian darted up a massive boulder and took a flying leap onto the dead man's horse. He careened to the side, but latched his fingers under the pommel to keep from falling. Ian pulled himself up and threw his torso onto the horse's neck. He gathered the reins. "Gar, come!"

Sliding his toes into the stirrups, Ian slammed his heels into the horse's barrel, galloping after Merrin and Niall.

"Arrggh!" Rewan's frustrated war cry echoed off the mountains. Ian glanced over his shoulder—his archenemy stood, a bulky image growing smaller in the path, sword in hand. Thank God. Gar galloped on Ian's heels, tongue lolling to one side, eyes wild as a wolf's.

The passing trees blocked Ian from her sight. Merrin couldn't help her frequent glances over her shoulder. She hated being forced to run while Ian stayed behind to fight. How would he battle out of this one? Rewan had too many men—and Gar? One sweep of a sword, and her beloved dog would be dead.

Both horses she and Niall rode were old. Her gelding kept changing his gait to a trot, raising his chin and shaking his head with agitated snorts. She'd kicked her heels until the horse became unresponsive.

"Keep on," Niall urged, his mare showing the same exhaustion.

Merrin threw another look back. Tingling rippled across her skin. Ian galloped straight for them with Gar right behind. *Praise God.*

Ian quickly approached. "We cannot slow down."

Merrin tried to kick harder. "The horses are spent."

Ian's steed didn't look much better. He frothed at the mouth, with white sweat lathered along its neck. "We need to ride a safe distance away—somewhere we can defend ourselves if need be."

Ian took the lead, the other horses following the younger steed. Not much time had passed when Ian's horse stumbled. He slowed it to a walk and circled behind the others. "Rewan's cavalry rode most of the night. Their horses need to be rested as well."

Niall pointed ahead. "There's a waterfall yonder. Perhaps there's a pool up above."

"Whether there is or nay, 'tis a good place to rest."

Merrin's stomach growled. "I'm starved and ever so thirsty."

They followed Ian up a rocky slope and through the sparse wood, the ground covered with moss. At the stream, Ian dismounted and led his horse to Merrin. He reached up his arms. "Let me help ye down."

Her robe opened as she placed her hands on his shoulders. Her breathing stuttered when his fingers grasped her waist. She slid down his body until her toes touched ground. Merrin pulled him into her embrace and squeezed. She didn't care if Niall balked. "I was so worried."

He cradled her head against his chest. His heart beat a reassuring cadence in her ear. "I couldn't let Rewan overtake ye. Are ye all right?"

She was breathless. "Aye."

Ian kissed her forehead. Needing more, Merrin raised her chin and guided his lips to hers. His kiss breathed life into her soul. She wanted Ian to hold her in his arms and never let go.

"Ahem." Niall cleared his throat.

Merrin arched her brow at her father. "He could have died, Da."

Niall frowned as if trying to look stern. She'd seen that look a hundred times. "I've some rope now. We can hobble the horses and let them graze."

No lecture telling Ian to keep his hands to himself? Good.

Ian pinched Merrin's robe between his fingers. "What's this?"

"A friar gave it to me." She bit her bottom lip. "Right afore he saw me scar."

Niall chuckled. "Then he cursed her and threw us out of God's house."

"And Da cursed him back and stole the friar's horse."

Ian laughed. "I was wondering where ye got the horses."

Merrin patted her gelding's back. "We found this old fella last night. Took us straight to the chapel, he did." She pulled Ian's hand. "We've some cheese, and this stream looks pure."

"Good." Ian crouched, splashed his face and drank. "You eat. I'll climb the crag to see if it's safe first."

Merrin ran her fingers across his shoulders. "I'd like to go with ye." His muscles tensed beneath her touch.

"Stay. Ye're safer here." He pressed her palm to his lips and stood. "I'll no' be long. Save a morsel for me. I could eat a salmon raw."

Merrin gulped a handful of water and helped Niall hobble the horses. Ample clumps of grass sprouted from the moss. They'd eat their fill in no time. Merrin massaged her gelding and ran her hands down each leg to ease his muscles. She glanced at the other two horses. Should she remove their saddles? No. They may need to make a fast getaway. The ole fella didn't have a saddle, but Merrin preferred it that way. She liked to feel the horse's movement beneath her.

Niall found a fallen log and sat. He held up a slice of cheese. "Ye'd better eat. I'm guessing there'll be no rest."

"Ta." She took it and nibbled at the corner.

"You've grown awfully fond of Ian."

Merrin broke her cheese in two and gave Gar half. "Aye." She shrugged, hoping her father wouldn't scold her. She held still for a moment, waiting. Fortunately, he said nothing more.

Niall carved off another slice and popped it in his mouth. Merrin watched him. He stared at the pool of water as if deep in thought. She took a larger bite and sat beside him. She hadn't time to appreciate the fine day. The sun shone straight above while puffy clouds floated with a gentle breeze. A brook tumbled into a small pool, just as they suspected, and the waterfall sang a relaxing lullaby.

Merrin closed her eyes and took in a deep breath. *How nice it would be to camp here for the night.*

Footsteps neared. Gar wagged his tail and Merrin looked up expectantly. Ian marched through the wood, powerful legs stretched against his kilt, his hands fisted with purpose. The hilt of the claymore jutted over his right shoulder, the bow over his left. Tall, broad and well-muscled, he formed an idyllic picture. Merrin's chin ticked up as she watched him. It gave her great pride to be riding with Ian, to know he protected her.

If Ian hadn't come along, Rewan would have run them down and shown no mercy. She'd watched Ian take out two. Rewan's numbers were dwindling. Would it come down to a fair fight between the warriors? Merrin shuddered. She hated fighting—hated the thought of Ian facing that beast of a henchman. Yes, Ian was big and strong, but his muscles were chiseled. From her glimpses of Rewan, that man was built like a bull, with a barrel chest and thick legs, which probably made him strong beyond anything she could imagine.

Ian smiled. Blessed be, his grin lit up her insides as if the sun radiated clear through the tips of her fingers. Merrin took the cheese from Niall and held it up. "Did ye see anything?"

Ian grasped it. "Nay, we must have caused quite a stir." He scratched Gar behind the ears. "Ye're an angry beast when Ye're riled, are ye not?" The dog wagged his tail and leaned in for more. Ian rubbed the length of his back. "Merrin, ye should have told me Gar was a trained war dog."

"He is?" Merrin shrugged and splayed her palms. "I think it comes natural. He's always been a lazy hound around the cottage."

"How did ye come to find him?"

Niall shrugged. "Picked him up at Brochel Castle. He was eating scraps off the floor and no one laid claim, so I took him home to keep Merrin company."

Ian bit into the cheese. "I think he's had some training—he looked like a bloody wolf today." The warrior looked off into the trees, as if he could see beyond them. "We've made good time. I think we'll reach Eilean Donan by nightfall."

"Nay." Niall shook his head. "Merrin cannot approach a castle dressed in a friar's robe."

Ian gave Merrin a studious once-over. "Well." He scratched his chin—his beard had grown longer than Merrin had ever seen.

It really must be itching him now.

"I'll go in and explain first. I think that might be our best option. Besides, I'm the son of a chieftain—that has to account for something."

Merrin clamped her hand over her mark.

"What about her neck?" Niall asked. "She lost her scarf."

Ian glanced across the clearing and back to Merrin. "Can ye tear a strip of cloth from your shift?"

Merrin shrugged. "I suppose. 'Tis already ruined anyway."

"But 'twill be too far above her ankles," Niall said.

Merrin pulled the dagger from her boot. "Mayhap Ian can negotiate a new shift for me? After all, I've mended this one so many times, I think it has more woolen thread than flax." She made a cut and tore, but once it hit the seam the cloth wouldn't budge.

"Let me." Ian bent down and finished the job.

Merrin glanced at Niall. Her father shook his head and rolled his eyes toward the sky.

Ian pulled her hem down then smoothed his hand over Merrin's robe.

Niall stomped his foot. "Enough. You've had your hands on me daughter far too much for a man who has not proposed marriage."

Merrin's hands flew over her mouth. *How could Da be so brash?*

Ian stumbled backward, his face red. "Apologies." He handed Merrin the cloth and straightened his shoulders. "W-we'd best ride and make good use of daylight."

Chapter Twenty

T hough Ian hadn't been to Eilean Donan Castle in years, the winding path along Loch Alsh was familiar. The MacKenzie and MacLeod of Raasay clans generally were on good terms, and as a boy, he often attended gatherings when the MacKenzie chieftain visited his "lesser" estate.

The setting sun sparkled off the saltwater loch, a tributary to the Sound of Raasay. Once things settled, it would be easy for Niall and Merrin to sail back through the loch and up the sound, straight to Fladda.

"Are we nearly there?" Merrin asked. "The sun just dipped behind the hills. 'Tis twilight."

"Not far now—one more long bend in the trail, then 'tis a straight run to the castle."

Niall rubbed his belly. "I hope we arrive in time for supper."

Gar yowled, as if complaining about his empty stomach as well.

By the time they rounded the last hillock, the sky had turned violet. Ian's spirits soared. Torches blazed on the castle walls. What a lovely sight. Shadowed galleys and small boats moored sleepily in the water, surrounding the castle grounds.

Ian urged his horse to a canter and called over his shoulder, "Come. I can smell the roast lamb from here."

Merrin's gelding dragged his hooves. Ian circled back and took charge of her reins so the old fella would keep pace with his younger mount. Gar loped beside them, excitement lighting up his dark brown eyes. Ian looked back. Niall kept up. Thank heavens they'd made it in one piece. Once they gained entry to the stronghold, Rewan might lurk about for a sennight or two, but after Ian convinced the clan to help him, Ruairi's henchman wouldn't stand a chance. He didn't have enough men, for one. He'd be forced to sail back to Stornoway for reinforcements, and then his uncle would need to decide if a full-on feud was worth Ian's head.

The hair on the back of Ian's neck pricked when they passed the first galley. No light hung from its mast—the owner most likely enjoying the laird's table. Ian couldn't shake the icy tingle slithering around his neck. He looked again.

Three musket barrels slid over the rail.

Ian slammed his heels into his horse. "Get down!"

Merrin's gelding tugged against Ian's hold. He wrapped his hand around the reins and jerked with all his might.

"Da," Merrin shrieked. "Hurry!"

Crack. Crack. Crack.

A thud shook the ground.

Merrin turned and pulled up. Niall lay flat on his back. "No!" She whipped her horse around. "Da!" He didn't move.

Ian reined in beside her. "Go before they can reload. I'll see to him."

"I cannot!"

Ian threw his hand back and slapped Merrin's horse so hard the steed would stop for nothing. Her shrieks of protest diminished as the gelding galloped toward Eilean Donan with Gar alongside.

Ian leapt down to Niall's side and tugged him behind the security of a massive boulder. The old man's breathing wheezed. Blood frothed on his shirt, directly under his lung.

"Come, Niall." Ian shoved his arms under the healer's body and heaved.

Niall groaned. "No."

Blood trickled from the corner of the healer's mouth. Ian couldn't stop. He had to spirit him to safety. "I must take ye to the castle."

"Leave me."

Ian hefted Niall into his arms. "I cannot."

"Promise me." Niall tried to swallow. "Promise you'll care for her."

Three muskets clapped in quick succession.

Ian hugged Niall tight against his body and ducked. Lead balls hissed through the air around them. Before Rewan's men could reload, Ian hefted the old man over his pommel and jumped on the steed's back, digging in his heels. "Get up."

"Promise me." Niall's voice gurgled.

"Aye. Ye have me word." Ian leaned forward to urge the horse faster, one hand keeping Niall from bouncing off. "But ye'll be here a long while yet."

The muskets cracked, but Ian knew they were out of range.

Merrin's gelding stood rider-less at the gate. Merrin sprinted to meet them. "Da!"

"He's hurt bad." Ian knew full well what frothy blood meant. He only hoped Niall could stay alive long enough to hear his last rites. "We need to carry him inside."

Merrin turned and pounded on the portcullis. "Help us. Me da's dying!"

Ian dismounted and hauled Niall into his arms. Vacant eyes glared, accusing him of murder. God help him, it was too late.

Merrin spun around.

A hundred emotions distorted her features. "Noooooo!" She ran to her father and cradled his head to her breast. "Da. It'll be all right." Tears burst from her eyes. "I'm here for ye." Her mouth pulled down in the most painful grimace Ian had ever seen. "Da. Ye cannot leave me. I need ye."

Ian clenched his jaw and pounded on the gate. "Open. I am Ian MacLeod of Raasay, a chieftain's son." Never had he been so ashamed of those words.

He blinked his eyes and choked back against his urge to bellow with remorse.

The chains of the castle portcullis groaned as the old wooden gate began to rise, black spikes pointed downward.

Ian didn't wait for it to draw up fully. When it reached his waist, he ducked under with Niall's body. A sentry dressed in a steel helm and mail faced him, sword drawn, targe held across his chest. "What is your purpose, Ian MacLeod of Raasay?"

Wailing, Merrin held Niall's hand to her chest. Gar stood protectively at her side, eyes darting around the scene.

Ian inclined his head toward Niall's body. "This man was shot by Rewan, henchman of Lewis. We seek sanctuary."

"Granted." A woman's voice came from the wall-walk above.

Ian's gut twisted in a million knots. He'd recognize that voice anywhere.

Janet.

Iron chains clanked and the portcullis slammed down behind them.

The sentry waved other soldiers forward. "I'm Henry MacRae, the man-at-arms." He cast his gaze to Niall. "Take him to the chapel."

Janet descended the stairs. Ian locked eyes with her, his heart shredding into a million pieces. "Thank you, m'lady." He glanced to the weeping woman who'd now become his charge. "Come, Merrin."

Ian followed the sentries to the chapel and rested Niall's body atop a long table. Merrin fell to her knees. "Please, God, do no' take him away. There is no one else who'll take me in."

Ian rested his hand on Merrin's shoulder and squeezed. "I must avenge him."

She snapped up and grasped his shoulders. "No more bloodshed."

Ian ground his teeth and looked to Niall. "Ye must pay your respects. I'll fetch the priest."

He couldn't utter the words, but Rewan would never give up until one of them was dead, and by God, Ian would finish it this night.

He couldn't tell Merrin she'd be safe, he couldn't tell her of the pledge he'd made to her dying father—not until the battle with Rewan was over. He hated to leave her like this, but it was the only way. He clamped his lips and left.

Janet waited outside the chapel, wringing her hands. "What are ye doing here?"

Ian choked back his gasp. "Moreover, what are *ye* doing here?"

"Me father thought I'd be safer tucked away at Eilean Donan. Rewan cannot discover my presence."

Merrin's cries resounded through the door. Ian's shoulders dropped. It should be him laid out on the table. Niall was innocent. "I've got to make this right, else Rewan will be chasing us forever."

Janet's lithe fingers caressed his cheek. "What can I do?"

Ian shuddered. Her touch soothed his troubled soul, but Ian raised his chin. He could not succumb to those deft fingers, not again. "Merrin needs a bath and clothing. 'Tis a long story, but know she's a good and honest woman. She and her father plucked me from the sea with a musket ball in me back and healed me."

Janet's gaze shifted to the chapel doors. "I shall see to her comfort."

"Thank ye." Ian started off then turned. "Bring the priest to her. If I do no' return, see to it that Merrin is cared for. The last thing her father heard on this earth was me vow to protect her."

"If you vowed it, I will make good your promise."

Janet would be true to her word. She owed him at least that.

Once in the courtyard, Ian turned full circle. The castle grounds were smaller than both Brochel and Stornoway, but it didn't take him long to spot the armory. Similar to most keeps, weapons were kept near the gate. He tested the latch. Unlocked, the door creaked as he slipped inside. Running his fingers along the wall, he found a quiver full of arrows. After slinging it over his shoulder, he pushed outside. His memory kicked into gear and he headed up the stairs to the west tower.

Up and down stairs, it was as if he had to maneuver through a maze to reach the rear gate. Ian drew his dirk and sidled up to the guard. "I aim to return this night. See to it the gateway opens without me having to make a racket."

"Aye, m'lord."

Ian didn't correct him. He was no man's lord, but perhaps it was better for this man to think him nobility—for now. At least the gate might remain tended.

Chapter Twenty-one

S till wrapped in the musty robe with the piece of linen tied around her neck, Merrin could no longer feel her knees driving into the chapel's stone floor. Her whole body had gone completely numb. Her father's lifeless body stretched across the table with his lifeblood pooling on the floor beneath. A priest had come and gone, making the sign of the cross and uttering imperceptible Latin prayers. He had left her with nothing but emptiness.

How could she go on? This couldn't be happening. When her home burned, she thought she'd lost everything, but now she truly had. Merrin's tears bled down her face as she rocked her quaking body.

A woman placed a hand on Merrin's shoulder. "Come. Ye need to tend to yourself."

Merrin's breath stuttered, her eyes raw. "I cannot leave him."

"He would want ye to rest." She tugged Merrin's hand and helped her stand. "I've ordered a bath drawn for ye and a change of clothes. Ian asked me to see to your comfort."

Merrin looked at the woman for the first time. Dressed in a gown of finely spun cloth, she was young, small boned and lovely with blonde hair—she looked like a queen. "Where is Ian?"

The woman shifted her gaze sideways. "He's stepped out for a bit."

"No." Merrin yanked her hand away. "Do no' tell me he's gone to face Rewan."

The woman's stricken eyes gave her secret away.

Merrin clutched her arms around her stomach. This could not be happening. "I told him no' to go." She doubled over. "I cannot lose him too."

A fresh bout of tears poured from her eyes. Merrin howled like a wounded dog, but she didn't care who heard. A sentry picked her up and cradled her against his chest. Merrin pounded her fist against his rigid chainmail. "No." She hit him again. "No, no, no."

But the man marched forward. "Easy, lass. We'll set ye to rights."

Merrin didn't want to be set to rights. He marched on and the door to the chapel slammed closed behind them. Through bleary eyes, it registered he was taking her above stairs. Unable to continue to struggle, Merrin covered her face with her hands and wept.

He pushed into a chamber and set her down in the center of the room. Merrin took her weight and swayed.

He grasped her shoulder firmly. "Will ye be all right, miss?"

Merrin nodded.

"Leave us," the woman said.

"Aye, Lady Janet."

Merrin's back stiffened. "Ye're Ian's Janet?" It came out like an icy whisper.

Janet beckoned two maids with a wave of her hand. "Ian cast aside everything he held dear to help me escape from a tyrant—and now I'm repaying the debt by helping ye."

Before Merrin could blink, the friar's robe fell from her shoulders. She crossed her arms over her breasts. "I do no' need your charity."

Lady Janet's gaze slipped down to Merrin's boots and back up. "From the tattered state of your shift, I disagree." She pointed to a large wooden basin. "Bathe and dress her. I'll send up food and a tonic."

Merrin jerked her arm away from the maid's grasp. "What tonic?"

"Something to make ye sleep."

"I do no' need sleep."

Janet offered a faint smile and slipped out the door.

Merrin faced the maids. Her stays dropped to the floor, followed by her shift. A maid lifted her arms to untie the bit of cloth around Merrin's neck. Her hands flew up and covered it. "This stays."

Ian found a skiff and silently rowed through the shadows behind the line of moored vessels. A watchman stood at the helm of Rewan's galley, panning his spyglass across the scene.

"Anything?" Rewan's disembodied voice asked.

"Nay. Looks like the yellow-livered bastard's hiding with the MacKenzies for the night."

"Unfurl the sail. I do no' want to come under their cannon fire come dawn. We'll moor behind the shelter of a cove and sleep."

"How do ye expect to ferret him out of Eilean Donan?"

"Patience," Rewan growled.

Ian steered his boat behind a pinnace and moored only feet from the galley. He pulled himself up the ship's rigging, hand over hand. Crouching on the deck, he scanned for signs of life. No one.

Ian tiptoed across to the starboard rail, keeping his head below it. The small ships were moored so closely, he could practically reach out and touch the enemy galley.

He reached back, pulled four arrows from his quiver and leaned them against the hull. He prayed he'd have time to fire them all. Peering over the rail, he eyed his first target—one of the two men unfurling the single-masted sail.

Ian's stomach turned as he loaded his bow. He didn't care for killing, but Rewan had left him with no other choice. He silently slid his weapon over the rail. With a clear shot, he pulled the string taut. Ian only had one chance. He must hit his mark every time. Holding his breath, he released.

The arrow hissed through the air. In a blink of the eye, the man grunted and clutched his chest. Without a cry, he fell forward.

"Man down!"

Before the second sailor could hop from his perch, Ian fired an arrow into his heart. Another dashed across the deck. Ian snatched a third and loaded his bow. He timed it with the man's pace and released. With a gurgling cry, the man dropped.

Silence. Waves slapped the hull, but tension hung thick in the air. Rewan and at least one other kept quiet, awaiting their chance to strike. Ian wasn't about to give them an opportunity to counter his attack.

He yanked his sword from his back and took a running leap over the hull. Ian sailed through the air, the water of Loch Duich passing beneath his feet. With a jarring thud, Ian landed on a bench of Rewan's galley and stumbled sideways. Scrambling to scoot his feet beneath him, Ian swung his claymore in a circle.

Two men faced him. Ian's calculations were right—only two remained—Rewan and Alick. Rewan chuckled, sword drawn, sauntering close. "Ye've finally seen fit to face me like a man."

Ian backed against the rail, his eyes shifting between both. Rewan swung down. Ian deflected and spun. He snatched his dirk. Alick raised his sword, laughing. But Ian stopped him with a thrust of his dirk, straight to the gut. Ian yanked and twisted it up to finish the kill.

Stunned to lifelessness, Alick dropped between the two vehement enemies.

Rewan leveled his sword, circling. "Ye killed all me men."

Ian watched for a twitch—any sign to signify a strike. "Why can ye no' leave me alone?"

"Ruairi needs proof of your death. I cannot return to Lewis without it."

"We were friends. Does that no' count for anything?"

"I've pledged me life to Ruairi. Have ye forgotten ye did too?"

"Fealty, aye. But I did not sign on to stand by and watch an innocent lass suffer at his hand."

"It is no' our place to question our laird."

Ian circled with deadly intent. "As knights, "tis our place to protect women and children."

Rewan's eye twitched. He lunged in, brandishing his sword like a madman. Ian's muscles jarred, deflecting the larger man's brute force. Rewan advanced relentlessly, hacking his blade with downward thrusts. Ian backed against the rail. His heart raced, his arms burned. Rewan slashed harder. Ian rolled to the side. Rewan's blade sank into the ship's rail.

With a bellow, Rewan heaved up to release his claymore, but the sword stuck. Ian stepped in and pressed his dirk against Rewan's throat and twisted until it drew blood.

Rewan held up his hands. "Wait."

Ian pulled the big man's dirk and hurled it over the side. "Ye need proof of me death?"

Rewan swallowed, his Adam's apple sliding against the blade. "Aye." His voice quavered, nowhere near as self-assured as it had been moments ago.

Ian held his dirk still. "I do no' want to kill ye."

"Please. I'll do anything ye ask."

"Vow it."

"I swear on me father's name and to the Almighty God."

Ian's gaze met the man's black-eyed stare. He'd never known the henchman to go back on his word—though now he no longer could be sure. "I'll spare ye if ye take me dirk back to Ruairi, but I need your pledge to never come after me again."

"I cannot—"

Ian dug the blade into Rewan's flesh until blood streamed down his neck. "Ye will or die this night."

Rewan blinked. "I swear it."

Keeping his blade trained on the henchman's neck, Ian backed toward the rail. "I'll hold ye to it. For ye will no' live should ye ever cross me path again." He yanked away his dirk from Rewan's neck and tossed it astern. "Leave now. If I do no' see the backside of your boat by the time I reach the castle, I'll order the guard to blast ye with cannons afore the sun rises."

Chapter Twenty-two

I an trudged through the castle gate. He couldn't face Merrin. Not yet. He'd killed before, but that didn't lessen the bile burning in his gut. He probably should have finished Rewan, but couldn't do it. He abhorred the unsavory task of killing a man with whom he'd shared a table, a man he once fought beside. He only prayed he knew Rewan well enough to believe the henchman would own up to his word.

Ian stopped at the chapel door and slipped inside. A lone candle burned on the candelabra beside Niall's body. They'd covered him with linen cloth. All color had drained from his face and it looked like sallow cream, but peaceful.

Ian walked to the table and knelt. "I failed ye." He reached out, but held his trembling hand in midair. Unworthy to touch the healer who'd taken him in, Ian clenched his fist and pulled it into his chest. "I'm so...agonizingly sorry."

He half expected Niall to pat his head and utter a comforting word, but he lay motionless, his life drained before his time—dead because of Ian's actions. He'd let Niall down, and now Merrin was without her father—an orphan.

Ian looked to the cross above the altar, tears streaming down his cheeks. "Forgive me." He rested his head against the table and tried to regain control, but his shoulders shook. He should have sent Niall and Merrin back to Brochel with Friar Pat. Blast her mark. Once anyone got to know her, they'd realize she couldn't possibly be a daughter of the devil.

And if they hadn't gone with the friar, Ian should have faced Rewan and let him do what he must. Niall should not have been the one to lose his life.

Gradually, Ian's breathing returned to normal.

A small hand rested on his shoulder. "Ye've returned to us."

Though he couldn't deny fond feelings for Janet MacKenzie, she wasn't the woman he wanted to see. "Rewan will bother us no more, m'lady." He stood, bowed and kissed her hand. "Thank ye for your hospitality."

A sad smile turned up the corners of Janet's lips. "'Tis the least I can do."

"And how are ye?"

"I've been better." She glanced toward the door as if she feared being overheard. Grasping Ian's hands, she stepped closer. "Once Ruairi sent word of divorce, Father arranged for me to wed into the MacNeil Clan."

Ian swiped his hand across his face. He didn't want to have this conversation now. "So soon?"

Janet ran her hands over her belly. "I'm with child."

Ian tugged at a knot in his shoulder. "Ye are?."

"Me da believes 'tis Ruairi's babe."

Ian gasped. He'd made love to Janet once—right before he agreed to spirit her away. He'd been her guard. Often she would invite him in to play chess or just talk. The poor lass had been so lonely, locked in the tower, and then the inevitable happened. "Is it...mine?"

"A babe that makes me heart swell with joy as this one does could only be yours, Ian."

He should have been happy. He'd fathered a child. But he owed his life to Merrin. He *loved* Merrin.

Ian blinked. Merrin's lovely face filled his mind—but he had to make this right. He forced his eyes open and meet Janet's gaze. "I cannot allow ye to marry the MacNeil when ye carry me child."

Janet shook her head. "The agreement is signed. Robert MacNeil kens I'm with child and will raise it as his own."

Ian paced in a circle. "How could ye do this? Ye must have known I'd want to raise me own flesh and blood."

Janet pattered to him. "But I cannot marry ye. I'm the first daughter of a chieftain. Me dowry is worth more than your brother's entire island of Raasay. Ye ken. We've talked about it."

"Aye, but that was afore I realized ye carried my bairn."

She wrapped him in an embrace and rested her head upon his chest. He felt...nothing but remorse. She held him tighter. "Ye will always have a place in me heart, but I will do as me da commands. And one day, I'll tell the babe of the brave warrior who spirited me away from a tyrant laird—and his heart will discover who his true father is."

Ian forced himself to cradle Janet's back. How could she do this to him? And all because he was a second son? Only good enough to fight for a lady—never good enough to marry one?

Janet held him at arm's length. "There's a lass above stairs who's wrought with despair."

Ian clamped his jaw and ground his teeth. "I must see to Merrin. I promised her da I would take her into me care."

Janet led him to the chapel door and told him how to find Merrin's chamber. His heart dropped to his toes as he climbed the stairs. Janet never had any intention of marrying him. She'd used him to spirit away from a miserable life and too many men had died because of it. Would he have done the same again? He most certainly would not have stood idle while Ruairi's abuse continued.

He waited outside Merrin's chamber with his hand on the latch. The news he'd fathered a child, together with the day's events, weighed heavily on his mind. He thought to head to the stables and make a bed of straw in the loft. But he couldn't leave Merrin alone, fretting about his return—he must face her. Ian opened the door.

Gar growled from across the room.

He stepped inside. "'Tis only me."

The dog bounded up to Ian and rubbed against him. Ian ran his fingers over Gar's wiry coat. "Merrin?" he whispered. "Are ye awake?"

The coals in the hearth cast enough light for him to see Merrin's form curled under the bedclothes. The poor lass desperately needed sleep. Ian started back for the door when the tub caught his eye. Aside from swimming in frigid water, he hadn't had a bath since the day Merrin had sponged him in his half-conscious state. How long ago that seemed now.

Ian stripped and sank into the tepid water, his knees against his chest. He found a cake of soap at the bottom of the barrel and held it to his nose. *Primrose*. Merrin's smell. He used the cloth to scrub every inch, to scrub away the death and violence.

Merrin stirred.

He cast his gaze to the bed. Her eyes remained closed, the duvet rising and falling with her breath.

Ian toweled off and wrapped the drying cloth around his waist. He lit a candle with the embers of the fire and set it in the iron holder beside the bed. The light flickered across Merrin's face. In slumber, she was as beautiful as a white rose.

Ian bent down and kissed her forehead.

She moved ever so slightly. "Ian?"

"Aye, my love. 'Tis me."

"Ye're...back." Her words slurred.

He shifted his hips onto the mattress. He moaned—the softness of feather down calling to his stiff limbs. "Rewan will never bother us again."

Merrin's eyes widened. "Ye killed him?"

Ian laced her fingers through his and pressed her hand to his lips. "I spared him on the promise he'd take me dirk back to Stornoway as proof of me death."

"Ye lost the beautiful dirk your da gave ye?"

"Aye, 'twas more than worth the price of peace."

Merrin tried to sit, but dropped back to the pillow. "Do ye think he'll do it—tell Ruairi Ye're dead?"

"Aye. Rewan was me friend for years. He'll honor his word. Of that I'm certain." He prayed it would be so, but didn't want to think about that right now. Ian ran his hand across Merrin's forehead. "Ye look flushed."

"They gave me a tonic of potent chamomile. It made me ever so sleepy."

Ian pulled her head into his lap and stroked her long tresses.

"I suppose ye'll be leaving me now." Her voice was strained. A tear pooled on Ian's arm.

His hand stopped. "What?"

"You've found Janet—and I saw the way she looked at ye." Merrin bit her bottom lip.

"True, Lady Janet is here, but only for a time while she awaits her new husband."

Merrin struggled to sit. "Are ye planning to marry her so soon?"

"Nay, lass. Her da's betrothed her and her dower lands to Robert MacNeil, Chieftain of Barra."

She blinked, gazing at him with those intoxicating, almond-shaped blueberry eyes. "Ye're not leaving me?"

He cupped both her cheeks between his palms. "I will never leave ye, Merrin. I love ye."

She tried to speak, but Ian covered her mouth and showed her how deeply his love ran. He would not be there for the birth of his first child, but he would stay beside Merrin, and by the grace of God, when they found a home, she would bless him with many bairns. In the days to come, he would share his plans and listen to hers. But presently, they needed to mourn. "Ye must rest. Ye've been through a terrible ordeal."

Merrin nodded. "I dunna ken how to feel. I'm happy ye're here, but me heart aches for Da."

"I ken, *mo Bana*." Ian stood. "I should let ye sleep."

Merrin tugged on his hand. "Stay." She scooted over and patted the bed. "'Tis large enough for us both, and I'd feel so much safer with ye here."

He knew he shouldn't, but by her side was the only place he wanted to be. Ian dropped the cloth from around his waist and slid beside her.

Merrin's breath caught when Ian released the cloth. Yes, she'd seen him naked in the cottage, but she'd never seen him standing before her with his face stricken by tragedy and eyes filled with desire.

His manhood lengthened. Full, masculine, but not yet erect as it had been in the forest. Desire flooded her body. A tickle of guilt needled at the back of her mind. Merrin could no sooner stop her physical reactions as she could dampen her sorrow.

Ian smoothed his hand over her new linen shift. "This is much heavier than the other."

"'Tis new. The other was but in tatters."

"It smells like spring rain." He nuzzled into her neck.

She curled into him. "Everything is so grand. I've never slept on anything as nice as this bed, and the chamber? Why, I believe 'tis as large as the entire cottage on Fladda." A gasp caught at the back of her throat. "But...that's gone too."

"Do no' think on it tonight," Ian purred. "Right now, in this moment, all that exists is you and me and this wonderfully soft bed."

Merrin's body radiated with heat as Ian ran his lips along her neck. "Ian?"

"Aye?"

"I want ye to show me how a man breeds with a woman."

A low chuckle rumbled from his throat. "Only ye would find the words to attack me most basal desires."

She brushed the hair from his face. "I want ye to."

"Make love to you?"

"Is that what they call it...making love?"

"Aye, lass."

She met his gaze. "I may live in solitude for the rest of me days, but I will nay forget how ye make me feel. When ye lay your hands on me, me whole body comes alive, and yearns for more."

"'Tis the same for me."

"Truly?"

"Ye are so fine to me, Merrin. Do ye not know what ye do to me?"

She smiled, not quite sure how to respond.

"I shouldn't be naked and lying in bed beside you, but there's no place I would rather be." He took her hand and led it under the bedclothes. He showed her how to wrap her fingers around his manhood. Merrin gasped. It was hard as a bedpost.

"Ye stroke it like this." He led her hand along his shaft in a gentle, rhythmic motion. His breathing sped. "But not too much or ye'll make me come too fast."

She pushed the bedclothes aside to better see him. "Come?" Her thighs quavered, right at the spot where he'd touched her in the meadow. The place where he'd caressed her flesh and she'd come undone in his arms.

"Spill me seed."

"Ah, and make a bairn."

Ian frowned and pressed his hand to his eyes.

"Have I said something wrong?"

"Nay." He pulled her atop him and closed his mouth over hers. His kisses were more forceful than ever before. 'Twas as if he could hold back no longer.

Merrin straddled Ian's hips. The column of his manhood pressed against her sacred spot. That same hot desire screamed for friction and she rocked her hips as if they were controlled by a force outside her body. Up and down she slid against him, her own moisture spilling over him.

Ian grasped Merrin's waist and held her firm. "I cannot take your innocence. Not when I have nothing to give ye."

Merrin arched her back and met his gaze. "We have nothing but our bodies and our lives." She smoothed her hand over his rugged cheek. "That's what I want to give."

He untied the cloth that hid her scar. "Do ye ken what Ye're saying?" The slip of linen fell to the floor.

"Do ye no' want me?"

With a chuckle, Ian rolled her onto her back. Pressing the length of his body into her side, he kissed her again. "Can ye no' tell I want ye more than life?"

"Then take me." Merrin reached between them and found his manhood. "Show me what 'tis like to be a real woman."

"Ye are a real woman and more," Ian growled as he tugged her shift up and over her head.

He cast it aside and pushed her legs open with his knees. "I do no' want to hurt ye."

"Nothing ye can do would hurt."

"It might at first." He placed his hand on her belly and smoothed it down to her mons. He slipped his thumb across her womanhood and teased her with quick flicks over her soft folds. With a quick inhale, Merrin bucked against his hand. He went further and slid a finger inside her core. "Ye're so wet for me."

Merrin ground her hips around him. "Is that good?"

"Aye, it excites me to the brink of madness."

She uttered a throaty growl and reached down, covering him with her fingers. She stroked as he'd shown her.

Ian grunted and threw his head back with a stirring moan. He then dipped his chin and tapped his tongue to her breast. He suckled and massaged both her breasts. Merrin moved restlessly beneath him, as if her nipples were attached to her sacred place. She wanted him everywhere. Ached for him.

Merrin pulled his manhood toward her, craving it.

Ian gently tugged against her grasp. "I cannot hold back any longer."

"I do no' want ye to."

"But a woman's pleasure should come first."

"Can we not come together?" The words seemed erotic, strange on her tongue, but enticing. She wrapped her fingers around him again and guided his manhood to the very place where his hand had been. He clenched his eyes shut. Merrin sucked in a quick gasp. "Are ye hurt?"

"I wanted to wait, but me flesh is too weak." The rounded tip of his manhood stretched her entrance—so much larger than his finger. Ian's breathing came faster. Merrin watched his beautiful lips part with desire. Merrin sunk her fingers into his buttocks and pulled. He slipped further inside and held himself still.

A sharp pinch caught her breath. "Ian."

His muscles tightened. "Am I hurting ye?"

"Nay." Hurting? Aside from a little discomfort at first, she'd never felt anything so wonderful in her life. She could utter not another word. Noises she'd never heard before emitted from her throat. All she could do was tug him deeper, needing more of him, forcing him to an unknown destination. On his elbows, Ian held himself above her, tense, trembling as he allowed her to pull him until he filled her completely.

With a stuttered breath, he looked into her eyes. Merrin had never seen a more beautiful sight as Ian's face, sky-blue eyes intense, mouth parted. She rocked her hips around him. He eased his lips over hers. Gently, he pulled back, then thrust deep.

Merrin cried out. She'd never before felt anything so staggeringly pleasing.

He held tight again and hovered over her. "Are—"

"Do no' stop!" She strengthened her grasp on his buttocks and showed him what she wanted. The twinge of pain forgotten, she spread her legs wider and dictated the pace.

Ian's breathing sped. Merrin curved her hips into him. Her cries came faster until everything burst into thousands of brilliant stars. Her body convulsed over and over and over. Ian threw back his head and roared, shoving himself deep within her, pulsating along her inner walls.

His breath easing, he met her gaze again, his intensity replaced by tranquility. "I love ye, Merrin."

She wrapped her arms around Ian's back and kissed him. They had bonded, connected by the intimacy of love. Only this moment mattered. She would cherish this merging of souls for the rest of her life.

Chapter
Twenty-three

I an opened his eyes. The only thing that told him a new day had arrived was the faint beam of light shining through the space where the furs didn't quite cover the window. It had been a long time since he slept in a bed as grand and a chamber as large. He'd forgotten what it was like to be a son of privileged nobility. His uncle certainly hadn't paid a mind to his lineage during Ian's fostering.

Deep in slumber, Merrin nestled into him. After finally succumbing to the chamomile tonic, she most likely wouldn't wake until the midday meal. Ian hoped not. She would need all her strength to face the task of laying her father to rest.

Ian closed his eyes and inhaled. He would carry the cross of Niall's death for the rest of his life. How could Merrin even bear the sight of him? Would she grow to resent him, even now that she'd given him her innocence? He smoothed his hand over her hair and let his heavy eyelids close. He'd be there for her, protect her, always. No matter what.

But his mind refused ease. What was next? How could he provide for Merrin? With all that had happened, dare he approach Alexander and seek a place at his brother's table? Could he allay the suspicions about Merrin that pervaded Brochel Castle? Would Alexander stand beside him, or take the side of the superstitious?

Could he talk to Janet about providing a recommendation to the MacRae constable? Could they remain at Eilean Donan? Ian did wield a steadfast sword—few could best him. He'd make a fine henchman or man-at-arms for any clan. But with Ruairi spreading rumors about, he might be forced to settle for a position assisting a smithy, or worse.

Ian pulled Merrin closer and inhaled her scent. It calmed him—told him they would pull through. Somehow.

The door latch clicked. Ian held his breath and reached for the hilt of his sword. The door creaked and light flooded the chamber. He held perfectly still. A servant hadn't entered his chamber to light the fire since he was a boy. Memories flooded back. His loving mother, his older brother who challenged him at every turn. Calum, his imposing father, a man to respect and to revere.

Footsteps pattered inside.

Gar barked and leapt to his feet.

Before Ian could react, Merrin sat straight up with a shriek. "Gar!" She clutched the bedclothes to her chest. "Why are ye here, sneaking around and scaring me dog?"

"I..." The maid faced them. Horror darkened her eyes. Her hand flew over her mouth. "Blessed Jesus, spare me." She crossed herself and sprinted for the door.

Ian jumped out of bed and yanked the cloth off the floor. As the door slammed, the maid's muffled cries echoed through the corridor. "She bears the mark of the devil! Haste ye—call the guard..."

Ian turned to Merrin, her hands clutched around her throat. "I shouldna taken it off."

He snatched her shift from the floor and handed it to her. "Dress quickly."

Ian raced to his clothes, pulled on his shirt and belted his kilt. Merrin reached for a set of stays hanging over the chair.

He strapped his sword in place, the ache in his back becoming easier to ignore. "There's no time for those."

Merrin nodded and slipped into a kirtle. She fumbled with the laces.

"Come." Ian handed her the bow and arrows. "Can ye use these?"

"Aye."

"Good, cover me back."

He tugged her along by the elbow and cracked the door open. Below stairs, the deep bellows of the guard accompanied innumerous booted footsteps. Christ, the whole MacRae force was ascending the tower stairs.

"Wait." Merrin dashed across the room, picked up her neckerchief and hastily tied it around her neck. "What will we do?"

"I cannot fight them all." Ian drew his sword. "But I'll die trying. Stay back and train your arrow on the first man up the stairs. If ye must shoot, aim to kill."

"Heaven help us."

They crept forward. Merrin shushed Gar and made him heel behind her. The bloody dog had done enough.

The footsteps approached, clamoring up the winding stairs. Ian would rather meet them in the narrow stairwell where he'd only have to fight one or two at a time.

Something grabbed his arm. He sliced his sword around, aiming the point at…Lady Janet's neck.

She released him and inclined her head. "Come."

They ducked through a door hidden behind a landscape tapestry.

They followed Janet through a dank, poorly lit passage. Confused, Ian tried to find his bearings. Were they heading to the south wall?

Janet stopped at a case of stairs. "This leads to the water gate. Moored alongside it is a small galley—the one that ferried me here from me father's lands. Take it. I'll cause a distraction."

"Thank you." Merrin clasped Janet's hands. "Please. Promise me ye'll see me da has a Christian burial."

"I will."

Ian ran his thumb over Janet's tear-splashed cheek. "I'll no' forget this."

She nodded and pressed her hands to her belly. "Go. There's no time to waste."

Ian took one last gander at Janet's flat stomach—his future child, one he'd never meet. Regret was a bitter potion to swallow. Taking Merrin's hand, he ran.

Merrin raced behind Ian, barely able to think of anything but the wild shouts of men outside the walls. They were after her—because she was marked. Ian squeezed her hand and dragged her along the dim passageway. She had put him in enough danger already. But she wouldn't make it to the boat without him.

They came to a solid wooden door dotted with black iron nails. Ian pressed his ear to it and levered the latch. A gust of wind snagged the door and blew it wide. "Quickly." Ian grasped her hand so tightly, her fingers ached like they would break.

Just as Janet said, a galley moored in the water, tied to the tiny jetty behind the water gate. Ian lifted Merrin by the waist. Flying through the air, she clamped her lips shut against her urge to scream. Her feet hit the deck. Thank heavens, the arrows and bow stayed slung over her shoulder.

Gar scrambled to find his feet behind her, then Ian jumped over, rope in hand. "Can ye man the rudder?"

"The what?"

"'Tis that handle astern. Push all your weight into it on a course out to sea. I'll unfurl the sail."

Shouts filled the courtyard.

Merrin looked at the arm of the rudder sticking out from the hull. The oak shone smooth from use. Wind caught her hair and pulled it across her eyes, her kirtle fluttering and slapping between her legs. She shoved her hair away and leaned into the rudder. It hardly moved. She glanced over her shoulder. Ian already had the sail down. It flapped and cracked angrily, like a sheet hanging out to dry. Ian dove for the sail ropes and tied them to belaying pins.

Merrin levered her feet against the bench and forced the rudder to move.

"There they are," a guard yelled.

"Muskets, where are the muskets?" another voice bellowed.

Merrin held the rudder firm and peeked over the rail.

Waving her arms, Janet ran to the front of the mayhem. "Stop this. They're my guests."

The boat lurched forward. Merrin snapped around to ensure they were on course. The sail billowed, filled with the blowing wind.

She could no longer hear what was being said on the shore, but Janet shook her finger under a warrior's nose. That woman had grit, though Merrin was thankful she wasn't aboard. The way she looked at Ian had Merrin's insides twist in knots.

Ian tied off the ropes and climbed over to Merrin. "Ye're doing well."

"It isn't so hard now that we're at sea."

"I can take it from here." He took the rudder under his arm and gave her a good once-over. "What are ye wearing?"

"A blue kirtle, silly." She reached inside her bodice and pulled out the stays she'd stuffed down the front. "And a lass cannot leave behind a new set of stays."

He laughed. "Only a woman would worry about her figure in a time of crisis."

She clutched the garment to her chest. "And where to now? Is there any place I can go where they'll not see me as a monster?"

Ian cast his gaze north. "I reckon 'tis time we paid Fladda a visit. We'll set it to rights as a memorial to your da."

Chapter

Twenty-four

C louds rolled in with the howling wind. Without a cloak, Merrin clutched her arms around her ribcage and watched the islet of Fladda near. The sheep's white wool contrasted with the brilliant green. How she loved the colors of summer. If only Niall were there to enjoy it too. Her chin trembled as she choked back her urge to cry.

Ian sailed the boat onto the smooth-pebbled beach. With an excited bark, Gar bounded over the side. Merrin bit her bottom lip. "He's no' going to like what he finds."

Ian hopped over and assisted Merrin to disembark. "Nor shall *we*, I reckon."

Ian tied the galley and Merrin stared up the grassy hill, clutching her arms across her midriff. Trepidation crawled along her skin, intensifying the wind's chill. She didn't know how she'd react once they got to the cottage.

Ian put his arm around her shoulders. "Come. We shall face this together."

At the top of the hill, Merrin stopped and clapped her hand over her mouth. She knew it would be bad, but nothing could have steeled her nerves for the sight ahead. The thatched roof was gone. Black char fanned out from the windows and stained the stone walls. A hen squawked in the garden, her back feathers missing.

Ian pulled Merrin along. "It looks like the workshop wasn't touched."

She glanced to the old lean-to with Niall's drying herbs still hanging from the ceiling. She could almost see Niall bent over a mortar, crushing herbs with his pestle. A cry caught in her throat. "Da."

The bells hanging from the entrance jingled, *tink, tink.* Niall had been so proud of himself when he'd hung them. *"These'll keep away the fairy folk. I'll no' have them messing with me potions and turning them bad."*

He had rigged every charm known to man, but none of them saved him in the end.

Agonizing tears streamed down her face as Ian led her to the cottage threshold. The door had been reduced to cinders. Merrin stood and stared at the burnt-out remains of her home. This was the only place she'd ever been where she didn't have to live in fear—where no one cared about her mark, where her father taught her to sing and dance, and cook.

Her shoulders curled and she bent over, pressing her hands to her face. The pain welled inside and crippled her. "Heaven help me, how will I survive? I feel like I cannot go on."

Ian pulled her into his arms. "There, there, *mo Bana*. We'll make it right." He rubbed her back and rocked, back and forth.

Merrin had held it in for too long. Her knees buckled as she gave into her sobs, weeping from the bottom of her soul—a gut-wrenching wail. Her insides burned and cramped at the raw memory of Niall's life's blood draining from the horrid musket shot. She wanted to die. She didn't care about the cottage or the workshop or chickens without feathers. She prayed for God to send down a bolt of lightning to strike her dead. How could Ian stay with a woman marked by the devil? Must everyone she love die? Aye, Ian said he loved her, but she would only ruin his hopes to find his place.

She pushed away. Ian reached out, but she batted his hands down. "Leave me be." She ran with no purpose but her need to be alone—her need to come to grips with everything that had happened. As fast as she could, Merrin ran for the north side of the isle and fell to her knees. Gar bounded beside her and leaned in. She pushed him, but he refused to budge. "Oh, Father, Father, why did ye leave me? First Ma, now ye, but it always should have been me."

Ian watched Merrin flee. His first inclination was to run after her, but his feet didn't move. She'd pushed him away. Perhaps she needed time to come to terms with all that had happened. She hadn't much time to mourn her father's death.

Ian scratched the beard that had grown in since they left Fladda. She might be resenting him, as he thought she would.

Ian turned full circle. Perhaps he should leave her alone for a time. He needed to start cleaning up the mess so they could rebuild.

Tam, the old gelding, snorted behind him. Ian turned and ran his fingers along the old nag's nose. "She'll come round. Do no' worry."

Ian pulled the remains of the door away and walked inside. It was a bloody mess. Black soot charred the walls—most of the furniture was unrecognizable. He strode to the hearth. At least Merrin's iron pots and kettles were still in working order, though they'd have to be scrubbed clean.

Ian heaved a sigh. *May as well start.* He pulled Niall's old wooden barrow from the shed and hauled load after load to a burn pile out back. He looked around for scraps of wood, but found nothing of use for a rebuilding effort. A few spindly birch trees grew in a grove, but were not what he needed to reconstruct the roof. He gazed across the narrow *caol*. Unless they wanted to sleep in the lean-to, they'd have to go to Brochel.

The sun touched the western horizon and peeked between a gap in the heavy clouds when Merrin and Gar walked through the lea.

She held an open palm out to him. "I found some strawberries."

Ian snatched one with blackened fingers. "Looks delicious."

"Ye're covered with soot."

"Aye, cleaned out most of the mess. But if we're to rebuild, we need to go to Brochel and ask me brother for supplies."

Merrin touched her throat. "Ye best go on your own."

Ian clasped her hands to his sooty chest. "Nay. I promised I'd take ye." A splash of rain slapped his forehead. "Besides, I cannot allow ye to stay here alone."

She jerked back. "Ye cannot *allow* me? Since when did ye start making me decisions?"

"Since ye lost your da."

Her face fell and she swiped away a tear, but didn't argue.

"I've a chicken on the boil. We'll leave at dawn." Ian popped the strawberry in his mouth. The sweet made his stomach rumble.

Merrin grasped his wrists and surveyed him from head to toe. "Ye'll need to wash up first. We've plenty of ash to leach out some lye and I can make soap from lard."

He pointed to a clump of yellow flowers. "I'll bet those primroses will add a pleasant fragrance as well."

Merrin nodded and went to work. Ian watched her. Her movements slow, she said nothing. Had she realized he was to blame for everything? Had she begun to hate him?

Raindrops splattered his face. Ian pressed his hand on to her shoulder. "Come, we'll eat in the workshop."

She nodded and hefted the pan from the fire in the cottage hearth. "It only needs to set now."

Ian got her under the shelter before Merrin's gown soaked clean through. He portioned out the chicken on a breadboard—one Niall obviously used to chop herbs.

They stood alongside the bench to eat. "We'll gather oats and flour at Brochel as well."

Merrin took a bit of chicken and passed a morsel to Gar. "Will we sail?"

"Aye, that makes the most sense. We can put the supplies in the galley. The roof will need a fair bit of timber." He rubbed her kirtle between his fingers. "And ye need more than one gown."

She glanced away. "This is enough for me."

He took a step into her and reached out. He wanted to pull her into his arms. Would she push him away? Ian settled for smoothing his fingers through her hair.

She turned her head. "I'll fetch the kettle. I'm sure the soap has set by now."

"Let me help ye carry it."

She held up her hand. "Nay. I'll manage."

The rain had stopped. Droplets sprinkled down from the rafters, but the shed was dry. Ian found a tallow lamp on the workbench and lit it with the flint and knife. He turned full circle. The wood outside was too wet to build a fire with, but a pile of hay was stacked against one wall. He spread it evenly and made a pallet.

Merrin returned carrying a heavy pot, the water sloshing over the side. Ian jumped up and grasped it. "Och, 'tis too heavy for ye to carry."

She brushed off her hands. "I've done it afore. I'm no' helpless."

Ian placed the pot on the workbench. "I did no' say ye were."

She pointed to the stool. "Sit."

"Aye, m'lady." He complied.

She frowned, but then stepped into him and pulled his shirt lace. Ian's heart fluttered. He allowed her to take the lead, raising his arms when she tugged the shirt. Merrin stood between his legs and moistened her bottom lip. Her fingers brushed across his bare chest. Gooseflesh stood proud. Ian closed his eyes and moaned.

Merrin pulled a cake of soap from her pocket. "Scented with primrose, per your request."

Ian inhaled. The scent intoxicating—almost as powerful as her own. "Gratitude." He squeezed his fist so he wouldn't grab her by the waist and tug her into his arms.

She rested the soap on the workbench. "Before I can start, ye must be bare, because right now, I'm making the decisions for *you*."

Asserting her position as lady of the house, was she? Ian chuckled and reached for his belt.

Her hands stopped him. "I'll do it." He liked that even better.

Staring into his eyes, she unfastened his belt and let it slip to the ground. Her breathing labored. Ian sat motionless, his heart threatening to burst through his chest.

Merrin's gaze slowly inched down his body as if her stare was palpable. Ian shivered. He wanted her hands on him again. She drew in a deep breath and grasped his plaid. Her eyes met his again while her hands pulled the plaid open. He lifted up enough to let her tug it away. Her eyes dipped to his swollen member, only for a fleeting moment.

She turned her back, folded his clothing and placed it on the bench.

The cold breeze blew, chilling his skin. If only he could reach out and pull Merrin into his lap. But something told him he must wait. The anticipation drove him mad. He wanted her more now than ever before, more than anything he'd ever wanted in his life.

She picked up the soap and dipped it into the water. She took a long, ambling look at his naked body before she grasped his hand and ran it around his palm. "Do ye remember the last time I bathed ye?"

"Aye." His voice rasped. His heart stuttered, ever so grateful for her resumed touch. "I shall never forget."

She ran the cake up his arm. "It turned me insides into a raging fire."

Ian couldn't resist. He pulled her in his embrace and covered her mouth. Merrin returned his kiss, but slid her palms between them and pushed away from his chest. Parting from his mouth, she sighed. "Ye must wait until I've finished."

A droplet formed at the tip of his cock. She wanted him. Thank God and all the angels in heaven. Ian could think of nothing sweeter than to pleasure her. He closed his eyes and held out his arms and let Merrin work her magic while his cock stood rigid between them.

She washed every inch, avoiding the one place he wanted her to touch most of all. When she stepped away, he hoped she might be finished. She scrubbed her hands in the basin and turned, soap bubbling between her palms. Her hips swung suggestively when she stepped up to him again and clasped her fingers around his turgid cock.

She tilted her head back, her eyes shuttered, half cast and dark. Gently, she stroked him. Ian thrust his hips forward and willed himself not to come. Her fingers slipped to his ballocks and cleansed him with a swirling motion that took him to the edge of his self-control. He reached for her.

"No' yet." She pulled the cloth from around her neck and wet it. "I'll rinse ye now."

Ian trembled as she tortuously meandered through the whole process again. By the time she finished, he needed to jump into the cold sound to regain his mind.

She draped the cloth over the bench and faced him, licking her lips again.

He tugged open her kirtle laces. "Now ye."

She sucked in a sharp breath. "Ye do no' intend to bathe me?"

"Nay." He waggled his eyebrows. "But I'll strip ye bare."

Aroused to within a hand's breadth of his sanity, Ian couldn't take his time and savor peeling every strip of cloth from her body. He shoved the kirtle from her shoulders and pulled it down around her ankles. She held up her arms and he tugged the shift over her head. Thank God she hadn't gone and bound her breasts with those constricting stays.

He grasped her bare breasts between his hands and suckled. More than a mouthful, he buried his face between them and melted. He had never been so hard, so aroused or so ready to pleasure a woman—and pleasure her he would. Merrin would have no question of his love for her by the time he finished with her.

Still thinking she was in command, Merrin slid her hands around his waist and ran her hands up his chest. Ian growled. She pulled his mouth to hers. He parted Merrin's lips with his hungry tongue and devoured her, pressing his cock against her abdomen. She rubbed against him, side to side.

Unable to wait a moment longer, he cradled her naked body in his arms and carried her to the pallet. His fingers strayed to her womanhood and she moaned. Gently, he caressed her wet treasure until he rested her on the hay.

Kneeling between her legs, he smoothed his fingers over her sex. "Are ye sore?"

"Mayhap a little—'tis no' bad."

"I want to taste ye."

She gasped and rose up on her elbows. "Can ye do that?"

"Aye. But first I want to kiss ye again." He slid up to her face and kissed her, his tongue searching, his hand finding her breast. He flickered kisses down to her nipple and circled his tongue around her sensitive bud.

"Please."

He chuckled. "'Tis my turn to make ye squirm." He changed his attention to the twin, that pink, erect nipple. Merrin's back arched, her moans already increasing. On the edge of control, Ian forced himself to keep his head. He swirled his tongue around Merrin's belly button and continued down.

She closed her legs tight and he met her gaze. "Open."

Wide-eyed, she gasped and shook her head.

"Open," he demanded, shouldering her knees apart. God help him, she smelled of an entire field of wildflowers laced with woman. He slipped out his tongue and licked her. *Sweet mead of the gods.*

Merrin bucked. "Merciful Father."

He chuckled and tasted her again, kissing her with languid strokes of his tongue. She rocked against him. He thrust his tongue inside her.

"Higher."

"Ye like this better?" He licked her tiny nub.

"Aye." She swirled her hips. "It...feels so...good."

She moved hypnotically against him, her mewling cries filling Ian with desire. Ian relentlessly suckled her womanhood, watching Merrin come undone. With a gasp, her entire body went rigid, and then her thighs shuddered. Merrin tried to catch her breath as Ian ran his tongue up her body until it found her mouth.

He pushed between her legs and slid his cock across her womanhood in languid strokes until her moans showed him she was ready. He positioned himself at her entrance and slid inside until his head was covered. It took every ounce of willpower he could muster not to thrust all the way to her womb. Her body yielded to him so much more easily this time. But he still wanted to be careful. Exercising as much control as possible, he let her guide him with her hands on his buttocks and gradually filled her.

Ian arched his back. He wouldn't last long. Merrin drew up her knees and dug her fingers into his buttocks. "Come for me, Ian."

He moaned, leaking his seed. She moved in tempo with him, gazing into his eyes. A woman had never before looked as beautiful. Her locks glistened in the lamplight, her eyes focused only on him. He thrust harder. His cry caught in his throat. On the ragged edge, his seed burst, pulsing into her. Blinded by ecstasy, he thrust with each surge as Merrin arched against him and cried out, her silken flesh rippling around him.

Ian dropped to his elbows and nuzzled into her neck. He would never tire of the heavenly fragrance that defined her. "I shall love ye forever, Merrin."

"As I will you."

Chapter Twenty-five

M errin stood on the deck of the galley and stared up at the cliff-top fortress of Brochel Castle. Though Niall had described the enormity of the stronghold, it still shocked her to see it. The keep was even grander than Eilean Donan.

Ian stepped behind her, his body molding to Merrin's back. He wrapped his arms around her. "I've no' seen the keep since I was a lad."

"Is it as grand as ye remember?"

"Aye—nearly as big as Stornoway. If there's one thing the MacLeods are known for, 'tis the size of their keeps. As long as Ye're putting stone to mortar, ye may as well build the biggest fortress ye can afford."

Built atop the natural rock crag, the tower loomed over the beach. Merrin craned her neck to see the top—so high, it nearly touched the clouds. Ian pointed. "Ye see the window, second down from the top?"

"Aye."

"'Twas me chamber. I spent many an afternoon gazing across the sound, waiting for me da to come home."

"Ye were no' afraid to be up so high?"

"Nay." He batted the air. "I was born to it." He pointed to an enormous ship moored in the bay. "Ye see the galleon there?"

"Aye."

"I won many a race climbing its rigging." He pointed to the castle curtain. "I used to chase me brother around the wall-walk with no fear."

Merrin nestled into his chest. "I think I'd be afraid to be up so high."

The bailey walls surrounded the fortress, notched by crenels for archers and cannons. The beach was covered with smooth stones like the beaches on Skye. Ian sailed the boat at a slow tack into the cove until the galley's hull stopped with a resounding scrape.

Ian took her hand. "Welcome to Brochel, m'lady."

Merrin hesitated. "Do ye think I should wait here whilst ye go find your brother?"

"I want ye with me." Ian straightened the cloth around her neck. "Ye look fine."

She giggled. "Do ye think they'll have a gathering tonight?"

"Of course." He hopped over the side and reached for her. "If Alexander does no' order a feast, me ma will see to it."

Ian carried Merrin to the edge of the beach and set her down. He pointed straight up to a thatched roof building outside the bailey walls. "That's Sir Bran's cottage—he's Alexander's henchman."

"'Tis big compared to me home on Fladda."

Ian pulled her hand. "'Tis about the size of the laird's chamber in the castle. Come, I want ye to meet me mother."

People poured out the gate, filing down the zigzag path. Women, warriors, children. Merrin had never seen anything like it. "So many."

Friar Pat stood at the top of the hill and waved. Merrin's heart skipped a beat—a familiar face. She flapped both hands. "'Tis the friar!"

Ian released her hand and broke into a run, straight into the outstretched arms of a large redheaded man. "Brother. Och, 'tis good to see ye."

Alexander. The chieftain, laird of this land. Merrin clutched her hand to her throat. Perspiration stung her underarms.

Alexander shook Ian's shoulders. "I feared I'd never see ye again."

"Did ye doubt me?"

"No' you. But Rewan outnumbered ye by far—we must talk."

Ian waved, beckoning to Merrin. "But first I want ye to meet the woman who rescued me from the brink of death."

Alexander's eyes widened when he looked her way. "A warrior woman?"

Heat crawled up her face. "Nay, a healer."

"Ah. Welcome to Raasay." He bowed and kissed her hand. "Any friend to my brother is a friend of mine."

Merrin bit her lip. Would the laird be as cordial once he discovered her true identity?

Alexander shepherded them up the hill. The crowd closed in on them, everyone asking a barrage of questions. Merrin's head spun. She clutched Ian's hand as he pulled her alongside him. He pressed his lips to her ear. "I've got ye. Relax."

Easy for him to say.

They neared the top of the hill, where stood a beautiful woman, dressed in the finest cloth Merrin had ever seen, her head covered with a veil of golden silk. She stepped forward so gracefully, Merrin could have sworn she was floating. "Son. I am ever so happy to see you." Her English accent took Merrin off guard. And though Niall had told her Lady Anne was the daughter of an English earl, Merrin hadn't expected her to look like a queen.

Ian took the fragile lady's hands and kissed her cheek. "Mother, Ye're as beautiful as ever." He pulled Merrin to his side. "I'd like ye to meet Merrin. Without her, I'd no' be standing here today."

Merrin curtsied deeply and bowed her head. Her heart fluttered. She'd always dreamt of curtsying before nobility. "M'lady."

Lady Anne clasped Merrin's shoulders and smiled. "My, you are lovely." She fingered a strand of Merrin's hair. "I have the perfect veil to match your gown. You must come above stairs with me."

Her warm smile made Merrin feel as if she'd known Lady Anne all her life.

Friar Pat stepped in and wrapped his arm around Merrin's shoulders and gave Lady Anne a wink. "I see ye've already grown a fondness for this bonny lassie."

Anne turned to another beautiful woman behind her. "What say you, Lady Enya? Shall we take Miss Merrin above stairs?"

"Aye." Enya stepped forward with a huge grin. "A blue veil will make her eyes shine like precious stones."

Merrin shot a panicked look toward Ian. "I do no' think—"

Ian touched her shoulder. "Go with me mother. She cannot resist an opportunity to primp. I'll be along after I meet with Alex."

Merrin nodded and looked at Pat. "Do ye want to come with us, friar?"

He sputtered. "Me? In a lady's chamber? I think not." He leaned in and lowered his voice. "But I'll be in the garden should ye need me."

Lady Anne clapped her hands. "'Tis settled, then. Come with me, Miss Merrin. I do think we shall have a grand gathering tonight. It is not often my youngest graces me with his presence. We must celebrate."

Ian followed his brother to the laird's solar. Alexander had grown serious since Ian last saw him. He'd hardened, his face weathered. He wore his red beard long, ending in a point. Alex closed the door and moved to the sideboard.

Ian watched him pour two tots of whisky. "I hear ye have a son."

"Aye, Malcolm. He's nearly a year old."

"A fine lad, I have no doubt."

Coughing, Alexander handed Ian a cup. "He has the MacLeod coloring."

Ian sipped. "And how is Ilysa?"

"Bossy. It appears birthing the laird's son gives a woman unmitigated confidence." He gestured to a chair. "Now sit. We've much to discuss."

Ian complied and looked straight into his brother's hawk-like stare.

"Ye crossed Ruairi," Alexander blurted with a frown.

Nothing like moving straight to the point. Ian kept his back straight. "He beat her."

Alexander eased into his red upholstered chair. "But it was no' your place to interfere."

Ian swirled the amber liquid in his glass. It was important to choose his words carefully, though he wanted to slam his fist on the table and roar. "As a man of honor, I had nay choice but to protect a mistreated woman. She's with her kin now."

"I wanted to blast Rewan and his galley out of the water with me cannons, but it would have meant ruination for the clan. I feared Rewan would kill ye for certain."

Ian sipped, savoring the fine spirit. "He nearly did."

"What happened?"

Ian relayed the story of Rewan's relentless pursuit. "...I had him under the knife and made him promise to leave me be. He took me dirk back to our uncle as proof of me death."

"Ye mean to say ye let him live?"

"And why no'? Before this mess with Janet, Rewan was me friend." Ian drained his whisky. "Besides, Ruairi's found another woman. She'll keep his mind off trivial matters such as me whereabouts."

"If ye stay here, he'll eventually find out Ye're alive—and ye'll put the whole clan at risk from Ruairi's cannons."

"I'm no' planning to stay. I came to ask for supplies so I can take Merrin and rebuild her cottage on Fladda."

Alexander leaned forward, one hand braced on his armrest. "Ye mean to say Merrin is the witch from Fladda? Niall's cursed bairn?"

Ian held up his hands. "Merrin is no' the devil's spawn. She's—"

Alex shoved his chair back and paced, coughing with every other step. "I cannot believe ye would bring her here. The elders still tell tales about her mother's death—all because the bairn was marked."

Ian stared at his hands. He hated superstition in a man, but he loathed seeing it in his brother. "I need some wood to rebuild the cottage. We need grain and food stores. We've nary a piece of furniture. Everything was burned. Merrin can weave, but her loom was lost. Anything ye can spare, I'd be obliged and we'll be on our way."

Alexander grasped the flagon from the sideboard. "Her da came to Brochel for supplies—had something going with a widow. He'd trade tinctures and herbs. But he never brought *her* with him."

Ian held up his cup and Alex filled it. "I'm no' asking for much. And ye ken ye have me sword. I faced down Rewan and all his men. I can bear your arms. On that ye have me pledge of fealty."

Alexander sipped and moved to the window. "Ye can use your old chamber this night. On the morrow, I'll see what supplies we can spare." He coughed.

Ian stood and bowed. "Thank ye, brother."

"Laird." Alexander pulled a kerchief from his sleeve and launched into a coughing fit. "Blast this cough. It grows worse by the day."

Ian poured him another tot of whisky. "I could ask Merrin to make ye a tonic."

His brother snatched the cup and threw the brew down. "Nay," he barked. "The only person who'll tend me is Friar Pat." He slammed the cup on the table. "I'll see ye in the hall for supper."

Merrin sat, mesmerized, in an incredibly comfortable armchair while Lady Anne and Lady Enya flitted around an upstairs solar Anne called her craft room. The dowager lady threw open the lid of one of the many trunks that lined the wall and pulled out a brilliant blue gown.

Lady Enya grasped the skirts and held them up to the light. "This is perfect."

Anne tossed the gown on the table, which sat in the center of the room, then dug in the trunk, silks and woolens flying everywhere. "There's a matching coronet and veil in here somewhere."

"But I cannot wear your things," Merrin said. "It wouldn't be right."

Anne chuckled. "I could wear these dresses before my sons were born." She shook her finger. "And I blame Ian for thickening my waistline the most."

Enya found a lovely silk scarf. "This will perfectly match your kirtle."

Merrin puzzled. The younger woman sounded different, not as formal as Lady Anne. "Where do ye hail from, Lady Enya?"

She smiled. "I'm the daughter of Lord Ross of Renfrewshire."

Merrin fanned herself. "My, 'tis a bit overwhelming to be amongst such nobility."

Anne grasped the scarf from Enya's fingers. "Hogwash. You are our guest, and welcome." She pulled a wooden stool in front of Merrin and sat. "Let me remove that rag from around your neck."

Merrin clutched her neck and recoiled into the cushions. Her hands trembled like a sapling in the wind. "Nay, I cannot take it off."

Anne lowered her hands and cleared her throat. A most serene expression crossed her face. "Merrin. You have the look of your mother."

Gooseflesh spread across her skin. "Ye knew her?"

"Yes. And 'tis the reason why I sent the servants away. Tonight only Lady Enya and I will attend you."

Enya sat on a stool by the table and leaned her chin into her hand, as if she was settling in to listen to a good yarn.

Anne glanced back at Lord Ross's daughter. "What I'm about to say shan't be repeated by anyone. Agreed?"

Enya offered an eager nod. Merrin lowered her hands to her lap and folded them.

"You were a beautiful babe, born with a full head of dark curls. My dear friend Mara and I attended your mother through the long and difficult birth. When she died of childbed fever, a few superstitious members of the clan shouted for you to be burned on account of the little pink mark you had on your neck."

Merrin slapped her hand around her throat. "'Tis no' so little anymore."

Anne wound the blue silk around her hand. "My husband, Laird Calum, had to do something, and quickly. Your mother was well liked, beautiful, full of life. But I could not bring myself to believe an innocent child had anything to do with her death. I asked Calum to send you and your father to Fladda, where he could hide you away from the naysayers."

"Ye did that?"

"Neither Calum nor I could stand by and watch an innocent soul be shunned by the clan. They called for you to be..." She cleared her throat. "Our biggest fear was that someone might murder you in the dark of night." Lady Anne patted Merrin's hand. "You see, I understand how important it is to keep your neck covered."

Merrin untied the tattered cloth around her neck and slowly pulled it away, her hands trembling.

Lady Anne examined it closely—her face expressing concern, but no fear. "'Tis not all that bad, and it does nothing to detract from your beauty." She set the scarf on the table and stood. "Tonight we shall celebrate my son's return. You shall wear the sapphire gown. It has a fashionably tall neck and the lace will frame the slim lines of your jaw superbly."

Lady Anne held up a dress of such exquisite beauty, Merrin had never seen the likes. The ornate embroidery on the flat stomacher must have taken months to sew, and the sleeves puffed at the shoulders, with white silk pulled through diamond-shaped openings.

Merrin didn't know what to say. "I...I cannot."

Enya pulled her arm. "Come. It will be fun, and tonight Ian shall not even recognize you when you glide down the stairs to the great hall."

"But I want Ian to recognize me." And she also wanted to attend the gathering. She wouldn't even have to hide behind a curtain. Merrin held out her arms and let the two women set to work.

Ian turned full circle in his boyhood chamber. It had been so long since he'd occupied this room, it seemed surreal to him to be back after he'd spent a decade away. He was concerned about Merrin. She was still grief-stricken by Niall's death and the state of her home. He'd stopped by his mother's solar ages ago, and she'd shooed him off, telling him to go to his chamber and dress for supper. Of course, fresh clothing awaited him on the bed.

He'd see Merrin at the laird's table tonight. Hopefully Lady Anne wasn't being too overbearing.

A tap came at the door. So faint, it had to be Merrin. In two strides, Ian opened it wide, grinning. His face froze. "Mother?"

"You were expecting Miss Merrin, were you not?"

He bowed and beckoned her inside. "I could never hide anything from you."

Lady Anne smiled and kissed his cheek, then led him to the worn settee. She'd grown older since he last saw her, but the faint lines on her face and the touch of grey that peeked out from the sides of her pink wimple did nothing to detract from her classic beauty. Like a preening swan, she flared her silk skirts and sat, patting the seat beside her. "We have much to discuss."

Ian complied. "Aye." He took her hand and kissed it. "'Tis so good to see you. Are ye well?"

"Yes, though I doubt I'll ever cease to miss your father."

"Has no one else offered for your hand?"

She chuckled. "Several—I suppose being born an earl's daughter makes me a worthy match." She leaned forward and tapped her fingers to her lips. "I daresay, however, I fear my childbearing years are over."

Ian cringed inside—discussing his mother's womb made him a tad uncomfortable. "At least ye have Alexander and his babe to tend to."

"True, and now you've returned. I cannot tell you how happy that makes me." She cleared her throat. "And it appears Miss Merrin has become quite fond of you."

"Aye, and I of her."

"Oh?" Mother eyed him with a pointed look. "She is lovely, but carries a heavy burden."

"I ken." Ian's gaze drifted away and his jaw hardened. "I promised her father I'd see to her care. He died because of me."

"Because of you or because of your uncle Ruairi's selfishness?"

Ian combed his fingers through his hair. He could place the blame of Niall's death upon no one but himself. "If I hadn't washed up on Fladda, Niall and Merrin's lives would be untouched."

Mother reached for his hand. Her fingers were so frail, her skin paper thin, but her touch was soothing, just as it had been so long ago. "You do know, when I sent you to Ruairi for your fostering, I believed I was doing right. He once was an honorable man and a venerable chieftain."

"I ken." Ian smiled, adoring his mother's concern. "Do no' worry, he may have been a tough bastar—task master, but he turned me into a man, a warrior. I will honor me promises and keep me word."

She squeezed his arm with a proud glint in her eye. "Tell me what happened with Janet MacKenzie. Where did you go after Fladda, and why is it Ye're here without fear of retribution?"

Ian took in a deep breath and started at the beginning. He relayed the entire ordeal, including his final battle with Rewan. "I could never stand for a scoundrel who abuses women and children."

Anne patted his hand. "You were always the child with the most compassion. And of you, I am the most proud." She held up her palm. "Do not take me wrong, Alexander makes me proud as well, but you have kindheartedness that is rare to find in a man."

"Aye? I'm afraid 'tis too soft." Ian would only ever admit that to his mother.

"I disagree. You can use your capacity for empathy to do great things. So tell me, do you think Rewan, and moreover Ruairi, will leave you in peace?"

Ian shook his head. He'd thought a lot about Rewan since they'd faced off. He'd convinced Merrin there would be no retribution, but truth be told, he could not be sure. Leaving Rewan alive was a risk...and his damned compassionate heart made him do it. "I hope so. I thought about sailing to Ireland or the Americas, but I want to live here, close to Brochel. This land is me home."

"That it is—and I'm ever so glad to hear it." She lightly touched his shoulder. "And your musket wound, how is it healing?"

"'Tis coming good. The pain doesn't needle me as much now—just a sharp pang now and again."

"I cannot tell you how relieved I am to hear it." Mother sighed. "Tell me. What are your plans for Miss Merrin?"

Ian looked his mother square in the eyes. She might try to stop him, but if he didn't tell her, she'd uncover his plans in some other way. "I want to marry her." Ian watched Lady Anne's face and held his breath.

She blinked, but otherwise, any shock she felt was unreadable—so English of her. "Truly?" She tapped a finger against her chin. "But I do not believe it is a good idea for her to live in the castle."

That was it? No lecture on finding a wealthy daughter with a dowry? A surge of excitement shot through Ian's blood. "Nor do I. Besides, Merrin would prefer to live on Fladda. I've asked Alexander for some supplies to help us rebuild."

"Fladda's not far. You'd be able to attend gatherings often." She smiled, her eyes calculating, but then her brow furrowed. "Once you have the cottage finished, what will you do? Have you plans to support a wife who some consider *marked*?" She uttered "marked" as if it were blasphemous.

"I thought I'd carry on with Niall's trade, but grow it. I acquired a galley from the MacKenzie. With a ship, Merrin and I can trade herbs and remedies all over the isles. I'd wager I could grow his business tenfold."

"It sounds as if Ye're brewing quite an ambitious plan." She stood and pointed to the red woolen rug in front of the hearth. "Roll back the carpet, please."

"Now? I thought ye wanted me to dress for supper."

She flicked her wrist impatiently. "I have something to show you first."

"Very well." Ian complied. He knew of the trapdoor under the rug. He'd stowed his favorite toys there when he was a lad to keep them hidden from Alexander's thieving hands.

Once the rug was neatly rolled and pushed to the side, Lady Anne pointed. "Open it."

Ian played along, wondering what the devil she was up to. He'd probably left a meat pie in there that had petrified. He pulled back the lid and gaped. "What is this?"

"'Tis part of my dowry."

Ian filled his hand with silver sovereigns and gold crowns. Beside the coins was a full set of silver goblets and a ewer, and inside them were gems—rubies, sapphires and pearls. He saw the glint of something familiar. He pushed aside the coins and grasped the hilt of a broadsword, a full-sized likeness to the dirk he'd given Rewan as proof of his death. "My word." He turned the beautiful weapon over admiringly.

"That, your father aimed to give you upon turning one and twenty." She brushed her soft fingers across his cheek. "I apologize for the tardiness. I'd hoped Ruairi would have released you from his service by then."

"Not at all—no apology necessary. If ye'd given it to me, this magnificent piece may very well be in me uncle's hands." Ian ran his finger over the magnificent blade. "I only wish I still had me dirk."

Anne patted his arm. "I'd rather have you back here, safe and healthy, son."

Ian glanced back at the hole in the floor. "This is astounding. Why are ye storing all these treasures here?"

"After your father passed, your brother was to inherit all—have you any inkling of our family's wealth?"

"Vast, I ken."

"We try to keep it quiet to avoid attack...but I digress." She cleared her throat. "After your father passed, I sat Alexander down and showed him what I had brought with me, intended for that horrid man."

Ian sucked in a whistle. He knew well the story of mother's proxy marriage to Lord Wharton, and how his father had fought for her hand.

"Nonetheless, since I never had a girl for whom Calum and I were to provide a dowry, I told your brother I wanted to save these things for you. We both agreed to keep it hidden until you finished your term with Ruairi or married, whichever came first."

Ian stared at the treasure of such wealth most men would never earn in a lifetime. "Ye're giving this to me?"

"With my blessing."

A lump formed in his throat. He lowered the sword and pulled her into an embrace. Mother always smelled of sweet biscuits. "I dunna ken how to thank ye."

"You already have." She sniffed. "You are a son in whom any woman would be proud."

Chapter Twenty-six

M errin had never been so corseted and crammed into a gown in her life. She could scarcely breathe. When Lady Anne told her she must climb down the steps and enter the great hall alone to make a grand entrance, Merrin actually swooned.

She stood on the first-floor landing off the stairwell, her hand on her chest, trying to breathe deeply, which wasn't easy given the stays tightly laced around her ribcage. She never would have guessed Lady Anne was so strong by looking at her small stature. But she pulled the stays tighter and tighter until she was satisfied Merrin had been cinched within an inch of her life. And though the stomacher tacked over her bodice looked divine, it felt like she had a wooden plank attached to her chest—not to mention the stiff lace that crawled up her neck. The three buttons at her throat were a work of art, though the lace separated and framed her bosoms as if they were a portrait hanging on the wall. The stays and the stomacher ensured her breasts defied gravity and stood proud for all to see, her nipples barely covered by the stiff silk.

Merrin groaned. Ian would think her a harlot. Then she chuckled. He most likely already did after she'd thrown herself at him with shameless fervor. A man pattered down the steps as if in a hurry. He gave her a passing glance and nearly missed the next step.

The voices from the great hall rose in volume. So many people talking and laughing at once made her head spin. Or was it the gown? No matter, her head spun like never before.

Merrin fanned herself and breathed as deeply as she could manage. *If I do no' go now, they'll send up a search party.*

She placed a slippered foot on the first stair. Her ankle twisted a bit. *Blast. If only Lady Anne would have allowed me to wear me boots.* Merrin braced her hand on the wall and continued downward.

When she rounded the corner, the voices stopped. Merrin looked up. Heaven help her, all eyes stared. She glanced over her shoulder to see if anyone was behind. No. They were all gaping at her. She clasped her hand over her cleavage. She knew it stuck out far too much. *Blast Ian's mother.*

Speaking of the dowager lady, she stood at the far end of the hall, smiling from ear to ear. The laird's party presided all the way up on the dais, exactly like Niall had described. Lady Anne led a polite applause, while Ian closed his gaping mouth and shoved his chair back.

Merrin wrung her hands, baffled by what she should do next.

Everyone watched in uncomfortable silence while Ian marched down the dais and crossed the long hall with purpose. He'd changed into a fine plaid that stretched across his powerful thighs as he walked toward her. His clean linen shirt hugged his chest, his taut muscles rippling beneath it. Across his shoulder, he had a thick woolen tartan pinned at the shoulder with a brooch of silver.

He grinned as he approached. A finer Highlander she'd never seen. He could have passed for the laird himself.

Merrin's stomach dropped to her toes.

Bowing, Ian took her hand and kissed it. "Ye are stunning, Miss Merrin."

She lowered her lashes, heat burning her cheeks. "Thank you, sir." She leaned in so only he could hear. "I'm wrapped up so tight I could swoon at any moment."

He smiled and offered his elbow.

Taking it, she remembered to breathe. "I see ye found a fresh change of woolens—quite an improvement from your sooty kilt."

"We can both thank me mother."

The conversations in the room began to resume. Merrin sighed, much more comfortable when there weren't hundreds of eyes watching her. He led her to the dais and she stopped. "Only high-ranking clan members can sit at the chieftain's table."

Ian smiled. "And his guests."

"Niall never got to sit beside the laird."

He tugged her arm. "Come, they're waiting for you."

As if playacting one of her dreams, Ian held a chair for Merrin and made introductions. Merrin had met most everyone, except Sir Bran, Lady Enya's husband. The clan below the dais sat on benches, but she got her very own upholstered chair with Ian on one side and Lady Enya on the other.

The kitchen doors opened and the air filled with rich aromas of roasted meats. Servants filed through the door, each carrying a tray laden with food. They proceeded to the dais first. Ian leaned in. "The chieftain's table is served first, then the trenchers are passed down the hall. The people at the farthest end are the lowest ranking and take what remains."

Merrin craned her neck to see all the way to the back of the hall. "Aye, Niall sat down there, but he said there was always plenty."

"Usually there is."

The trenchers overflowed with lamb, beef, chicken and Merrin didn't know what else. A servant offered her a platter with a selection of breads. They all looked so delicious, Merrin took one of each.

When at last the trenchers were passed along to the other guests, she looked at her pewter plate. It was piled high with enough food to feed her for a sennight.

Ian sniggered and tore off a bit of bread, dousing it in sauce.

She shrugged. "It all looks so good."

"I'll help ye with what ye cannot eat."

Ian was right, of course. What was she thinking? Merrin's laces were bound so tight, she could scarcely eat a thing.

She turned to Lady Enya. "Where are your children?"

She pointed. "They're sitting with Friar Pat."

Sir Bran gave his wife a squeeze. "We've too many to fit up on the dais."

Merrin found the friar and counted twelve children of varying ages. "Are they all yours?"

"Aye." Bran looked like he could stand atop the bailey walls and beat his chest with pride.

Ian filled her goblet with ale. "Are ye enjoying yourself?" His eyes dipped to her exposed bosoms and his eyebrows jumped up with a wolfish grin.

"'Tis like a dream, except this gown is like being wrapped in a wooden box."

"Ah." He winked. "We'll make good sport of removing it later."

Merrin covered her mouth to hide her laugh. How could he be so brash in front of all these people?

Alexander coughed. So did his wife. Merrin glanced between them both. The coughing stopped, thank heavens. She recalled Niall had recently mixed up a tincture to cure a cough that had spread at the castle. Hopefully it hadn't returned.

At the far end of the hall, benches scraped across the floor. A fiddler and a piper moved to a corner near the stairs and began to play. Merrin clasped her hands and looked at Ian. "Och, 'tis marvelous—even better than Niall described."

Ian chuckled. He grasped her hands and held them to his lips. "I could watch ye all night. Ye're more vibrant than a harvest moon." He pulled her up. "Come. Dance with me."

Merrin gasped. "Here? In front of the entire clan?"

"Ye told me once ye wanted to see the castle and go to a gathering. Remember we danced around the campfire to Niall's flute?"

"Aye, but that was just us."

"Do no' worry, just focus on me face. 'Twill be as if were alone."

But it wasn't. Couples filled the hall, dancing to reels and strathspeys. Laced up in her suffocating stays, Merrin could scarcely catch her breath, but she wouldn't sit down for anything. Ian knew all the steps, and moved her around the floor with expert finesse. Fortunately, the ample skirts of her gown hid her feet, and in no time, she was laughing and following Ian's lead as if she hadn't a care in the world.

The friar tapped Ian on the shoulder. "May I have the next dance?"

Ian frowned, but Merrin patted his hand. "I'd like to hear ye play the pipes."

Ian shook his head. "Nay."

"Come, Ian," one of the dancers said. "I'd like to hear ye too."

The friar held his belly and laughed. "I hope your piping's improved since ye left for Lewis."

Ian clapped Pat's upper arm. "Ye always had knack for bending me to your will." He gave Merrin a wink and headed toward the musicians.

Merrin looped elbows with the friar. "I cannot imagine Ian being bad at anything."

"Learning to pipe isn't easy. At first it always sounds worse than a chicken yard full of squawking adolescent roosters."

Ian filled the bagpipes with air, his fingers at the ready. Merrin held her breath. The last thing she wanted was for the love of her life to be embarrassed, though she couldn't wait to hear him play.

Pat stood across from her, lining up for a strathspey. At least this dance wouldn't be too strenuous for poor Friar Pat's rheumatism.

The pipes filled the hall with light, reedy tones. Merrin smiled. Ian wasn't good—he was excellent, even better than the paid piper whose instrument Ian had borrowed. Merrin floated through the dance, uplifted by Ian's magical music. Yes, the hall was crowded with people, but she danced for Ian. His gentle tone skimmed the air and touched her heart. She danced for him as if they were the only two people in the hall.

The friar brushed past her shoulder, opening a clear view of her big Highlander. His foot tapping, hose tied at his knees with black flashes, the neatly pleated red and black kilt hung from his hips—he was a picture of masculine beauty to behold. Ian focused on her, his gaze intense. Merrin stopped, his beautiful melody filling her soul. The strength of their gaze was so powerful, she forgot about the dance partner behind her. Merrin stepped forward, reaching her hand out to Ian. His gaze darkened, beckoned her closer. A shudder coursed through her insides. The tune caressed her skin, as if Ian had his hands on her, undressing her and baring her soul.

A hand grasped hers and tugged. Merrin blinked, snapping out of her trance.

Friar Pat grinned. "I think ye missed a step."

"Did I?" She'd probably missed half the dance. The friar graciously led her through the remaining steps until the music ended. The two neat lines of dancers became a mob of people talking and laughing. The crowed closed in. She was unaccustomed to being in such close proximity to so many, and her chest tightened. She had difficulty catching her breath. Seeming not to notice her discomfort, the friar took her hand, but she pulled it away. "Where's Ian?"

Fortunately, he appeared and bowed. "M'lady, your dancing was as graceful as a swan."

She stepped into him, his closeness easing the anxiety of being surrounded. "I daresay I'm no' as skilled as the other ladies here. But your piping was magnificent."

The friar clapped Ian's shoulder. "Ye learned a thing or two at your uncle's keep."

Ian's smile waned and he pulled Merrin to his side. "Do ye think Ye're up for another dance?"

Aye. "With you as me partner, I'll never want to stop."

Friar Pat cleared his throat. "Well, I believe there's a flagon of whisky calling me name."

All too soon, the numbers in the hall began to dwindle. Bran and Enya stopped by between songs with their brood in tow. "'Tis time we retire," Bran said.

Ian shook his hand. "I'll see ye on the morrow. I could use a back as strong as yours to help me with the cottage roof."

"Ye can count on me."

A few songs later, the piper's bellows blared with dissonant tones. He rubbed his hand over his mouth. "That's it for me. My lips feel like blubber."

Merrin glanced around the hall. Only a half-dozen couples sat at the tables. The laird and his party had all gone above stairs. Ian wrapped his arm around her shoulders. "Alexander's put us in me old chamber for the night."

"The one that overlooks the cove?"

"Aye."

"But is it proper? Will your mother not be upset?"

"Do no' worry about her. She'll understand—and once I have a chat with Friar Pat, we'll make arrangements to make it right."

"Ian?"

He grinned. "Aye?"

"Are ye saying ye want to marry me?" Merrin's hands flew to her cheeks. Ian couldn't marry her. Not when he had all that Brochel had to offer. He was a chieftain's son, a fierce warrior. What would he do married to a marked woman? They'd enjoyed their time together, but Merrin couldn't keep her secret hidden forever. Eventually she must return to Fladda, and Ian must take his place beside Alexander.

He grasped her hand. "If ye'll have me."

"But ye cannot. Ye can go anywhere ye want—do anything ye want. I'd be like an anchor around your neck."

He picked her up and marched up the stairs. "I'll make me own decisions about where I go and what I do."

Merrin's heart nearly burst out of her stomacher. Did he know what he was saying? Did he drink too much ale? Surely he would come to his senses in the morning. But all her doubts didn't make her less euphoric. She slipped her arms around Ian's neck and leaned into him—he smelled of fresh rosemary soap and rugged male. Unable to resist his charm when he had her in his arms, she decided to worry about his sanity on the morrow.

The stairs wound up and up, until finally he pushed through a large oak door. He set Merrin in the middle of the room and went about lighting the candles. Merrin turned full circle. The chamber was larger than the one she'd stayed in at Eilean Donan. A huge four-poster bed sat in the middle of one wall, festooned with emerald-green drapes. Tapestries of seascapes lined the walls. A massive hearth filled the space across from the bed, its peat fire already stoked for the night.

"Did ye light the fire?"

Ian blew out his twig? "Nay, the servants see all the fires are lit whilst we're at supper."

"Unbelievable." Merrin turned full circle again, taking in every nook and cranny. She pattered to the window and pulled back the furs. "Ye have an alcove with sitting benches built into the stone?"

"Aye, 'tis called an embrasure." Ian came up behind her and nuzzled her neck. "I never said I had it rough as a lad."

"I'll say." She faced him. "Ye must think me cottage on Fladda awfully drab."

"Not at all." He popped one of her stomacher tacks free. "Brochel is no longer me home. Remember? Me elder brother is chief of this land." He popped the other side. "But I do no' want to talk about that now."

Merrin backed to the wall. "Ian, I cannot—"

Clasping his big hands to her face, he smothered her words with a deep, possessive kiss. Her eyelids fluttered closed. On a sigh, she gave into the pleasure of his soft lips. Heat flooded through her entire body and coiled in the one place she desired his touch most.

"Ye cannot what?" he rasped.

Merrin cast her doubts aside. She couldn't think when he pressed his manhood against her and rubbed. She ran her hands up the outside of his arms. She would take him tonight, and as many times as he was willing to make love to her until he came to his senses and realized he belonged in another place. Yes. She was being selfish, but Ian was too—he just didn't know it yet.

In a blink of an eye, her stomacher was gone. Ian pulled her into in front of the hearth. "I want ye to stay warm while I remove this contraption."

A shiver coursed up her spine, one that had nothing to do with the temperature in the chamber. "Aye?"

He stood back and fingered the fine silk of her sleeve. "Do ye ken how many times I dreamt of having a woman in here when I was a lad?"

"Many?"

He pulled the gown from her shoulders and let it drop. "More than I can count."

"But ye never did?"

He shook his head. "No' in here. I was still a virgin when I left Raasay."

Merrin saw Janet's face when she blinked. "Did ye make love to *her*?" Merrin bit her lip. She wished she could take her words back, but it was already said.

Ian stopped unlacing Merrin's stays and looked at her, his face serious. His Adam's apple bobbed when he swallowed. Her question really bothered him. He pulled her into a tense embrace and inhaled. "When I saw Janet at Eilean Donan, the only person I wanted in me arms was ye"

It was Merrin's turn to swallow. He'd made love to her for the first time at Eilean Donan. Janet was somewhere in the castle, but not in his bed. "Did ye love her before ye met me?"

Ian smoothed his hand over her hair. "Not really. She lured me into helping her by inviting me to her bed." He sighed heavily. "I thought she loved me—but she only needed a warrior bold enough to spirit her away from Ruairi."

Merrin nodded. His words were barbed. She grimaced as if she'd been struck in the stomach. The thought of sharing Ian with anyone tore her insides to shreds.

He reached out his hand and cupped her cheek, but Merrin stepped away—and nearly fell over the heap of fabric around her ankles. She looked down. Her stays were half unlaced, cinched atop a new linen shift.

"It grows worse." Ian rubbed his face and turned away. "She's carrying me child—and Robert MacNeil is going to raise the bairn as his own."

Too stunned to speak, Merrin stared until her trembling knees knocked. Had she heard him correctly? He'd fathered a child? In one move, she bent down, pulled the gown over her shoulders and ran for the door.

Chapter Twenty-seven

I an stared after her with a wicked ache under his kilt. He ground the heel of his hand into his forehead. What was he thinking? He wanted to tell Merrin about the babe, but his timing couldn't have been worse. She'd just lost her father, for Christ's sake. Her home had been reduced to stone and cinders, and though a relatively mild affair, this was her first gathering—her first time at Brochel. And he had to ruin it for her. No matter what his mother said, he had to be the biggest lout in all of Scotland.

He barreled through the door and listened. Faint footsteps clapped the stone steps below. Taking three stairs at a time, he bounded after her. Ian wanted to call out, but he'd wake the whole damned castle.

He skidded into the great hall and turned full circle. Empty. She couldn't have gone far, not in the contraption she wore. Ian could scarcely believe he hadn't overtaken her in the stairwell.

A whimper squeaked above stairs. Ian looked up. It came again. He darted up one flight and listened. Muffled sobs came from the corridor. He tiptoed toward the door, ears ringing with the silence.

The sob came again, much louder this time. He gripped the latch to Mother's solar and cracked the door open. "Merrin?"

Her breathing stuttered. "Go away."

He stepped inside the darkness. Having not been inside this chamber for a decade, he skittered along the wall until he bumped into the hearth. He ran his fingers over the mantel and knocked over a candle. Then his fingers found the flint. Retrieving the candle from the floor, he lit it.

Across the room, Merrin curled into Mother's overstuffed armchair, surrounded by blue silk. Her head hidden in the crook of her arm, she slowly rocked, whimpering. Ian's throat tightened. He left the candle on the mantel and stepped forward.

Merrin threw out her hand. "Come no further." Tears glistened on her cheeks, her eyes pleading.

He spread his palms. "Please. Allow me to explain."

"I kent ye loved her, but ye lied to me."

"Ye are wrong." Ian took another step toward her. "I said I *thought* I loved her, but then I met you." She drew in a stuttered breath and Ian crossed to within an arm's length of her. "I do no' want there to be any secrets between us. I told ye about the bairn because it is tearing up me guts."

"Stop." Merrin shook her palms, then clasped them to her face. "'Tis too much to bear. I'm but a simple lass. Me head is spinning out of control."

"I want to hold a bairn in me arms." He knelt in front of her. "Our babe, Merrin."

"How can ye say that when she has your seed growing in her belly? Och," she wailed. "Me insides ache like ye reached in and pulled them out with your bare hands."

He rested his palm on her shoulder. "I'm so very sorry."

She jerked away. "Do no' touch me."

Ian clenched his fist. "Please." He hesitated. "Come above stairs with me."

She snapped her head up, the corners of her mouth drawn down as if she were in unimaginable pain. "Just go and leave me be."

Ian stared. He hated to leave her like this. What more could he say?

"Go, I said!"

"If ye do no' want me here, I'll be in me chamber. Do ye remember how to find it?"

She nodded once and dipped her head into the crook of her arm.

Ian's shoulders slumped as he dragged himself up the stairs. He loathed leaving her alone, but she'd been so insistent. God, her face reflected the torture he bore in his heart. He should have kept his mouth shut about Janet. What good would come of it? Janet was headed to Barra with a new husband—and he thought her unborn child was Ruairi's spawn. Ian grumbled under his breath—he'd never meet the babe he'd fathered. How many other men in the world had fathered bastards they knew nothing about?

Never again would he be in this predicament. He'd make Merrin forgive him. She just needed time. He'd rebuild her cottage—better and stronger. He stopped mid-stride. He had the coin and jewels. Niall's herb business could become renowned throughout the Hebrides, mayhap even all of Scotland. He now had a galley worthy of sailing the open waters. In addition, he had the money to purchase healing essences from all over the world. His stomach flipped. He'd discuss his ideas with Merrin in the morning—surely she would come round by then.

Ian paced his chamber, his thoughts bouncing between Merrin's upset and his idea for their new venture. He must marry the lass straight away. He'd discuss Merrin's sudden melancholy with his mother in the morning. Lady Anne would know how best to proceed.

He tried to lie down, but couldn't even close his eyes. *Sweet dawn come soon, there is far too much to do to simply lie abed.*

He jumped up and crossed to the door. Holding his hand on the latch, he hesitated. Merrin had told him to stay away. He needed to give her time. Besides, she was most likely asleep—Ian knew full well how his mother's overstuffed armchair could lull a person into slumber.

He traipsed back to the bed and kicked off his boots. He crawled under the bedclothes and stared at the green drapes above. The bed was more comfortable than he'd remembered, and after a time, his eyelids grew heavy.

He must have fallen asleep, because he sat up with a jolt. Blood-curdling screams resounded through the window.

Merrin!

Chapter

Twenty-eight

M errin's eyes were still swollen from crying herself to sleep when they flew open. Guards burst through the solar door.

"There she is," a burly, mail-clad man yelled.

She jolted in her seat, tugging the silk across her chest.

Two guards latched on to her arms. Heart in her throat, Merrin twisted and tried to yank away. "No!"

The largest one sneered. "Ye're going to burn, witch."

The hair at her nape stood on end. Merrin's hand flew to her neck. The gown's lace still tightly enclosed her mark. *How did they know?*

A grey-haired woman dressed in black pushed through the door and pointed. "'Tis her—she killed her ma, then she killed me Niall, and now she's brought the ague onto us all."

Merrin's eyes darted between the angry faces in the growing crowd. "What? No. Ye're wrong."

"Ye should have been burned at birth." The woman sauntered forward, eyes narrowed. "Take her to the courtyard," she spewed with bitter bile.

"Nay! Where is Ian? Where is Lady Anne and the laird? This is madness." Merrin struggled and tried to fight, but the soldiers lifted her off her feet. Without the stomacher, the gown's front pulled open, her stays still wrapped around her torso, partially unlaced, exposing her shift. God in heaven, why hadn't she righted herself during the night?

As they yanked her through the corridor, Merrin struggled to break free. "Nay," she cried over and over.

The guards muscled her down the tower stairs and pushed her into the great hall.

Barking and yowling, Gar strained against a rope that tethered him across the immense room. Ice coursed through her blood. Someone had thought this through. Merrin glanced over her shoulder. The old woman smirked. *What did she mean, "her" Niall?*

But there was no time to think. Merrin's arms wrenched under the guards' heavy-handed grasp. When they burst out the heavy oak doors, the sunlight blinded her. Merrin tried to tug up her arm to shade her eyes, but the man holding her dug her fingers into her flesh like a tourniquet.

Her heart thudding against her chest, Merrin squinted at the faces through the bright light. "Ian! Where are ye?"

The steely-eyed sentry roared with laughter. "He's no' coming. No honorable man would rescue a witch."

Merrin flinched as if the heartless guard had punched her in the gut. "Help! Someone. I'm no demon."

"Light the torches," a woman screeched.

"Burn her." A man's voice rose over the crowd and started a chant. "Burn her...burn her..."

Screaming, Merrin's throat grated and her knees buckled. Over and over she shrieked until her voice went raw. The courtyard whirled around her as people lunged in with their hideous taunts. Niall had warned it was too dangerous to go to Brochel, and now she would pay with her flesh.

"Ian," she shrieked, wrenching her arms to no avail. Where had he gone? Why had she sent him away in the dead of night? And now he'd forsaken her. Merrin's gaze darted across the faces—there was not one from the dais the night before, not one with a sympathetic eye. They all shouted and jeered, calling for her to be mercilessly burned.

Two men marched ahead, bearing torches. Merrin struggled harder. "Nay!" Bile burned the back of her throat. This couldn't be happening.

"Stop." A deep voice echoed across the bailey walls.

Merrin gasped. *Ian!*

The love of her life barreled into the courtyard, barefooted, sword trained on the largest guard. "Release her."

"I cannot." The ugly man puffed out his chest, weighed down with a coat of mail.

"Ian," Merrin whimpered. If only she could say she was sorry. If only she'd gone with him last night.

Pulling her away, they dragged her toward the stake, wood piled underneath—ready to burn her alive. Merrin's trembling flesh bristled.

A half-dozen sentries marched into line, swords drawn.

Baring his teeth, Ian faced them all, panning his sword across the scene.

The old hag raced forward. "She's brought the ague upon us. Our own laird is fevered—nearly half the clan is abed with the sweat." The woman pointed at Merrin. "And all since *she* arrived." Her voice accusing, hateful.

Merrin trembled. How could she have brought an ague upon them?

"Widow Bethag, still looking to cause a stir?" Ian growled as he pointed his claymore at the big man's throat. "Me brother had a cough before we arrived. He told me himself."

Bethag sauntered up to him with confidence, fearless of the deadly weapon Ian held in his hand. "Aye, but what of all the others?"

A serving maid ran into courtyard, her hair covered by a white coif. "Lady Anne's fevered as well."

Friar Pat raced in beside Ian, a damp sheen over his face. "'Tis no' Merrin's doing." He coughed. "Alexander was sick before they arrived. I can attest. He asked me for a tonic."

Bethag's hands flew to her hips. "And how can we trust your word?" She shook her finger. "If ye think I do no' know ye've protected the witch all these years, Ye're wrong. Niall told me everything."

The friar shook his fist. "Merrin wouldn't—"

"Stop this madness." The ground shook as Sir Bran marched across the courtyard, his mammoth claymore secure in his hand.

"She's brought the ague upon us all." Bethag rushed toward him, ensuring she was heard first.

Merrin's shaking breath burst in and out, heaving through the huge gap in her gown.

Bran glanced at Ian. "What proof?"

Bethag shook her finger. "Alexander, Lady Anne and half the clan—they're all fevered."

Friar Pat stepped forward, all color drained from his face, sweat beading at his temples. "'Tis no' her, I swear it."

The old woman whipped around. "There ye go, a man of God swearing an oath."

Merrin glared at Bethag. She was the reason Niall visited Brochel so often? What on earth did her father see in *that*?

Bran ignored the old woman and focused on the friar. "How do ye ken?"

The friar smoothed his palms over his brown robe. "She's no witch, never has been—but she can heal us."

Ian kept his sword and eyes trained on the guard's throat. "The friar's right—she's learned her father's skill."

Sir Bran stepped up to Merrin and focused his dark gaze on her face. "Can ye prove it?"

Trembling, Merrin looked to Ian. He raised his chin. She knew what he was asking—what she must do. "Take me to Fladda. I can make a tincture."

Ian touched his razor-sharp sword to the guard's neck. A line of blood trickled. "Release her now or Ye're the first to die."

Bran held up his weapon. "Do it or every man who defies Ian will feel the cold iron of me blade."

"Let there be no bloodshed." Pat coughed and held up his hands. "Go to Fladda. Niall taught ye well, lass. Ye ken what must be done."

Bethag grabbed Bran's arm. "Ye mustn't let her slip away."

He shoved the woman aside. "While the chieftain is ill, Ian is acting laird and I pledge me fealty to him, as stated in the chieftain's charter. I will accompany Ian and Merrin to the healer's workshop on Fladda."

"Burn her," a man shouted from the rear of the crowd.

"I said no," Sir Bran roared, stepping up to the guard. Enormous, he towered over them all.

Ian reached in and grasped Merrin's hand while holding his sword level. "I *am* chieftain and ye will never in your life touch me woman again, or I will cut ye down and show no mercy." The blade in his hand trembled with the deep tenor of his voice.

As soon as the guard's grasp eased, Merrin slipped under Ian's protective arm. Never again would she doubt him. He clutched her tightly as he backed away and panned his sword across the crowd. "I am ashamed of your actions this day. Ye will tend the sick until we return with a remedy."

Merrin clamped her teeth. God help her. Yes, she knew how to prepare a tincture for the ague, but even Niall didn't know a surefire cure.

"Come," Bran ordered, leading the way to the beach.

"Gar?" Merrin shouted. "Release me dog."

Ian backed toward the gate, keeping Merrin behind him. When they cleared it, he turned to her. "Stay between us." With a bark, Gar bounded through the portcullis and raced in beside them. Ian glanced to the sentry on the wall-walk above. "Close it. I do no' want anyone coming after us."

It didn't take long to sail the galley around to Fladda. Merrin's entire body still shook. "I never want to go there again."

"Ye must." Bran steered the rudder to the beach as Ian manned the sail. "They'll fear ye forever if ye do no' return."

Merrin clutched her arms tight around her ribs. "But what if they try to burn me again?"

Ian removed his plaid. "As acting laird, I'll grant ye sanctuary until this ague has passed. If anyone crosses me, they'll receive the same treatment."

Bran's eyes turned dark as coal. "Ian will have me sword, and I shall cut any man down who stands against him or you."

Merrin didn't doubt he would do it. The man was more fearsome looking than Rewan, truth be told.

Ian glanced back. "I'm grateful to ye, Bran. At least someone has a clear head." He draped the plaid across Merrin's shoulders. "This will cover your gown until we return to Brochel."

She glanced down to his feet. "Ye left without your boots."

He chuckled. "'Tis a good thing 'tis summer." He batted the air with his hand. "Do no' worry about me, I'll be right. Just focus on making the tincture."

Merrin nodded, her gut squeezing. What would happen if it didn't work? A cool blast of wind blew her hair back. She steeled her resolve. She'd apply herself to this task with everything she had, and, God willing, she'd prepare a remedy that would see them through to good health.

Bran pulled hard on the rudder and pointed the galley toward the *caol*. The two men moored the boat in no time and soon the trio headed up the hill to Niall's workshop with Gar sticking close to Merrin's heel.

She recounted the remedy in her head. She'd use a mixture of angelica and alder bark. She'd also add anise for the cough. If only Niall were here, she'd be sure of the measurements. But she couldn't worry about that now. Her biggest concern was the bark. Niall traded with passing merchants for it, since it wasn't prevalent nearby. She looked skyward and prayed there would be enough.

Once they reached the workshop, Ian placed his hand on her shoulders. "What do ye need us to do?"

Merrin turned full circle, looking at the herbs hanging from the beams above. "We'll need a good-sized batch. Light a fire in the cottage hearth and put the large kettle onto the grate. We'll need it half full with water."

"We'll see it done."

"Aye," Bran said. "And I want to have a look at the damage Rewan did. I have half a mind to make him pay for the repairs."

Ian led the big man away, leaving Merrin alone in Niall's workshop. After her ordeal in the courtyard, and now faced with a daunting task, her chest was so tight, she wanted to vomit. Everything under the lean-to reminded Merrin of her father—including the tinkling bells. She reached out a trembling hand and picked up his pestle. *Father. I need ye with me now. Show me what to do. Please, please help me heal these people and prove to them I'm no' evil.*

She pulled Niall's largest mortar into the center of the table and filed through the herbs hanging from the ceiling until she found the angelica. *Grind the whole plant, roots and all—the fruit yields the strongest results.* Merrin heard Niall's voice clearly in her head, as if he'd only given the lesson yesterday.

She reached up and untied a clump from the line and inspected it. The angelica had impressive clusters of dried fruit pods. Methodically, she ground them to a fine powder and scraped it into a stoneware pot. Merrin found the alder bark piled on a shelf. As she suspected, there wasn't as much as she'd like, but she rigorously ground it to a fine powder to ensure equal distribution through the mixture. Niall kept dried anise pods in a stoppered jar with others at the back of his table.

Merrin pulled off the cork and poured all of the pods into the mortar. She bit her lip. She could use more anise, but this would have to do as well. Once she had all of the medicinal ingredients she needed, Merrin took the shears to the garden and snipped some mint leaves for taste.

Ian slipped up from the cottage. "The water's boiling."

"Good, I'm nearly ready." Merrin dropped the mint leaves into the mortar. "Where's Bran?"

"Tending the fire." Ian kicked the dirt with his big toe. "I wanted to talk to ye alone."

Merrin's heart squeezed. "Ian—I'm sorry."

He tugged her into his arms and cradled her head to his chest. "Nay, lass. 'Tis I who should be sorry. I never should have left ye alone last night."

"But I told ye to go."

"I shouldna listened." He ran his fingers through her hair. "I kent it was dangerous for ye, but I just went back up to me chamber and paced half the night."

"I was daft." Merrin squeezed him tighter. "I was so angry when ye told me about Janet, I couldn't think straight."

"I do no' want to talk about her anymore. I'm going to marry ye, Merrin. I love ye."

She closed her eyes and savored the warmth of his strong arms. "I love ye so much, but what if me tincture doesn't work?"

"It will. Ye can do it, and once everyone's cured we'll rebuild. We have the galley now—and me mother's given me an inheritance. I've been so excited to tell ye about it. We can build upon your da's herbal business—buy herbs from all across Europe at the market in Glasgow, and sell them at a marked-up price along the Hebrides."

Ian's eagerness helped her spirits. For the first time since she'd been abducted, Merrin felt an inkling of hope. "If only it could be."

"It will. I will make it so. I promise."

Tears burned Merrin's eyes. She wanted to be a part of Ian's dreams so much, but she must return to Brochel.

There was every chance she'd face her death.

Chapter

Twenty-nine

T he men moored the galley on Brochel beach. Bran handed the three ewers of tincture to Ian, who carefully steadied each one into the smooth stones without spilling a drop. Merrin stood on the deserted shore, wringing her hands, still wearing Lady Anne's fancy gown. Of course it was all but ruined, having been sprayed by salt water and smudged with soot from the cottage. Thank heavens Ian had given her the plaid to wear over the stomacher-less bodice until she could change.

Sentries clad in steel helms watched from the bailey walls, but no one came down to greet them. She fingered the lace at her neck, ensuring it sufficiently covered her mark. Aside from a handful of gracious souls, the clan hated her—and worse, feared her. Merrin jumped when someone placed a hand on her shoulder. She whipped around, ready to defend herself.

Lady Enya snapped her hand away—of course, she lived in the cottage up the hill, not behind the castle walls. "Apologies." Her gaze darted to her husband. "Three of our bairns are fevered and down."

Merrin hefted one of the ewers. "Take me to them."

Bran hopped over the galley rail. "Nay. Merrin must tend Alexander first."

Merrin held the ewer out to Lady Enya. "Take this. Give each child a tot, and keep a pint for later, then bring the ewer to me. I'll go check on them as soon as I can."

"Thank you." Lady Enya grasped the heavy vessel with both hands. "I'll not forget this."

Bran tapped his wife's elbow. "Can ye handle the children on your own? There's been a grave skirmish at the castle."

Her brow furrowed, her eyes darting to Merrin. "Aye."

"Godspeed."

Merrin offered a shy smile and looked to Ian. He lifted the two other ewers and gave her a grim nod. "Come."

Calling Gar, she walked between the two men as they climbed the steep zigzag path to the castle. Near the gate, Bran drew his sword.

Merrin stopped. "Do ye think there'll be trouble?"

He balanced the hilt in a firm hand. "I'll see to it there's no'. Open the gate," Ian bellowed.

Merrin held her breath as the chains above creaked, slowly revealing a busy courtyard.

The smithy's shop clanged, the guard sparred, women chased children and people coughed. But when Merrin stepped into the light, silence cast an eerie pall over the scene. Everyone stared.

Lady Anne burst through the great hall doors, her eyes wide. "Thank heavens Ye're back. Nearly fifty people are afflicted—the whole castle will fall if you cannot stop it."

Ian grasped her shoulders. "Mother? They said ye were ill."

"I was tending Alexander when the commotion broke out. I am yet unaffected."

Lady Anne gave Sir Bran a firm nod. He moved to the center of the square and faced them all. "We'll start with Alexander. Everyone will be seen."

"I'll no' have me son touched by a witch," Bethag crowed.

"Nor will I," another said.

Bran slammed his sword against the side of the well. "Silence! The laird and lady will be tended first. Miss Merrin has been granted sanctuary until Alexander is well enough to hear her plea." He glared at Bethag. "The rest of ye, bring your sick to the great hall and curses to any who refuse treatment because of stupidity and foolishness."

The old hag spat.

Bran eyed her, then trained his claymore across the crowd. "If anyone lays a hand on Miss Merrin whilst she's under me protection, they'll answer to Ian. And no doubt their punishment will fit the crime. On that I give me oath."

Ian stepped forward and made a show of slowly drawing his sword. "Anyone going against me decree of sanctuary will pay in blood, mark me." He pointed his claymore toward the skies. "Any action toward Miss Merrin will be punished by Sir Bran and multiplied tenfold by me."

Low grumbles dispersed throughout the crowd. Merrin hated the way they looked at her. She stepped closer to Ian. He wrapped his arm around her protectively. If nothing else, she prayed her tincture would cure them.

Ian and Bran shepherded Merrin up to the solar, where she quickly changed back into her kirtle. After collecting Ian's boots, they proceeded to laird's chamber. Lady Anne followed closely behind. Bran led them down a corridor and stopped outside a large door. "Ye go in. I'll stand guard."

Merrin glanced between the two men. "Is it not safe now that ye've declared sanctuary?"

Bran knit his thick brows. "We must take nothing for granted. Ye cannot be left alone—not until this ague has passed."

Ian opened the door and Merrin clasped her hand over her mouth. "Mercy, 'tis so grand."

Ian pulled her inside. Merrin's gaze darted from the ornate tapestries and rich woolen rugs to the carved stone hearth, across from which was the biggest bed she'd ever seen. Ian tugged on her arm and she stumbled on the edge of the rug.

"'Tis all right, lass. Me brother needs ye."

Merrin gulped and followed Ian to the laird's bed.

Alexander opened his eyes. "Where is Friar Pat?" His voice rasped and a bead of sweat rolled from his temple.

"The friar asked me to tend ye. He's got the ague as well." Though the friar put on a brave face when they captured her, Merrin had recognized the signs. She'd bet her life Pat had taken to bed once they set sail for Fladda. Merrin felt Alexander's forehead. "Ye're burning up."

Alexander turned his head away.

Lady Anne stepped beside the bed and grasped Alexander's hand. "You must allow Miss Merrin to treat you. She's prepared her father's tincture."

The laird pursed his lips and gave a single nod.

Ian helped support Alexander's shoulders while Merrin gave him a tot of her brew. "Ye'll need this once every couple of hours until the fever breaks. Someone needs to tend him with damp cloths to his forehead."

Lady Anne turned the hourglass on the bedside table. "I'll see to it myself." Lady Anne pointed to an adjoining door. "Go tend Lady Ilysa, then you'll be needed most in the great hall."

Merrin followed Ian through the strange door. "Do no' they stay in the same chamber?"

Ian shrugged. "They have their own rooms when they choose."

This chamber, decorated in lavish purple velvet and silk, was every bit as extravagant as the laird's own. "How could anyone possibly need so much luxury?"

A serving maid, seated across the room, hopped to her feet, clasping her shaking hands.

Ian faced her. "Fetch some water and a cloth. Lady Ilysa's head mustn't be without a damp rag until her fever breaks."

The woman curtsied. "Aye, m'laird." She let out a quick breath and crossed herself, mumbling, "Heaven help us all—I cannot believe a witch..." The door closed and blocked her utterance.

Ian gave Merrin a reassuring pat. Merrin shook it off, trying to control her urge to run after the lass and give her a good shake. With a deep breath, she poured a tot of tonic into a glass cup. "They're all nervous about me."

Ian helped Ilysa sit up. "Do no' worry about what they think. This ague is bad. Ye must stop it quickly."

Merrin held the cup to Lady Ilysa's lips, but she burst into a fit of coughing. Patiently, Merrin waited. "I've added some anise for your cough, m'lady. Ye'll feel much better once ye've taken it."

"Thank you," Ilysa said weakly, shivering from fevered chills.

"Lady Anne will oversee your comfort. If ye need anything, I'll be tending the others in the hall."

Rumbling voices echoed up the stairwell as Merrin descended, with Ian leading and Bran behind. But these were not the same angry voices from the morning. These were tones of concern and worry.

Benches had been pushed to the walls. Coughing people were strewn across the floor, every shade of plaid imaginable draped over them. Merrin clutched Ian's elbow. "There will no' be enough tincture for all these people."

Ian glanced back to Bran. "I've never seen anything the like."

"Nor I." His mouth pulled down in a grim frown. "Pray 'tis not the Black Death."

Merrin shuddered and made the sign of the cross. "Do no' even speak it."

Ian beckoned a serving maid. "Bring out trays of cups. We'll need ye to help us tend the sick."

Her eyes darted to Merrin. "She's trying to kill us all."

Ian stepped up to the maid, his nose an inch from hers. "If I hear ye utter one more falsehood about Miss Merrin, I'll see to it ye tend the chamber pots for good. Now be gone with ye."

Merrin took in a deep breath and watched the maid disappear into the kitchen. She brushed her hands off on her kirtle and went to work. Bran stood on the dais like a statue, his arms folded over his massive chest. Ian had given him one task—maintain order. Ian stayed beside Merrin, fetching everything she asked for, barking at the healthy to lend a hand. But it seemed more often than not, the healthy clansmen and women cast sideways looks and curses under their breath.

Merrin knelt down and held a cup to an older man's lips. "Drink."

He shook his head. "I'll not take it from your hand."

Merrin cast an exasperated look to Ian.

He tapped the man's hip with the toe of his boot. "Let him suffer."

"I cannot do that." Merrin held the cup to Ian. "You give it to him. Please."

Ian's jaw ticked, but he took the cup and knelt. "If the laird will take it from Miss Merrin, 'tis good enough for anyone in the clan."

"Aye?" The man coughed. "What sorcery did she use to mix this brew?"

Ian held the cup to the man's lips. "Ye do no' deserve this—'tis only at Miss Merrin's insistence I give it to ye, but I'll no' forget your words."

Merrin had no idea how much time had passed after they'd worked down the line of patients. She picked up a cloth from the table and wiped her hands. "I do no' see Friar Pat—he was fevered afore we left for Fladda."

"He's most likely on his cot in the chapel."

"We should have tended him first." Merrin picked up the last ewer and swirled the contents. "We've not much left."

Merrin entered the chapel and rushed to the friar's side. "Oh me heavens. I'm so sorry it has taken us so long to find ye."

He reached out a shaky hand. "Do no' worry overmuch for me."

She felt his forehead. "Ye're burning like a fire."

"I've the chills. Do ye have another blanket?"

Merrin cast a worried look to Ian. "Fetch him a blanket—and send someone to tend him. 'Tis deplorable he was left alone."

Ian shook his head. "I cannot leave ye here."

"Do it, I say. I'll not leave the chapel until ye return, and with Sir Bran outside, no harm will befall me."

Ian's jaw tensed. "I haven't liked the rumblings I've heard."

An icy shiver crawled over Merrin's skin. She didn't want to think about the taunts. Every single one needled at her heart.

"Have they been unkind?" the friar asked, his voice weak.

Merrin's shoulder ticked up.

Ian crossed his arms. "I'll say—even after I declared sanctuary. I dunna ken why she's bothering to help some of them."

Pat licked his dry lips. "Because she's a kindhearted lass."

"Go." Merrin shooed Ian away. "I'll be right with the friar."

Ian gave a curt bow and took his leave.

Merrin knelt beside Pat. "We're nearly out of the tincture—and I need at least another batch. Do ye have the herbs here?"

He ran his tongue across dry lips as if trying to muster the energy to speak. "Check me workshop—'tis in the garden. What do ye need?"

Merrin counted the ingredients with her fingers. "Angelica, alder bark, anise."

Friar Pat closed his eyes and coughed. "I do no' think I have the alder—mayhap ye can use willow?"

"'Tis not as effective for the ague."

"But it will have to do in a pinch and will help with the fever."

Merrin buried her face in her palms. "I wish Da were here. He was a much better healer than I."

The friar rested his hand on her head. "Do no' worry yourself, lass. He taught ye well, and now ye must step into his shoes." He took a labored breath followed by a weak cough. "I wish I could rise from this cot and help ye, but the fever's knocked me flat."

Merrin met his gaze, her chest tight. "What if it does no' work?"

The friar closed his eyes, but before his eyelids completely hid his emotion, the flash of fear was unmistakable. He'd tried to hide it from her. Pat coughed again. "Keep Ian beside ye—he's right. Ye shouldn't be alone. He'll protect ye with his life."

Merrin shook her head. "I do no' want anyone else killed for the likes of me. Ma, then Da. I couldn't bear to lose Ian too."

Pat reached out and Merrin took his hand. "The good Lord reveals his path for us one day at a time. Follow it, and put your trust in God."

Merrin ground her teeth. She wanted to help, to tend the sick, but they hated her. If only everyone could recover quickly—mayhap they'd even stop their cruel remarks. But she couldn't fail, and she wouldn't put Ian in a position where he'd be forced to fight to defend her.

How she would do that, Merrin had no idea. But one thing was for certain—once she was assured the clan was no longer in danger, she would not remain to await their ire.

Ian could have hit something when he discovered Sir Bran had de-serted his post outside the chapel door. He'd been gone far longer than he'd wanted—practically every blanket in the castle was in use. He'd finally had to take the plaid from the foot of his bed. Blanket clutched under his arm, he pushed inside.

God's teeth, Merrin was nowhere in sight.

He darted to the alcove. Friar Pat hadn't moved. The holy man dozed, but his body shook with fevered chills. Ian draped the plaid over his body.

The friar's eyes opened. "Thank ye, Ian."

"Where has Merrin gone?"

"The workshop."

Ian pulled the blanket to Pat's chin. "She should have waited until I returned."

Pat nodded weakly and closed his eyes.

"I'll send someone to tend ye after I've had words with Merrin."

Ian dashed through the door and headed to the garden. Bran stood guard outside the friar's workshop. He loved the clan's henchman like a father, but the decision to allow Merrin to leave Pat's side needed to be addressed. "I said no' to leave the chapel until I returned."

Bran cast his thumb over his shoulder. "Aye, but did ye say it to her? I either let her come out here, or tie her to the altar, she was so determined."

Ian stammered. Bran was one of the few men for whom he was forced to lift his chin to meet eye to eye. Known throughout the Hebrides as a man who could not be bested, the henchman was the difficult to argue with. Ian took in the stretched seams across Bran's chest. 'Twas best not to challenge him to a test for strength. Not today, anyway—especially knowing how headstrong Merrin could be.

Ian tugged up his belt. "I'll go talk to her—why do no' ye go check on your bairns?"

Bran shook his head. "I—"

"Go. I'd like to speak to Merrin alone."

"Very well. I will no' be long." Bran clapped Ian's shoulder. "Ye've a good lassie there. I've never seen a woman work harder than she has today."

"Aye, and 'tis not over yet. Do ye ken what will happen if the ague worsens?"

Bran's expression turned grim. "The problem is, it very well could. Many a man has lost their lives to it. I saw it meself in the South Seas." Bran shook his head. "And they're blaming it on the lass."

Ian returned the clap, resting his hand on Bran's shoulder. "We'll weather it—or it may be you and me against the entire clan."

"I pray no'."

Bran headed down the path and Ian peered into the workshop. Similar to Niall's, a lean-to with three walls, this one had a bit of lattice covering about three-quarters of the front opening, with ivy winding its way through the gaps.

Merrin bent down, inspecting the contents under the shelves. The blue kirtle she wore hugged her bottom. The feminine curves presenting to him robbed Ian of the chastisement he'd intended. Yearning heat spread below his navel. He stepped inside. Oh how delectable it would be to raise her skirts and take her right there in the holy man's workshop.

Heady fragrances of mint and rosemary flooded his nostrils as he walked toward her. "Merrin."

She stood with a jolt, nearly dropping the jar in her hands. "Ian, I need your help."

He puzzled. Was she not going to apologize for deliberately going against his wishes? "Ye agreed to stay in the chapel."

She set the dusty container on the table. "Aye, but ye took so long—and Bran was there." She craned her neck and smiled. Damn, she was so adorable when she did that. Ian's anger fled.

"I sent him to check on his children."

"Good. 'Twas the right thing to do. I certainly do no' need two brawny knights guarding me."

Ian chuckled. As a lad he'd always held Sir Bran in high esteem. His chest swelled to be compared to him as an equal.

Merrin blinked, her eyes endearing like a baby seal's. She used a cloth to wipe the dust from the jar. "There's a note inside this container, but it smells like it could be alder. 'Twas hidden so far back, I wonder if the friar forgot he had it." She reached inside and pulled out the note. "Can ye read it?"

Ian turned the parchment toward the ray of light streaming from the entry. "'Tis in Latin."

"Oooh. That sounds old."

Ian chuckled. Latin was the language of kings—one all nobility across Christendom could use to communicate, no matter what language they spoke. Fortunately, he'd paid some attention to his mother's lessons. "It says Jesuit's Powder, the year of our lord fifteen-fifty-one." He glanced at Merrin. "This powder is thirty-three years old."

A lovely crease formed between Merrin's brows. "Jesuit's Powder? I do no' think I heard Niall mention *that*." She pointed to the note. "There's something scrawled on the other side—did ye see it?"

Ian turned it over. "Ah, this must be the friar's hand. 'Tis in Gaelic." He read. "*Calum plundered from a Spanish ship. Bark of the cinchona tree. Unproven.*"

Merrin narrowed her eyes. "Cinchona bark?" She drummed her fingers to her lips. "Niall mentioned it—said he'd like to lay his hands on some. Yes, I remember—it was not long ago. He said a passing merchant mentioned it on one of his Wednesday visits to Brochel."

"Do ye ken why he wanted it?"

"He said it was touted as a miracle cure."

"For what?"

Her shoulders ticked up to her ears. "I'm such a mutton-heid, I didn't ask—it could be rats bane for all I ken."

"But 'tis a cure, aye?"

Merrin looked at the jar and dipped her finger inside.

Before she put it in her mouth, Ian grasped her hand. "Nay."

"I wouldn't give anyone something I didn't try first.

Ian glanced to the jar and dipped his finger in as well. "I'll try it, then you."

Merrin shook her head. "Together." Simultaneously they tasted the tiniest morsel. Merrin clicked her tongue on the top of her mouth and looked to the rafters. "'Tis bitter."

Ian stuck his tongue out then spat. "'Tis awful."

She looked at the other jars lined up on the table. "Me tincture is missing something. I think we should add a few spoons of Jesuit's Powder to the mixture. If they show improvement, we can add a touch more." She pointed. "We've plenty of angelica and anise, but even his cache of willow bark isn't enough. We need a miracle."

"And Niall thought this might be it?"

She bit her bottom lip and gave Ian an insecure look. "Aye, he did. Mayhap Niall is giving me a sign."

"Then ye must try."

Chapter Thirty

The sun had set when they left Friar Pat's workshop. The few servants who tended the kitchen fire scattered like cockroaches exposed to light when Merrin stepped inside with Ian.

"We've work to do," Ian barked. "I cannot believe this."

"Never mind them. We made the tincture without servants on Fladda, we can do it again here." Merrin pulled a linen apron over her head and tied it back. "We need plenty of wood. Get every pot boiling we can. We'll make as much as possible."

Together they worked quickly. Ian took cast-iron pots to the well and filled them while Merrin ground the herbs to a fine powder. The kitchen at Brochel was well stocked and large. Even the hearth was tall enough for her to walk inside. A large iron grill sat atop the embers, which made it easy to stir all three brews at once.

Ian handled all the heavy lifting and Merrin measured, poured and stirred. One batch was nearly ready when Bran arrived.

Merrin stopped stirring for a moment. "How are your bairns?"

"No change." With dark circles beneath his eyes, Bran looked as tired as she felt. "At least no one else has come down with it—Enya's keeping the sick ones separated."

"Good." Merrin tapped her spoon on the edge of a kettle. "This one's ready."

Ian picked up a ewer and dipped it in. "We'll take this new brew to Alexander and Ilysa first."

Merrin held up her hands. "Only after I taste it."

"I'll do it," Ian said.

Merrin snatched a cup from the counter. "Nay, Ian. The healer must."

He reached for another cup. "Then we'll both taste it, just as we did in the workshop."

She didn't like the idea of Ian tasting her brew—God only knew if there would be some sort of adverse reaction when the cinchona tree mixed with the other ingredients. She didn't expect anything bad, but Niall had always cautioned her to be careful. *Do no' use too much of a new herb and increase the dosage gradually...*

Dear Lord, help us. Merrin closed her eyes and sipped. The hot liquid scalded her tongue as it went down. It was definitely bitterer than the last lot, barely palatable.

Ian blew on it, sipped his and swished it around his mouth.

"Well?" Bran asked.

Merrin held her palms out to her sides. She felt fine—no dizziness, no blurred vision. "I'd like to take it to Friar Pat first."

"But me brother is our chieftain."

Bran took Merrin's cup and swallowed the rest. "'Tis a good idea. He'd want to try it afore we give it to Alexander."

Ian was relieved to see the serving maid he'd sent to tend the friar was still there. He'd been furious at the clan's reluctance to help with anything where Merrin was concerned. She stood when they came in, but swayed a bit.

Merrin eyed her. "Are ye well?"

"Not so much." She wiped her forehead with the back of her arm and cast a worried look at Ian. "Did ye bring the ague upon us all?"

Ian stepped between them. "Can ye no' see she's trying to help? Do ye no' understand that without Miss Merrin the sickness could overcome the entire clan?"

The maid hung her head and scratched a bump that looked like a mosquito bite on her hand. "Mistress Bethag says—"

For the love of God, how did the clan come to rely on the word of windbag who was reputed for her ability to twist a trifle rumor into a momentous scandal? "Do ye know Bethag to be a gossip?"

"Aye," she whispered.

Ian placed his hand on her shoulder. "I suggest ye try thinking for yourself. Would a woman such as Miss Merrin have returned from Fladda if she wanted to see us all fall to the ague?"

The woman coughed weakly. "Nay."

"Of course not." Had he finally gotten his point across? *Please, God, make it so.*

Merrin poured a tot of the tincture into a cup and offered it to her. "Drink. It may stop the sickness from becoming worse."

"Merrin?" the friar called from his cot in the alcove.

Merrin dashed to his side. "How are ye, father?"

"Mayhap a bit better."

Merrin felt his forehead. "Ye're still fevered." She beckoned Ian. "We've a new brew. I found some Jesuit's Powder in your workshop."

His face blanked as if he couldn't recall it. "Jesuit's Powder? I think Calum brought it back from one of his adventures."

"Aye," Ian said. "Ye left a note in the container."

His breath caught. "I recall—'tis the bark of the cinchona tree. Impossible to find in these parts." He swiped a hand across his brow and closed his eyes. He shivered, still gripped by chills.

Merrin knelt beside him and held the cup to the friar's lips. "Ian and I have both tried it. Drink."

Pat could barely swallow. Merrin glanced back to Ian. "We must pray."

Ian bowed his head and recited the twenty-first psalm, then silently he offered up prayers this new tincture would work. The first one had been administered with little effect. If they didn't see signs of improvement by the morning, things could become very grave.

Merrin stopped by the serving maid on the way out. "How are ye feeling now? Any change?"

"No different."

"Any worse?" Ian asked.

The lass shook her head.

Ian and Bran escorted Merrin to the laird's chamber, where they found him much in the same condition as the friar. Though his condition hadn't worsened, he was still fevered and in and out of consciousness. After administering the tincture to Alexander,

Merrin handed the cup to Lady Anne. "We must all drink me new tonic. I do no' want to see another soul sick, and it may ward off any further bouts of ague."

Lady Anne drank and passed the cup to the serving maid.

Ian put his arm around his mother's shoulders. "Ye look exhausted. Let the maid tend him."

His mother shook her head and cast a worried glance to the bed. "But he's my son."

"Aye, anyone can dampen a cloth and place it upon his forehead." He tipped up her chin. "Please, Mother. I cannot bear the thought of ye being sick as well."

By the hour of the clock on the mantle, it was well past midnight when they left the laird's chamber.

Merrin turned to Bran. "I want to check on your bairns, and then we can tend the rest."

"I'd like to see them as well," Bran said. "It isn't often I've seen Lady Enya distraught, but she was fraught with worry when I was last there."

Merrin hurried to the stairs. "Come, then."

Bran carried the torch as they approached the cottage. He tapped on the door and then opened it. Ian peered inside. It was bigger than he remembered. "Did ye add on?"

"Aye, a few years back. Needed a place to put all the bairns."

Enya jumped up from the rocking chair by the hearth.

"How are they?" Bran asked.

She rubbed her hand across her face, making her wimple skew. "Still fevered."

Merrin grasped her hands. "We've brought a new tincture."

"Good. Come." Enya led her into the next room, leaving Ian and Bran alone.

Bran gestured to a chair. "Sit. Ye look like shite."

"We all do." Ian pulled up a chair while Bran poured two tankards of ale.

Bran sat across the table. "Merrin's tough. She hasn't batted an eye at all the taunts being thrown her way."

"It bothers her, though. She just does no' let on." Ian wiped his mouth with the back of his arm and spotted a sealskin cloak hanging by the door. "I'd like to do something for her once the ague leaves us."

Bran drank and clanked his pewter tankard on the table. "'Tis a good idea."

"She's lost everything because of me. I told her I'd make a seal-skin cloak like the one over there."

Bran looked. "I've some seal pelts curing in the stable if ye want them."

"Could I buy them from you?" Ian realized he could purchase sealskins and a great many other things for Merrin. The thought made him sit taller.

Bran batted the air. "They're yours."

"Ye're a good friend, Bran. Ye ken the only dress she owns is the one she's wearing—ye saw it, Rewan made sure the whole cottage was completely wrecked. I aim to make it up to her as soon as I can."

Bran pounded his fist on the table. "Bloody bastard. And he was a friend."

"Aye, but Ruairi put him up to it."

"It does no' make it right."

"What would ye have done if Alexander ordered ye to do the same?"

Bran refilled the tankards. "I would have gone after the culprit, not punish everyone else along the way—Rewan's tactics were pure cowardice if ye ask me."

Ian took a swig of ale and stared into the cup. "What do ye reckon will happen if someone dies of this ague?"

"I hate to think of it." Bran frowned. "I've swayed the guard to our side, but if the mob grows out of control, we cannot fend them all off on our own—ye best put Merrin in your galley and set sail for Ireland."

Ireland? And all Ian had wanted was to earn his place beside his brother. The ague probably struck the clan on account of him—not Merrin.

The women came in. "Enya, ye look like Ye're at death's door." Bran pulled her onto his lap.

She rested her head on his shoulder and closed her eyes. "It has been a long day, that's for certain."

Merrin still stood in the doorway. "But it looks like your bairns are coming good, thank heavens. Willy's fever has broken." She glanced at Ian. "We'd best go back to the castle and tend the others."

Bran waved her to the table. She didn't look any spryer than Enya. "Come, have some ale and a slice of bread."

Ian pulled Merrin beside him. "Sit. Ye haven't eaten all day."

She slid onto his lap in a heap. "Mayhap one slice of bread."

Her soft bottom pressing against him made Ian's mind blank. Oh how delectable it would be if they were alone. Ian would be in heaven if only they could find a bed rather than head back to the great hall.

However, it was a pleasant respite to be in a cottage where Ian didn't have to have his guard up. He'd been watching Merrin's back, arguing with clansmen and women who grumbled curses under their breath. Each jibe attacked his heart. He couldn't strangle every naysayer, but he did what he could to prove his point. Ian thought he got through to some, but others might never come around.

He must keep his ears piqued. If he sensed anarchy, he'd move quickly and spirit Merrin to the galley before the mob could marshal her to the courtyard as they'd done before.

The melodic rumble of the surf on the shore cast a calming shroud over the dark night. Together Merrin and Ian crossed back through the castle gates. Bran would join them after he got a bit of sleep. He promised he'd return at dawn.

Dimly lit, the bodies of the sleeping ill strewn on pallets of straw across the spacious hall reminded Merrin of seals on the beach.

"Water," a boy called.

Merrin squeezed Ian's hand. "I'll bring it—please fetch the tincture. We must give it to them all."

Together they tended the fifty or so patients. After she gave the last man his tot, Merrin could scarcely stand. She arched and kneaded a knot in the small of her back.

Ian wrapped an arm around her shoulders. "It will be daylight soon. We need to rest."

"Aye." She pulled him toward the kitchen. "And I must check on me brew. I pray we have enough for the morrow."

Ian needed a shave, and dark circles had taken up residence under his eyes. But he said not another word to convince her to rest. Driven to do everything possible to beat this sickness, she moved to the sideboard and examined the contents of Friar Pat's herb jars. She could strengthen the mixture with Jesuit's Powder, but she'd be short of angelica and anise—and that would be the end of it until they could collect more herbs.

Ian hefted up the kettle and carefully poured the contents into a ewer. He didn't spill a drop.

Swaying on her feet, Merrin watched. "We need to prepare more."

"Aye?" He held up the jug. "This is three-quarters full."

She pulled a mint leaf from its stem and popped it in her mouth. "Ye want one? Tastes fresh."

Ian slid one onto his tongue. "Ta." How he made such a simple motion look so wonderfully tasty, Merrin had no idea. A familiar longing stirred inside her breasts. Oh how she regretted running from Ian's chamber. If she could have that moment back, she'd show him the love he deserved—show him how much he meant to her.

Gar sauntered in from the great hall and plopped in front of the fire. Merrin chuckled. "Ye're making yourself comfortable are ye not, ye giant mop?" The dog opened one eye and closed it. Merrin snorted. "He has nary a care in the world."

"He'd do anything for ye, though." Ian poured a bucket of water into the kettle. "He fought like a lion when Rewan was chasing us."

Merrin gave the dog a fond glance. "Aye, he did." Gar whimpered in slumber. "But that does no' make him any less of a sook."

While they set the kettle to boil with a new batch of tincture, a hint of daylight lit the sky cobalt through the window. Ian wrapped his arms around Merrin's waist and pulled her against his body. His stubble tickled her ear. "I cannot wait to have ye alone—someplace where there's a bed."

She closed her eyes and inhaled his masculine scent. "If I found a bed, I'd sleep for a sennight."

"But only after I ravished ye." Ian lifted Merrin by the waist and set her on the sideboard.

He ran his lips along her neck. Gooseflesh erupted over her skin as Merrin closed her eyes and gave into the gush of hunger stirring to life in her midsection. "That feels so good."

Ian nudged between her legs and rubbed against her. Heat flared with her need, reacting to the hard manhood crushed to her mons. Merrin tried to regain control. "Are ye always standing like a stallion?"

His low chuckle brought another wave of gooseflesh across her skin. "Only when Ye're near."

"All day?"

He arched his brows with a devilish grin. "Aye."

Merrin couldn't resist latching her ankles around the back of his thighs. Ian covered her mouth and swirled his tongue, tantalizing her with succulent mint and male. He slid his hand over her breast and kneaded. "I like it when Ye're not wearing your stays."

"Ye're a wicked man, Ian MacLeod." Merrin arched her back and shamelessly ground against him. Her breath quickened. "I wouldn't run from your chamber if I had it to do again."

"I wish ye were there now."

"I love ye, Ian."

"Show me how much."

His pale blue eyes bored through hers, stripping her soul bare. Tapping her tongue to her top lip, she slid her hand inside the front of his kilt and touched him.

Ian rocked his hips and moaned, his half-cast gaze still focused on her. "Stroke me."

Merrin grasped him with her fingers, though his belt hindered her movement.

He chuckled again and raised his kilt. Merrin could scarcely breathe. It was as if she was seeing him for the first time. Longer than a hand, his manhood stood proud, demanding her attention. Merrin fondled him with long, languid strokes, her own need building, coiling with desire.

He leaned into her. His hand knocked a stoppered jar. It teetered noisily.

Merrin slipped her hand away, suddenly aware of her surroundings. Holy fairy feathers, Ian was ravishing her in the kitchen. "What if someone finds us?"

With a playful grin, he lifted her from the counter. "Pick up the candle."

Gripping her legs around his hips, Merrin did as asked.

Ian carried her into the larder and locked the door. "No one will bother us in here."

He set her down and Merrin placed the candle on a barrel. Ian spooned his body behind her and slid his hands over her belly. Swirling upward, he cupped both breasts. Merrin arched and met his mouth over her shoulder. Ian ran his palm down the length of her body and slowly hiked up her skirts. The hem tickled her legs as he pulled it up, one agonizingly erotic tug at a time.

He pushed the wool aside, his fingers caressing her bare flesh, her need reaching a pinnacle of expectation. Merrin's breath stuttered as he fondled through the soft mound of curls at her apex. She moved with his motion, her skin sizzling with each encroaching touch. "Please."

Finally his fingers slipped between her sacred folds. "Open your legs for me."

Yes, merciful mercy. Merrin slid her ankles apart and gasped when he stroked her wickedly hot, sinfully sacred place. Nearly coming undone, she cried out, grinding her buttocks against the long column wedged to her backside.

Needing to see him, she twirled around and loosened his belt. She watched his face while she let it drop to the ground. With a growl, Ian snatched her up and walked her against the wall. "I can wait no longer."

He grasped her buttocks and lifted her. Merrin cupped his face with her palms and moved her bare legs up over his hips. The thick column of his manhood stroked her. Back and forth, the friction built. "Take me."

Right there, Ian tilted his hips and entered her. Merrin circled over him as he gradually buried himself within her. Their mouths joined, completely on fire. Ian started with languid strokes, sliding into her wet womanhood and pulling out, driving her to the brink of insanity. Merrin clamped on to his shoulders. "Faster." Her hips slapped against him as she rode him like a galloping stallion, completely out of control. Ian's hands clamped on to her buttocks. Growling, he drove into her with wild thrusts that matched her own.

A sharp cry caught in the back of Merrin's throat—her eyes flew open and then rolled back, unable to focus. Her entire being went completely rigid, followed by the shattering of blessed release.

Chapter Thirty-one

A serving maid gave Merrin a haughty glare when Ian tugged her back into the kitchen. All too quickly, the reality of their plight came back. She would treasure fleeting moments shared with Ian, but Merrin also would not soon forget her treatment by the clan. As soon as she could, she'd slip away and let Ian return to his life. He dreamt of supporting his brother and adding value to the clan. That was something Merrin could never do.

"What have the cooks got planned for the morning meal?" Ian asked.

The woman pointed toward the great hall. "I dunna ken what to do. They're all out there on their backs, crying for food."

Ian pointed toward the larder. "Fetch the oats."

"I can cook," Merrin volunteered.

Ian looked at her in disbelief. "But ye haven't had a wink of sleep."

Merrin pinched the bridge of her nose and closed her eyes. She had to stay awake. "Who else will do it?"

Bran pushed in through the back door. "Any change?"

From the grim line between his eyebrows, Bran really meant to ask if anyone had died during the night. Merrin took in a deep breath to clear away the ugliness of her horrendous thought.

Ian shook his head. "Nay."

Merrin grabbed a water bucket. "There's no use standing around." She handed the pail to Ian. "Can ye fetch the water? Bran, can ye bring in some sausages from the larder if 'tis not too much trouble?"

She glanced at the serving maid, who came in with a small barrel of oats. After setting it down, the wench shook her head, held up her hands and walked back to the great hall.

Bran started after her. "I'll no' stand for rudeness."

"Let her go." Merrin groaned. "'Tis no use having a backstabber in the kitchen."

Still heading after the woman, Bran called over his shoulder, "Then I'll see to it she tends the fires."

Together the three of them prepared a grand feast of porridge and sausages, while rumblings grew in the great hall. Ian and Bran ran trenchers of food out to the tables and above stairs for the laird and ladies—at least, anyone who was well enough to eat.

After administering another round of tonic to the sick, Merrin returned to the kitchen, thinking she'd find Ian there, but things had been so frantic with only a few people tending to the ill, they'd had no option but to spread the work and go their separate ways.

Merrin glanced at the mound of dirty pots, trays and trenchers. She nearly dropped. Her vision blurred and she rubbed her eyes. Now that the morning meal had been handled, mayhap she could slip above stairs and sleep. Gar looked up from his mat in front of the hearth. She bent down and gave him a scratch behind the ears. "'Tis much fancier than our home, hey, big fella?"

A woman cleared her throat from the outside doorway.

Merrin's skin crawled. She glanced back in hopes that Ian would come from the great hall. Bethag was one of the reasons he felt it necessary to be so protective.

The old woman glanced around the kitchen and raised her chin. "Ye think you've come in here to take over, aye?"

"Of course not. There was no one here to cook the morning meal."

Two more women stepped in behind the old crow.

"What kind of sorcery did ye use to mix the tincture?" one asked.

Bethag cackled, nodding her head. "She has our Ian bewitched, that's for certain."

"Nay." Gar bounded beside Merrin and growled. "Can ye no' see I'm trying to help?"

"No one was sick afore ye arrived."

Merrin shook her finger toward the tower. "Alexander had a cough. I witnessed it meself."

Bethag sneered. "*Ye* witnessed it? Ha. That means nothing."

"We should put her to the floating test," said the plump one.

Merrin's heart raced. The three stepped closer, hate in their eyes. Gar leaned toward them, growling, baring his teeth.

Bethag recoiled, clasping her fists against her chest. "Your dog does no' scare me."

The plump one shot a worried glance at the dog. "She'll kill us all."

The third wicked woman joined in. "Burn her."

Merrin's entire body shook. She hadn't slept in more than a day. She'd put up with taunts and jeers and sideways looks, all the while trying to help. She could take no more. Her eyes filled with tears. She grasped Gar's collar and ran for the door. The cackles of those hateful women followed her all the way to the rear gate. Once outside, Merrin turned full circle. Fladda was northwest—the only place in the world she'd ever been safe. Her father and Friar Pat had walked to and from the castle many times. She could do it as well.

Gar rubbed against her leg. "Come," she said. "We shall never return to this hateful place again."

Ian took the cup from Alexander's hand and felt his forehead. "I think your fever's broken."

"I'm definitely feeling better—mayhap I was wrong about Merrin."

The heavy burden upon Ian's chest lightened for the first time since he regained consciousness. "I concur with that."

"Are ye planning to keep her at Brochel? I could use your sword beside me."

"The clan proved they do no' deserve her." Ian shook his head. All this time he wanted to earn a respected place beside his brother, and now that he had, he no longer wanted it. "I doubt she'd like the idea either. I think it would be best if we rebuilt the cottage on Fladda."

"Very well." Alexander yawned. "But I ask ye to think on it afore ye make a decision."

"That I will."

Alexander sat up and stretched. "I've been abed long enough."

"Ye're rising so soon?" Ian could have hugged him. "I must tell Merrin. She's been sick with worry—some in the clan have been blaming the ague on her."

"Honestly?" Alexander's joints creaked as he crossed to the basin and splashed water on his face. "And ye allowed it?"

"We called for sanctuary until ye could hear her plea. I must confess, 'tis near impossible to enforce punishment on so many at once."

Alex picked up the drying cloth. "I'll put an end to it straight away. The last time the ague spread through the castle, it took ages to clear—and two good men died."

"Merrin was so worried—never stopped working, did no' even sleep."

"By the looks of you, ye did no' as well."

The corner of Ian's mouth ticked up. "I'll fetch her and see to it I remedy that."

Ian clamored down the tower stairs. Bethag came from the kitchen with a two other women on her flank. Ian ignored the prickle at the back of his neck. He scanned the hall for Merrin. He hadn't meant to leave her alone, but he needed to check on Alexander and she was busy ministering her tincture. He'd thought a few minutes above stairs shouldn't matter—besides, Bran was there.

Alexander traipsed down the stairs behind him. "Bloody hell, how long have I been abed?"

The hall was a shambles with straw and bodies everywhere. Ian spread his palms. "No' too many folks were willing to help, given their fear of Merrin's mark."

"Deplorable," Alexander said and marched ahead.

Ian looked to the rafters. If his brother had given Merrin a bit more support before he took to his bed with fever, it would have made things far easier.

Clansmen and women began to cluster around the stairwell, everyone commenting on how good it was to see the laird up so soon after the ague struck him. Oh how easily their attitudes changed once their chieftain was solidly on his feet.

Bran burst through the hall door. "Alexander? This is a surprise. I did not expect to see ye in the hall for days."

Alexander fisted his hips. "No fever's going to keep me abed for long."

Ian puzzled at Bran. "Where's Merrin?"

The big man looked like he'd been kicked in the knee. "I thought she was with ye."

Friar Pat's walking stick clanked through the kitchen door.

The holy man was mobbed at the entrance. Ian tried to push his way through, but the door was completely blocked.

He craned his neck to see over the tops of heads. "Friar. Did ye see Merrin in the kitchen?"

Pat glanced back over his shoulder. "Nay, she's no' there."

Ian spun around, looking for Bethag and her following. *Damn, damn, damn and double damn.* The woman was nowhere to be seen now things had turned for the better.

"Ian, ye and Merrin are to be congratulated. The tincture worked," Alexander hollered over the crowd.

Ian pounded his fist on a table. "Where is Merrin? Has anyone seen her?"

A lad pointed. "I saw her and that big dog running for the back gate. She was crying too."

Ian snapped his gaze to his brother. "This is Bethag's doing, mark me."

Alexander fisted his hips again with that same powerful look their father used. "Go after your woman. I'll dig to the bottom of this menacing disrespect."

Ian pushed out the door. How long had Merrin been gone? Spying the stables, he took a quick detour. He could cover more ground with a horse. He raced inside and nearly ran over a lad with a rake.

The boy scurried out of Ian's way. "Ye want to ride, m'lord?"

"Aye, and I'm no' your lord."

"Yes, sir. How about a chestnut Galloway?"

"Just give me a fast mount—a stallion. Put a bit in his mouth and forget the saddle."

"In a hurry, aye?" The lad's eyes popped, but he snatched a bridle off the peg and marched into a stall door.

"Thanks." Ian took charge of the reins and launched onto the stallion's back. The horse bolted before he found his seat. Ian gripped with his knees and the stallion raced toward the back gate. Only problem—It was closed. Ian relaxed his legs and tugged on the reins. "Easy, boy." He called to the sentry, "Open the gate."

The horse reared and kicked his front hooves. *Bloody hell, this colt is hardly broke.*

The portcullis opened and Ian lowered the reins to give the stallion his head. Ian steered him toward the path to Fladda—the only place Merrin could hide.

Gar trotted beside Merrin, his tail wagging as if he thought running through a forest with branches slapping at his face was fun. Merrin gasped for air, tears still streaming down her face. The cramp in her side felt like someone had skewered her with a dagger. She slowed to a fast walk, swiping the tears from her face.

She'd tried to be helpful. She'd done everything she knew to cure the ague, but there were so many people. It would probably take all the known herbs in the north of Scotland to cure every one of them. And yet she was blamed for it.

Merrin dragged her feet. She'd watched the coast of Skye across the sound and knew she had to be nearing Fladda. With any luck, the tide would be out and she could walk across the *caol*. If the tide was in, she'd swim. She could sleep in Niall's workshop and cook in the hearth—winters might be a bit rough, but she'd figure it out. She was tough. Anything was better than staying at Brochel Castle and listening to their evil taunts.

She clapped her hands over her eyes and rubbed. Her toe caught on a protruding root, sending her stumbling forward. Flinging her arms out, she fell right into a muddy bog.

Flicking the mud from her hands, she sat. A frustrated shriek grated her voice box. Gar stood on the bog's edge and wagged his tail as if he wondered why she'd thrown herself in the mud. "Ye can go ahead and say it. I'm clumsy as well as a wretched outcast."

Something snorted behind her. Inhaling a sharp breath, she turned. A mob of feral pigs barreled down the hill. Gar barked and launched his body over the top of her head. Guarding her, fierce as a lion, he snarled at the giant pigs—the largest nearly twice his size. They stopped on their stubby legs and flicked up their snouts as if sniffing for danger.

Merrin pulled her dagger from her boot and stood. Facing the pigs, she slowly backed away. Gar stood his ground, snapping his teeth, putting on an impressive show of fearlessness.

Once her feet met dry ground, she called him. "Gar, come behind."

The deerhound backed as the pigs sauntered forward. Merrin picked up a fist-sized rock and hurled it at the biggest one. "Get away, ye mongrels!"

The big fella shuffled aside. Gar bounded beside her and she picked up another rock. The pigs stood and looked at her with beady eyes. She knew a mob would attack a small human if they considered her an easy kill. She put the rock in her pocket and grasped Gar's collar, holding out her dagger with the other hand. Together they retreated until well into the trees, and then Merrin ran.

Her heart leapt to her throat when behind her, a beast crashed through the wood at an alarming pace. Could pigs move that fast? She didn't look back to find out.

"Merrin," Ian's voice boomed over the snapping twigs.

Her head spun—one part of her heart wanted to run and the other wanted to shout for him to save her. But she'd made her decision. She couldn't shirk from it now. She forced her legs to keep running.

But she couldn't pump them fast enough. Her side cramped like her guts had been ripped out, mud sloshed through her boots and her lungs were on fire.

Ian reined his horse to a skidding stop beside her. "Merrin. Why did ye no' stop?" He hopped down.

Merrin kept going, pushing her muddy hands through her hair. "Go back to Brochel, Ian."

Dismounting, he rushed in and grasped her arm. "Merrin."

She tried to yank away, but he held fast. "I said go."

"Why are ye turning me away? What did they do to ye?" His gaze scanned the length of her. "Did they do this?"

She pulled as hard as she could and he released her arm. "I used ye to discover what it's like to be loved—to be a real woman."

Ian blinked, standing stunned as if she'd dealt him a savage blow. "Is that what ye think? Ye're not a real woman?" He stepped into her, his pale blue eyes turning dark as coal. "Well, I've news for you."

Merrin slid her foot back, but before she could blink, he had her wrapped in his arms.

"Ye're a living, breathing, bonny woman." His lips neared, dangerously close. "Ye're more woman than any lass I have ever met."

Merrin's knees turned to mush, but she could not let him change her mind with his blasted charm. Not this time. "Ye belong at the castle...and I..." She gestured toward her muddy dress—the only one she had and most likely would ever again own. "Me place is on Fladda. No one taunts me there."

She tried to push away, but Ian's arms of iron clamped her to his chest. Heaven help her. Fresh linen, a touch of horse and a great deal of spicy male. Merrin turned her head from his enticing allure.

He grasped the back of her neck and leaned in, kissing her temple. "I'm so sorry I left ye. Those dreadful women will be punished, mark me."

Merrin shook her head. "I do no' want anyone punished—I must face it. I'm a monster and I always will be." She swallowed against the tears. She would not cry.

"Ye're no monster—ye never were. Your tincture has worked. Alexander and the friar are both up."

A gasp of relief caught in her chest. Thank heavens at least something had turned for the better. She blinked. She needed to stand her ground and be strong. She'd resisted him even though he chased after her on a shiny steed like a fabled knight.

Ian cupped her chin with his finger and turned Merrin's face so she'd have no choice but to look him in the eye. *Why did he have to do that?* His gaze pierced through her, sapped her resolve.

"Come back to the castle with me. Alexander wants to thank ye."

Merrin shook her head. "Can ye no' see? Ye're meant for a life in a big castle, working beside your brother, but 'tis no' the life for me. Ye must go back and leave me be."

Ian dropped his arms. A cold shudder coursed across Merrin's skin. This was it. This is what she needed him to do. Why did it feel so mercilessly wrong?

"And what if Ye're with child?"

Merrin felt the blood drain from her face. *A child?* A breeze blew her hair away from her face. Again she could scarcely breathe. "It would be the most blessed gift imaginable." Her words were but a whisper.

Ian reached for her hand and brushed his thumb across her palm—*such a gentle touch for a warrior.* "When I said I loved ye, I meant it. When I said I wanted to marry ye, I meant it." His hand trembled—he was as upset as she, yet there was no anger behind his eyes. "Merrin—I will take ye to Fladda if that is what ye wish."

"But I cannot force ye to stay."

"I'll stay because me heart is yours—and ye're certainly no' going to bring my bairn into the world without me."

She swiped a hand over her belly. Was she with child? Her courses hadn't come in a while, but that didn't mean anything. She'd go for months without seeing them. Her mouth went dry. If she could bear Ian's child, she would be the happiest woman in the Hebrides. If she could have Ian beside her—as a husband—well, Lord only knew how happy she would be.

"Do ye love me, Merrin?" The great, beautiful warrior stood before her, looking a bit shy—afraid, even.

"There's never been a question of me love for ye, Ian." She laced her fingers around the back of his neck. "I'll love ye until I take me last breath on this earth."

His mouth met hers with ferocious passion. Merrin closed her eyes and melted. She could have kissed him forever.

Chapter Thirty-two

Alexander MacLeod, second chieftain of Raasay, sat in his up-holstered chair—the same large throne his father had oc-cupied before him. He held a fist to his mouth and coughed. He hated the way sickness sapped his strength. Fortunately, this bout of ague ran its course quickly. Very few of the ill remained in the great hall. And they could thank his brother and Merrin for that.

Any reservations he'd harbored for the lass had vanished. His mother's explanation of what had occurred upon Merrin's birth, combined with her miraculous tonic, allayed his trepidation. If Merrin had the "gift", God meant it for the good of the clan, no question.

Friar Pat lumbered up the dais steps and took a seat at Alexan-der's right, as he always did upon hearing supplications.

Sir Bran pushed through the door, pulling Bethag behind him, his jaw set in a hard line.

The woman struggled against his grasp, wailing imperceptible woes. Why Bethag had to continuously cause a stir, Alexander couldn't fathom. She'd been widowed for years and he'd done the right thing offering the woman and her son protection within the walls of Brochel. But no one cared to have her work beside them. She'd failed in the kitchens, failed as an assistant to the tailor. Alexander had next put her in charge of keeping the courtyard clean, which she managed to do without bothering others too much.

Bran released Bethag's shoulder and she stumbled toward the dais.

Alexander folded his arms and frowned down at the pathetic hag.

She cowered, touching praying fingers to her lips. "Please, have mercy on a poor widow."

"Did ye have mercy on a lass who worked through the night for the clan?"

Bethag held out her palms. "But I remember when her mother died, and the bairn's red mark shone bright."

Friar Pat pounded his staff on the floorboards. "And where is it written that a red mark always indicates the spawn of the devil?"

"It has always been so—ye ken I cannot read."

"Silence." Alexander sliced his hand through the air. "I cannot tolerate your treatment of a lass who tried to help us, no matter what happened when she was a babe—only a few hours old when the false judgment was passed. Ye shall be muzzled with the iron branks bridle for your gossip."

Bethag recoiled, hands clutched to her chest. "Nay!"

Alexander stood. "I'll no' abide gossipers and slanderers in me keep. If any of the rest of ye disagree, come forward now and ye'll have the same as Mistress Bethag." He flicked his wrist toward the door. "Take her away."

The hall erupted in a low grumble. Yes, iron branks hurt, and restricted a woman's tongue so she couldn't talk. But that was better than a sentence of burning. Alexander didn't care to burn any woman—though Bethag had wanted to do exactly that to Miss Merrin.

Friar Pat stepped in beside him. "'Twill do her good to be put in her place."

"Aye, but I do no' ken if it'll change the woman."

"We can only pray it does."

A sentry stepped into the hall. "I've a missive for the laird."

Alexander fisted his hips. "What are ye standing back there for? Bring it up."

The lad hastened to the dais and handed the letter to Friar Pat. After examining the seal, he gave it to his chieftain. "From Ruairi of Lewis."

"Aye?" Alexander ran his thumb under the red wax. "Mayhap me uncle needs a tincture for the ague."

He read and passed it to the friar, pursing his lips.

Pat scanned the note and shook his head, a deep frown darkening his features. "Will he never give up?"

"Ian wants to build a home on Fladda—but I'd rather have me brother at Brochel. We can use his sword."

Pat tugged on the rope surrounding his ample waist. "Fladda is no' so far, and 'tis a good place for Ian to hide."

Ian led Merrin into the workshop and sat her on a bench. "I hate to say it, but ye smell like a swine's bog. How did ye end up covered in mud?"

Her head swooned with exhaustion. "I was running for Fladda, and the next thing I knew, me foot twisted and I was flying face first into the mud." She pushed the heel of her hand into her forehead. "Worse, it *was* a real swine's bog—a mob of feral pigs nearly had me for supper."

Ian brushed a strand of hair from her face. "Ye should never have run without me. Ye could have been hurt or killed."

Merrin nodded, though Ian would've had no idea what it felt like to face Bethag and her minions. "I think I'll stay right here. I've had enough trouble to last a lifetime."

Ian grinned. "Ye need a bath."

"Aye, but I'm so tired I can hardly hold up me head—and besides, the barrel burned with everything else."

"Then we'll improvise—as ye did with me. Ye stay here and I'll heat some water by the hearth. It will no' take long, and then we'll rest."

Merrin wanted to protest, but her aching muscles prevented her rebuttal. She let out a breath of air and her spine curved. She cradled her head in her hands and closed her eyes. Her lids were so heavy, she didn't think she'd be able to open them again.

Everything had gone wrong. Mayhap not *everything*. At least her tincture worked. *Thank ye, Niall. I felt your presence with me—at least I saw the castle and dined like a lady for a night.* Her eyes opened, her heart fluttered and she rubbed the outside of her arms. How could she be thinking of self-pity at a time like this? Everything had *not* gone wrong. Iron pots clanged within the cottage walls. Ian honestly intended to stay. She'd given him every opportunity to turn tail and go back to Brochel, but he remained.

Not only was he there, but he was tending to her needs, as opposed to the other way around. She tried to stand, but her muscles hurt too much. She plopped her elbow on the workbench and rested her head in the crook of her arm. A moment or two with her eyes closed couldn't hurt.

The next thing Merrin new, Ian was kissing her cheek, his stubble lightly scratching her skin. "Your bath's ready, m'lady."

She chuckled. "I'm no one's lady."

Ian tapped her nose, his eyes filled with love. "Ye're mine—always will be."

He warmed her heart in every way, but Merrin could hardly move. "Ian, I think I'm too tired for a bath."

He pulled the string on her kirtle. "All ye need to do is sit here. I'll manage the rest." He got that dark, dangerous look on his face—the one where he eyed her and made her feel like the only woman in the world.

"I do no' think I can do that either."

He knit his brows. "What?"

"Ye ken." She nodded toward his unmentionables. "*That.*"

"Ah." He winked—such a wicked mind he had. "Mayhap we can do *that* after we've both had some sleep."

He slid the kirtle from her shoulders. With a few more tugs, he pulled it away, neatly folded it and set the dress atop the workbench. It was mostly covered with mud.

The sleeves and hem of her shift were also filthy. Ian untied the bow. "Hold your arms up."

Even raising her arms was difficult, but Ian lifted her up and pulled her shift from under her, then made swift work of tugging it over her head. The day was warm, and Merrin felt not a twinge of embarrassment sitting on the stool completely nude.

She closed her eyes while he dipped a cloth in the warm water and ran it over her face. It was invigorating. He cleansed her fingers and up each arm, then moved to her back with languid swirling motion. Merrin closed her eyes and melted into his gentle touch.

"Does it feel good?"

"Mm hmm."

Ian's cloth ran over her chest, the warmth soothing with the slight chill after tingling preventing her from completely drifting into slumber. Merrin sucked in a quick inhale when he cleansed her breasts. Instantly heavy, desire shot through her core. Only moments ago, she didn't think she could manage lovemaking, but now her body ached for it.

Ian suckled her while he bathed her belly.

"Ye're torturing me."

"Am I?" He sounded none too concerned, and circled the cloth over her womanhood. "Open your legs."

"But—"

"There too."

She opened her eyes long enough to give him a knowing look. Hot fire burned in her loins, but he didn't linger. Slowly, he continued down her legs and forced the warm water between her toes. She reached for him and pulled his body close. The column of his erection pressed between her breasts. All she needed to do was hike up his kilt, and she could suckle him too.

But Ian patted her hair and stepped away. He pulled his shirt out from his kilt and over his head. "Put this on. I'll go wash your things."

She held the linen against her naked body, a tad disappointed. "But I can do that."

He picked up her clothes. "Aye, ye can." In a blink of an eye, he was gone.

Merrin tugged Ian's shirt over her head and exhaustion returned full force. Inhaling Ian's masculine scent, she headed for the pallet of straw they'd made at the back of the workshop.

Ian would be along soon. He had to be every bit as tired as she.

Well rested, Ian took one last swing with the axe. The gnarled birch tree crashed to the ground.

Merrin clapped her hands. "Ye did it."

Did she think he couldn't? Ian chuckled. "Only ten to twenty more to go."

"That many?"

"Ye want the roof sound, do ye not?"

"Aye."

He gestured to the small grove of trees. "These are not the best for building, so we'll need plenty of them."

Merrin used a hatchet to chop off the limbs while Ian started on another birch.

After felling it, he wiped his brow with the back of his shirt-sleeve. "I'll need to go to Brochel and fetch the galley and me inheritance soon. It is our key to a better life. We will be able to sail to Glasgow and trade for seeds and plants—mayhap even start a grove of cinchona trees." He laughed. "Do ye ken how rich we'd be if we invented a surefire cure for ague?"

He watched her lovely hips as she bent to cut off another limb. "I've no idea, but I do no' care about wealth so long as we've a roof over our heads, clothes on our backs and food in our bellies."

They'd made love all morning, but he still could go another round with Merrin—or forty. "That's no' the only thing I want in your belly."

She held up her palm. "Oh no, Ian. We've a roof to build afore bairns come."

He swung the axe to dissuade his errant thoughts. "I want ye to go with me."

"Where?"

"To fetch the galley."

"Nay." She shook her head firmly. "I'm no' going back to Brochel."

He took a swing at another tree. "I do no' want to leave ye here alone."

"Why? Da left me alone plenty."

"Aye, but that was afore half the clan wanted to see ye burned."

Merrin snapped up straight. "Do ye think they still want that?"

"Nay." Ian slammed the axe into the trunk so hard the tree crashed to the ground. "I just do no' want ye to be alone. Not ever."

Merrin's hands found her hips in a defiant pose. "I—"

Gar's bark resounded from the direction of the cottage. It wasn't one bark, but a barrage of hysterics.

Ian picked up his scabbard from the ground and drew his sword. "Ye stay here."

"I thought ye didn't want me out of your sight." She always chose the damnedest times to argue.

"Ye kent what I meant."

Merrin hastened to his side. "Ye're no' going without me."

The back of Ian's neck burned. Why couldn't she understand this was different? "What if it *is* a mob?"

"I'll stay hidden." She urged him forward with a flick of her hand. "I'll creep behind ye until we reach the coop. I've a bow and some arrows hidden there."

Holy Mother, he could have used those when they ran from Rewan. "Ye're full of surprises." He hastened forward, mindful of his footfalls. He didn't want to snap a twig and make undue noise. "Do no' forget ye promised to stay out of sight."

Chapter
Thirty-three

G ar's barking grew nearer while Merrin marched behind Ian until they reached the chicken coop. He placed a firm hand on her shoulder. "I meant what I said. Stay out of sight."

Though she didn't like it one bit, she nodded. "Can ye no' stay here and wait for whomever it is to come up the hill?" Yapping, Gar barreled around the corner. "Wheesht." She grasped the deerhound's collar and pulled him to her side. He yowled and tugged. Merrin shook her finger in front of his nose. "Stay."

She turned to Ian, expecting a hug, but he was already twenty paces beyond the coop. Her gut clenched. "Ian," she whispered as loud as her voice would allow.

He snapped his head around and held up his palm, commanding her to stay. But he didn't miss a step.

Merrin's stomach roiled. She should be by his side, not hidden. She slipped behind the coop door and found the bow and arrows she'd placed there years ago. Honestly, she'd completely forgotten about them until Gar had launched into his maniacal barking. She grabbed the dog's collar. "Come."

Pulling Gar beside her, Merrin crouched behind the rock wall and made her way up to the stony crag that overlooked the *caol*. She crawled onto the moss-covered crag—the one where she'd often sit and stare across at Raasay, dreaming of what it would be like to visit the big castle. On her belly, she pulled herself to the edge and looked back at her dog. "Down." Gar dropped and crawled beside her. "Stay," she growled with her lowest, fiercest voice.

Her hands shook. She didn't care for facing death daily, weekly or ever—how men went to war, she couldn't fathom. She spread a clump of heather with her hands and peeked down to the shore. *God no*. She could never in her life mistake the sleek lines of Rewan's galley.

He promised to leave us alone. He took Ian's dirk. What more does he want? Merrin clenched her teeth. Rewan MacLeod had to be the lowest backstabbing bastard she'd ever come across. He was in a league with the hideous pirates from Rona.

Out of the corner of her eye, she caught Ian creeping toward the crest of the bluff. She opened her mouth to warn him, but before she could utter, Ian bellowed a sound so frightening, Merrin thought he'd been skewered. Then he ran ahead full tilt, braying like a mad bull.

Gar growled. Merrin yanked down on his collar. "Wheesht. Stay. I mean it."

Men poured over the side of the galley, all roaring their battle cries, hellbent on murder.

Ian didn't stand a chance against so many. Merrin snatched an arrow from the quiver. Niall had taught her to shoot well, but her lessons were eons ago. Still on her stomach, she tried to steady her shaking hands and aim. Releasing, the string grazed her arm. Worse, the blasted thing missed her man by ten feet. He ran through the surf without noticing an arrow hit the water behind him.

Gar whined and stood.

Merrin grabbed another arrow. "Stay."

This time she rose to her knees. Her hands steadied. She could do this—she must help Ian. Merrin pulled the bowstring to her ear and eyed her mark. The arrow darted through the air faster than peregrine falcon dives. In a blink, the evil man hurled backward. The arrow lodged in his chest.

She'd killed a man. She wanted to vomit. Her hands shook violently.

Ian's sword clanged. Merrin's resolve returned with full force. Rewan got to him first, with five men behind. Merrin snatched another arrow, and another, each one hitting its mark with more accuracy than she'd ever had at target practice. Three men down.

Ian spun, his claymore catching the light. It clanged as he fought Rewan and the other two warriors, all at once.

Gar stood and whined. Merrin snatched an arrow and glanced at him. *A trained war dog? He could save Ian.* Making a quick decision, Merrin pointed to the skirmish. "Go."

Gar bounded ahead, snarling. He latched on to a warrior's arse and dragged him from the circle of swinging blades. Ian swung his sword, fighting like a machine. Rewan and his man encroached upon him. Ian constantly stepped backward as he fought. Merrin held her bow to her cheek, but had no clear shot. If she released, there was every chance she'd hit her dog or Ian.

Things moved so fast, she could only glimpse flashes of Ian and Gar. Merrin's mind raced. Ian couldn't fight them off much longer.

Gar yelped and staggered out from the center of the fight. "No!" She tried to run, but hands grabbed her from behind.

Ian's muscles burned. Gar's yelp knifed at his gut. If the dog was in the middle of the fight, where was Merrin? He couldn't avert his eyes, else Rewan's sword would lodge in his gut. Why was the bastard here, damn it all? He'd ask, but couldn't stop gnashing his teeth and grunting with each deflection. Ian could scarcely blink. In fact, he didn't.

He could take Rewan man to man, but the two other warriors flanking him proved deadly. He couldn't see around them, but prayed an army of men wasn't pouring out of the galley moored in the *caol*.

Every sinew in Ian's body strained to defend an attack by a battleaxe from the right. He didn't recognize the beast hacking his blade with the strength of a warhorse. Ian swung his sword across his midsection and deflected Rewan's thrust. The brute to his left raised his weapon over his head. Ian used the momentum of his sword, levering it into the exposed gut. Thank God seafaring men didn't wear mail. Ian's blade tore through flesh as the stunned fighter fell forward.

Ian yanked his claymore free and spun around.

Christ. As if three weren't enough, the battle cry of an entire army roared from the shore.

Ian girded his loins, praying they'd treat Merrin well. He'd fight and defend her with his last breath, but no man could take down an entire army with nothing but a sword and a dirk. Savagely, he wielded his weapon. Muscles burning, he had no idea how much longer he could last. Rewan hacked at him, eyes blazing, every jab targeted for a kill.

Spinning, Ian flinched to dodge a blow from the battleaxe. Rewan's sword clashed with the downward thrust of the axe. Ian's eyes snapped to the henchman. *What? The brute just defended me from being cut in two?*

Ian found his breath. "Why are ye here?"

"A spy saw ye at Brochel, ye bastard."

Ian shoved the man with the battleaxe to the ground and circled Rewan. He had an inkling men were fighting along the shore, but couldn't take his eyes off the Lewis henchman. His mind clicked. *Why are so many fighting each other and not bearing down on me?* He tried to glance to the *caol*, but Rewan lunged in with a sparring move.

"Ruairi cut me loose."

"Then why are ye trying to murder me?"

"Because he's in the galley. If I kill ye, he'll let me live. If ye fall by another's blade, I'm a dead man."

Ian slashed downward with a move that could kill if he let his sword slice close enough, but he held it back. "Is that it? Life or death?"

"Aye." With a toxic roar, Rewan lunged. Ian jumped aside, but not fast enough. The blade nicked his flank.

At Eilean Donan, Ian had held the milk-livered bastard's life in his hands. He chose not to take it because he rued killing a man who'd been a friend. He had no choice now. Either he killed Rewan or he'd risk losing Merrin. Ian bore down and spun, leveling a blow to end it all. Rewan dropped to his knees. Ian's blade hissed over the henchman's head.

Expecting Rewan's offensive attack, Ian swung his sword back to defend a strike. No blow came.

Rewan fell face first into the dirt. Ian looked up. Sir Bran grinned beneath his embattled helm with a crooked nosepiece, his face splattered with blood. The big man had knocked Ruairi's henchman unconscious with the pommel of his claymore.

A slow smile spread across Ian's face as he lowered his sword. "Where the hell did ye come from?"

Bran moved in beside him, training his weapon across the scene. "I thought I might receive a warmer welcome, considering I just saved your arse."

Only men from Brochel remained standing along the shore. Ian breathed a sigh of relief. "Och, I'm glad Ye're here. More than glad, but what brought ye?"

"After all ye and Merrin did for the clan, Alexander thought he'd pay ye a visit."

Merrin's shriek fired like an arrow on the wind. Gar yelped. With effort, the dog stood, favoring his front right. He barked and bounded, as if unscathed, toward the *caol*.

Leaving Rewan writhing on the ground, Ian and Bran ran. Old Ruairi stood at the helm of the galley, beckoning two men to carry Merrin to the ship.

She twisted and struggled against her captors. "Get your hands off me."

Ian bellowed his war cry and raced ahead, his chest heaving He'd risk everything to save her. He'd never wanted to cut a man down so vehemently. Any man who touched his betrothed would pay in blood. Water splashed in all directions as his feet plunged into the surf. He barreled between Merrin and the ship. Sword held level, ready for a killing blow, he faced them. "Release her."

Ruairi's grating voice crackled behind. "Me wife-stealing nephew has risen from the dead."

Gar latched on to the arse of one bastard and whipped his head from side to side. The man yelped with pain, but Gar held on. He dropped to his knees, reaching for his dirk. Gar shuffled away. The man started after him but fell to the ground, rubbing his backside.

Ian kept his sword trained on the guard who had his hands latched to Merrin's arm. He could kill him just for touching her.

Ruairi chuckled behind. "Lower your weapon, nephew. I've an archer aiming at your back."

Bran barreled behind Ian and held up his targe. "Nay. Tell your men to stand down, or Alexander will blast your wee boat out of the water."

Ian snapped his gaze to the sound and back. God bless his brother. *The Golden Sun* was moored in deep water with all eighteen of her guns at the ready. Alexander had lowered a skiff and two men manned the oars, rowing him ashore with Friar Pat astern. The Raasay chieftain stood in the boat with fists on his hips.

Alexander mirrored the fierce image of their father. "Uncle, 'tis time ye stop this madness," he hollered over the roaring surf. "I'll stand beside ye through the bowels of hell, but Ye're no' killing me brother or Miss Merrin." He pointed back to his ship. "I guarantee me cannons are aimed at your galley. Ye do no' stand a chance."

Ruairi's eyes darted across the scene. He motioned to his man. "Ye may have won for now, but do no' forget, I have more guns and men. I'll be back."

Alexander shook his finger. "Do ye really want to start a feud between our clans? All because of a wayward woman? A woman you've divorced and ruined before all the world?"

Ian pushed Ruairi's man aside and pulled Merrin into his arms. Closing his eyes, he squeezed until she might break. Her warm body molded to his side. He never wanted to let her go—never wanted to see another man touch her in any way. "Are ye all right, my love?"

She drew in a ragged breath and nuzzled against him. "Aye."

He held her by the shoulders and met her gaze with determination. "There's one thing I must do. Stay here with Gar."

She nodded.

Ian grasped the arse-bitten man by the shoulder and marched through the thigh-deep water to his uncle's galley. He grabbed the guard by his bleeding backside, hefted him into the boat and faced his uncle. "Before ye leave, I'll have me dirk returned."

Ruairi folded his arms. "Ye do no' deserve it, ye thieving bastard."

Ian's nostrils flared, heat flushing through his blood. "Ye call me a thieving bastard?" he yelled. "What about ye? Ye're a wife beater, and gloat about it. I'm ashamed to call ye kin."

Ruairi launched himself over the side with Ian's dirk aimed to kill. Ian snatched his uncle's wrist and twisted. The dirk dropped into the shallow water. Grasping his uncle by the crotch, Ian hefted the old man back into the galley. "Get him out of here afore I lose me temper."

He bent down and fished his dirk out of the sea. Rotating it in his hand, he shoved it in his belt and he turned. Merrin stood on the shore, her arms reaching out to him. He'd fight all of Scotland to have those loving arms surround him.

Sir Bran tied Rewan to a post rather than send the bastard back to Stornoway to face certain death.

After the Ruairi's galley sailed out of the sound, Merrin rushed to Gar. The dog wagged his tail and spun in a circle as if nothing had happened. She pulled him to a stop and examined his shoulder. He was cut, but not too deep. "I'll need to stitch that up once I take ye to the workshop."

"I'd be proud to have him fighting beside me any time." Ian gave him a scratch behind the ears. "Ye are a war dog, are ye not?"

Alexander cleared his throat and pointed to the *caol*. "They've all come to help rebuild your cottage."

Merrin's jaw dropped. Ian's galley and three others sailed into the sound. Aside from Bran's men, who already lined the shore, she could have bet the entire clan was standing in the boats waving at them. "What on earth?" She shot a panicked grimace to Ian. "We've not even a roof."

Alexander beckoned the procession of clansmen and women up the hill. "Miss Merrin, it is I who must apologize first. Ye and Ian performed a great service for the clan. Without ye, our people could have died—the ague could have spread through the entire castle."

A pair of men walked past, laden with wood. "Hello, Miss Merrin, Sir Ian."

Alexander chuckled. "We've come to see your cottage has a new roof—among other things."

A woman, one who'd taunted her, carried a rocking chair. "Apologies, Miss Merrin. I hope this will help make amends. Ye're the best healer in the Hebrides, I'll attest to that in front of a magistrate if need be."

Merrin didn't know how to respond.

Ian smiled. "Thank ye."

Each man, woman and child came ashore, laden with everything imaginable from cloth to barrels of oats to thatch for the roof, a table and benches—her cottage would be whole again before the day was out.

Merrin threw her arms around Alexander. "Thank you, m'laird. I cannot believe it. All this. For us?"

Ian's brother gave her a squeeze. "Aye, and ye deserve it all and more. Not a one of us would be fit to put up a roof if it weren't for ye and your tincture." He beckoned the marching line of people. "Come, everyone. Time's wasting."

Sir Bran followed with a heap of fur over his arm, a big grin shone from beneath his dark beard. "This is a wedding present from Lady Enya and me." He draped a sealskin cloak over Merrin's shoulders. "Ian said ye lost yours."

She smoothed her hand over the exquisitely soft fur. "Aye, but it wasn't as nice as this...and we're no' married."

Friar Pat hobbled up with Lady Anne on his arm. "But ye will be afore the day is out."

The lady gave him a polite whack. "I beg to differ. Much preparation is needed, and we'll have the ceremony at Brochel." She smiled at Merrin. "Besides, you'll need to be fitted for your gown."

"A real wedding gown?" Merrin giggled like a giddy child. "I cannot believe this."

"Of course, my dear. Why do you think I have all those bolts of exotic fabrics in my solar? Any woman fit to marry my son deserves to be clad in the finest silk on her wedding day."

"Thank you, m'lady."

Lady Anne smiled and fondly touched Merrin's cheek. "My thanks to you, dear."

Ian clutched his arm around Merrin's shoulders and glanced at his brother. "Ye arrived just in the nick of time—and with your guns too. How did ye ken Ruairi would show up?"

Alexander walked back to the cottage with them all. "I received a missive from our notorious uncle—it said he'd received word from one of his informants. It appears someone reported your piping in the great hall—he found your rise from the dead quite amusing. I only figured it was a matter of time before he set out for revenge."

Ian shook his head.

Alexander smoothed his hand over the plaid draped across his shoulder. "I would have told ye about it today if me spies hadn't reported him sailing south."

Rewan turned his bloodied head as they approached.

Ian stepped forward, clasping his hand around his hilt, and elbowing his brother. "What do ye aim to do with *him*?"

The chieftain frowned. "He cannot be trusted at Brochel, no' after I witnessed this barbarous attack."

Bran tapped Rewan's hip with his boot. "Mayhap we should put him on a ship for the Americas. After all, he was a friend once."

Alexander fisted his hips. "The Americas or death by hanging—what will it be, Rewan?"

The man's Adam's apple bobbed. "I've no' much choice, have I?"

"Then let it be done," Ian said.

They left Rewan tied to the post and headed toward the cottage. Bran clapped Ian's shoulder and pulled a flask from his sporran. "Let us drink to our success."

"Agreed." Ian took a healthy swig and Merrin slid her fingers into Ian's hand. They watched as the rooftop beams were levered into place. "We are the luckiest couple in all of Scotland."

Chapter Thirty-four

One sennight later

Alexander stood beside Merrin as she turned one last circle in front of the looking glass. "Ye're lovely—quite honestly the prettiest bride I've ever seen."

Warmth spread across her cheeks. "How can ye say that? I'll wager Ilysa was far more beautiful."

He tapped a finger to his lips. "Never repeat this, but ye are far lovelier, my dear. Do no' take me wrong, Ilysa made a pretty picture indeed, though I'd never set eyes on her before our wedding day."

"Och." Merrin shuddered. "Ye must have been mortified."

"I was a wee bit—but I daresay she was more so. Fortunately, the match worked."

Merrin nearly asked him if he loved his wife, but held her tongue. That would have been an awful thing to say. She couldn't imagine marrying someone without knowing him first. How awkward it would be—especially the wedding night. She could hardly imagine being in bed watching her husband undress while trembling with pure fright under the bedclothes. She shook off her thoughts. Fortunately, she'd never be forced to face that kind of terror.

Alexander reached out his hand. "Are ye ready, Miss Merrin?"

She took it. "I'll no' be a 'miss' much longer."

"Perhaps 'tis the last time ye'll hear it."

She laughed. "I do prefer Mistress Merrin—I always thought I'd die an old maid, and then Ian washed ashore."

"I only regret Niall isn't here to see ye. He'd be proud, so very proud."

Merrin's heart squeezed at her father's name. But he was watching over them and he would approve of this marriage.

Ian had already made contact with merchants in Glasgow, and they'd be sailing south on the morrow to fetch a long list of herbal remedies and supplies. She hated to leave the cottage after the clan had done so much to make it homey again, but Ian estimated they'd only be away a fortnight. She didn't mind, as long as they were together.

Lady Anne had given her an assortment of high-necked kirtles designed to cover her mark, though the blue silk gown she wore today scooped low over her breasts. No one at Brochel would dare comment about her mark with Laird Alexander giving her away.

He led Merrin down the winding stairwell to the great hall. Before they rounded the last bend, she stopped and pulled the lace veil over her face.

He winked. "Are ye ready?"

Unable to speak, she nodded.

When they stepped into the enormous hall, benches scraped across the floorboards. Everyone stood. Merrin couldn't breathe for a moment. 'Twas a bit overwhelming for a simple lass to be on the arm of her chieftain with the whole clan standing and smiling at her with oohs and ahs filling the room.

But her initial trepidation fled from her shoulders as if a waterfall had splashed over her and taken all worries away. Ian stood upon the dais, smiling, staring directly at her. An imposing warrior, he exuded power beneath his vibrant kilt of red and black. He had one foot planted forward on sturdy legs while his jeweled claymore hung at his hip. His plaid was draped over one shoulder, clasped by a large brass brooch.

Alexander led Merrin beside her betrothed.

Reaching for her hands, he grinned wider than he'd ever done before. She'd never seen a man more handsome—how on earth did he fall in love with her, and thank all the stars in heaven he had.

Merrin gazed into Ian's adorning pale blue eyes and her breasts swelled. There could be no other man on earth for her. Ian had shown her unbridled love, and though she'd been an outcast, her mark had never brought him pause. He loved her with all her flaws as she did him.

They held hands as together they spoke their vows, declaring their love with an everlasting promise. In Ian's arms she would live forever.

Also by

Amy Jarecki

Highland Force Series:
Captured by the Pirate Laird
The Highland Henchman
Beauty and the Barbarian
Return of the Highland Laird (A Highland Force Novella)
Devilish Dukes Series:
The Duke's Fallen Angel
The Duke's Untamed Desire
The Duke's Privateer
Secret Longings of a Duke (a novella)
The MacGalloways series
A Duke, by Scot
Her Unconventional Earl
The Captain's Heiress
Kissing the Twin
A Princess in Plaid
Charmed by a Wily Lass
The Kings Outlaws series
Highland Warlord
Highland Raider
Highland Beast
Highland Defender Series
The Fearless Highlander
The Valiant Highlander

The Highlander's Iron Will (a novella)

Lords of the Highlands Series:

The Highland Duke

The Highland Commander

The Highland Guardian

The Highland Chieftain

The Highland Renegade

The Highland Earl

The Highland Rogue

The Highland Laird

Guardian of Scotland (Time Travel) Series

Rise of a Legend

In the Kingdom's Name

The Time Traveler's Christmas

Highland Dynasty Series:

Knight in Highland Armor

A Highland Knight's Desire

A Highland Knight to Remember

Highland Knight of Rapture

Highland Knight of Dreams (a novella)

Blitzed series:

Defenseless

Unintentional

Tackled

ICE Series (romantic suspense)

Hunt for Evil

Body Shot

Mach One

Pict/Roman Romances:

Rescued by the Celtic Warrior

Celtic Maid

Stand Alone Titles:

My Genes Don't Fit

Time Warriors

Defenseless

Virtue: A Cruise Dancer Romance

The Chihuahua Affair

Boy Man Chief

About the Author

An Image

Known for her action-packed, passionate romances, *USA Today* Bestselling Author Amy Jarecki has received reader and critical praise throughout her writing career. She won the prestigious RT Reviewers' Choice award for *The Highland Duke* and a RONE award from InD'tale Magazine for Best Time Travel for her novel *Rise of a Legend*. In addition to being a *USA Today* Bestselling Author, Amy has earned the designation as an Amazon All Star Author. She holds an MBA from Heriot-Watt University in Edinburgh, Scotland and now resides in La Crosse Wisconsin with her husband where she writes immersive historical and contemporary romance novels. Become a part of her world and learn more about Amy's books on amyjarecki.com!